WINGS SO WICKED

A GOLDEN CITY NOVEL
BOOK ONE

EMILY BLACKWOOD

Cover design by MoonPress www.moonpress.co

Editing and proofreading by Enchanted Author Co

Interior graphics by Etheric Designs

✸ Created with Vellum

AUTHOR NOTE

Please check your triggers—
Wings So Wicked is a new adult fantasy romance novel with
dark themes, violence, cursing, and explicit sexual scenes.
Characters are harmed in ways including whippings and
stabbings. Death of parents, abusive father figures, depressive
thoughts, self harm, deep betrayal and blood sharing/biting are
themes in this novel.
This story will get dark and contains an epic cliffhanger, but the
series will ultimately have a happy ending.

For readers who enjoy the wicked pleasure of a slow burn.
Buckle up. This one's for you.

PROLOGUE

The fall of Scarlata Empire

C laudia Fullmall Gawerula stood tall amongst her falling kingdom without shedding a single tear. Aggressive, fuming fires ripped apart building after building in the distance, the growing roar and crackle of burning wood vaguely disguising the horrified, gutted screams of her people as they took their last breaths.

She blinked at the stench of burning flesh that wafted through the slight breeze, but she did not shed a tear.

Claudia flinched when she heard the hungry, animalistic growls of her people—people who were once kind and patient— as they ripped into innocent bystanders on the streets with their sharp teeth. Even so, she did not cry.

The Queen of Scarlata Empire only lifted her chin, beholding the crumbling walls of everything she had worked so hard to build over the last fifty years. She had created peace, created a home not only for herself and her new daughter but for the thousands of other vampyres who counted on her.

For once, vampyres were living in harmony, kingdoms away from any fae who might feel weary about the habits of her people.

It didn't matter how much good she did in the world, though. It never did. She could never stand a chance against the hunger.

She sighed and removed the heavy golden crown from her head as she stood atop the tallest hill that surrounded the kingdom, away from the war below. The second the fae invaded, she had summoned her wings to find her way here. Not to escape the fight, no. She would never leave her people to fight alone. She merely needed one moment—one last look—to remember Scarlata Empire as it once was.

For she knew deep in her bones, like the most primal foretelling of any attack, that their time as a kingdom was over. The fae would never let them exist for so long without retaliating, especially when the hungry ones had been growing more and more.

Being a vampyre herself, Claudia understood the nearly impossible cravings to sink one's teeth into another's flesh, but those cravings must be controlled if one wished to remain sane. Giving into that bloodlust—letting the hunger take over and control your senses until you were its slave—was what she had lost so many of her people to. They turned into monsters, into the vampyres that most of the fae feared.

Claudia was not like that. Her sister was not like that, nor was her neighbor or the baker who rose at dawn daily to make bread for the kingdom.

But it did not matter to the fae. They would take and take and take, killing whatever they feared because they knew no better.

Below her, the fighting intensified. She looked down, holding her crown between her hands as she watched fae attacking vampyres, and vampyres draining the blood from fae.

Some of the vampyres, understand, were innocent. They were not the soulless, hungry monsters that fed on the flesh of their attackers. Those innocent vampyres tried to run, tried to escape, but they were surrounded.

The queen's heart hurt, not just for the innocent vampyres but for the vampyre with lost souls, too.

She knew her kingdom would fall eventually. The numbers of the hungry ones had been increasing for decades. It did not matter how much she begged the goddess to save her kingdom; it was only a matter of time.

But the Queen of Scarlata Empire did not fear death. She set her crown upon the grassy hill, drew her sword, summoned her wings, and flew to fight with her people against the invaders that wished them all dead.

Perhaps she would die today. She would fight with her people against the fae, and she would wield her sword with honor and with respect for the ones who had already fallen. She would fight until her very last breath with her chin held high, because perhaps her kingdom was falling, but she would die remembering what Scarlata Empire stood for.

CHAPTER
ONE

"Begin," Lord's order rang through the stone cave walls before he retreated, backing into the protection of shadows.

My opponent emerged from that same darkness, one step after the other. Even in such little light, I could see the raw, primal energy beneath the cloth mask that hid his features.

I was sure his energy matched my own.

My feet were lithe feathers beneath me, ready to move at my will. My heart beat steadily with power, reminding me of my strength.

Reminding me of my *purpose*.

Another opponent, another fight, another test.

Another opportunity to prove to Lord that I was the best, the strongest, the most violent.

I counted to three, waiting for my opponent to make the first move. Over the last twenty-two years, I had learned how to spot a male's intention to fight.

They could hardly restrain themselves from lashing out within the first three seconds.

But when they did, when they hesitated, it showed me their greatest weakness.

I lunged forward with a wave of lightweight agility, watching his body, observing his reactions as I threw my first punch.

He swatted it away, his robust arms having no problem deterring my force.

I punched again; he blocked me again.

Leaving his midsection wide open.

Too easy. Too predictable.

My fist swung through the opening in his center and contacted my opponent's face with a satisfying *thud*. I ignored the pain that thundered through my knuckles, no doubt from the splitting skin on my bare hands. The scabs hadn't had time to heal since the last time they had split open. They never did.

The male before me hissed, baring his sharp fae teeth at me while blood trickled from his nose.

Males. They always had such uncontrollable tempers.

"Again!" Lord shouted from the far wall of the underground den.

Fuck. He did not sound pleased. I obeyed instantly, unable to rest for a single second before my opponent advanced, swinging his dagger toward my torso.

This guy was temperamental *and* cocky.

I *hated* cocky.

I inhaled sharply before launching myself forward, narrowly avoiding his silver blade, before I pulled my own from my waist and grazed it across his chest, leaving a trail of blood behind.

One quick glance at Lord in the shadows told me he was still not impressed.

He rarely was.

Think, Huntyr. Focus. You should have taken him down by now.

I stepped backward while my opponent recovered, giving myself a second to collect my thoughts. The den was dark and offered minimal lighting, but I could still see the way my opponent gripped his blade tightly. Each finger flexed around the hilt as if letting go would spell his death. As if the blade would save him from failure.

That was his weakness. He relied too heavily on his weapon and likely had weaker combat skills without it.

"Stop dancing around," Lord ordered, his voice booming off the rock walls around us. "You're supposed to be killing each other, not playing games."

He was right.

Lord's voice was enough to send a chill down my spine, raise the hair on my arms.

It distracted me just enough so that when I busied myself with blocking the fist that suddenly flew toward my face, I did not notice the second punch ready to hook into my ribs.

I doubled over and staggered backward, gasping for breath.

Fuck.

I sucked in air once, twice, then straightened myself, ignoring the screaming in my ribs.

Swiftly and without a sound, I ducked and rolled forward, tumbling toward my opponent's feet. He stood still, ready for me, but he was surprised enough at my advance to leave his legs unguarded.

The second I landed in a crouched position, I swept my foot beneath him, sending him falling to his back with his weapon scattering. Before he could climb back to his feet, I jumped on top of him, pinning his shoulders with my weight while I straddled his torso. He writhed beneath me, scrambling for an escape, but with my weight centered and my knees planted firmly on the ground, he wasn't going anywhere.

My blade found its way to his neck, hovering above the delicate skin.

"You're dead," I growled through clenched teeth. My breath came out in pants, exhaustion beginning to take over my limbs as I held him there, waiting for Lord's order to end the fight.

For a few seconds, time stopped. The cramped, damp den disappeared, leaving just me and my opponent, our breaths blending together, both with our faces covered by a thin cloth, with slits just large enough for our eyes so we could see without revealing our identities.

Of course, I could identify a male with much more than his features. I could identify him by the way he walked, the size of his shoulders, the sharpness of his fae ears, the sway in his stance.

But it didn't matter who he was. It didn't matter who I was, either. We were simply pawns, simply weapons in this wicked, dark world. With one swift motion, I could end his life.

We were all that fragile.

A low growl came from my opponent's chest, reminding me of who and where I was.

I turned my attention to the back wall, where Lord lurked in waiting.

"Sloppy," he muttered.

I scrambled off my opponent and sheathed my weapon, standing tall with my hands clasped behind my back, waiting for more instruction.

My opponent did the same.

Not so cocky now, are you?

That had been another key component I had learned during my lifetime of studying killers under Lord: *Everyone bowed to someone.*

Lord stepped forward with a lazy amount of patience, making us wait every torturous second. His typical dark, perfectly creased trousers and spotless shirt nearly blended with the underground stone around him, the tiny stream of moonlight reflecting off the shine in his hair. He stood with his shoulders back and his hands relaxed, but he towered over everyone in Midgrave with no effort at all. He was aging, yes, but his presence alone still made even the most ferocious fighters tremble before him.

"I expected more from you both," he drawled. I dipped my chin, unable to look at him as he continued. "If he were a vampyre, you would have been torn to shreds."

"Yes, Lord," I replied, keeping my head down.

I stared at the ground in front of me, not wanting to see the lingering doubt that would be all over Lord's face.

"And you," he said, turning his attention to the male beside me. "You let a female half your size take you off your feet. That is an embarrassment, and not one I will allow here. Do you understand?"

"Yes, Lord," he grumbled.

I tried not to smile.

Being satisfied by my opponent's criticism would not lessen my own, and my punishments did not end here with words.

I was not just another assassin being trained by Lord to kill any and every threat that entered Midgrave. Lord had made killing vampyres his life purpose. He gave everything he had to protect the fae of Midgrave from those monsters, and he expected more from me. He expected *perfection*.

And that fight was nothing close to perfect.

The male was strong, stronger than most. It was hard to tell with the disguised faces, but I was certain I hadn't fought one that strong before.

Maybe Lord was testing me, finding stronger opponents to push my strength.

When I looked up again, Lord was already staring at me. I had learned the meaning behind most of his facial expressions over the years, either from all the hours we spent together or as a form of protection.

Either way, I was always expecting, always watching, searching for those clues.

Like when his lips tightened into a thin line, curling slightly in the corners as he squinted his eyes.

That meant I was royally fucked.

It took everything in me not to cower away when I saw that expression grow on his mouth, followed by the darkness of disappointment in his aged eyes.

"Do you two think killing vampyres is easy?"

"No, Lord," we answered in unison.

Lord stepped forward. "Do you believe Phantom is a waste? That fighting against the blood-sucking creatures is below you?"

I shook my head, biting the inside of my cheek. *Of course I didn't think that.* I, too, had given everything to become the best vampyre killer in Midgrave—aside from Lord.

Lord's gaze shifted from us to the shadows of the underground den. I felt the weight of his golden, piercing eyes physically lift away from me.

"When I started Phantom after the war, I saw it as the only way fae in Midgrave would survive. Many of the surrounding fae kingdoms had already been ravished by the fall of the vampyre kingdom. Nobody stood a chance." He paused for a few seconds. My chest tightened. "But I was not going to back down like the others. This place was my *home*. I decided to stay and fight against the depraved beasts, and I trained as many as I could to stand and fight with me.

"Phantom was not created with weak attempts at fighting and ill-prepared assassins. Phantom was forged out of perfection, crafted with a desperate desire to survive, to kill as many vampyres as possible and to remind those blood-thirsty monsters who was in charge here. I did not become the master of vampyre killers by allowing my fighters to make mistakes and train with sloppy punches. When I tell you to kill, you damn well better be prepared to kill. When I tell you to fight, it better be the best damn fight I have ever seen. Do you understand what I am saying?"

"Yes, Lord." I knew what Lord had done to protect Midgrave, what he had done to protect me. Hearing him say the words himself, however, pulled the air from my lungs.

He was the only reason Midgrave survived. He was the only reason *I* survived. When my parents were killed during the war, Lord found me. He took me in, protected me. He did not raise me to be soft. He did not raise me to be just another victim the vampyres could drain of blood.

No, he raised me to be unstoppable.

I flinched as his eyes slid back to us.

"You both may go," he said, sounding nothing but bored.

That was it. No second chances. No do-overs. I had one chance at showing Lord how strong I was every week, and this week? I let that male get multiple blows in. Hells, he almost *won*. Lord did not expect me to fight like all the other Phantoms. No, I was supposed to be the best. I was supposed to be his mirror, fighting like the goddess herself and making not a *single* mistake.

My instinct was to stand up for myself, to tell Lord I could be better. Could *fight* better. But arguing with him only made him angrier.

Words won't help you, he would say. And he was right.

My fighting would help me. Getting better, stronger, faster would save me from his punishments.

Not my words.

I dipped my head and followed the male out of the den, walking in silence through the small, tunneled entrance of the underground cave until the cool night air hit my face.

The male did not hesitate before bolting down the alleyway, away from Phantom, away from me. I turned on my heel, running into the night, through the dark alley-ways and covered entrances.

It was one of Lord's first rules. Nobody knew the other Phantoms. Nobody revealed their identity. We fought for training purposes, but we never uncovered our faces.

We all remained safe that way. Becoming friends with the others, building relationships with them, it would only distract us. It would take away from our true purpose of killing the enemy.

I continued running from my opponent, my black combat boots guiding me through the damp alleyways set out before me. The route was so familiar now, and I loved being outside at night after the streets emptied and the moon rose.

Midgrave wasn't nearly as hideous when the shadows took over, hiding the harsh reality of what really remained in these streets.

The homeless children, the starving animals, the mounds of rubbish. They barely stood out now, when the only thing to be seen was darkness.

I trudged past a building that used to be a school, now with only two walls still standing and a pile of rubble where fae children used to learn. Beyond that were a few newly built homes, each with four walls and a roof. It wasn't much, but around here, it was practically a luxury. A few of the older residents lived there now—ones that had survived long enough to earn those new homes.

A few voices and a fit of laughter rang out in the alleyway next to me, but I lowered my head and continued walking. Making friends was not a skill of mine, and I found that keeping to myself was the best way to stay focused. The smell of burning wood and cooked meat wafted through the wind, making my stomach flip.

Midgrave was not small by any means, but it felt that way to me. It felt constrained. Those walls surrounding the perimeter that were once built to keep the vampyres out sometimes felt like my personal boundary in the world—a boundary I could never escape.

I neared the familiar brick building at the edge of our run-down city, the same brick building that had been a beacon for me for over two decades. It was the tallest building left in Midgrave, nearly three stories high. I enjoyed the vantage point; it made me feel protected. Prepared.

This was home. As shitty and rugged as it was, this crumbling space still brought me comfort.

Almost as much comfort as the familiar figure I saw in the shadows, already lounging on the roof with her booted foot dangling off.

Rummy.

A smile spread across my face as I slowed my jog, ducking into the hidden doorway at the bottom of the building and striding up the stone stairs two at a time until I reached the top. The shattered window that led to the roof remained open, and I ducked my head to step through.

Rummy and her smooth golden hair didn't move as I walked up beside her, careful that my boots didn't slip against the few slick remaining shingles before sitting down.

We let silence linger between us for a few minutes. That was one thing I liked most about Rummy: She understood how comforting the night was. I breathed, taking in the cooling air that somehow seemed cleaner up here. Fresher.

I let my foot mimic Rummy's, hanging off the edge of the roof as I reclined onto my back.

"You look like shit," she remarked, twisting her neck until her dark green eyes met mine. "Bad fight?"

I blew out a puff of air. "You really have a way with words," I joked. Peering out at the city, I shrugged. "It was fine. I won."

She propped herself onto her elbow and scanned my face in the darkness. Her pointed ears twitched as she focused in on me. "Fine isn't good, Hunt. Lord isn't going to let that go."

"I know," I answered, trying not to snap at her. "I did my best. He was a lot bigger than me and a hell of a lot stronger. But I still won."

Rummy shook her head. "How long has it been since your last punishment? Two weeks? Has your skin even healed?"

"It's healed enough," I said stiffly.

My mind wandered to the lingering pain on my back, the dull stinging that hadn't quite disappeared since I lost a fight two weeks ago.

It was rare for me to make a mistake.

It was even more rare for me to lose a fight.

Lord didn't approve.

Rummy knew Lord. She wasn't a Phantom, but she had been my friend since I was a child. If Lord knew she existed, he didn't show it. Sometimes, I thought he knew about our late-night meetups and hidden conversations in the shadows, and maybe he let me have this. Let me have this friendship.

Rummy was strong and fierce and loyal, but she despised him. She hated that I was a Phantom, and she hated that Lord controlled me. She was smart enough to pick up on a few things over the years: bruised fists, lashings on my back, days where I went missing with no contact.

I saw it in her eyes, in the way she flinched slightly when I told her about my fights and my training sessions.

"Don't say it," I sighed.

"Say what?"

"Whatever judgmental and incredibly unhelpful comment you're about to make."

She huffed, throwing a hand up. "I just don't understand why you don't leave. You could run, Huntyr. You could escape, and he would never find you!"

I squeezed my eyes shut and shook my head. "You know I can't do that, Rummy."

"But why?" she demanded.

We had the same conversation every few months, but lately, they had gotten more and more frequent. Rummy had a certain desperation about her she could hardly contain.

Lately, though, my training had grown more intense. My fights were harder, my punishments fiercer. Lord had been leaving no room for error, not from me or from any of the Phantoms.

But Rummy didn't understand. Nobody could. Lord may have been just a teacher to the rest of the Phantoms, but not to me. He had taken me in when I needed him the most. He had raised me as his own daughter.

It wasn't as simple as leaving Midgrave. I would be leaving the closest thing I had to a father. And worse, I would be disappointing him.

That was something I couldn't bear to live with.

"I need him," I said, my voice barely above a whisper. "He's made me strong. He's made me a survivor."

"He's made you his pet." Rummy turned her face back up to the sky, spitting out the word *pet* as if it were poison. "Are you going to let him control your life forever?"

She didn't get it. She didn't understand. Every fight, every punch, every whipping—it was all to strengthen me. It was all so I could survive out there in the world with *them*, the bloodsucking vampyres who took everything from us.

Those creatures killed my parents. They took my family away from me. The only reason they didn't kill me as well was because of Lord. I couldn't help but wonder if this was all part of some wicked plan from the goddess, if I wasn't meant to live this fate so that I, too, could protect people from those killers.

But darkness crept closer to Midgrave every day. Soon, it would take over.

Lord only wanted to prepare me. He wanted to keep me alive long enough to save Midgrave, to save myself.

"Forget it," Rummy mumbled, shaking her head when I didn't respond. "You're going to need this tonight." She reached into the cloth satchel beside her and pulled out a silver flask, twisting the top open and taking a long pull of whatever was inside.

I sat up as she passed the flask to me, hissing as she swallowed the liquid.

Strangely, I found peace in these encounters with Rummy. "Thank you," I murmured. Even in the dark night, I caught a glimpse of her smile. "I don't know what I would do without you."

I put the flask to my lips and drank, letting the liquid burn my throat and stomach. I didn't cough, didn't grimace. The burn was a pleasant distraction.

Rummy laughed. "You'd have to take your whippings without our liquid friend, for one," she said.

"I take it back," I mused. "You *are* cruel." I passed the flask back to her. "And who knows? Maybe Lord is feeling particularly kind this evening."

Her smile slowly disappeared, all hints of amusement swiftly wiped from her face. "Yeah," she said, her snarky tone replaced with a genuine one, "maybe."

CHAPTER

TWO

My senses were comfortably dulled by the time Rummy slipped from the roof, disappearing into the night and leaving me alone.

Without her presence, my mind wandered. Lord usually came home later in the evening, well past midnight. Maybe something would keep him busy tonight. Maybe he would wait until tomorrow to reprimand me for my mistake during the fight.

Or, if I were lucky, perhaps he would come home and send me on a mission instead, teaching me a different lesson by putting me in the face of danger.

It had been weeks since he sent me on a mission, and my hands shook with the need for another fight.

A real one this time. A true fight. With one of *them*, the monsters that lingered in the depths of the shadows.

I shook my head. *Stop thinking that way, Huntyr. If Lord punishes you, you'll take it. Tomorrow will come, and it will be done. You'll be a better Phantom because of it.*

I slipped my body back through the broken window and wandered down the stone steps until I reached the bottom floor.

Home.

I ignored the sinking feeling in my stomach, ignored the way every instinct in my body told me not to go inside the small room I called my home. That was natural. I had to get over that fear of pain.

With a deep breath, I pushed the wooden door open and stepped inside.

Aside from my half-rotted mattress on a cot near the wall and chair in the corner, the room remained empty. It wasn't much, and I never cared for many material things, but it was home. This space was *mine*, and that was enough.

Not this time, though. This time, as my eyes adjusted to the darkness, a lantern lit up the back corner of the room.

Shit.

Lord was already home.

I closed the door behind me with a slow certainty and stopped, standing and waiting.

"Lord," I greeted, swallowing over the newfound lump in my throat.

He sat in the chair beside the lantern, his legs stretched out before him and his arms draped over the sides. His short hair, always perfectly greased back, shined in the dim lighting. Not a single piece ever strayed from its position. Not a single piece of black clothing wrinkled, not a single speck of dirt on those slacks.

Always perfect. Always the master.

"You disappointed me today, Huntyr," he began.

I dropped my head. "Yes, Lord. My opponent was stronger than I expected him to be."

Lord stood from the chair with unexpected speed, crossing the room in two big strides. "Now you make excuses? You think it is his fault that you struggled during the fight?"

I stumbled over my words, "No, Lord, I–"

A hand cut across my cheek. The stinging on my face was nothing compared to the shame that crept through my body. I deserved it.

"It cannot happen again," he commanded.

I squeezed my eyes shut to keep the tears from seeping out. "I understand."

"Do you?" Lord challenged, his musky breath brushing over the now-sensitive skin on my face. "I've tried, Huntyr. I've tried to protect you, to train you for the dangers of the world. Do you understand how much I have sacrificed for you? How much I risked by saving your life? Do you know just how special you are?"

I did not answer.

"Many of the Phantoms would take your place in an instant to be brought up by me, to be personally trained by me from childhood. You are a weapon, Huntyr. A sword. There is no room for error here."

"I can do better," I mumbled. "I'll train harder, I'll get stronger."

The silence that lingered between us seemed to last for

minutes. "You will," he replied finally. "You have no other choice."

Lord turned to walk toward the back of the room once more, only pausing for a second to tilt his head toward the ceiling and exhale, long and slow. Perhaps he wouldn't punish me this time. Perhaps his disappointment would be enough.

But he reached for the whip that always sat in the corner, propped against the wall. I knew then that I was very wrong.

What came next was no surprise.

"Turn around."

Another beat of silence. My heart stuttered in my chest.

"Yes, Lord." I did as I was told, moving in slow-motion as I turned and lifted my training garments, peeling away the black leathers and matching black undershirt until I stood facing the door with nothing on but my chest wrap.

The first lash came quickly, unexpectedly. I hissed in pain when the leather snapped through the air, smacking against my scarred, bare back. My hands slapped against the wooden door, holding me up as I braced myself.

"Do you think I enjoy this?" Lord demanded. "Do you think I want to hurt you, Huntyr?"

Another smack of the whip, lower this time. I bit my tongue to keep from crying out.

"I do this for you!" he pushed.

Another lash.

Another.

Tears streamed down my face now, and I was happy Lord could not see my lapse of strength.

Tears were weak. Showing pain was weak.

I eventually lost count of the lashes. Seven, maybe eight.

My vision blurred, my head grew heavy. My forehead fell against the wooden door in front of me as I struggled to stay upright. They were just lashings. This was the punishment I deserved, no worse than any of the others I had received.

I nearly cried out in relief when I heard him drop the whip to the ground. "Look at me," Lord ordered.

I wiped my face quickly before turning to face him, lifting my chin to meet his steely gaze. I only saw a quick glimpse of anger in his eyes before it melted away to a soft expression of pity, of care.

"Oh, Huntyr," he cooed. "You have so much potential." He stepped forward and caressed my cheek. "You could be the one to save us all, you know. It is why I put so much pressure on you."

I fought to stay upright.

"You understand why it must be this way, right, child?"

I bit the inside of my cheek before answering, "Yes, Lord. I understand."

He smiled softly, tilting his head to the side as he scanned my face. "Good," he replied. "Get some rest. I have a very special task coming for you soon. You'll want to be ready."

His hand slipped from my cheek as he stepped away, walking out of the door. I listened as his footsteps quietly disappeared, the sounds of him slipping into the room below mine affirming he was really gone before I let myself crumble to the floor.

Hells, I hated him at times. I hated him for hurting me, for turning me into this weapon—into this shell of a fae.

But I also hated myself for disappointing him, for bringing this punishment upon myself.

Darkness swarmed my vision. I could no longer see that lantern in the corner of the room. I knelt on the floor and pressed my forehead against the cool wood. My tears dripped and dripped and dripped as I allowed myself pity, only for a moment.

And then I stopped. I sat up, pushing myself onto my knees. I wiped the snot and tears from my face with the back of my hand.

I was better than this. I could overcome anything.

My back screamed in agony, the blood trickling down my skin until it hit the waistband of my training pants.

I was better than this.

If I could just do what I was fucking told and fight better, fight stronger, this wouldn't happen. It was my fault, I reminded myself. My fault that Lord was upset. My fault that my skills were not perfect.

Mistakes would get me killed.

This pain? At least I still lived to feel it.

I woke up in my bed, unsure of when I had finally managed to crawl the few feet to the low cot. My shirt was still off, but that was a good sign. That meant my back was getting some air.

My mouth grew stiff with dryness and my muscles ached. I had to get up.

I wasn't sure how long I had been asleep. Sometimes, the lashings would cause me to pass out for days. The worst was when they grew infected, or during the hot months when I couldn't keep the sweat from seeping into the wounds.

This wasn't so bad.

I pushed myself up to my feet, stifling a groan as the scabbed skin on my back cracked. The sun crept through the fabric that covered the window, bright enough to be past mid-day.

I had to get up, had to drink water and eat something before I passed out again.

Don't be weak, Huntyr. It's just a whipping; it will heal like it always does.

I stumbled to my feet and almost fainted when the blood rushed from my head. I just had to—

A rush of pain hit me, followed by an unexpected wave of nausea. I half-ran, half-stumbled to the tiny bathroom connected to my nearly empty room, vomiting up nothing but stomach bile as I dropped to my knees near the toilet.

Fuck. That was not a good sign. I tried to spit in the toilet to cleanse the bile that now covered my dry mouth, but it was nearly impossible. I hadn't eaten anything. My body needed fuel if I was going to regain my strength anytime soon.

A knock on my door made me tense.

"Go away!" I yelled as I threw a hand up and flushed the toilet. Rummy was probably coming back to check on me, and I was in no mood for her antics. She needed no more reason to hate Lord.

The door opened anyway.

"It's me," Lord called out as he slipped inside. "I brought you ointment and something to eat."

My eyes shot open. *Thank the goddess.* I would normally be ashamed for Lord to see me like this with my head hung over the toilet and sweat plastering my black curls to my forehead, but I was in absolutely no condition to argue with that.

Lord was the one who had inflicted these wounds, yes, but he was always a provider to me when I needed it, too. He kept me at his mercy; I was smart enough to know that.

But I wasn't strong enough to fight it, especially not now.

I sagged in relief.

Lord stepped forward, pausing at the bathroom door to take in what he saw. "Here," he said, extending his hand and hauling me from the floor. "You need to eat, or you'll get too weak."

I let him help me back to my cot. He set me down gently, careful not to touch any of the open wounds on my back.

Once I was fully seated back in my bed, he turned to

dig into a paper bag he brought with him. "This will help your back heal," he said, pulling out a glass container.

It wasn't rare for Lord to bring me food, especially after a rough training day. But healing ointment? "Why would you bring me this?"

He exhaled loudly, showing me a small sliver of the stress that I suspected ran in his veins at all times. Protecting the entire city from vampyres had weighed on him over the years. His once jet-black hair now had tendrils of white laced throughout, his fierce eyes now accompanied by fine lines etched into the surrounding skin. "Like I said, child, I need you to be prepared for anything. I raised you to be a fighter."

I didn't object when he opened the container and knelt beside me, the dirty floor getting dust all over his pristine black pants as he strategically applied the ointment to the ripped skin of my back. I hissed and flinched away at first, but Lord's touch grew softer.

These were the moments—those soft, caring times in between brutal fights and slaughtering vampyres—that Rummy would never understand. Lord *did* care for me, even if it did not always appear that way on the outside. The way his fingers barely contacted my poor skin, the way he pretended not to notice my sigh of pain.

It was our version of love, our unsaid message that we were family, we would take care of each other.

After a few seconds, the stinging pain in my back turned to a dull ache.

Relief flooded my senses as the healing herbs and tonics seeped into my skin. It was easy to forget what my body felt like without the pain until the nonstop agony finally subsided.

"Thank you," I whispered through my cracked lips. I took a pain-free breath for the first time since before my punishment.

"You don't need to thank me," Lord replied. His voice held no malice or anger. This wasn't a visit from the assassin master, it was a visit from the man who took in a child when she needed help. "I'm here to talk to you."

I peered at him over my shoulder. "About what?"

He finished rubbing the ointment across my back, then returned it to the paper bag, tossing it onto the cot.

"Eat," he ordered.

I obeyed, digging into the bag and pulling out a loaf of bread and an apple. I immediately ripped the bread open with my teeth.

Lord pulled the chair from the corner closer to my cot. "What do you remember about The Golden City?" he asked as he sat down casually.

The Golden City. I quickly recalled everything I had been told about the place. It was a hidden society, one that only the strongest fae could get into. Angels used to live there too, but that was before they became nearly extinct.

The ones that were too good for this life, the ones that were strong and wealthy and smart, they all made it to The Golden City. Of course, you couldn't just walk right up to it and ask to be let in. It was completely secret, from what it took to enter to what happened once you were inside.

All I knew was that for people like me, for people like the

citizens of Midgrave, it was too far out of reach. We were raised here, with crumbling buildings and starving children. We did not possess the skills required to make it into The Golden City. They lived like the goddess herself while the rest of us suffered.

We would never be good enough. We would never be like *them*.

"It's an elite society," I replied, swallowing another bite of bread with a shrug. "Only the strongest fae can get in, only the absolute best."

"That's correct," Lord said. "Do you know what's so special about The Golden City?"

I pursed my lips. "No homeless children. No sick mothers. No unsolved crimes. They're all perfect, apparently. Better than us, that's for damn sure." The words felt bitter rolling off my tongue. I had never met anyone who lived in The Golden City, but I couldn't understand why anyone would want to live with such ridiculous luxuries while fae like us barely survived.

"They are untouchable," Lord continued, nodding his head. "Because they possess special gifts. They wield magic freely, pulling power from the archangels."

I paused my chewing. "Magic? How is that possible?"

Years and years before the war, fae like us had free rein to wield magic whenever they pleased. I've heard stories of mothers using fire magic to warm their children, of farmers using magic to adjust the winds and save their crops.

But now? Not a scrap of magic existed in Midgrave. I had a hard time believing it existed anywhere, even in The

Golden City. The magic came from the archangels, and without them, we had nothing.

"There are a lot of things that go on there, Huntyr. Things the rest of us could not even fathom."

I set down the rest of my bread. "Why are you telling me this, Lord?"

He took a long breath. My nerves erupted, tightening my chest. It wasn't like him to act this way, so unsure. He braced his elbows on his knees and clasped his hands together as he said, "I'm sending you there, child. Your next assignment is to make it into The Golden City."

My blood froze in my veins. "Is this some sort of test?"

Lord smiled softly. "No. This is no test. You must pass a series of challenges with others who are attempting to become one of the elites, and you'll be one of the very best."

I shook my head. It was all way too much information. "But why? Why now, and why me?"

He leaned forward, seeking my face with his eyes. "You are the one I trust the most out there, my child. There's something I need from you once you are inside, something I cannot trust with anyone else here."

My heart fluttered. "What is it?"

"Don't worry about that now," he said, sitting up straighter. "For now, we must worry about getting you inside."

I took a deep breath and nodded. "Okay. How am I supposed to do that?"

Lord explained the process, starting with a special academy I would be forced to attend. I had never heard of the academy, but I suppose I never wondered much about the exact process of making it into The Golden City. Living there was never an option for me, and thinking about how to get in was a monumental waste of time.

The academy, Moira Seminary, would push me to my limits, physically and mentally. I would learn even more physical combat, as well as how to wield magic, magic that we had only heard about in legends from our elders.

"Why?" I asked, my brow creasing. "What are they preparing us for?"

"The Golden City is home to the strongest, most powerful fae and angels that exist, Huntyr. The city is a frequent target for enemy attacks and vampyres. They have become so elite because every single citizen within those towering walls can defend themselves. They earned the right to be there."

I considered his words. "You're saying we'll be training to protect The Golden City before we're allowed to live there?"

"Yes," he confirmed. "That's right."

"And what if I fail? What if I don't make it through Moira?"

Lord leaned forward again, coming a mere few inches from my face, so I could feel his breath on my skin when he whispered, "Failing is not an option, child. You'll make it through Moira, or you will die like the other students who are not strong enough to pass. Do you understand your assignment?"

Fear threatened to infiltrate my senses, but I pushed it

away and lifted my chin. "Yes," I answered. "I understand the assignment. When do I leave?"

Lord sat back in his chair, apparently pleased with my answer. "Three days. Get plenty of rest. No more training for you; you have everything you need."

He stood to exit, leaving me speechless on my cot.

Three days? How was I supposed to prepare for a secret elite academy in just three days? My back certainly wouldn't heal in that amount of time, even with ointment, and I was in no condition for combat training. Not after what Lord did to me.

"Wait," he said before he reached the door. "I forgot something." He returned to the chair before unclipping the sheathed dagger from his belt and handing it to me. "Here. I want you to have this."

I glanced at him in disbelief. This was so unlike Lord, even now. "You're giving me your dagger?"

He nodded. "Her name is Venom. She's been with me through many life-or-death trials, and now she'll be with you."

I took the weapon from his grasp, stunned by the solid weight of it. I slowly removed it from the black sheath, amazed by the green emeralds embedded into the perfectly sized silver handle. "She's beautiful," I whispered. "But I cannot accept this, Lord."

"You can, and you will. Let it remind you of why you're in that school, of what your end goal is. You are the only one who can do this, Huntyr. It must be you." His words held a certain desperation. "This is what your entire life has been leading up to."

I nodded, hesitantly accepting the weapon. I still didn't know why it had to be me, why he couldn't trust one of the other assassins to do it. But Lord was not a trusting person at heart, and whatever he needed me to do inside The Golden City seemed to weigh heavily on his shoulders.

It was just another mission. I could handle it.

Lord stood and left me alone without another word. I placed the sheathed weapon—Venom—under my pillow, scarfed down the rest of the bread and apple, and drifted into a deep, deep sleep.

CHAPTER

THREE

The pain that screamed in my back had dulled to a constant yet manageable burn as Rummy and I made our way through Midgrave. We walked the same route every week around this time; just as the sun was setting and the beautiful rays of gold and orange flickered over the fallen ruins of our town.

Normally, Rummy and I would talk over each other, explaining every detail of our lives since we last spoke.

This time, though, we walked in silence.

I shoved my hands into my black jacket, my boots crunching over the dirt and rocks as we listened to the sounds of surrounding life: the constant thud from Midgrave's only metal welder in the distance, cries from a screaming baby, the cheerful voices coming from the half-crumbled but still functioning bakery.

And, of course, the half-drunk fae who grew louder and louder with every glass of golden ale they consumed at the tavern.

That's where Rummy and I were headed—the local watering hole.

Like most of the establishments in Midgrave, there was no longer a door. Just an opening in the grey stone that we quickly ducked into before being greeted with a usual cheer from the other fae inside.

"There you are!" the barmaid, Sophia, yelled as soon as we made our way to our usual table near the back. A cloth hung over her shoulder as she set two ales down for the men at the bar, quickly flashed that perfect smile, and made her way in our direction. "I was starting to think you both forgot about me."

"Please," Rummy scoffed. "If we ever forget about you, that means the entirety of Midgrave has crumbled, and you can find our bones with the ashes."

Sophia rolled her eyes, quickly busying herself with pouring our ales. Rummy made herself comfortable across from me, slipping off her black leather jacket and leaning forward with both elbows on the small wooden table.

"First round is on me," she said as she returned, placing the large mugs in front of us. Her bright gaze lingered on me. "You look like you need this."

I said nothing as I picked up the mug and took two large gulps. I felt their eyes on me, but I didn't care. They had both seen me in much, much worse condition. A few bruises and a stiff back were nothing.

I set the mug back on the table with a clank. "I'm feeling better already," I said with a wink.

Sophia pulled the cloth from her shoulder as she spun

around, her icy hair trailing behind her as she got back to work.

Rummy, however, eyed me for a second longer. My sarcasm wasn't nearly as effective on her. She knew me too well. "What's going on with you?" she asked. Her bright green eyes scanned my face, piercing my soul. "Was Lord's punishment that bad?"

My foot tapped against the bottom of the table. I was thrilled that Lord wanted me to go to The Golden City, even more so that he trusted me to complete whatever this mission entailed.

But leaving Rummy?

She had no one else. Like most of the fae who used to live in Midgrave before it turned to...well, this crumbling, pathetic excuse for a home, her parents were killed by vampyres years ago during the last large attack. Her and I had a lot in common, actually. We both had nobody.

Nobody except each other.

But the train to the academy would leave in days, and I had to tell her, eventually.

"I'm leaving," I said, fighting to keep my voice steady.

Rummy's dark brows drew together. "Okay..."

I leaned in, matching her posture with both elbows on the table, and I lowered my voice. "I'm going to The Golden City."

It took a few moments for my words to register. She quietly picked up her mug, taking the first sip of ale since we arrived. The rest of the tavern seemed to disappear entirely as I watched her, waiting for her response.

She set her mug down and met my gaze. "I'm waiting for more of an explanation here," she started, "because there is no way in all hells that you randomly decided to get into that place. You do know that most fae don't even get in, right?"

Another few heavy seconds passed. I tapped my fingers against my mug. "Lord is sending me on a mission there."

Rummy leaned back in her chair, rolled her eyes, and threw her hands up in the air. "There it is. There's the truth behind this horrifically idiotic idea."

"It's not idiotic," I retorted. "Can you hear me out, please?"

Her nostrils flared, and I knew Rummy well enough to know that her temper was raging within her right now.

She crossed her toned arms over her chest. "Fine. Start talking. And this better be good."

"I've been training for this all my life, Rummy. Lord made sure I was prepared. I'm the best damn fighter in Midgrave. I've killed hundreds of vampyres, if not more, and this could be my ticket out of here."

A flash of hurt crossed her features. "You want to leave that badly?"

I shrugged, taking another sip of ale. "If it were up to me, I would be perfectly happy staying here and protecting Midgrave from those bloodsuckers. You know that. But Lord needs me to do this, Rummy. We both know I owe it to him."

She scoffed before looking away.

"What?" I pushed.

She shook her head before finally meeting my gaze, an intensity I had never seen before lingering there. "You can't keep letting him control you, Hunt. Yeah, he took you in as a baby and raised you as his own, but was it fucking worth it? I mean, look at you! I bet if I looked at your back right now, it would be covered with reasons you shouldn't give a shit about him or his orders."

I shushed her, quickly glancing over my shoulder to make sure no one had heard. "Keep your voice down!" I whispered.

"My bad, wouldn't want the big, scary Lord to hear me talking this way to his precious Huntyr."

"Goddess," I mumbled. "I thought you might at least be the tiniest bit happy for me. I'm actually getting out of here, Rummy. How many times have we talked about leaving this place? How many times have you urged me to run away from here? Well, here I am, finally doing it. And you're so angry, you can't even fake a tiny smile for me."

She gave me a half-laugh. "Please, when have I ever been one to fake anything?"

I waited for another argument, another retort, another piercing glare, but none came. Rummy's smile lingered long enough to break the tension building between us.

Hells. She wanted the best for me. I knew that. Nobody truly understood the relationship I had with Lord, the life debt I would be forever paying back. He took me in and saved my life, giving me the strength and skills I needed to stay alive in a vampyre-riddled kingdom.

I would do anything he asked of me. It was that simple.

"I *am* happy for you," Rummy said after a while. "I'm going to miss you like fucking crazy, but if anyone deserves to get into The Golden City, it's you."

Heat rose to my cheeks. "I'll come back and visit you once I'm in," I added. "Moira Seminary only lasts a couple of months, and as soon as I'm finished with this mission, I'll come back home. Lord says I have to learn magic, but I have no clue how that will be possible."

Her eyes widened at the mention of magic. "You're kidding, right?"

I shook my head. "Not in the slightest."

She tossed her head back and laughed. Her shiny hair fell over her shoulders as she leaned forward, the grin on her face spreading from ear to ear. "Okay, tell me everything."

So I did. I told her everything Lord and I discussed, from the combat training, to the magic that existed in The Golden City. I told her about the strongest fae that would compete with me to get in, about how mysterious everything was, how secretive. Her face lit up as I told her about the magic, about how I would be able to use it after they trained us at the academy.

By the time our conversation was over and two more mugs of ale were emptied, any arguments lingering between us faded entirely. That was another thing I loved about Rummy. No matter how much we fought, it was quickly forgiven.

"I fucking love you," she mumbled as we both stood from the table. She slipped her black jacket on and threw an arm over my shoulder. "And if you don't make it back here alive someday, I'm really going to be pissed."

That, I believed.

With only one day remaining until I left Midgrave for an unknown amount of time, I trekked out to the woods that surrounded the city. I found it much easier to clear my head out here, with nothing but the tall masses of trees and trickling water of the river to distract me.

Rummy would kill me if she knew I was coming out here alone. *There are vampyres outside of the city*, she would argue. *You shouldn't be going out there by yourself!*

I wished a vampyre would try to attack me. It would give me an excuse to tear their heart out.

Besides, Lord trained me to be a killer. Vampyre or fae, I would be perfectly fine.

I kept walking, my black combat boots crunching over the cold forest ground, until I found the familiar, secluded spot beside the narrow river. *Thank the goddess.*

Even with the ointment Lord had given me for my back, I needed the cold, refreshing water of the river to relax my muscles before my journey tomorrow.

The sun was still setting, but I didn't care. Nobody else would dare to wander this far from Midgrave.

I dropped my bag and stripped off my leather jacket and boots, followed by my shirt and pants. I tossed everything into a pile until I stood in the forest with nothing but my underwear and chest wrap.

Those, I would leave on. Just in case.

I quickly knelt, sitting on the edge of the riverbank as I dipped my feet in first. It was cold, but I needed cold. I needed *clarity*. After telling Rummy about my new mission, a weight lifted from my shoulders. Now, I had nothing holding me back. This was really happening. I was about to leave my entire life behind to throw myself at the mercy of an elite academy.

Lord chose me for this. I wouldn't disappoint him.

If I had to learn magic, if I had to pass special tests and become one of the elite, I would do it.

I had to admit, it sounded like an adventure. Something deep in my stomach flipped every time I thought about The Golden City, about what might be lurking inside.

The water ran at an easy pace down the stream, tumbling over rocks at the far end of the bank. This area was deep enough for me to bathe in when I needed it, which I appreciated, but not deep enough that I would have to swim. After rain, the river would only be as high as my chest.

Not knowing how to swim was foolish, I knew that, but taking time to learn such things was a luxury I didn't have.

Finding shallow portions of the river had become a skill of mine anyway.

With one push off my hands, I slid from the grassy ground of the riverbank and into the water, dunking beneath.

My bodily instincts were always the same: tensed muscles, frozen lungs. It was shocking to enter the uncomfortably cold water, the icy underworld of the river. But after a few stunned seconds, I resurfaced, gasping for a breath.

The skin on my back screamed at the temperature until, slowly, the heat dissipated from the wounds.

Finally, I thought. A few minutes in this water would be enough to calm my body for tomorrow. The chill of the river combined with the ointment from Lord would make me almost as good as new.

And yet uncertainty still swarmed in my mind. Lord explained so much to me, adding details I could have never imagined. I'd barely even heard about The Golden City before two days ago, and now? It was all I could think about.

I was strong, yes. Lord made sure of that.

But elite?

It wasn't only the fae of Midgrave that would fight with me for a chance to make it to The Golden City. It would be fae from all over Vaehatis, from kingdoms I didn't even know existed. How was I supposed to compete against them? Be stronger than *everyone?*

I shook my head, ridding myself of those thoughts. It didn't matter. Lord needed this from me, so it would be done. I would find a way to survive, to make it through the academy. I had no other option.

It sounded ridiculous; I knew that, but after everything Lord did for me, I would risk my life for him.

I cupped the freezing water in my hands and threw it over my mess of dark curls that were now plastered to my forehead and against my neck. I reached over my shoulders and brushed my fingertips across the wounds there. It wasn't as painful as I expected, which was a good sign.

A twig snapped in the distance.

I froze.

Nobody ever wandered this far into the forest. Nobody fae, anyway. Nobody from Midgrave.

Another crack of a leaf echoed in the tense silence. My pointed ears instinctively flickered in the direction, and my already rapid heart sped up, pumping a lethal amount of adrenaline through my blood.

Someone lurked out there.

As quietly as possible, I crept to the edge of the river, keeping everything below my mouth hidden beneath the water.

My eyes scanned over the forest, landing on my clothes and bag in a pile by the river. Even if I was hidden, my clothes were not.

Dammit, Huntyr. You just had to go for a dip today.

I waited a few more seconds, making sure no fae or vampyre bolted from the woods to attack me, before slowly slipping from the shallows and crawling toward my clothes. I threw my black shirt on and slid my black trousers up my wet legs. Shoving the rest of my clothes in my bag and carrying my boots, I crept backward, back toward the city lines of Midgrave.

Not even five footsteps in, I heard the rustling of leaves, followed by a low, animalistic growl. Everything in my body screamed at me to run, which could only mean one thing. *Vampyre.*

I grabbed my new knife—Venom—and dropped my bag.

Come and get me, you blood-sucking bastard.

My heart pounded in my chest, just as wild as my breath, as I waited for my attacker. Vampyres were naturally instinctive creatures, but their bloodlust made them idiots. Even the smartest among their kind would turn into rabid animals once they were hungry enough.

That's why they couldn't be trusted.

"Come on," I mumbled to myself. "I've got plenty of warm, fresh blood pumping through these veins. Come and get it."

I rotated the dagger in my hand, getting used to its weight. It was heavier and more solid than any of the cheap, handmade blades I had used during training, but it would work.

Anything would work if you were strong enough.

I waited and waited and waited, frozen in my crouched position with Venom in my hand.

But nothing came. No vampyre bolted from the woods, aiming their nasty teeth at my neck.

Nothing.

I sat there for a few more minutes, ensuring the vampyres had moved on, before throwing my boots on, sheathing Venom, and silently making my way toward Midgrave.

If vampyres were this close, Midgrave was the next target.

And the Phantoms were the only ones standing between them and a slaughtered city.

CHAPTER

FOUR

Midgrave came into view ahead of me as I traveled back toward the city, with the tops of the crumbling walls shining through the thinning line of trees from the surrounding forest. I could see the short wall that circled it, just fifty paces away, but every instinct I had screamed that something was very wrong.

I picked up my pace, my jog soon morphing into a full-blown sprint. A scream split the air in the distance. Another followed shortly after. *Shit.*

The sound of glass shattering echoed, making my blood run cold.

I yanked Venom from my sheath and ran faster.

A million scenarios ran through my mind as the crumbling walls of the city grew closer and closer. The logical explanation would be the local bandits breaking into someone's house.

But this early into the night?

I didn't want to admit the other option. Because that meant more death. More violence.

If the vampyres made it into the city, I might be too late.

The barely standing stone wall that separated Midgrave from the forest taunted me, just a few feet away. My heart pumped quickly but steadily, my lungs sucking in a powerful breath every second.

I used my free hand for leverage and swept my body over the waist-height wall in one motion.

Two more screams erupted, followed by an unmistakable growl of a hungry, soulless monster. My boots hit the dirt ground again.

Again.

Again.

Dammit, Huntyr. Get to them. Get to Lord.

Vampyres had invaded before, of course, but with Lord and the rest of us Phantoms living within the city, they never got far.

The buildings grew more and more dense. Eventually, I began running into people—other fae who had heard the screams and instantly panicked. I didn't blame them; I would have done the same if it weren't for my training.

Instead of running away from the danger, however, I ran toward it.

Straight fucking toward it.

The crowd grew thicker and thicker as I forced myself onward, pummeling through the narrow streets and around sharp corners. Half the damn buildings were nothing but fallen stones that only made it harder for me to maneuver quickly.

But I made it work.

Closer and closer to Lord, closer and closer to home.

The pain in my back was nothing but a memory now, adrenaline pumping through me with every trained motion.

Another scream.

I stopped cold.

I knew that one. It sounded familiar. It sounded like...

Rummy.

Nothing else mattered. I changed direction and pivoted straight for it, my hand gripping my weapon like my entire fucking life depended on it.

Hells, maybe it did.

I heard the first vampyre before I saw it: grunts and half-breaths from a stumbling, rotting corpse. And that smell...

The aura of death pulled me in the direction of the monster, beckoning me ever-closer. I spotted it around a corner, stumbling after an unnatural need for blood.

Disgusting.

It took me three strides to make it to the vampyre and one swift motion to slide my dagger into its back, piercing it through the heart.

Killing it.

That's one.

The body crumbled and fell to the ground with a sickening thud. I stepped over the body without looking. My eyes focused in the darkness, looking for the next beast.

Two more came sprinting out of the nearby alleyway, surprisingly fast for the lack of muscle on their bones. I threw myself into action and slid Venom across the gut of the first one, not slowing down for even a second as I spun and stabbed the second one in the neck.

That wasn't enough to kill it, though. Vampyres still required fatal blows, and I wasn't taking any chances. I pulled Venom from the neck and pierced the closest vampyre in the heart before shoving the body aside and doing the same to the gutted creature.

They both fell to the ground with sick grunts.

I held back my vomit. More screams rang out in the air around me, which meant more vampyres. Many, many more.

I didn't miss a breath before jogging down the street and locating the next vampyre.

And the next.

There had been vampyres in Midgrave before, sure, but these seemed to be after something. Unless they had aimlessly followed each other to this portion of Midgrave, they were all searching for the same thing.

I swallowed those thoughts; I would worry about it later.

Right now, I had to worry about killing.

By the time I reached Rummy's house, I had slain five more decrepit beasts. Old, rotting blood now splattered my face, smeared down my chest.

I spit to get the foul taste out of my mouth.

My feet marched one after the other, hardly controlled by me but rather by the desperate need to get to her. To kill anything in my way.

I'm coming for you, Rummy.

EMILY BLACKWOOD

I turned the corner, finding two vampyres in the street outside the door to Rummy's unit.

My limbs screamed in exhaustion, my palm blistering from holding onto Venom so tightly.

The vampyres both turned and locked their attention onto me. My shoulder now bled from one of the dead creature's claw marks, which practically made me a beacon.

I spun Venom in my palm, raised my arm, and attacked.

They weren't fucking touching her.

My limbs screamed at me, but my anger was stronger than any exhaustion. I would stop at nothing to protect these people from the beasts that had taken everything from me.

These two vampyres were fresh—they still looked sane. One of them had long brown hair and wore a thick red dress, one that made me wonder what she had been doing when she lost her sanity and became this.

It didn't matter. Once the vampyres lost themselves to the bloodlust, there was no turning back.

I reminded myself of that as I let out a battle cry and pierced her in the chest.

Her friend—a male with blood dripping from his mouth—clawed in my direction. He was tall, an entire foot taller than me, but it didn't matter. I ducked below his outstretched hand and stabbed him in the chest.

Missing his damn heart.

He cried out, almost as if he could feel pain. He couldn't. Once the soulless creatures became these monsters, all emotions and feelings left them.

50

This vampyre wanted nothing but blood. My blood.

His long arms got to me before I could pierce his chest again. His disgusting fingernails raked themselves across my neck and chest, ripping the front of my shirt and drawing even more blood.

Did I mention how much I fucking hated vampyres?

I screamed out, more in anger than in pain, and stabbed him again, my aim true to his heart. He froze for a moment before falling to the ground, his body slipping away from Venom as I stood over him.

Another scream pulled my attention away from the couple—Rummy's scream. I bolted up the few wooden stairs to her unit and kicked the ajar door fully open.

Rummy struggled on the ground, a vampyre seconds away from ripping into her throat.

I threw Venom, and the blade landed in the side of the monster's neck, spewing blood.

"In the chest, Rummy!" I screamed.

I made my way over to her, grabbing the beast by the arms and hauling it backward so she could grab Venom and dive the dagger into its rotting heart.

She struggled at first, her hands shaking as she tried to grip Venom. Eventually, though, she did, and her screams echoed off the walls as she delivered the fatal blow.

Rummy and I both froze there, waiting to ensure the creature was really dead.

Two seconds passed. Three. I threw the corpse to the floor beside us and dropped to my knees, heaving for breath after the ordeal of running and fighting to make it in time.

"Thank you," she gasped, her own chest rising and falling with adrenaline as well. "Thank you, Huntyr."

"You can't die," I said between breaths. The words came out angrier than I meant them. "Who else would keep me sane, Rummy? Hells, that was too fucking close."

She scoffed. "I was asleep. I didn't even realize one had entered my room until those cold, lifeless hands clawed at me!"

"They're all over Midgrave." I swallowed, pushing myself back up to my feet. "I've killed at least seven, but there are more."

"Go," she said with a nod, immediately understanding what I had to do. "I'll be fine here."

My forehead creased with worry. "Are you sure?"

"Go," she insisted, loosening Venom from the creature's chest and handing it to me. "They need you more than I do. I'll stay out of trouble, I promise."

"Close the door behind me," I ordered. "Barricade it if you have to."

She reached forward and pulled me into her arms—quickly but harshly—before shoving me toward the door. I took one more breath, letting the cool night air fuel me, and ran back into the streets of death.

My feet were silent on the crumbling dirt. My fae ears begged for a sign, a signal. I stepped over the two kills from earlier.

Where are you, you bloodsuckers?

The hair on my arms rose, and it wasn't from my wet clothing and the cool breeze of night.

Someone was near.

"You must have a death wish." The male voice behind me made me jump. I spun around, dagger raised, ready to stab him directly in the chest.

But what stood behind me wasn't a vampyre. Not in the slightest. A tall, hooded man was before me, one so tall that I had to bend my neck to look up at him, but that wasn't the surprising part. Massive black wings spanned the sides of him and cast a shadow on my face.

Not fae wings, either. They were not leathery and sharp but fell softly with hundreds of black feathers.

Angel wings.

Black angel wings.

He was not just an angel, which was already nearly impossible because they were supposed to be *extinct.*

He was a *fallen* angel.

I gripped Venom even tighter. "Who are you?" I asked in a hushed tone.

He smiled, and I noticed the way his icy blue eyes glowed against the shadows of his hood. "I could ask you the same thing," he replied.

What was he...? Why did...? My mind ran through a dozen different questions but landed on one in particular. "You're an angel," I breathed.

His smile only grew, though it was simply a sign of his

apparent arrogance. "Fallen angel, actually. You're quite observant."

"What are you doing here?" I pressed. I had to admit, I was tempted to throw Venom at him and run as quickly as I could back in the direction I came.

I had seen many vampyres and killed even more. But an angel?

My heart continued to pound in my chest. Angels were powerful—more powerful than any fae that lived. They were descendants from the archangels, and they possessed magic and very rare abilities that I was certain I did not want to find out about here.

Plus, his wings were black. He did *something* to piss off the archangels, and I had no interest in discovering what that was. This creature was dangerous. A threat.

The angel's eyes raked down my still-wet body, lingering for a moment on the dagger in my hand before he dragged them back up to my face. Every one of my instincts lit up, much too aware that I hadn't been trained to fight an angel.

They were stronger than fae and could wield magic freely. They had gifts I had never seen before, had never trained on before. Mostly because—for a reason I was now questioning—angels did not exist in Vaehatis anymore.

Angels had been dwindling in numbers for decades, but lately it was rare to see one in the flesh at all. The angels that *did* exist were meant to be living with the archangels in The Golden City.

I slowly backed away, instinct all but forcing my footsteps backward, until the angel bolted forward, grabbing me and spinning me around while he wrapped a hand around my mouth and dragged me off my feet.

I wanted to scream, wanted to fight, but the angel's impossible strength kept me pinned to his body as I thrashed under his grip.

He pulled us into an alleyway, deep into the shadows of darkness.

"Shhhh," he hummed into my ear. "Your blood smells like cherries. The second they hear you, they'll attack."

I elbowed him in the ribs and thrashed out of his grasp, making a dash back into the street. I made it two steps before the angel wrapped an arm around my waist and hauled me backward, pinning my back against the crumbling wall with another hand on my throat.

Yeah, I fucking hated this male.

"Is this what gets you off?" I seethed. "Saving random females from getting their throats ripped out by blood-suckers, only to use your brute strength against them while you do whatever you please?"

He bent down so his nose barely nuzzled my neck. I would have taken an assassin's tongue for doing something that ignorant back at Phantom. It was a blatant show of power, of strength.

But he was vastly stronger than me. There wasn't much I could do as he ran his thumb up and down the front of my throat.

"There are a lot of things I get off on, little fae. I could show you sometime if you'd like to see."

Footsteps in the street came closer, followed by the gutted grunting of the vampyres around us. Four, maybe five, based on the number of steps. They usually traveled in groups, increasing their odds of feeding.

It was sick. Their insatiable need for blood, for the taste of flesh.

The angel leaned back and held a finger to his lips, motioning for me to be silent. I wanted to bite his damn finger off. I didn't need him to save me. Him, or anyone else. I was a trained assassin, the deadliest fae in Midgrave.

I could kill all five bloodsuckers at the same time if I needed to.

But there I was, back against the crumbling stone in the depths of the shadows, wavering under the hands of this fallen angel.

The urge to kill took over, pulling me like a beacon toward the streets, toward the vampyres. If I could just get my knife up to his throat...

"Don't even try it," he hissed in my ear. "You clearly know nothing about killing my species." He glanced behind me at the trees. "You seem to know plenty about getting yourself killed, though, after what I just witnessed."

I shoved his chest. Hard. "Get away from me. I should gut you for putting a hand on me."

He took a few steps back, and part of me wondered whether I actually had the ability to shove him, or if he was simply humoring me. "Gut me?" he repeated with a slight scoff. He crossed his arms over his chest, dropping his chin to look up and down dramatically with those piercing eyes. Again. "Careful, killer. I like my females violent, you know."

"Shut up," I hissed. The cool winter air now clung to

my wet locks, my skin freezing with every breeze that blew past. "You're lurking in the streets and hiding from the vampyres. What do you want with me?"

He raised a brow. "What makes you think I want something from you?"

"The fact that you're still here!" I sputtered.

The corner of his mouth lifted, and all hells, I couldn't deny that he was attractive. With his hood now pushed back, I could see his skin was dark and full of life, his black hair falling messily around his cut cheekbones. His eyebrows were thick, and they shaped those magnetic blue...

What was I doing? I lifted my knife and charged, aiming Venom directly at his chest.

The angel caught my wrist with no effort and pressed forward, backing me up once again, his hand pinning mine above my head. "Careful," he sneered. "I bite."

My back screamed in agony.

How the *fuck* did this keep happening?

Angel boy had to go.

"Get out of my way before those vampyres slaughter this entire city," I bit back.

"You mean what's *left* of this city? I hate to break this to you, but if I can hear and smell you," he said, giving me a look that sank my stomach, "so can they."

I opened my mouth to defend myself, but his massive black angel wings spanned the sides of him, sucking any unformed words from my mind.

I moved to shove him again, to squirm out from under his grasp and run into the street, but two more vampyres stumbled into the alleyway. We both turned to look. The creatures distracted the *angel boy* just enough for me to slip from his grasp, bolting in front of him.

Right toward the bloodsuckers.

The angel sighed behind me, but I kept my focus on the rotting flesh ahead. With Venom readjusted in my hand, I lunged.

But so did the monsters.

I only had one weapon, one small slice of death separating me from them. Normally, that wouldn't be a problem, but the alleyway caused me to adjust my usual maneuvers, limiting my movement.

I dove Venom into the first vampyre's chest, holding her there while it struggled, all while kicking the second one away from me with my black boot.

Its disgusting claws sliced the skin on my arms, aiming for my face, my throat. The bloody wounds only forced them into a frenzy, leaving pain wracking through my body.

"Need some help?" the angel called from behind me.

"Fuck you!" I yelled back.

He laughed, but a few moments later, the second body dropped. Angel boy had tossed one of his own daggers, landing perfectly in the center of its rotted chest.

Both vampyre bodies slumped to the ground.

I yanked Venom out of the corpse.

"I just saved your life," the angel whispered, now much closer than he needed to be. "You're welcome."

"I didn't need your help," I argued, narrowing my eyes at his proximity.

He shrugged. "Sure."

I turned my ears to the streets, listening for any more movement, any more signs of vampyres.

Silence.

The angel's breath tickled the back of my neck, all of my senses heightened from the rush of the kill.

I turned around and met his gaze.

He stared down at me with a twinkle of amusement in his electric eyes, his black wings now narrowed to fit the thin alleyway.

The vampyres, I could handle. The killing, I could handle. But the way he stared at me, the way his eyes flickered to my wet, sliced-open shirt that exposed my chest wrap, to the cuts that now scattered my chest and my upper arms... That was something new.

More footsteps caught my attention, but they weren't from vampyres.

"Huntyr!" Lord yelled, searching the streets. "Huntyr, where are you?"

My eyes widened. The angel took a step back.

"I'll be seeing you soon, little huntress," he whispered.

And as soon as Lord arrived, the angel boy was gone, deep in the shadows, as if he was never really there at all.

Lord stood at the entrance of the alleyway a few moments later. His pristine appearance now radiated with hatred and violence. His dark skin dripped in sprayed vampyre blood, the moonlight glistening off the wetness of it.

Every breath he took sent his massive chest rising and falling. "This way, Huntyr," he ordered, beckoning me closer. "There are a few more vampyres approaching Phantom."

I snapped myself out of the fog and ran after Lord, ready to kill.

Ready to fight.

Ready to protect.

By the time Lord and I had covered the entire city of Midgrave, my feet ached in my boots. The blood on my skin had dried, my palms bruised from gripping my weapon.

At least I had something to remember this place by.

Once the attack was over, once we were sure no vampyres survived, we burned the corpses, sending the ashes into the air. I spent the few hours until morning washing the vampyre gore from my clothes, preparing for tomorrow.

Tomorrow, everything would change. Tomorrow, I would have much greater enemies than the vampyres.

CHAPTER FIVE

"Welcome to Moira Seminary. I hope you're all prepared to die."

Okay, not the best start to the academy.

I spent all day and night on a train with absolutely no clue where I was headed. I kept to myself, though it wasn't hard. I was one of the few people on the damn thing. Most fae would come from other places in Vaehatis, not Midgrave. They would take trains from the north, from the kingdoms that actually produced elite-worthy fae.

Midgrave didn't exactly have an overwhelming number of fae fighting to get into The Golden City. Most fae from back home had lost hope a long, long time ago.

I only saw one other fae board my train—a younger male I had never seen before. He had red hair that reminded me of the sunset, and he looked much too fragile to be involved in something like this.

Perhaps he was trying to escape the dull life that

existed in Midgrave. Maybe he thought Moira Seminary was his way out.

Moira Seminary, however, lived up to its expectations. Stunning, ancient architecture with towering arcs of stone and terrifying black gates grabbed my attention as soon as the train escaped the thick cover of the deep green forest. White and gray walls ascended into dozens of massive peaks, creating an intimidating and religious experience as I walked through the front doors with my bag slung over my shoulder.

I had never seen anything so beautiful. Every stone, every detail, was assembled with care. Nothing was left unattended to, even the thick green vines that twisted and sprawled across the arching ceilings.

The place felt *alive*.

I wandered forward, following the dozen others who had traveled in on other trains from neighboring kingdoms and appeared just as clueless as myself.

But all of that beauty and awe vanished when a woman walked through the massive arched doors at the end of the hall. Her dark skin and piercing green eyes drew me toward her like a drug. She commanded power, demanded respect. There was no doubt in my mind that she was the one in charge here.

"Hello, recruits. I take it your journeys here were comfortable enough?"

I glanced around the room. Nobody answered.

"Quiet." She clasped her hands before her. "Good. The last loudmouth that came through these doors died the first day."

The first day? She was just saying that to scare us, right?

"My name is Headmistress Katherine. You can call me that, or Headmistress, but not Katherine. You'll address the rest of the mentors here with respect, as they can end your time at this academy with zero reasoning at any time at all."

Again, the room was silent.

Headmistress Katherine smirked. "Follow me."

We obeyed, silently trailing after her. My back ached with the lingering pain of Lord's whip, only amplified by last night's fighting and the long train ride.

I didn't see the angel again, though I spent half of the night looking for him. Not for any reason, of course, other than the fact that angels were incredibly rare.

And a fallen angel in Midgrave? It wasn't normal.

I thought about telling Lord, but what was I going to say? That I let a fallen angel save my life? That I needed help out there against the vampyres?

No, I didn't need to give Lord any reason to pull me from this mission.

The Headmistress took us through a maze of dark, narrow hallways with towering ceilings and perfect stone floors, not slowing down for a second. I lingered near the back of the group, trying to keep my head down.

Don't draw attention to yourself, Lord had ordered. *It will only make things harder.*

I adjusted the strap on my shoulder and kept walking, ducking down the final hallway and into a larger room littered with training equipment. I was familiar with some of it, such as the large bags used for practicing punches. But others looked damn near lethal.

"This is where we'll be spending every other day," Headmistress Katherine announced, turning on her heel to face us. "The rest of your time will be spent with your mentors, learning magic, fighting tactics, and the history of The Golden City."

I swallowed.

"An inability to show up will result in your removal from the program. An inability to keep up will result in the same. If you disobey any of the rules, you're out."

A murmur began in the group. I kept my lips sealed, ducking my chin.

"Is there a question?" the woman directed toward the group of whispers.

One student—a young male who appeared too soft and innocent—stuttered to answer. "We were just... what are the rules?"

Damn, this woman was terrifying. Even her eyes held a promise of death. I didn't trust her one bit.

"We have two rules here at Moira Seminary. Rule number one: Don't kill your fellow recruits outside the classroom. You'll have plenty of time for that in training. Rule number two: Stay alive. This program is not for the weak, and we will not show you mercy. You fight. You live. You make it to The Golden City. It's that simple. Do you understand?"

Everyone nodded.

"Good," she announced, clapping her hands together. "There will be a test, the Transcendent, at the end of your time here. A series of tests, rather, however you wish to look at it. It will be nearly impossible to pass, and most of you will not make it."

I clenched my fists. I wasn't about to cower in the face of death. I had prepared for this. Lord had ensured I would be ready.

There was no test I could not pass. No trial I could not overcome.

"You're all here for a reason," she continued. "Remember what that reason is. Every year, students gather here for the chance to make it into the elite society. Every year, lives are lost. You all know the risks, yet you chose to come here anyway. There was a time when hundreds of students would line the halls of this academy, all fighting for a chance to get into The Golden City." She surveyed the small group of us. "Just because the numbers have dwindled does not mean your entrance will be taken any less severely.

"You've been randomly assigned roommates, and your names are listed on the doors through that corridor." She pointed to her left. "I feel the need to repeat this, but if you kill your roommate in their sleep, you're out."

You could have heard a damn angel feather dropping in the room.

"Get some sleep," Headmistress Katherine ordered. "The Blessing is this evening, and you'll all be required to attend. But listen to me when I say this: The tests to enter The Golden City began once you walked through those doors. I'll see you all this evening."

Okay, so I'm probably going to die.

That was fine. I'd made peace with death a long time ago. It was how I became so fearless, so lethal. No sane female would launch themselves at the back of a vampyre simply to get the approval from their assassin Lord.

Maybe there were a few things wrong with that statement, but nevertheless, I was probably going to die here regardless.

I followed the crowd, keeping my face down as we all funneled through the dark stone hallway, where everyone would be sleeping. It reminded me of corralling sheep. Dangerous sheep, but sheep all the same.

We might have been the strong, capable fae in our respective homes, but here? We were nothing but prey. They wanted to test us. They wanted to see us break.

By the time I reached the end of the hallway, I thought they had forgotten my name. Until I spotted the very last door.

HUNTYR GWENEVIVE
WOLF JASPER

My brows furrowed. What type of name was *Wolf*?

I reached for the door handle when the shadow of a colossal figure cascaded over me. I froze, watching a tanned, massive arm reach over me, gripping the knob I had just been reaching for.

Something about that presence felt so familiar...

"I hope you're good with the bottom bunk," the grumbling voice whispered in my ear. "I like the top."

I spun around to find the fallen angel from Midgrave looming over me, staring down into my face.

"What are you doing here?" I hissed.

"I'm here to get into The Golden City, same as you, I presume. Surprised to see me?" He smirked.

This was not happening.

"Yes! Are you following me?"

He cocked his head to the side. "What makes you think that?"

"The fact that you were in Midgrave and now you're here, trying to enter my bedroom!"

"Of course I'm here. We're roommates." He pointed to our names on the door, as if the fact were obvious. "And it's *our* bedroom."

"No, we aren't," I argued.

He continued reaching forward, his chest almost brushing against me as he twisted the knob and pushed it open, all while maintaining an infuriating level of eye contact.

"The names on this door tell me otherwise," he replied. "Now,"—he waved his hand toward the room—"after you, roomie."

This could not possibly get any worse.

The weight of the dagger strapped tightly on my thigh was only reassuring until I remembered Wolf was an angel, and I knew nothing of killing his kind. A fact he'd so respectfully reminded me of himself.

I backed into the room, squinting my eyes at Wolf— who was absolutely *not* my roommate—before turning around.

The room was bare, as I expected. Two beds—not bunks, thank the goddess—flanked each side. A small window with black bars let in a few rays of the setting sun. The rest of the room was depressingly bare.

Even my dirt pile of a bedroom back home had more personality than this.

"Cozy," Wolf murmured from behind me before brushing past and throwing his bag onto the left bed. "I guess there's no need for pleasantries when half of us will be dead at the end of this anyway."

I tossed my bag onto the other bed. "That's morbid."

"And if what I saw in Midgrave taught me anything, you'll be one of them."

We stared at each other for a minute, neither one backing down. Wolf's expanded angel wings took up nearly the entire room. His arms fell lazily by his sides, and he looked at me as if he were utterly familiar with my every move.

I glared back, arms crossed over my chest. "Get out."

He smiled. "Don't be rude."

"Trust me, *angel*, when you see me being rude, you'll know."

He sauntered forward, closing the small amount of space that existed between us. "I think I saw plenty of it last night while you were impaling vampyres in the chest."

My blood froze. "How long were you watching me?" I gaped.

He shrugged casually. "You intrigued me. And I was bored."

I swallowed and slowly reached for my dagger, finding

comfort in the warm, rough handle that fit perfectly in my palm. "I'll tell you one last time before I lose my damn patience. This is my room, and you're not staying here. Get. Out."

My heart pounded in anticipation, waiting for his response. He somehow irritated and terrified me all at once, causing my body to react in ways I had never felt before.

Wolf ignored me, crossing his arms over his chest. "Just so you know, I prefer to sleep naked."

That's it.

In one swift motion, I pulled Venom from her sheath at my thigh and aimed her toward Wolf's chest with a cry of frustration. Nobody was going to get in my way of completing this mission. Not Wolf, not anyone.

But just as quickly, Wolf's unbelievably powerful hand stopped me. His fingers wrapped around my wrist, just a few inches from his chest, and squeezed to the point of pain.

He twisted his grip, sending my dagger scattering across the floor and my body falling against his. Hard.

I gasped as he pinned my body flush against his. The amusement that lingered on his face before was long gone, now replaced by a flash of both shock and anger.

"Don't ever," he snarled, his lips curling to reveal those perfect predator teeth, not as sharp as a vampyre's but certainly sharper than the fae, "do that again. I don't think Headmistress will appreciate you breaking her number one rule."

He held me there a second longer, and my body heated

at our proximity. I had been this close to males many times during training, but this was different. It was intimate and brutal and so, so wrong.

"Get away from me," I whispered before shoving at his chest, forcing him to release me.

"Trust me, Huntress. I have my own motivations for surviving Moira. I have no plans to crawl into your bed late at night, as much as you may dream of it."

I nearly choked. "Then do us both a favor and mind your own business."

He smiled, but this one beheld no niceties. "Gladly. See you tonight at The Blessing, *roommate*." His jaw tightened as he sauntered out of the room, going goddess knows where. But with him out of the space, I could finally breathe. This was an unexpected challenge, but it was nothing that would interfere with my orders.

Survive Moira. Make it to The Golden City.

Rooming with the only damn angel in this academy would not help me keep my head down. But maybe nobody noticed, maybe nobody saw us walking to the end of the hall.

I waited a few seconds, ensuring Wolf was gone, before cracking the door back open and peering down the hallway.

Only to be met with dozens of eyes doing the same, staring right back at me in awe as if they had just watched Wolf exit from this same room.

Great, just great.

I shut the door and squeezed my eyes shut, trying to settle my racing heart. This wasn't me. I wasn't the person who got flustered by arrogant pricks. I was focused, determined.

This was a minuscule, non-existent bump in my plan. A blip on my roadmap to success. It would not change anything, and it sure as all hells would not affect my mission.

I walked over to my bed and opened my bag, pulling out the two extra sets of clothing I brought with me. They were simple, easy. They wouldn't get in my way. A small leather tie that Rummy gave me lay in the bottom of the bag. She was always insisting I tied my black curls away from my eyes, something I wholeheartedly agreed with.

I picked the tie up and pulled my messy, unmanaged locks away from my face. The cool air instantly hit my neck, soothing the heated skin there.

From the stress of the new environment, I reminded myself. *Not from the damn angel.*

A knock on my door made me jump. I pressed against it instantly, a hand hovering over Venom.

"Who's there?" I asked.

A light, annoyingly cheerful voice responded, "It's Ashlani! Open up!"

Deciding anyone who sounded that chipper would likely not attempt to kill me, I opened the door.

Ashlani stood expectantly with a hand on her hip. Her doe eyes batted at me as she quickly looked me up and down, pausing only for a second at my hand still hovering over my weapon.

"Hey there," she started. "I was coming to see if you wanted to head to Blessing with us tonight."

"Um, why?" I asked.

She shrugged. For a place that trained people on how to be deadly and fierce, she seemed much too nice. "We're going to be living together, so we might as well be friends."

"I don't think making friends is such a good idea."

"Oh, please," she scoffed. "We'll have plenty of time to kill each other later. I'll see you tonight, okay? I'll find you there!"

Ashlani didn't give me time to respond. She turned on her heel, flipping her light hair over her shoulder, and bounced back through the hallway.

At least one person here wouldn't actively try to kill me. *Yet*. But I had to keep my guard up. Someone like Ashlani was hard to read. On the surface, she was kind. Bubbly, even. But nobody was truly happy on the inside.

Too much darkness lingered in this world.

People like Ashlani were only denying their true paths, covering up the shadows with layers of fake light.

I would trust a blatant asshole before I trusted someone like her.

With Ashlani gone and the rest of the hallway empty, I retreated into my room. The Blessing would be tonight, and I needed to prepare.

Like Lord always said, plan to fight and plan to survive. Trust nobody. Death would wait around every corner.

SIX

I spent the rest of the day playing many different scenarios in my mind as to what would happen at The Blessing. I envisioned a blood-covered trap, wild animals chasing us through the academy, a fight-to-the-death competition at the dinner table.

Anything but *this*.

I followed the voices through the academy until the narrow stone paths opened up to a massive square courtyard. The white and gray flanks of the castle walls still towered above me as my feet moved from the rough stone to the soft grass below.

I wasn't used to grass. Dirt, maybe, but no grass. I bit the inside of my cheek to stop myself from smiling.

"You're from Midgrave, right?" The younger male with sunset-red hair pulled my attention away from the courtyard. "I saw you on the train."

I nodded, keeping my features still. "I am."

The male eyed me. He was maybe eighteen, barely old

enough to qualify for The Golden City. "I thought I recognized you. You and Rummy would come to the bakery every once in a while."

The mention of Rummy instantly made me feel more relaxed. If he knew her, I had a chance of liking him. A slim chance, but a chance nonetheless. "You worked at the bakery?"

He shrugged. "Sometimes. My father owned the place. I only helped here and there."

I recalled the way the bakery always made even the darkest days of Midgrave seem less cold. The man who worked there—this male's father—always wore a smile on his face. I wondered time and time again what someone like that would have to smile about in such a shitty world, but I also envied it.

"And you know Rummy?"

He blushed and looked away. "Not really. I tried speaking to her once or twice, but she can be..."

"Scary as all hells?" I finished.

"Yeah." He smiled. "Scary as all hells."

I let my tense shoulders fall, the corners of my mouth twitching upward. "What's your name?"

"Nathaniel." His face instantly lit up. He held his hand out for me to shake.

I shook it lightly. "Right. Well, it's nice to meet you, Nathaniel. It seems we're the only two people from Midgrave that made it here this year."

"If I stick by your side, I just might make it through," he said with a wink. I watched as Nathaniel turned and walked to the other side of the courtyard, where he attempted to mingle with even more of the new students.

He was brave. That, or a total idiot. I watched him until his bright red hair got lost in the sea of people, fading away into the crowd.

I was beginning to like Nathaniel.

"There you are!" Ashlani cheered as she walked over to me, looping her arm through mine.

She isn't a threat right now, I reminded myself. *Be friendly. Blend in.*

I forced a smile. "Yep, this *is* mandatory, you know."

She began pulling me further into the courtyard. Most of the other students had already gathered, along with a dozen others who I assumed to be the teachers here. One quick scan, however, told me Wolf had yet to arrive.

He wasn't in our room all day, either.

Ashlani ignored my comment and guided me over to a male leaning against the stone wall. His features were warm and welcoming, practically glowing beneath the lantern light of night. His face lit up when he saw Ashlani approaching.

"This is Lanson," Ashlani announced, pulling me to a stop before him. "Lanson, meet..."

"Huntyr," I finished for her, shifting uncomfortably on my feet.

"Huntyr," Lanson repeated. He extended a large hand in my direction. He had soft, golden hair that curled around his face and sharp cheekbones that accentuated his smile. He looked like the type of guy you *wanted* to trust, even though his sculpted muscles flexed against his black training shirt. "It's a pleasure to meet you."

I slid my hand into his and he shook it quickly. He kept his hand clasped in mine for an extra second, causing my heart to sink. But his eyes held nothing but kindness. Odd.

"Likewise," I said as I pulled my hand away.

"You must be skilled at hunting, then, with a name like that," he remarked.

I shrugged. *Don't let them know anything, certainly not your strengths or weaknesses.* He may have appeared soft, but just like Ashlani, that was never the case.

Never.

"I can hunt when needed," I said, crossing my arms over my chest.

"Noted," he replied with a smile. "Maybe we'll be seeing more of each other around here, then."

"I think, given the circumstances, that's highly likely."

I stared into his green eyes, looking for a shadow. A demon. A secret. Anything. But all I saw was a friendly fae looking back at me.

A small, hopeful part of my mind thought that maybe this was it. Maybe Lanson was simply a welcoming fae. Maybe not everyone hid their darkness deep in their souls, waiting for the time to burst from keeping too many shadows at bay.

But those thoughts quickly dissipated.

"Look!" Ashlani interrupted. "It's starting!"

I followed her gesture to the middle of the courtyard, where Headmistress Katherine stood near a male who prepared to speak. But my attention was stolen by an abnormally large, black-winged creature leaning against the stone wall with his arms crossed over his chest.

Glaring at me.

Wolf's dark eyes could have sliced through skin. His jaw was set, his shoulders sharp. He looked *pissed*.

I fought the urge to look over my shoulder. Was he pissed at me? What in the hells could I have possibly done to piss him off? I was the one that should be pissed. Not him.

The male preparing to speak looked like a fighter. He was aged, with long white and grey hair pulled away from his tanned, rugged face. He wore all black training gear, much different than Headmistress Katherine's formal gown. He clasped his hands together as he spoke. "Welcome to Moira Seminary. Your first day begins tomorrow, but not all of you will make it through tonight."

A few gasps filled the air. I caught myself double checking the weight of Venom at my thigh, snug and secure against my black training pants.

Wolf still leaned against the wall, relaxed as ever, but his attention now lingered on the male speaking.

"Drink," he continued, as if he hadn't just dropped something massive and mysterious on us. "Relax and enjoy your evenings. But let this be a warning to you that you must always keep your guard up. I'll be your combat trainer starting tomorrow. If you don't see me again tonight, which I truly hope you do not, I'll be seeing you at sunrise."

And with that, he was gone.

Okay... That was weird...

I looked around the courtyard again, making sure no obvious threat lingered in the shadows.

Nothing.

Besides Wolf, who had re-focused his attention on me once more.

"I'll be right back," I said to Lanson and Ashlani before taking off in his direction. His brows furrowed even more as I approached, weaving through the now-mingling crowd of students and teachers before stopping in front of him with a hand on my hip.

"Do you have a problem with me?" I demanded.

Amusement flashed over his features. "Many problems, actually. Why do you ask?"

"Because you've been glaring at me ever since I got here."

His jaw tightened. "How do you know I'm not glaring at those friends of yours?"

"They're not my friends," I argued, hating that I suddenly felt defensive enough to say anything.

"They sure seem like it, Huntress. I thought you were smarter than that."

"They're not threats."

He tsked, "You just met them."

"Well, I just met you too, and so far, you've been more of a threat to me than anyone else here."

His expression changed—torturously slow—from his grumpy scowl into an arrogant smirk. "You forget I saved your life from those vampyres not too long ago. Is that what makes me a threat?"

"You absolutely did *not* save my life," I spat.

Hells, Huntyr. Are you really letting him get to you? He was trying to rile me up. It was so fucking obvious.

I took a long breath, attempting to calm my rising temper. "You are a threat because you're a fucking *angel,* clearly the only angel here, and probably the only angel most of these students have ever seen. I'm trying to keep my head down, and you're drawing way too much attention to me."

"Is that so?" he retorted, tilting his head. "Because I believe you were the one who walked over here to me."

"Only because you were staring at me!"

He smirked. "Allegedly."

A groan of frustration escaped me before I ran my hands down my face and started backing away. "Just stay away from me, okay?"

"Sure thing, roommate."

I spun on my heel and marched back through the crowd, acutely aware of the eyes that now lingered on me.

Wolf was right. I was the one who had marched over to him. It was a mistake I wouldn't be making again. My emotions could not impede getting through this academy. Through this mission.

Ashlani and Lanson talked in hushed voices as I rejoined them.

"Oh good," Ashlani chimed. "You're back."

"Sorry about that. I had to have a word with my... with him." *Not* my roommate.

"Do you two know each other?" Lanson asked, scrutinizing my face. "I didn't know angels still came here."

"No, no. We only just met, but I'm the unlucky one who was paired in his room, I suppose."

"Wow," Ashlani whispered, taking on a look of pity. "That is very unlucky. If it helps you at all, you're always welcome in my room! My roommate is that girl over there."

I followed her gaze to a short yet strongly built female fae standing by herself near the mentors. She had a drink in her hand and busied herself with pacing in small, lazy circles while she observed the details of the courtyard.

She seemed smart. Calculated.

"That's very kind of you," I admitted, forcing a smile. The truth was, sleeping with an enemy who outwardly disliked me was a safer bet than sleeping with two I wasn't sure I could trust. "I'll keep that in mind."

I took a second to observe the rest of the recruits. Lanson, Wolf, Ashlani, and I made up four. Nathaniel from home made five. I tried to scan the faces and put them in my memory.

A group of fae—strong ones, it seemed—stood whispering a few feet away. They were tall, nearly as tall as Wolf. They stood with their shoulders back and their chins up. Arrogant, I could already tell. They had likely been training for this school for some time.

So had I. I just hadn't known it.

"Do you know anything about them?" I asked Ashlani and Lanson, who quickly glanced in their direction. They shared a tentative look before returning their gaze to me. "What?"

"They're bad news," Ashlani whispered. "Do yourself a favor and stay away."

"Why? Are they dangerous?"

"Lethal," Lanson answered. "They grew up near me. We used to be friends, actually, when we were children. But they'll do anything to get into The Golden City. They'll cut you down in an instant if they think you're a threat."

I stole one more glance. Two of them were nearly identical; they both wore sleek black clothing with shaved hair. Their fae shoulders were sculpted and massive, and if what Lanson said was correct, they likely spent a lot of time killing.

Practicing.

"Well, that's terrifying," I said. It was a lie, of course. I couldn't wait to challenge them. They would underestimate me without question.

Everyone always did.

"Alright," Ashlani sighed. "I'm going to get a drink. Want anything?"

"No, thanks," Lanson and I replied in unison.

With a shrug, she was off.

"What about you?" Lanson asked. "Have you been training for this?"

I slipped my hands into my pockets. "Not exactly. It was a bit of a last-minute decision. Frankly, I never imagined trying to get into The Golden City. It seemed too good to be true."

"I know the feeling," Lanson said. He mimicked my body language and slid his own hands into his pockets, which I noticed immediately. "It's a dream. We aren't actually supposed to get into The Golden City, right?"

"That's what I was raised to believe."

"In Midgrave?" he asked. My eyes snapped to him in surprise. He pulled his hands from his pockets in a defensive shrug. "It was a guess," he said. "You seem like the type with some survival instincts."

"I should probably be insulted that you guessed correctly." *Okay, Lanson. You've been paying attention. I'll give you that.* "Where are you from?" I replied, flipping the conversation. "I can tell by your clothing that it's not Midgrave."

He laughed, flashing his perfectly straight teeth. "You're right. I'm from a larger town up north. Ashlani and I came here together, actually."

"Oh, I didn't know you two were..."

"We're not," he corrected. "No, we're just friends. We weren't that close before, but from what I have seen, she's one of the good ones."

I turned my attention to the rest of the courtyard again. "That's good to know," I breathed. "So far, it's hard to tell."

Lanson may have been convinced, but I still wasn't sure. Between the cocky fae, Ashlani's roommate, Lanson, and Wolf, I had no idea who to trust. Lanson seemed to like me, which was a good sign.

A scream cut through the chilling air, followed by a roar of what sounded like water pouring.

"What in the hells is that?"

SEVEN

ater cascaded from the four corners of the courtyard, flowing from nowhere specific and rushing toward us in powerful waves.

My first instinct was to panic. It took me all but two seconds to swallow that fear and think.

Think, Huntyr. Think.

This must be The Blessing, the test to weed out the first round of recruits.

And I couldn't fucking swim.

The tutors had all left, leaving just the apprentices behind to panic in the courtyard. Some twisted, evil magic must be forcing the castle to bleed water.

A few screams rang through the air as soon as the water hit our feet.

And it quickly climbed our legs.

"Don't panic!" Lanson yelled. "They want us to fight."

"I can't swim," I admitted. "I don't know how."

"You won't have to," he pushed, grabbing hold of my

wrist. I didn't shove him away. "They're trying to scare us, that's all."

"It's working!" Ashlani screeched as she sprinted over to us.

The water rose, cascading in waves around the courtyard, pushing us all toward the center.

"Hold on to me," Lanson said. "I won't let go of you."

I wasn't sure why a complete stranger would help me, nor why I would let him, but all I could focus on was the freezing water lapping at my knees, my thighs, my hips.

By the time the water hit my chest, fear had taken over.

"Are they trying to drown us all?" I seethed, my pulse skyrocketing in my ears.

A few of the fae began to swim against the spiral current, as if that would help anything. As if that would stop the water that continued to pour.

Only a few seconds went by before we were forced off our feet, too.

I kicked as hard as I could, trying with everything in me to keep my head above the water. But even with Lanson pulling me upward, I couldn't avoid the bodies that shoved into me, all of us helpless against the strength of the current.

We circled, fighting against the water with sheer panic and instinct.

I inhaled a mouthful of water and immediately coughed it up, cursing at myself for losing the vital air.

Hells, I needed air.

My legs burned from kicking, my chest tightened with panic.

This was it. Not even day one of this fucking place and I was going to die, was going to drown like the weakest of the weak.

"Kick!" Lanson screamed, though the water now roared around us, making it hard to hear. Ashlani bobbed her head in front of us.

I kicked. I kicked as hard as I fucking could.

Someone screamed.

It has to end soon; they can't keep doing this forever.

Water roared, and a massive wave came from nowhere, crashing into us.

I lost my grip on Lanson.

And the water pulled me under.

No amount of kicking would send me upward. No amount of fight, of will, would propel me toward the surface.

I held my breath as long as I could—which wasn't long, due to my racing heart and exhausted limbs.

I had cheated death many, many times in my life. Fought hundreds of vampyres. Killed males twice my size.

But to leave this world by way of water?

No fucking thank you.

I kicked and kicked and kicked, moving against the dark water blindly, desperately.

Then something was grabbing me around the waist, hoisting me upward with strong, rough hands.

Not Lanson.

I was so close to inhaling water, to giving into my screaming lungs, when we broke the surface.

I gagged and coughed and spit up water, pulling fresh air into my lungs like I was breathing for the first time.

Then I realized who held me.

"Wrap your arms around my neck," Wolf growled into my ear, barely audible over the continued roar of the water.

The current moved in a tornado of chaos, sucking everyone toward the center.

Pulling everyone down.

In just a few seconds, we would be down, too.

I turned to face Wolf and wrapped my arms around his neck, holding on with everything I had. He was my fucking lifeline, as pathetic as that sounded.

His wings propelled us out of the spiral, dodging the bodies around us and pulling us to the outer edge of the courtyard. We were halfway up the castle walls now, water eating everything and everyone below.

Wolf reached the edge near the stone walls of the castle and hoisted himself—with me attached—out of the water and onto a window ledge.

He pulled me against his chest while I straddled him, holding on just as tightly as before. The water would not stop; it would not calm.

We were fucking dead.

But a few seconds later, while I clung to Wolf like a helpless, lost animal, the water began to abate its storm on those below.

A few cries of relief filled the courtyard, mixing with my rugged, panting breath as I peeled myself off Wolf.

Water ran down his face, dripping from his hair and his wings, rolling off his lips. "That's twice now," he panted.

I stared at him. "What?"

"That's twice that I've saved your life. I'll be keeping count, by the way."

If I wasn't paralyzed with terror of the death I had narrowly avoided, I would have had a comeback. Would have found a sassy remark to hide the brutal truth that he *had* just saved my life.

Instead, I let my head fall back against the stone wall.

"Huntyr!" Ashlani yelled, swimming over to us. Lanson followed.

"This way!" I said, moving as far as I could manage from Wolf in the confines of the ledge. "There's a window. I'll pull you through!"

Wolf didn't take his eyes off me as I kicked the window beyond the ledge, shattering the glass and slipping myself through, sprawling on the floor for just a second before pulling myself together.

It was only a test.

I was alive.

I was breathing.

A few seconds later, Lanson and Ashlani pulled themselves up and collapsed on the floor next to me.

All of us heaved for air in unison.

The sound of the once thundering water grew quieter and quieter, leaving only our breaths to fill the sound of the empty hallway we had fallen into. Besides Wolf, of course. He had hardly lifted a finger. Clearly, saving my life had been no laborious task for him and his fallen angel strength.

"The Blessing is now over," Headmistress Katherine announced from somewhere beyond the courtyard. Her voice seemed to echo off all four walls. "Those of you who have been deemed strong enough for the trials of Moira Seminary, welcome. You have a long road ahead of you, and this is only the beginning."

I pushed myself up and peered out the window, which now seemed much, much higher without the water lapping below.

The first thing I saw was Nathaniel's sunset red hair. He wasn't moving, and his limbs were contorted awkwardly beneath him.

My chest tightened before I reminded myself to breathe. He was from Midgrave, but he was not a friend of mine. Just because we came from the same home didn't mean I had to protect him.

Fuck.

I saw four other bodies lying motionless on the grass and countless others vomiting water and gasping for air.

One test down.

Countless more to go.

EIGHT

"Get out." I barked the order before Wolf made it two steps through the door.

He paused and smirked. "Really, Huntress? That's how you talk to someone who saved your life for the second time?"

"Don't call me that, and don't even try to act as if you actually get to sleep in here."

"Why shouldn't I?" he taunted. "You get the cozy bed while I'm exiled to somewhere else in Moira? How does that figure? I didn't ask to be assigned to this room any more than you did."

I crossed my arms over my chest and refused to look away. He wasn't going to charm his way out of this, wasn't going to talk me down. "I don't know you very well, but you don't seem like a complete degenerate. You're an angel. It's much safer for you out there than it is for me. We both know that."

He took a step closer. "Why is that?" The smirk on his face was now a full-blown smile.

"You're–You're…"

"Stronger than everyone else here? More powerful?" He took yet another step. "Taller? Faster?"

His closeness became palpable. He craned his neck to look down at me with his bright blue orbs, casting a shadow across his already dark features.

A delightful storm of madness.

"I—"

"What?" he pushed. "Tell me why you want me out of here, Huntress."

I huffed. "You know why."

"I want to hear you say it."

"Fine," I said, lifting my chin even further so my face lingered only inches from his. "You're dangerous. You're unpredictable. You're arrogant as all hells, and yes, you are stronger than everyone else here."

He stared at me, eyes flickering back and forth between mine like he was looking for something; a secret, a truth.

"I didn't expect a lethal vampyre assassin to be afraid."

"I am not afraid," I replied, the rush of words betraying me. *Stay calm, Huntyr. Stay steady.*

"Really?" he asked. His eyes flickered down to my chest, lingering on the spot just above my breasts. "Because your heart is racing."

Anger fired to life within me. Nobody made me lose focus like this. Nobody distracted me as much as he did, and nobody ever, *ever* made me nervous.

"Get out," I managed to whisper.

Wolf's eyes met mine again, and I could tell from the mischief lingering there that he wasn't going anywhere. "If I'm as dangerous as you say I am," he started, "then you'll be safer with me in here."

I laughed in his face, my nerves bubbling in my stomach in a way that made me want to vomit. "You're joking, right?"

"I hate to break it to you, but if I wanted to kill you, I would have done so in Midgrave."

"I'm still not convinced you won't."

Before I could blink, his hand found my throat, squeezing gently but still applying enough pressure to get my attention. His body pressed against mine, pushing me against my bedpost. His leg slid between my knees, pinning me in place. "I could kill you right now, Huntress. But I could just as easily kill anyone in this damn academy if I wanted to."

I held his wrist with both hands but didn't fight him. Something sharp in his gaze made me freeze. "You don't scare me," I breathed.

His hand adjusted on my throat, moving from restraining me to feeling my pulse. His hands were rough and hot on my exposed skin. "Good," he whispered back. "Then I guess this racing heart means you feel something else for me."

This time, I shoved him away. Hard. He finally let me go, sauntering back to his side of the small, stone room.

"It's going to be a long day tomorrow," he said, sliding his shirt up and over his head. I looked away at the last second. "Get some sleep. If it makes you feel any better, I promise I won't murder you in the night."

I stood there for a moment, not sure I could trust myself to walk without my legs giving out.

What the *fuck* just happened? Wolf intimidated me, put his hands on me.

Saw right through me.

When I was certain I wouldn't collapse, I hoisted myself into my bed. I didn't bother changing clothes, and I barely managed to slip my shoes off before burying myself beneath the thick covers. I turned my body to face the wall, away from Wolf. I couldn't think about him. Couldn't think about his breathing, his wings filling the room.

I had to think about myself. A few deep breaths later, my heart was finally slowing down. *Damn you for betraying me,* I thought to myself as I slipped my hand over my chest. I had mastered the skill of keeping a steady heartrate, even in the face of death.

But in the face of this fallen angel?

I guess I still needed to work on that.

I closed my eyes and tried not to focus on the dull pain in my back. Lord's lashings served as a reminder, though. I had a job to do. I had a mission.

Wolf could not distract me.

I kept my body facing the wall the entire night, kept the blankets pulled tightly under my chin. I didn't want to fall asleep with Wolf just a few feet away, but I didn't have much of a choice.

He wasn't going to kill me. Not in my sleep, anyway.

Not tonight.

"Yesterday, you were all simply students. Fresh recruits. New to this academy. Yesterday, you each held an identity; one that was created long ago, when you were growing up wherever you came from. Some of you are from poor cities with crumbling walls. Others grew up with wealthy families in castles with servants. Today, that changes."

I stiffened in my seat in the back corner of the room, one that allowed me plenty of space to see everyone else.

And gave them no space to see me.

Still, the energy with which Headmistress Katherine spoke sent a chill through the crowd.

"You no longer belong to yourself," she continued. "You belong to The Golden City. You'll identify as a defender of the city, as a part of the community. From today onward, you will lay your life down to protect The Golden City. Is that understood?"

The group remained silent.

"Is that understood?" she repeated.

"Yes, Headmistress," we answered in unison.

Everyone shifted, seemed to sit straighter. Everyone except Wolf, anyway, who sat casually splayed across his chair. With his wings relaxed on each side of him, he took up three seats instead of one.

Figures.

He was gone when I woke up this morning, which made me feel both comfortable and on edge. It was nice that I could avoid interacting with him today, but the fact that he was awake while I slept?

I reminded myself to slow down my heart.

"Today, you'll be stripping yourselves of those identities the hard way. You'll suffer. You'll hurt. Pain will cleanse you, will wash away the versions of yourselves that may have existed before you walked through the doors of Moira." Headmistress Katherine's gaze shifted to the fae in the front of the room, the ones who looked as if they were ready to run the place themselves.

I stifled a smile. I'd very much like to see them wash themselves in pain.

"Commander Macanthos will assist with your combat needs. We'll be training in the courtyard every other day at the minimum. You'll be in charge of your own recoveries on your off days. And don't think that the magic training will be any easier on you. Magic will take a deep toll on you, one that you won't see coming. So prepare yourselves."

Hells.

Commander Macanthos—the male who spoke at The Blessing last night—stepped forward. He was older, with wrinkles around his eyes and gray hair slicked into a knot behind his head. But even so, he looked as if he could kill any one of us without batting an eye. His shoulders were still large and lean, and he stood with his chest puffed out.

"Now that we're all settled, we'll head to the courtyard.

Find a partner. We'll be sparring until midday," he commanded.

Headmistress clapped her hands, and we all stood, quickly filing out of the room and down the towering halls to the courtyard.

"Hey," Ashlani whispered, falling into step beside me. "Be Lanson's partner. He'll go easy on you, I promise." She winked at me before moving to catch up with her own roommate, Voiler.

Voiler seemed just as shocked when Ashlani approached her, as if she wasn't expecting anyone to actually *want* to be her partner. They were similar in size, which would be an advantage for both of them.

Great. I really did not want to partner with Lanson, but I supposed it was better than my other options. I couldn't stop myself from glancing at Wolf, who sauntered alone toward the front of the group. Surely, a fae would not have to partner with an angel. Everyone knew that would be no match at all.

"Not that I'll need to," Lanson said, chiming in on my other side after Ashlani left. "I think you'll be able to handle yourself just fine." He grinned.

"Yeah," I laughed, feigning nonchalance. "Let's hope so."

The sun just peeked above the castle walls, warming the cold air around us. Morning frost covered the short grass of the yard, creating a glistening effect that reminded me of mornings in the forest.

"Spread out." Commander Macanthos's voice echoed

off the stone walls. "Get comfortable. Let's see what we're working with."

Lanson followed me to the far side of the courtyard. I tried to find a spot where we would draw the least amount of attention, but it was difficult. We were exposed out here.

"Ready?" Lanson asked, assuming his stance. His feet spread shoulder width apart and his fists loosely protected his face. He had done this before.

I mimicked his position. "Ready," I answered.

He took a half-step forward, a small, friendly smile still lingering on his features. It would take me two seconds to end this fight with him, but he didn't know that.

Nobody here knew that, and it had to remain that way.

Lord explained the plan clearly to me before I left. I had to survive, but I could not show too much skill in combat. Too much would draw attention, would raise questions. Questions would lead to Phantom, would lead to Lord.

No, I had to be good enough to survive, but weak enough to blend in.

Lanson would not hit me first, I could already tell. A male like him would wait for me, would give me the illusion of power.

Fine by me.

I moved slowly enough for him to block me, aiming a punch toward his gut. He defended my fist easily.

"Not bad," he cooed. "Go again."

Males. Always too cocky for their own good. It was always their greatest flaw: thinking I was weaker than them.

So I tried again, letting him catch my wrist this time and pull me forward, causing me to stumble into his chest.

I met his eyes, reminding myself to hide my anger. "I'm a little rusty, I guess," I mumbled.

He stole a glance at my mouth. "Don't worry," he whispered back. "We have all day to get you warmed up."

And he wasn't wrong. For the rest of the morning, I pretended like I couldn't land a punch. I restrained myself from tackling him to the ground, from pulling Venom on his throat each time I pretended as if he had really overpowered me.

After a while, though, I got used to it. We fell into a familiar rhythm, one that made me feel as if we were dancing together under the morning sun. Hells, I even found myself smiling and laughing for a bit.

I didn't even think about Wolf all morning, not until midday, at least.

Lanson had just tackled me to the ground, where he braced himself above me. I easily could have wrapped my legs around his waist and flipped us over, but I let him believe in his victory.

"You're getting better already," he whispered, his breath tickling my sweaty skin.

"Really?" I asked. "Is that why you're on top of me right now?"

He smiled but didn't budge. "I'm glad we're partners. This is going to be fun."

The intensity of his light green eyes made me shiver beneath him. He wasn't trying to hide his admiration in the slightest.

"Time for matches!" Commander Macanthos shouted, breaking the tension between Lanson and I. If that's what you would even call it. "Everyone, circle around. We'll be assigning random fighting matches every afternoon after we train together. There is no better teacher of combat than combat itself. You'll fight until one of you gives up."

Gives up? *Hells.* I half-expected the massive, terrifying commander to say *fight until death.*

Lanson climbed off me and hoisted me up after him. I glanced away from his soft gaze and walked to the center of the courtyard.

It's not that Lanson wasn't attractive. He was—anyone could see that. But I wasn't the least bit interested in someone like him, especially here. Sure, he could be an ally. But it would never be anything more than that.

He would only be a distraction.

And distractions would get me killed.

"Alright," the mentor announced, looking around the semicircle. "You." He pointed to one of the two large, arrogant fae that I *already* hated. "And..."

The hair on the back of my neck stood up.

No, absolutely not. This was not happeni—"And you."

He pointed directly at me. I felt frozen in time, unable to move.

But Commander Macanthos did not seem like a male to challenge.

"Hey," Lanson whispered behind me, placing a hand on my lower back. "You got this, okay?"

Got this? Hells, I wanted nothing more than to smash

this arrogant prick's teeth in the second this match started, but that wouldn't be an option.

Not on day one. Not with everyone watching.

Blend in. Don't win the damn fight.

I turned and gave Lanson a half-smile before stepping into the circle.

"Ryder and Huntyr, let's see what you've got. Fight like your life depends on it," the commander called out.

My opponent, Ryder, stepped forward, rubbing his hands in front of him. He looked me up and down, sizing me up like a toy to be played with. He had taken his shirt off, his glistening, toned body beaming in the sun.

He was strong and had clearly been training for this.

I planted my feet into the ground and lifted my fists. *Come on, you big brute. Hit me.*

The snarl on his face said it all; he was coming at me with everything he had.

A few seconds later, he did.

He towered over me in size, taking two long strides to close the gap between us and swing toward my face.

I ducked and rolled to the opposite side of the clearing before jumping back to my feet. My instincts screamed at me to do something, to fight back. To tackle him below the waist and throw him off balance.

Fucking hells.

"The Golden City needs fighters," Ryder snarled. "Not little rats like you." He finished his words with another swing, attempting to grab my shoulders. "Did you really think you would survive long enough to become one of the elite?"

I spun away from his grasp, giving his fingers barely enough time to graze my shirt before I escaped him.

He smiled and cocked his head to the side. "Can't run forever, rat."

My heart pumped adrenaline through my veins, only fueling the instincts that I tried so fucking hard to fight. Everyone watched us. Everyone waited for him to end me, to end this fight.

I wasn't *supposed* to win.

"End this, then," I said. "If you're so worthy, hit me already."

Ryder's eyes darkened, the primal fae instincts taking over. Instincts I knew all too well. This time, when he rushed forward and sent a fist flying toward my stomach, I let him hit me.

I was prepared for it, but the air rushed from my lungs, leaving me doubled over in the middle of the courtyard.

"Give up," he hissed. "You don't stand a chance."

I shook my head and braced myself with hands on my knees. *Strong enough to survive, weak enough to blend in.* I couldn't give up. Not on day one. Not like this.

"I'm not giving up." No, if he wanted to win this fight, he would have to earn it. I could only fight my lifetime of training so much.

"You want me to hit you again, rat? Fine by me," he growled. The next punch landed square on my jaw, sending me stumbling sideways.

My vision blurred. Blood filled my mouth.

I spit to the side and wiped my mouth with the back of my hand.

"Is that all you've got?" I whispered, straightening myself. I knew I should have kept my mouth shut, but the cockiness on his face lit a deep fire of hatred within me. "I thought you trained for this your entire life, Ryder. Isn't that what I heard about males like you?"

He swung again, aiming for my face, but I ducked and kicked my foot into his shin. He hissed in pain and whirled around, sending an elbow into my back.

I tried to stay standing, but Ryder came at me again, tackling me from behind and sending us both sprawling on the ground. His hands splayed around me, his full body-weight pinning me down on my stomach.

He was too heavy to push off, especially from this position.

His hand found the back of my head, pressing my face into the grass from the side. "Give up," Ryder hissed in my ear.

No, I wanted to yell. *Over my dead fucking body, you prick.*

"Relax, Ryder," Lanson called from the crowd. "The fight's over."

Oh good. *My knight in shining armor.* I wanted to vomit.

Ryder pressed my face into the ground even harder, grinding me against the dirt, before finally climbing off me.

I scrambled to my feet and retreated into the crowd, too embarrassed to look the commander in the eye. He wasn't Lord, but losing a fight embarrassed me all the same.

Even if it was part of the plan.

"Are you okay?" Ashlani asked, shoving herself over to me. "That asshole went way too hard on you."

"I'm fine," I whispered. Shame flushed my cheeks. I couldn't look anyone in the eye, not Ashlani, not Ryder.

I knew I could have taken him, but even losing the fight on purpose made me feel fucking pathetic.

"Alright," the commander said, finally breaking the tension. "Huntyr, learn to throw a solid punch. You won't survive without it. Let's move on. More fighting and less playing, please."

The crowd got busy watching the next two males fight, everyone all but forgetting about me and the brutal embarrassment they just witnessed.

I finally brought myself to lift my gaze, only to find Wolf staring back at me. His electric gaze changed, though. Something simmered there. I swore I saw something move in his deep blue irises.

But he blinked, and his eyes returned to normal. Perhaps I'd imagined the entire thing.

He lingered in the very back of the crowd, arms crossed over his chest and wings slightly expanded.

It was the type of gaze that made me feel exposed, naked. I didn't look away, though. Wolf seemed pissed off, and would probably look that way to most people, but I saw something else there, too.

Something enlightened. Something playful.

I forced myself to rip my eyes away as the next opponents began landing blows. So far, I had achieved what I needed to. I'd managed to blend in. People might remember my horrific failure of a fight, but at least they wouldn't be seeing me as a threat.

Although, my attention kept drifting off to Wolf, kept finding him standing there, staring back at me with fierce eyes.

He saw right through me. I knew he did. He had seen me fight before. Surely, he would know why I had to lose these fights.

Surely, he would keep my secret.

It's not like he was making friends here, anyway. The other students avoided him as if he were poison.

The feeling of unease washed over me every time we made eye contact, though. I tried to focus on the throbbing of my body instead, tried to think of the pain I felt every time I caught myself looking for his tall figure across the courtyard.

I can do this, I reminded myself. *I have no other choice.*

CHAPTER

NINE

By the time the sun set, my body screamed at me.

I had trained like this before many, many times with Lord, but I never took so many losses. I had two more matches after my fight with Ryder, each one weakening my body with hits and punches that I could hardly fight back. I found myself warring with my instincts more than I ever had, and if I was being honest, that was more painful than the physical torture.

Either way, I limped back to my bedroom when all was said and done.

It wasn't until the door closed behind me that I pressed my back against it, closed my eyes, and finally relaxed.

"Could've fooled me." Wolf's voice sang through the air.

I opened my eyes to find him lounging in bed above his covers, shirtless, with his wings splayed out. It was funny how relaxed his wings could look, so different from the fierce, sharp position they were held in during training.

"I'm not in the mood," I argued, limping toward the bathroom connected to our room.

"After watching you get your ass kicked all day, I must say, I have a few questions."

I gritted my teeth. "I said I'm not in the mood, *angel*."

I made it to the doorway of the bathroom and paused with a hand on the wall. My breathing came out labored.

Wolf sat up in bed. My instincts narrowed in on him, on his movements, as he pushed himself up and walked over to me.

"That's going to hurt tomorrow," he said matter-of-factly. "I'm dying to know if this was all part of your master plan, Huntress. Do tell."

I squeezed my eyes shut and tried to think of anything but how close he stood. I couldn't even get a minute of peace in this damned academy.

"That's none of your business," I hissed. Hells, even talking hurt more than I would have liked to admit.

The punches to my face weren't the ones that bothered me. They never were. It was the hits to my ribs, my shoulders, my back that lingered. I healed quickly, yes, but these bruises were going to take a few days. On top of the still-healing scars from Lord's punishment, I was in for an endless week of combat training.

I tried to take another step into the bathroom where I could close the door and fall apart without an audience, but my legs betrayed me. I stumbled forward, prepared to crash against the stone floor, but muscular arms hooked around my waist and hoisted me back up.

Wolf carried me into the bathroom and, within a

second, set me on the edge of the bathtub. I didn't fight him; I didn't have the energy to.

I hissed in pain when he removed his arms from my body.

"Damn, Huntress," he whispered, kneeling in front of me. "This doesn't look too good for you."

"It's fine. I just need to clean the blood off and get some rest before tomorrow."

From his position on the bathroom floor, he looked up at me, scanning my features the way he did way too often.

Hells. Wolf looked good on his knees. Especially when kneeling in front of *me*.

"Why didn't you fight back?" he asked. With his eyebrows raised and his eyes wide, he looked softer. Kinder, even. So much so that it was startling.

I let my eyes flutter closed. Wolf's hands lingered on my knees. I hated to admit it, but the heat from his touch distracted me from the pain.

"Answer me," he demanded. He didn't sound angry. No, he sounded confused. Desperate, almost.

"They can't know," I whispered, keeping my eyes shut.

Wolf's hands drifted down my legs, so light I barely felt it. He began unlacing my boots. Slowly, ensuring each lace was fully untied before beginning the next one.

I took a long, shaking breath. I blamed my unease on the pain, not the fact that he touched me with such an intimate delicacy.

"They can't know what?" he asked. "That you're a fighter? That you deserve to be here?"

I lifted my head and opened my eyes. Thankfully,

Wolf's gaze stayed focused on my boots, giving me space to reply.

I wasn't sure I could have said the words if he was looking at my face.

"That I'm a threat," I said finally.

The words sounded ridiculous after what had transpired in the courtyard today, but Wolf didn't laugh. His fingers stopped working on my laces as he looked up, pinning me beneath his gaze. "You don't have to torture yourself to get to The Golden City," he whispered. "You can show them how strong you are and still make it."

"You know that's not true," I replied. "They'll go after the strongest competition first. If not now, then they'll target me during the final test."

"Not if you become dangerous enough to scare them. If they knew what you were back in Midgrave—"

"Stop," I interrupted, my voice stronger than I meant it to be. "Nobody can know where I came from. Nobody can know what I am."

A trained vampyre assassin. A weapon. An undeniable slayer. A Phantom.

"They would respect you if they knew." He was trying to help, I knew that. Why? I wasn't sure. I had battled with the idea of showing my dominance in this academy, but ultimately, it would only create more problems.

"I'm asking you not to tell anyone," I whispered. My eyes pleaded, begged him to listen to me. I was at Wolf's mercy, which was the absolute last place I wanted to be right now.

He stared back at me for a second. I thought maybe he

would argue with me again, perhaps tell me how stupid I was to let them think of me as prey. But after a while, he busied himself with my other boot, untying the laces faster than before.

"Fine," he said, finishing his job and rising from his knees. "If you want to get pummeled into the dirt every day until the Transcendent, that's on you. But when you're too weak and injured to stop pretending you can't fight back, you're going to wish you had."

"We'll see about that," I muttered, kicking my boots off and trying to stand.

Wolf's hands shot out, ready to catch me if I fell. The worry on his face was unmistakable. "Let me at least help you."

"No," I argued. Wolf already questioned me. If he saw the scars on my back, he wouldn't look at me the same. "I can do it myself. Just go to bed."

His jaw tightened as he searched my face, no doubt waiting for me to change my mind.

But a few seconds later, he turned and left, closing the bathroom door behind him.

For fuck's sake. First, he threatens me. Now, he's unlacing my boots and offering to help me undress?

I didn't understand him, not in the slightest.

With Wolf gone, I peeled my black top off and surveyed my body in the small, rusted mirror that hung above the stone sink. Against my stark pale skin, bruises had already formed. Red marks littered my chest, my shoulders, my ribs. *Especially* my ribs.

My face had a nasty split, likely from my fight with

Ryder. It had already scabbed over, but the skin below was angry and swollen.

I turned around, glancing over my shoulder at my back.

The whipping scars had been healing nicely, but now? The skin split open, the bruises mixing with the damaged surface to create an anomaly of horrid, disfigured marks.

No, Wolf certainly would *not* want to see this.

Nobody would.

But that didn't matter, I reminded myself. I wasn't here to heal my back or to look nice for the males in this academy.

Stay quiet. Stay under the radar.

I peeled the rest of my clothes off and, somehow without audible grunting, sank into the hot water of the bathtub.

The bath felt like the goddess herself had blessed the water. I didn't have hot water back home. The cold water of the river had been the only way to relieve the screaming pain in my body. But this? This was better than all of that. This was better than the river, better than any ointment Lord could have given me.

I laid my head back on the edge of the tub, submerging my bruised body until everything below my chin soaked in the water's warmth.

I could do this. I could get through this. Just a couple months, right? A couple of months and I would be in The Golden City, ready for whatever Lord planned next. I would not let him down, even if bruises covered every inch of my skin.

The hot water eventually fell cold enough to force me out of the tub and back into my bed.

Wolf was gone when I re-entered the bedroom. But I'd grown too exhausted to care, too tired to wonder where he could possibly be. My eyes were heavy as I crawled under the covers and let my body relax into the soft mattress.

Tomorrow would be better. Tomorrow *had* to be better.

"Huntyr!" Ashlani called out as I entered the classroom. "We saved you a seat!"

Everyone else was too occupied with themselves to notice Ashlani and Lanson calling me over to their corner of the study room. I took a quick sweep of the other students, only partially looking for Wolf, but I didn't see his tall, winged figure anywhere.

Wolf wasn't in our room when I woke up this morning either, but a shiny red apple lay next to my head on my pillow.

In my right mind, I would have checked to see if he had poisoned it first. But I was exhausted and frankly desperate, so I accepted the gesture without fighting it.

"Hey," Lanson said as I took the seat next to him. "It's good to see you're up and walking. After yesterday, I was worried."

Ashlani leaned forward, surveying my bruised face with pursed lips. "Oh, honey," she started, voice laced with pity. "Yesterday was rough. It'll get easier from here on out, okay?"

I kept my mouth tightly shut and nodded. Ashlani was able to escape yesterday's training with nothing but a minor bruise on her cheekbone. She wasn't paired with one of the largest fighters on her very first day.

No, Ashlani fought her roommate once, and Lanson hadn't even been forced to spar.

Headmistress walked into the room, pulling Ashlani's attention away from me. Lanson's gaze lingered, though. His bright eyes scanned my face, pausing on the cheek that I know was bruised and split.

His hand reached up, almost as if he were going to touch my face.

I froze. I almost wanted him to.

I wasn't used to this blatant affection Lanson was showing me. Okay, to anyone else, it might not have qualified as affection.

But to me?

It was overwhelming.

The study room door slammed shut, making us both flinch. I turned in time to see Wolf sauntering forward, eyes glued on me. He stopped for a second, gaze sliding to Lanson and darkening, before he eyed the open seat on the other side of me.

All hells.

I turned my attention to the front of the classroom

while Wolf pulled the seat out and made himself comfortable next to me.

Lanson stiffened on my other side, also deterring his gaze.

"Looks like you're feeling better," Wolf whispered, loud enough for only me to hear.

I turned and gave him a death glare, only to find him smirking back at me. "Leave me alone," I mouthed.

He responded by stretching upward, pushing his legs out in front of him while he let his arm fall over the back of my chair.

Was he kidding? Even if Lanson was pretending not to notice, Wolf's motions were undeniable. He commanded everyone's attention in the room.

Everyone's.

I gritted my teeth and focused on Headmistress Katherine, who settled in at the front of the room. She wore a floor-length black dress fit to her body with sleeves that expanded around her hands, and she faced us in a way that made the hair on the back of my neck stand up. She tended to have that effect on me, even before a single word left her mouth.

"Good morning," she began. "Today, we'll be going over the basics of the magic used in The Golden City. Some of you may know about what goes on there, and some of you have only heard rumors and stories. Today, we'll learn the truth."

Magic? I shifted in my seat. I had wanted to learn more about magic since Lord mentioned it in Midgrave. Headmistress Katherine had my full attention.

"Who can tell me what magic is wielded in The Golden City?"

"The strongest magic in existence," Ashlani answered without missing a beat.

"That's right. And why is it so powerful?" The study chambers fell silent. "Anyone? What about you, Wolf Jasper? Any reason why the magic in The Golden City is unlike anything we have access to here in Vaehatis?"

All eyes turned to Wolf, mine included. His jaw tightened for one second before he answered, "The archangels allow it. They bless the lands with ungodly amounts of power."

"That's right." Headmistress grinned. "The archangels hold the power. So long as they live within the walls of The Golden City, that is where the magic remains."

"How are we supposed to learn magic if we aren't in The Golden City? I mean, what's the point?" Ryder asked from the front row.

"You'll learn the basics here," she replied. "Moira, as I'm sure you've all realized by now, is not an average seminary. This place was created on lands blessed by the archangels themselves. A magic lingers here that is not present in the rest of Vaehatis; it's what makes this entire academy what it is."

Chills rushed down my arms. I knew I felt something different as soon as we arrived here, something chilling and dark and *primal*.

Headmistress paused for a moment before a gust of wind appeared out of nowhere. I watched with my jaw

falling open as wings—dark, beautiful, leathery wings—
appeared on either side of her slim shoulders.

"If you are lucky," she continued over the gasp of the
classroom, "you'll even become strong enough to summon
your own fae wings. That's right. Angels are not the only
ones who can fly in The Golden City."

One male in front stood up. "Teach us how!"

Headmistress held up a hand, quieting the class.
Wings? I knew that fae long, long ago used to have the
ability to fly, but to summon the fae wings on command?
Goddess above.

"The first step in learning how to wield magic is to
understand your own limits. We'll be refreshing our
history on vampyres, fae, and angels before we delve into
magic training. It may not seem important, but it is. This
may in fact be the most important portion of this seminary, so pay attention. Lack of knowledge is just as deadly
as the inability to fight."

Headmistress moved on to discuss the two types of
magic: natural magic and blood magic. Both had their
benefits, and both had their downfalls. The way she spoke
of the raw, earth-shattering power contained within both
magics made my heart speed up, forced each one of my
senses to drink up every single word.

"Only fae and angels have been confirmed to wield
magic, but without the vampyres here to elaborate for
themselves, we cannot rule out their magic entirely. It's
possible that they, too, used to wield magic before the fall
of Scarlata Empire."

The two large fae—Ryder and his friend, who I now knew was named Espek—snickered.

"Why don't we just ask them?" Ryder asked.

I froze. The look in Headmistress's eyes would have made any normal apprentice still. "Tell me," she said, walking over to the males in the front row, "why can we not ask them?"

"They've all run rabid," Espek said. "The coherent, normal vampyres that used to live in Vaehatis are long gone. They've all given into their bloodlust, turned into those monsters."

"You're correct," she replied. "And unless you'd like to be thrown into the forest full of them, you'll show some respect."

"What happened to them?" Lanson asked. "If vampyres used to be coherent creatures, what changed?"

An eerie silence filled the room before she continued.

"Vampyres survive on the blood of humans and fae, yes, but they were not always monsters. The last two decades have changed everything, including the trajectory of their species."

We waited eagerly for her to go on, everyone glued to each word she spoke.

"Vampyres are not born with bloodlust, contrary to what you all might believe. Vampyres do not drink blood at all, actually, until they have lived a quarter of a century. Once a vampyre is twenty-five, their instincts kick in. That is when they need to feed.

"Vampyres can feed without losing control. They can

feed without killing. But when a vampyre gives in to the bloodlust, typically following the first time they drink from the vein, they begin to change. They lose control of their senses, of their ability to restrain themselves. They turn into the creatures who kill and attack and cannot be stopped."

"What happens before they lose control of their blood-lust? You're saying vampyres can be normal?" Ashlani asked, her brow furrowed in thought.

"That's exactly what I'm saying," Headmistress answered. "Some vampyres are still living out there somewhere, controlling their bloodlust, even after they drink from the vein. Not all of them have given into that monstrous side."

Ashlani leaned forward. "Where are they?"

She shrugged. "After the death of the vampyre queen and king, they scattered. War forced them out of their kingdom, sent them into hiding. All the more reason The Golden City must be protected. We don't know how many of them are out there. They could rebuild their kingdom from the ashes for all we know."

Hells. The fact that coherent vampyres—not the baffling bloodsuckers I had killed hundreds of times—were out there somewhere terrified me.

But it also put a hollow pit in my stomach that I couldn't seem to shake.

"Forget about vampyres. When do we learn to bond?" Ryder asked, rapping his pencil against his desk with a casual air. "We'll need it for the final test, right? Shouldn't we learn as soon as possible?"

The bond?

"Not now," Headmistress stated, narrowing her eyes at his pencil, which promptly stopped moving. She lifted her chin. "We'll learn to bond when you're ready, and none of you are ready. You must first learn to control your magic."

"What's the bond?" Ashlani spoke up. The fae in the front of the room laughed while others looked just as clueless as the rest of us.

Headmistress rolled her eyes before addressing the class again. "It's a way to share magic between two souls. When you must use magic to save yourself or your people and you aren't strong enough to wield it alone, the bond will allow you to split the burden with another. Many students choose to bond before the final test, although it isn't required."

"What does it mean?" Ashlani's roommate asked. "I mean, what happens during the bond?"

"Probably much of what you'd imagine. Aside from having access to another's magic, however, you'll also be hit with their thoughts, their emotions. Many students must already have a relationship with the one they choose to bond with, otherwise the mental sharing becomes too much to control."

Interesting.

Lord said nothing about a bond to me. Maybe it was because he knew I would never bond with anyone.

Or maybe he didn't know about it.

I shook that thought from my mind. Lord seemed to know everything about Moira and The Golden City. Surely, he knew I would have to bond with another if I wanted to survive. He trusted me to do whatever it took to complete my mission.

Lanson's foot slid out and tapped mine, just casual enough so nobody else would notice. Or that perhaps I'd think it might have been an accident.

"Enough of this," Headmistress announced. "Like I said, we'll learn more about the bonding when you're ready. For now, we'll focus on the basics."

We sat in the classroom all damn day. I tried my best to memorize everything that was said about the magic system, about the uses for it in The Golden City. Wolf sat and listened quietly next to me, not bothering to write a single thing down but also paying attention to the mentor in a shockingly respectful way.

Unlike the other fae assholes in the room, Ryder and Espek included.

By the time class was over, Wolf practically bolted out of his chair and into the hall.

"What's that guy's problem?" Lanson whispered to me, staring after him.

I shrugged. "If you find out, I'd love to know."

"I'm starving," Ashlani chimed in. "Come on, we're going to eat."

I grabbed my bag and slung it over my shoulder, trying not to grimace at the growing soreness in my body. Thank the goddess today was only a classroom day. The thought of sparring with someone else today and having to take punch after punch while the entire courtyard watched made me sick.

I would deal with that tomorrow. Today, I could relax and eat with Ashlani and Lanson.

We were two steps out of the classroom when someone slammed into me from behind, spinning me around and pinning me to the hallway wall so hard I saw stars.

"Where do you think you're going, little rat?"

CHAPTER
TEN

"What the *fuck* are you doing?" I growled. Ryder held me against the wall with all of his strength, his nasty fingernails digging into the skin on my wrists.

Espek did the same to Ashlani, while it took two other fae brutes to restrain Lanson.

"Are you kidding me?" Ashlani screamed. "I'm hungry! Let me go!"

The wounds on my back screamed from the pressure of Ryder's weight pinned against me. With every second that passed, I felt the skin of my lashings splitting more and more, once again demolishing the progress I had made on healing.

"When I say *give up* in a fight next time," Ryder hissed, his snarled words spitting into my face, "you give up. Got it?"

I should have backed down. Should have dipped my

chin, squirmed back against his grasp, and said whatever he wanted me to say.

But I'd had a long day. I was tired. And he needed to get the fuck away from me.

I didn't have time to think before I spit directly in his face.

"I think I got it," I replied, rage dripping like venom from my words. Any hope I had at withholding my temper was long gone, along with my ability to give a shit.

Lanson and Ashlani both quit fighting, staring at me with their mouths hanging open.

Ryder took one hand and wiped my spit from his chin, slowly and dramatically, before backhanding me across the face.

It barely stung.

I was too busy feeling my own satisfaction. In fact, I couldn't even control the bubbled laughter that slipped from my lips.

I laughed and laughed and laughed.

When Ryder raised his hand a second time, Ashlani screamed. Lanson struggled again against the other fae, cursing at them in a voice I could barely hear over the blood pumping through my veins. I flinched, waiting for the blow to land.

But it never did.

I blinked my eyes open to find Ryder's face morph with panic. "What the—"

He moved—was thrown, rather—off of me with a potent force and a flash of feathers. It took me a full second to realize what in all hells was happening.

Wolf was there, gripping Ryder's arm and slamming him against the wall.

Ryder fell, but Wolf didn't stop. He picked him up with a thick hand around the throat and pounded him so hard into the stone wall, the bricks crumbled around him.

The other fae froze, too. All of us, Ashlani and Lanson included, stood in awe.

And we all watched in horror as Wolf leaned down and whispered in Ryder's ear.

It was too quiet to hear, but the look on Ryder's face said it all.

Wolf was in charge here. Not Ryder.

After a moment, Wolf let Ryder go, watching him and his friends scamper down the hallway as if fleeing from a fire.

Interesting.

Wolf smiled at himself, which was not surprising at all. Cocky bastard.

"Go," I said to Lanson and Ashlani. "I'll meet you in the dining hall. I just need a second."

Lanson eyed me warily before turning his gaze to Wolf. I wasn't sure why, though. What was he going to do? Fight him? Stand up to him? After what we just saw, *nobody* could stand up to Wolf. The other students had avoided him since they first laid eyes on him, but now?

They would run in the other direction.

Part of me envied the fear he instilled in others, but I would never admit that to him. It would be nice to have others respect you at first glance instead of underestimating you time and time again.

"What in the hells was that?" I demanded once we were alone.

Wolf rubbed his fists in front of him. "I was looking for a *thank you*, but I suppose that will be fine."

"I don't need you to protect me." I ran a hand down my cheek where Ryder struck me.

He scoffed. "Really? You'd rather get pummeled in front of your friends by that asshole?"

"No, I—"

"You *what*? Are you finally going to stand up to him? Are you going to kick his ass the way I *know* you can?"

Anger fueled my senses, sharpening my instincts.

No, Wolf knew I would not do that. He knew I couldn't.

"I will not sit back while they kill you, Huntress."

"Why?" I asked, emotions leaking into my words. "Why do you even care if I die? You don't know me, Wolf! You know nothing about me! Do you get some weird satisfaction from helping me? Is that what this is?"

"Trust me," he said. "If you want to see me satisfied, there are other ways to—"

"I'm done with this," I snapped, pivoting on a heel and marching down the hall.

Wolf stopped me with a hand on my elbow, spinning me to face him. His face was so close to mine, full of an intensity that was almost too much to take in.

He stilled. "I don't want to watch you get hurt because I don't like it. Fair enough?"

My heart raced, my breath mingling with his in the few inches of space between us. *Fair?* No, none of it was fair.

123

Wolf wasn't making any sense, and the way he stared at me...

"I hate to break it to you, *angel*, but I'm already hurt. I've survived this long on my own, and I don't need you lurking in the shadows, ready to jump out and save me. You don't know me. You don't care about me, so let's stop pretending that you do."

When I ripped my arm from his grasp and stormed toward the dining hall, Wolf didn't bother following me.

"What does he want with you anyway?" Ashlani asked.

She and Lanson sat across from me at the end of the long wooden dining table. Thankfully, Ryder and his friends didn't bother coming after us.

Neither did Wolf.

"Nothing," I answered, lifting a shoulder. "Well, I don't know. We don't talk much, and when we do, he just pisses me off."

"It's clear he wants *something*," Lanson added, not looking me in the eye. "Nobody acts like that out of selfless intentions."

I shrugged. "Unless he really hates Ryder. That's a possibility."

"Did you see the way he looked at you?" Ashlani whispered. "I mean, he was about to kill Ryder just for touching you. I swear I saw smoke coming out of his ears."

My face heated. "No, it has nothing to do with me. You can trust me on that. Wolf and I aren't friends."

"You're sleeping in the same room, though, right? Has he said anything to you?"

"I keep to myself," I answered, perhaps a bit too fast.

Lanson's fork paused on his plate, and his eyes flickered to me. I could have sworn I saw something there; delight, maybe? Satisfaction?

"He's dangerous," Lanson added after a few seconds. "Nobody's messed with him yet, but they will. He's clearly the strongest one here, so he'll have a target on his back. He has those black wings for a reason. It's only a matter of time before we find out just how cruel he can be."

"Agreed," I said. "It's best if we stay away from him. Let's just forget about this, please?"

Lanson nodded, and Ashlani stared at me with a sparkle in her eye. "Whatever you say, Huntyr."

We ate the rest of our meal without any mention of Wolf or Ryder. Eventually, the conversation drifted to sparring tactics and discussion of magic bonding.

I tried to pretend like I cared about what they were saying, but it took more energy than I had left.

By the time I made it back to my room that night, Wolf was nowhere to be seen.

CHAPTER
ELEVEN

Ashlani surprised me the most. Over the next few days, the sparring session grew more and more intense. Everyone in the school sparred at least once—Wolf included, though it lasted only seconds.

When Ashlani was first called to sparr, I flinched at every punch her male opponent threw her way.

But she was surprisingly strong, and beneath those pretty eyes held an entire world of anger and aggression waiting to escape. She held her own. She threw punches fast and recovered even faster. She took a hit like a fae male, and she didn't pout like they would, either.

"Who taught you to fight like that?" I asked Ashlani over breakfast.

Her roommate, Voiler, joined us too, just like she had the last couple of days over breakfast, but she remained quieter than most. She didn't say a single word the entire time Ashlani and I ate, but I was okay with that.

Her presence wasn't entirely off-putting. She kept her large, dark eyes down and kept to herself.

Ashlani stuffed another piece of bread into her mouth, swallowing it entirely before answering, "I taught myself, mostly. When you spend enough time being on the wrong side of a fight, you pick up on a few things."

She pulled her blonde hair tightly into a braid that now hung loosely over her shoulder. She didn't seem like the type to get into fights, but then again, I was sure I didn't seem like the type, either.

"Is that where Lanson learned, too?" I asked. "You knew each other back home, right?"

She shrugged, returning her interest to the remaining pieces of bread. "Lanson's father was always very strict on him. I only met him a few times, but hells. He scared the shit out of me."

"Really?" It made sense. Lanson was a decent fighter, though not half as strong as the other fae.

I knew firsthand the type of things someone would do to impress the one who raised them.

Ashlani nodded. "Surprising, isn't it? Lanson seems so sweet. He's always been like that, really sweet and sensitive. It only made his father hate him even more."

"And what about your parents?" I asked. "Do they know you spent your free time learning to throw punches?"

When she smiled, her eyes didn't light up the way they usually did. "My parents don't even know I'm here. They couldn't care less about what I do in my free time."

Damn. I really *had* misjudged her.

We weren't all that different, it seemed.

Commander Macanthos walked into the dining hall then, and all eyes glued onto him as he approached the center of the room.

Straight toward our table.

"What?" Ashlani leaned forward and surveyed my worried face, completely unaware of the enormous man approaching from behind her. "What's happening?"

Even Voiler looked up, freezing right next to Ashlani and giving me the same helpless look.

"Shut up," I whispered, averting my gaze.

But two seconds later, Commander Macanthos stood directly behind her.

Staring at *me*.

"Huntyr," he greeted. His hands were tightly clasped behind his back and his chin remained lifted, as poised and professional as ever. "Take a walk with me."

My stomach sank. What would Commander Macanthos possibly want with me? I did nothing wrong. I carefully obeyed all the rules, in fact.

"Yes, Commander Macanthos." I plastered a polite smile on my face and stood, pushing the rest of my food in Ashlani's direction with a warning glare.

Every single pair of eyes locked on us—on me—as I followed Commander Macanthos out of the room and into the mostly empty hallway. My head barely met his shoulder as I fell into step beside him, clasping my hands behind my back so they wouldn't shake.

Hells, this male was massive.

"I've been watching you," he started.

My stomach sank. Fear screamed at me to run, to get as far away from this place as possible. But that wasn't an option. Lord made my mission very clear: Succeed, or die trying.

He paused. "The way you fight is... surprising."

"How so?" I tilted my head to the side in thought while I fought to keep my voice steady.

We took a few more steps in silence before the commander halted, turning to face me at the end of the hallway. With the light filtering through the tall glass window, I could see a thin scar on his face, narrowly missing his eye.

"You are calculated. Strategic." He reached out to grip my shoulder, surveying the muscle he found there. "Strong."

I swallowed. "Thank you. I suppose these are all good things?"

Commander Macanthos pulled his hand away and rolled his shoulders back, taking on a soldier-like stance that sent a chill down my spine. "I know what you're doing."

The corners of my mouth twitched upward, though I felt as exposed as ever standing before him. "And what's that?"

"You're hiding your true strength. You're losing fights on purpose."

My smile faded as I glanced over my shoulder, ensuring we were alone. Commander Macanthos did not seem like the male to lie to. "I'm sure you can understand why."

For the first time since I met him, his features softened. "Yes, actually, I can. But this place is vicious, Huntyr. You're only just beginning to see the dangers. Showing others you are strong may help you more than you think."

"Thank you, but I'll be fine."

"I hope so," he replied. "But do not think that you are the only one in this academy with masked intentions, Huntyr. You'll be forced to show your strengths eventually."

With that, he walked away, leaving me gaping after his massive figure as he disappeared into the hall.

Hells. If Commander Macanthos noticed my fighting, who else did?

And why would he care enough to warn me?

I made my way back to the dining room, trying to clear my head of the entire interaction.

But when I turned the corner and entered, my stomach sank.

All conversations in the dining hall ceased. Everyone stared in horror at the far end of the room, where Ryder pinned one of the students against the wall, a knife to his throat.

This student was one of the quiet ones. His name was Maekus, if I remembered correctly. He hardly got in anyone's way and surely didn't do anything to deserve *this*.

His eyes were wide in terror as he struggled against Ryder, but it was no use. He was half Ryder's size.

I jogged over to Ashlani and Voiler. "What's going on?"

Ashlani only shrugged and watched in horror. Voiler didn't even notice my presence.

Ryder sneered, "Do you think we want weaklings fighting beside us in The Golden City? Do you really think a coward like you will get in?"

Hells.

Maekus whimpered, still squirming as Ryder's knife pulled the smallest line of blood from his skin.

"Is anybody going to do anything?" I whispered.

"Don't." Voiler grabbed my wrist, her nails digging in. "I know you want to help, but you'll only make it worse. You can't save him."

She was right. Hells, I knew she was right. I couldn't do anything without putting a target on my own back.

But I had witnessed people like Maekus get fucked around by people like Ryder my entire life. And I *hated* people like Ryder.

Ryder summoned a small ounce of his natural magic then, using wind to pull the air from Maekus's lungs. I didn't notice it at first; only when Maekus began clawing at Ryder's arms, then his own throat, did I understand he was being suffocated.

Someone in the back of the room gasped.

Ryder was going to kill him.

"It's simple magic," Ryder announced, nearly gloating. More and more air whirled from Maekus. Ryder was horrifyingly talented at natural magic; even someone who could summon it would have a hard time pushing back. "If you're strong enough to get into The Golden City, you'll have no problem fighting it off."

Maekus struggled more and more until suddenly—torturously—his eyes rolled back in his head.

I was only slightly aware of Ashlani hissing something at me in a hushed whisper as I tore myself away from her and Voiler and drifted toward the conflict. I couldn't stop myself if I wanted to.

"What in all hells are you doing, Ryder? You can't hurt him outside of the classroom!"

Ryder pushed for a few more seconds, ensuring no air remained in Maekus's lungs, before he used his knife to finish the job, slitting Maekus's throat.

He fell to the ground in the dining hall.

Dead.

Ryder broke the first rule of Moira Seminary by killing Maekus outside of the classroom, and he didn't seem to care in the slightest.

He turned with a grin spread across his face. "Consider this a glimpse of your future, Huntyr. Weaklings won't be fighting by my side in The Golden City."

I clenched my jaw, trying to swallow my anger. *Weak?*

Maekus was sly and inconspicuous. He kept to himself. That did not make him any less of a fighter.

Ryder stepped closer to me, leaning down to my ear before whispering, "You're next."

He knocked my shoulder with his as he sauntered past me, leaving Maekus's body on the floor to finish bleeding out, and the entire dining hall silenced in terror.

I couldn't look away, couldn't tear my eyes away from Maekus. I should have done something sooner. Hells, *someone* should have.

"Come on." Ashlani pulled me from my trance, tugging on my wrist. Voiler followed tight behind her, looking just as horrified. "Let's get out of here before we attract any more trouble."

CHAPTER

TWELVE

As I made my way back to my bedroom that night, I caught a glimpse of Lanson leaning against the door frame of his own room. His shoulders were tense, his head hung low. He whispered something to himself under his breath in a way that made me slow down.

"Lanson?" I asked as I changed direction, making my way over to him. I wasn't sure why I felt pulled to Lanson. Over the last few days, I actually found myself enjoying his company during training. Things were peaceful with him. Simple. "Is everything okay?"

He stiffened further at the sound of my voice before spinning to face me. His eyes were bloodshot and rimmed with deep red lines. His soft curls were messy and disheveled, his normally tucked-in shirt falling messily down his torso.

"I've been better," he admitted.

I walked up to stand beside him, taking up the other

134

half of the doorframe. Maekus's bed was left unmade, his black bag strung over the bedpost along with his jacket.

My chest tightened. I'd forgotten they were roommates.

"He didn't deserve this," Lanson sighed. "Maekus wanted to get into The Golden City to be with his older sister who made it there last year. He–"

Lanson cleared his throat and turned away. Maekus and Lanson weren't that close, but anyone with a heart would be shocked by his death. He was quiet and kind, the type that nobody would have a conflict with.

Nobody but Ryder.

Ryder told Headmistress Katherine that the incident had been accidental, a simple mishap with his magic. If she planned to expel him, she was taking her sweet damn time.

He didn't deserve to be here. Maekus did.

Lanson stepped forward to the small table beside Maekus's bed, picking up a letter. "His mother put this in his bag before he boarded the train."

He passed me the paper. The edges were wrinkled and torn, as if Maekus took it with him everywhere and read it over and over again.

My perfect boy,
Your family is beaming with pride. Your sister awaits you in The Golden City, and I know you will do whatever it takes to be

reunited with her. Real life begins beyond those walls.

I have nothing but faith in you.

See you soon. Stay strong.

With endless love,

Mother

I sucked in a sharp breath. Not only was Maekus innocent, but he had family counting on him to make it inside.

All of that gone, an entire family shattered because of one arrogant brute.

I wanted to fucking kill Ryder for what he did.

"It must have been nice." Lanson shoved his hands in his front pockets. "He had so many people caring about him."

"Yeah," I whispered, passing back the letter. "People like him usually do."

I felt Lanson's attention slide from Maekus's letter to me. "I'm sure you have family waiting for you to get in, right? People who are rooting for you to get inside?"

"My parents are dead." The words slipped from my mouth in a single breath. I instantly regretted them, turning my attention to Maekus's bed. Lanson's gaze became too direct, too heavy as I stood there waiting for his response.

"I'm so sorry," he whispered. "I had no idea."

"I was young," I explained. "It's not a big deal."

The words were true. The death of my parents became a dull pain throughout the years. Now, I could think of them without feeling anything. I couldn't remember their faces, couldn't remember a single detail of my life with them.

Lord was my family now. Rummy was my family. They were everything to me.

My old life was dead, along with any memories of my parents.

"If it makes you feel any better," Lanson added, "I sometimes wish my parents were dead."

My attention snapped back to him. It was his turn to look away, to stare out of the tiny window in the bedroom. "What?" I asked. "Why would you say that?"

Lanson shrugged.

I stepped closer to him and placed my hand on his tense back. I wasn't sure why. Something within me pushed me to comfort him. Maybe it was because I had nobody to comfort me, had nobody consoling me when I really needed it.

Lanson needed somebody, too.

"I don't want to bore you with the details," he breathed.

I stepped in front of him until he was forced to look at me with his tired eyes. "That's impossible," I said, keeping my voice soft. "Tell me."

The air in the room grew thicker with every second. I knew exactly what Lanson was feeling; the internal battle on whether to admit the truth.

I slipped my hand down his arm, interlocking my

fingers with his. His eyes softened at my touch, looking slightly relieved, as he tightened his hand around mine.

"I was always a burden to them," he explained, "my parents. My father has always thought of me as a weak waste of space. I had an older brother for a long time, but he died a few years ago. My father blamed me."

I ran my thumb up and down the top of his hand. "Lanson, I'm so sorry."

"He was right to blame me. It was my fault."

My brows furrowed. "I'm sure that's not true."

He shrugged and shook his head. His shoulders moved with a deep breath before he continued. "None of that matters anymore. My father practically disowned me after that. I lived on the streets for a while, debated running away dozens of times. I didn't have a future to begin with, and without my brother, I felt lost. My father told me that the only way I could prove myself to the family was to get into The Golden City. He said once I did that, I would be forgiven."

A chill washed over me. "You're doing all of this to gain your father's forgiveness?"

He laughed, the sound dry and humorless. "It's ridiculous, I know."

I stepped closer. "I don't think it's ridiculous at all. We all would run through fire for the people we love. I guess that's what we're doing here, running through fire."

The corner of his mouth twitched. "That's one way of putting it."

"We'll get through this. Once we get into The Golden City, things will get easier."

He gave my hand a gentle squeeze. "Let's hope we don't end up like Maekus."

"We won't," I swore, more to myself than to him. "We won't."

I held onto those words as I made my way back to my bedroom, leaving Lanson alone with his grief. We wouldn't end up like Maekus.

We *couldn't* end up like Maekus.

I cracked my bedroom door open to find Wolf already sleeping in bed. I froze.

The last few days, he either disappeared all night, or he crept in after I was fast asleep. I rarely saw him in our bedroom, which I thanked the goddess for every time I entered.

But not tonight.

Tonight, Wolf lay shirtless—to no surprise—above the blankets on his back and his left wing hung off the mattress, grazing the floor with the silky black feathers. One knee was bent and propped up while the other relaxed over the full length of the bed.

I pushed the door open further, slipping inside and trying my best to click it shut silently behind me. My feet glided across the floor as I made my way over to my bed. The old mattress squeaked as I carefully sat down on the old mattress and slipped my boots off slowly, hesitating with every movement and ensuring I didn't wake him.

With my boots off, I pushed myself backward and reclined until I stared up at the castle ceiling in the darkness.

Hells, today was a mess. I knew some students would be competitive, but Ryder and his friends were blatant murderers. Killing Maekus and getting away with it?

It was time I started watching my back more diligently. These students were out for blood.

I took a long breath, inhaling the cool air and letting my lungs fill before exhaling the stress and tension of the day.

I took another long, relaxing breath.

Another.

My heart slowed, the rapid beats now low, soothing thuds.

"You snore, you know," Wolf announced in the silent room.

I snapped my head in his direction, though I could barely see in the darkness. "I do not."

"You do, and it's loud. I need my beauty rest and all. These wings don't stay this gorgeous on their own."

"Please," I scoffed. "I've barely seen you sleeping the entire time we've been here. You'll be fine."

"Again, it's your snoring."

I turned, propping myself up on my elbow and facing him. "One, I don't snore. Two, if you have a problem with my alleged snoring, you're welcome to sleep elsewhere. I'm certainly not begging you to stay."

Wolf mimicked my position, turning and resting his chin on his hand. In the dark shadows, his eyes lit up, almost glowing. I watched as his face slowly morphed, exposing his perfect white teeth in a massive, arrogant smile.

"What are you smiling at?" I pushed.

"Nothing," he replied. "Just imagining you begging. It's quite a vision."

"Ugh!" I fell back onto my pillow, ripping my gaze from him. "You're infuriating! Why did Maekus have to be the one to die and not you?"

"Careful, Huntress," he cooed. Even though I turned away, I felt his eyes lingering. "You're being rude again."

"I'm allowed to be rude," I sighed. "I've had a long day."

"What's wrong? Is Moira Seminary not the luxurious escape from the slums you thought it would be?" he taunted.

I didn't have to look to know that his annoying smirk splayed proudly across his face.

"I never expected this academy to be luxurious. I also didn't expect to be pummeled by one of the largest fae here on my first day of combat training, but that's beside the point."

Wolf huffed. "You're letting him get to you."

I turned my head in his direction. "He killed Maekus today. He used his natural magic to suffocate him before slitting his throat. I knew this academy would be dangerous, but Ryder's a problem that needs to be handled."

"He'll never make it into The Golden City, and if you

would've stopped him like you wanted to earlier today, you would be dead, too." He laughed to himself. "By the look on your face, I thought for certain Ryder was going to get a glimpse of the violent huntress."

"You were watching me?" My eyes widened.

Now it was Wolf's turn to fall backward and stare at the ceiling. The moonlight trickled through the small window, illuminating a path from his dark, messy hair tucked behind his ears to the sculpted muscles of his bare chest.

"Of course I was watching you. I couldn't look away for a moment, even if I tried." My cheeks heated before he continued. "It's quite embarrassing, the way you let Ryder antagonize you. The way you pretend you can't fight during our trainings only to let that weak male believe he's helping you. You haven't managed to summon a single ounce of natural magic yet, which would be somewhat understandable if it weren't for the entire class already learning the basics. I'm beginning to wonder if you ever really planned on surviving this academy to begin with."

Wolf kept his gaze glued to the ceiling while he casually hurled his insults.

I was glad his attention wasn't on me, though. I didn't want him to see my mouth falling agape as his words landed.

"I *will* survive this academy," I replied, voice soft. "We've only been learning how to use magic for a couple of days. I'll catch up soon. And standing up to Ryder is only going to put attention on me."

I felt his gaze fall on me then. "You think I'm the only

one watching you? I hate to break it to you, but *everyone's* attention is on you. Especially the males."

Chills arose on my arms at the way his voice lowered, vibrating through the air in those last few words.

"Why do you even care? Why don't you worry about yourself and leave me to do the same?"

I turned in time to see his blue eyes twinkle in the darkness. "I'm invested now. I'd be much too bored here without you chaotically spiraling through this academy."

"I'm glad my chaos entertains you, but I don't need an audience." I turned my body toward the wall and pulled my thin pillow beneath my head.

A few minutes passed in silence, and I thought Wolf might have drifted back to sleep. I let my eyes flutter closed before he whispered, "Sweet dreams, Huntress."

I said nothing in return.

CHAPTER

THIRTEEN

N atural magic was supposed to be simple and easy.

Easy my ass.

It took a couple of hours for the rest of the students to learn the basics. Everyone started with the power of the earth, learning to pull the grass from the ground as if it were nothing at all.

I tried, palms hovering above the ground like a damned idiot, but I never made the grass grow.

It's all part of who you are, Headmistress Katherine said. *Open yourself to the magic of the lands.*

Bullshit. It was all bullshit.

The sun set in the distance. I missed dinner because I had been in the courtyard hours after everyone else left.

I didn't care. If I couldn't summon even the easiest natural magic, I was utterly screwed.

"Try again." The female voice from behind made me jump. "This time, close your eyes."

I spun to find Voiler walking toward me.

"I thought I was alone out here," I replied stiffly.

"You were." She stuffed her hands in her pockets. "Until five minutes ago, anyway."

I rolled my eyes and refocused on the grass. "It's no use."

She kept approaching. "Funny. You didn't strike me as the type to give up so easily."

Her black boots—similar to mine—crunched the ground until she stood directly in front of me. I looked up at her from my seated position on the grass.

And then she surprised me by dropping to her knees in front of me.

This close, I could see the freckles that littered her white skin.

"Here," she said, gripping my palms and turning them down again toward the soil. "Close your eyes."

With a long exhale, I did as she suggested. Normally, I would have my guard up in a situation like this. But something about Voiler made me feel at ease.

She would not hurt me. She'd wanted to help Maekus earlier, too. I felt it.

"Now picture the magic stemming from your body. You are one with the grass, with the dirt. You come from the same goddess, and you belong together. Allow the grass to become one with you."

I tried to focus on her words, but I couldn't stop the doubt from creeping into my skull, yelling at me for being such an utter failure.

My shoulders slumped. Voiler released my hands.

"You have to try harder, Huntyr." Her voice was calming, not what I expected from her small fighter body.

"I'm trying."

"You're not, and it's because you're afraid."

I snapped my eyes to hers. "I am not *afraid* of magic."

She shrugged. "Then why are you closing yourself off? It is not *you* who holds the key to natural magic, Huntyr. It is the archangels who blessed this land."

"I'm aware of that, thank you."

Even with my attitude, Voiler smiled at me. "Try again."

And I did.

I tried again and again and again.

It wasn't until the sun fully set that I managed to pull one singular shred of grass from the soil beneath.

Voiler squealed in excitement.

I wasn't as convinced.

"Why are you helping me, anyway?" I asked skeptically.

She wiped her pants off after climbing to her feet. "I don't know," she replied in a murmur. "You remind me of myself, I guess."

I wasn't sure whether to be proud or offended. Voiler stood out to me as one of the strong, smart contestants from the beginning. She did not grovel for attention like some others, and she was not arrogant like Ryder or Espek.

She kept to herself.

I liked that about her.

Rummy would have liked her, too.

"Well, thank you," I mumbled as we turned down the

hall to the bedrooms. "Although I still have a lot of work to do if I'm going to catch up with everyone else."

"You'll get there." She winked at me before turning left, slipping into the door labeled *Voiler and Ashlani.*

Well, at least I wasn't a complete and utter failure.

I had the ability to wield magic. I only needed to learn to surrender to it.

Hours passed, yet I stared into the darkness of the small bedroom, wide awake. Every sound in the hallway sent my heart into an annoying, inconvenient flutter. Wolf wasn't coming back.

He clearly had no interest in running into me.

I should have been relieved, should have been overcome with joy at the fact that I didn't have to deal with his arrogant, self-righteous attitude.

I should have been so damn relieved.

Then why was I awake, waiting for him to come back? Wondering where he went so late at night?

Fuck it, Huntyr. It's none of your business.

But something pulled at me, awakened some sleeping piece inside of me that wouldn't rest until I found out where he was.

I got out of bed, still wearing my full training gear that

I slept in every night, strapped Venom to my thigh, slipped my boots on, and silently crept into the hall.

The castle was eerie enough during the day. Now? The sound of my pounding heart filled my ears, louder than even my own breath, my own footsteps.

Everyone is asleep, I reminded myself. It's not like I was breaking any rules, anyway. We were perfectly capable of handling ourselves at any time of the night. We weren't locked in our rooms like children.

Still, each step I took sent alarms off in my body.

I crept down the corridor of rooms, turning left and then right. I passed the hall with our classrooms, then the hallway that led to the courtyard.

I wasn't sure what I was looking for. Some secret meeting happening in the middle of the night? Wolf training by himself beneath the thick blanket of darkness?

My fae eyes were sharp enough to see everything that lurked in these shadows, but I had a feeling Wolf could see more.

He surprised me. He was a specimen of a fighter, that much I was willing to admit. He only sparred in front of the group a couple of times, but each time was like watching an artist.

He was calculated. Stronger than anyone I had ever seen. Elegant.

Violent.

I turned again, walking out of the castle and following the path to the trees that surrounded the place. It was strange; I had been at the academy for a while now and had only been outside in the courtyard. I hadn't even bothered to come back here.

The still air held a chilling coolness.

"Late-night walk?" Wolf's raspy voice interrupted the silence.

I spun on instinct and slammed straight into his chest. His hands gripped my upper arms as he backed me up into the bark of the nearest tree. I couldn't control the grunt that escaped my mouth.

Wolf moved his arms so one hand splayed flat against my torso, the other creating a bar across my shoulders, pushing me against the tree.

Once again, his strength shocked me. My stomach dropped at the sight of him.

It was divine and utterly sickening.

"Pretty much," I answered stiffly. There wasn't much I could say to get me out of this situation; Wolf pretty much caught me looking for him.

"Careful," he said with a tilt of his head. "It's beginning to look like you're following me."

I scoffed, "That's ridiculous."

"Really? Then what are you doing out here, Huntress?"

"I could ask you the same thing."

"Maybe, but you didn't."

We stared at each other in the darkness. I could still see the sharpness of his features. The ice in his eyes became illuminated in the moonlight. His eyes scanned my face, too, and I suddenly felt much too vulnerable. The hand pressed against my torso emitted a warmth that sent goosebumps down my arms.

"You've been gone," I managed to whisper.

He loosened his hold on me slightly but didn't let go. "I figured you'd prefer it that way. Miss me already?"

"No, I—"

"Because if your nights are getting lonely, I can always come back and—"

I stomped on his foot and shoved against his chest with all the strength I had left.

He barely budged, but then he grabbed both my wrists and pulled me to him until our chests were touching. He towered over me, bending his head above mine until all the moonlight was blocked from my sight.

There was nothing but him; dark and dangerous, glorious and confusing.

"Tell me why you're following me."

"I was curious," I whispered. It was a truth that gutted me to admit, but I wasn't sure why. "I mean, where have you been? I've barely seen you here at all over the last couple of days. I thought you might have left altogether."

He smirked. "And leave you here all alone? You aren't that lucky."

Wolf finally let go of me and backed away. A cool breeze replaced the heated buzz of his presence.

"Then where? Please tell me you're not sleeping in the woods like an animal."

"What's wrong with animals?" he asked. He craned his head and stared at the moon. "I'd rather sleep with the wolves most nights, anyway."

"You don't have to, that's all."

Wolf surveyed me, and it took everything in me not to back away from his intense stare.

"Fine, Huntress," he started. "I won't make you beg for me just yet, though I can't say I haven't pictured it."

I rolled my eyes and turned away. "You don't always have to be so—"

"Strong? Sexy? Alluring?"

"Arrogant."

I grunted but kept walking, convincing myself I didn't care whether he followed me.

But he fell into step beside me as I made my way back to the castle. His smug comments did not abate the entire way back to our bedroom. He even made a few more as I slipped in and out of the bathroom, and at least three as I lay in bed, willing myself to sleep.

But Wolf's annoying, pompous remarks filled that dark, soul-numbing silence. And for that, I was grateful.

CHAPTER

FOURTEEN

"Historically, there have been four individuals who made it into The Golden City without bonding. Four. The choice to bond is extremely personal and is not required, but the odds will be against you if you decide to go at this alone."

Even the mere mention of the magic bond made me sit up taller, made my instincts scream.

I didn't want to think about it. I absolutely didn't want anyone bonding with me, but I sure as all hells didn't want to fight those odds.

Lanson's knee brushed against mine. When I glanced at him, he was already looking at me, a soft smile playing on his lips.

"Today we will begin preparing for the final test—the Transcendent. All of you could pass, or none of you. The skills you'll be learning over the next month will help you, but you'll be pushed harder than you ever have. The Golden City is what it is because of the strength of those

152

living within. If you are strong enough, if you are worthy enough, then you have nothing to worry about."

Ryder and his friends whispered something amongst themselves and laughed.

Headmistress paused and gave them a death glare. "Many of you will view your classmates as competition. While we don't encourage you to turn on each other, you'll naturally be forced to fight one another during the Transcendent. This is simply to show which of you are worthy for admittance to The Golden City."

"What exactly is the final challenge?" someone asked.

"That's not something we can share with you. You'll find out with everyone else as soon as the challenge begins."

Silence filled the classroom. We hadn't talked much about the Transcendent, but we all knew we were preparing for something big.

Something dangerous.

Deadly.

A shiver crawled down my spine, but I sat up straighter.

"Today, we'll begin the training of summoning blood magic. Has anyone here learned of blood magic before?" Headmistress continued.

Ashlani's hand flew into the air. "It is magic that can only be used when a blood offering is made to the goddess," she answered.

My eyes shot to Headmistress. I knew an embarrassingly negligible amount about magic before I arrived, and I certainly did not know how to summon blood magic.

"That's right. Some fae—or angels—can have more access to magic, depending on bloodlines. We can all access magic here in Moira, thanks to the archangels who blessed these lands. But where you're all from, there is little to no use of magic. If any of you happened to descend from powerful fae, or the archangels themselves, you would likely have powerful blood that allowed you to pull more blood magic.

"Blood magic is much more powerful than natural magic. With blood, you'll be able to fight. You'll be able to summon the elements with only a thought. You'll even be able to heal or kill if you're strong enough, though those gifts are very rare. The limits to what you can do with blood magic are nonexistent, but be wary. With great ambition comes significant risk."

Headmistress pulled a small knife from her side and sliced it down her palm. Within seconds, blood pooled in her hand and dropped to the floor.

"Magic lives within us all." She lifted her other hand, palm down, and raised it. The blood droplets on the floor rose into the air. "Within the confines of The Golden City, you will wield magic to protect yourself and others when necessary."

She lowered her hand. The blood fell.

"Magic always, however, comes with a price. Each one of us has a certain limitation, a certain stopping point at which our blood magic source will stop giving to us."

"How do we refuel it?" Espek asked, pursing his lips in thought.

"Time," Headmistress responded. "Or, if you aren't

lucky enough to have time on your hands, the bond."

"What if you bond with someone who is weaker than you with their magic?" he pushed.

"You will only have access to whatever your partner has left when you bond. Therefore, the decision on who to bond with is an important one. Choose poorly, and it could be your life on the line. Now, everyone, stand up. I'm going to teach you all how to call upon your blood magic."

Great.

I stood in my seat next to Lanson. Wolf had thankfully chosen a seat near the far side of the study chamber, which left me room to breathe.

After our encounter in the woods last night, I found myself thinking about him nonstop.

But with Lanson talking to me and bumping my shoulder with his from time to time, I could at least pretend I was focused.

I pulled Venom from my thigh, watching as every other student with a weapon did the same. Some people, like Ashlani, didn't have a weapon of their own, so they were forced to share.

But nobody else was touching Venom.

"As you probably know by now, the very walls of this castle are blessed with the archangels' magic. Once your blood hits the ground with a clear mind and set intentions, you'll begin to feel the pull."

Ryder cut his hand first, followed by the fae around him.

I watched as Voiler did the same, followed by Ashlani and Lanson.

I placed Venom's blade on my skin.

And I cut.

Clear mind and set intentions.

It sounded easy, but my mind was absolute chaos, and my intentions were anything but set.

"Different bloodlines will feel different pulls to magic. This will differ greatly from natural magic, so prepare yourselves."

I tensed immediately. After barely summoning natural magic, my hopes were low, but my guard was up.

I fought the urge to turn to Wolf.

"Relax," Lanson whispered beside me. "You'll do great."

Blood pooled in his own hand, ready to fall.

Ready to test.

I flipped my palm, letting the droplets hit the stone, magic-infused ground of the castle.

My eyes squeezed shut in anticipation as I waited for it —whatever it was. A rush of power? Some magical light? Anything.

But nothing came.

Ashlani squealed, and I opened my eyes to find her holding a small flame in her bloodied palm.

Hells. *Focus, Huntyr.*

I shut my eyes again, focusing on my palm, on the light stinging and the warm blood that dripped from my skin to the floor below. I imagined the goddess herself looking over us, gracing us with her power. I pictured the archangels coaxing the magic from the blood, giving us everything we could ever want.

My fingers began to tingle. I squeezed my eyes harder, focusing on that drip of blood.

Drip.

Drip.

That's when I felt it. It was so subtle, I almost didn't notice. But when smoke filled my senses, when darkness filled my veins, I panicked.

I snapped my eyes open, looking around to see if anyone else noticed.

No, the others were too busy focusing on their own blood magic to notice anything about me. Everyone but Wolf, anyway, who stared at me with a raised eyebrow from the back of the room.

That couldn't be normal. To feel so much darkness, to sense so much power. There was no way that was supposed to happen. My stomach sank. What if I couldn't summon the blood magic like everyone else? What if some part of me was so fucked up, I could only call to the darkness?

For the next few hours, I tried and failed to summon the blood magic over and over and over again. Each time I started to feel that sultry, looming pull, I snapped out of it, afraid of what I might see on the other side.

My senses warned me against it, screaming at the dangers that lay within. Hells, maybe I was never going to summon blood magic.

Even Ashlani had no problem conjuring her small flame. Did she feel the shadows that called to her from her blood?

Did she give into the darkness as well?

I shook my head, wiping my bloodied palm on my leather pants.

I would try again, just not here. Not with so many witnesses, not with so many people to see if I screwed everything up.

Magic called to me. Later, when I was alone, I would answer with blood.

Blood poured from the sky.

The thick red droplets splattered the pristine kingdom with death and chaos, blinding soldiers and terrifying children.

I had never seen such a mighty place crumble so quickly.

I was in the vampyre kingdom, and though I couldn't remember ever being there before, it felt so right.

It felt like home... if home were burning to the ground.

Screams rang out in the distance; women and children fought for their lives.

War.

Suddenly, I was in the thick of it.

Vampyres, rabid and primal, rampaged through the kingdom as if nothing could stop them. They were out for fae blood, something they could feed on.

Of course, they wouldn't find any of that here.

Only the army fighting against us could give them what they craved.

So, they charged.

With every ounce of strength, the vampyres catapulted themselves toward the army that infiltrated the kingdom.

I didn't have time to question why I was here or why I couldn't remember anything before this moment. The battle grew closer and closer to the inner city.

I needed to run.

Run or die.

I staggered backward, forcing my lungs to suck in air as I ran down the dark streets. Others ran with me, and cries of panic filled the air.

Run or die.

Run or die.

Run or die.

I ran as fast as I could until I heard it: the sound that pulled me from my trance, pulled me from the chaos.

"Huntyr!" the voice said. "Come this way!"

I looked, seeing the most beautiful woman I had ever laid eyes on. Her hair was black and curly like mine, her eyes golden and filled with light.

I elbowed my way over to her, still fighting to catch my breath.

I knew this woman; I had seen her before, though I couldn't remember when.

"You're safe now," she whispered.

I shouldn't have believed her. Amid blood and war, nothing was safe. But a warm, serene blanket of comfort fell over me.

The woman leaned forward, opening her arms to hug me.

That's when I saw her change. Morph into one of the creatures we had just been fighting.

Her perfect, golden eyes faded into black, empty orifices. Fangs grew from her teeth like they had been there all along.

And then she aimed for my throat.

My own scream jolted me awake. I sat up in bed, panting, sweat covering my forehead and neck. I slapped a hand over my throat, feeling for a pulse. Gasping in relief when I found it, I swallowed.

It was just a nightmare. Those damn vampyre stories from learning history here had really started to get to me.

My breath came rapidly before I could start slowing it down.

Hells, I hoped I didn't wake—

I glanced over to Wolf's bed, expecting to find him asleep or not there at all, only to find him sitting up and staring directly at me.

But he said nothing. With his eyebrows drawn together and his mouth tight, he lingered in the darkness, not saying a single word about the obvious nightmare I had just woken from.

I rolled over, facing the wall as I pulled my sweat-covered blanket up to my chin. Hells, the dream had been so vivid. I could see the magnificent, towering castle, could smell the blood and decay in the air.

Just a dream, I reminded myself. *Your enemies are here, and you are nowhere near the vampyre kingdom.*

I did not sleep for the rest of the night.

And though I was certain he had seen my sudden outburst, Wolf never said a word.

CHAPTER
FIFTEEN

Days turned to weeks in a blurred series of classes, fights, meals, and restless nights. I got no better at magic, but I managed to keep my physical damage during class to a minimum, which was a relief.

The gashes on my back eventually healed into rough, raised scars, and day after day, I felt my body recovering. Rebuilding.

Preparing.

Wolf managed to keep to himself, mostly. Aside from staring at me across the courtyard or the dining hall, he kept his distance. I caught him slipping out of my—our—room every once in a while, but I didn't ask him any more questions.

Which is why I was absolutely *not* looking for him in the woods, but as I walked out of the castle and into the tree-filled night, I couldn't help but glance up with every snapped twig or crunched leaf I heard.

No, I was *not* looking for Wolf.

I had absolutely *not* stooped to that level of humiliation.

But when someone approached from behind me, every sense of mine electrified, anticipating him.

Only, it wasn't him.

Not even fucking close.

"I can't say I'm surprised." Ryder's voice crept through the air. "You are so weak, you cannot even summon an ounce of blood magic."

I spun to face him.

"Did you follow me out here?"

He stepped forward. "Maybe I did. I've been following you for the last few days, actually." Another step forward.

Fear ignited my senses, telling me to run. Ryder was a predator, and here? Like this? He stalked me like I was prey.

"See anything interesting?" I pulled Venom from my thigh.

Ryder stifled a laugh, crossing his arms over his chest. "It's more about what I don't see. No blood magic, no natural magic. Hells, can you summon at all? Or are you so weak that you'll never be able to use magic in The Golden City?"

"You're awfully concerned about how other people wield magic. Why don't you focus on yourself for once?"

"Like I said,"—he took another step—"I won't allow weaklings to make it into The Golden City."

"The Transcendent will get rid of the weak ones, anyway. It's not your personal job to sift through the students, Ryder."

"It is when some of them have angels pulling them through this academy."

I froze, my grip on Venom tight and ready.

Ryder was only a few feet away now, much too close for comfort. I couldn't run; he was taller and faster.

I could only fight.

Ryder did not know how much of a killer I really was, how much I had trained for this.

He'd underestimated me for the last time.

"Don't," I hissed, tightening my grip on Venom. "You don't want to do this, Ryder."

A few more steps and Ryder backed me up against a tree. I was out of options. It was time to *fight*.

"Why not?" he taunted. "Because your scary little angel will come after me? Well, guess what, rat? He's nowhere to be seen. He won't be able to stop me as I squeeze your last breath from your lungs, just like I did to the weak little boy in the dining hall."

"I don't need Wolf to protect me," I seethed. *Damn*, I hated Ryder. I hated him so much, I wasn't sure I could control myself anymore.

"Is that so?" he hissed. "Because you're so capable of protecting yourself, right?" He threw his head back and laughed, the sound cruel and grating. "The thought of you fighting me off is hilarious, and I've been dying for a good laugh. I'd like to see you try to—"

Ryder didn't finish his sentence before I kneed him between the legs. Hard. He grunted in pain and released his grip on me, doubling over.

I didn't hesitate. I stabbed him in the side.

He froze for a second, realizing what had just happened.

I pulled Venom out of his flesh before the blood came rushing from the wound.

Ryder stood up and pressed a hand to his side, pulling it away and watching the blood drip from his fingertips. "Oh, you're really dead now, you bitch."

Come and fucking get it.

I'd wanted to kill this bastard for weeks now and had come very close to snapping on many occasions. He wasn't worthy of The Golden City. Hells, he wasn't even worthy of Phantom.

"I'm not as weak as you think I am," I sneered. "But you? You're exactly who I think you are."

Ryder roared and tackled me to the ground. I braced for impact, quickly rolling our bodies so he wouldn't land on top.

He wasn't getting the advantage. Not this time.

The weight of him threw the breath from my lungs. We were a chaotic mixture of limbs and anger and hatred, grasping and clawing at each other with that desperation that always came right before death.

He wasn't leaving here alive.

If I could just slip my blade between us…

Hot blood smeared across my body, across my face, my chest. It made the grip on my blade slippery. Venom slid from my grasp as Ryder slammed me down against the ground.

"You think you're special? You think you can sneak around and nobody will notice? We notice, rat. We notice you lurking, creeping in the shadows."

He struck my temple so hard, my vision blurred. My hand stretched out, feeling the ground for my lost blade. *Come on, Venom. Don't leave me now. Not when I need you.*

His hands came down on my throat and squeezed. He was going to suffocate me. "Hells, I'm going to enjoy killing you. I've wanted to end your life since our first fucking fight. I could always tell you were a weak, cowardly rat."

Venom, Venom, Venom.

I was ready to give up, ready to give into that dark shadow creeping into my vision when I felt it against my fingertips: the cold hilt of my blade.

I picked it up clumsily before using my last ounce of strength to stab his side.

Ryder cried out, loosening his grip on my neck.

I stabbed him again.

Ryder sat up. I bucked my hips, throwing him to the side before climbing on top of him. I still couldn't breathe, could barely see.

I'm not dying here. You're not the one who gets to kill me.

I stabbed him again.

Every hit, every punch. Every fucking slight, every look he gave me. He deserved much worse than this.

I stabbed him again.

Again.

Eventually, Ryder stopped moving. Stopped struggling.

I stabbed him one more time, directly in the middle of the chest.

Ryder was dead.

I fell to the side, lying on my back on the ground next to

him. His blood pooled around us. I couldn't bring myself to care, couldn't bring myself to feel.

A strange calmness washed over me, like I had finally relaxed for the first time since I had been taken to this forsaken castle.

Good fucking riddance.

Each breath burned my throat, no doubt from the tight grasp he'd had on me. That bastard really was going to kill me.

Beat you to it.

Hells. I had actually killed him. I wasn't sure how long I laid there in the blood-soaked grass. Ten minutes? An hour?

All I knew was that by the time I stood up, my vision returned to normal.

Think, Huntyr. You can't leave him here. You're the first person they'll assume killed him.

Well, he did have many enemies here. He wasn't exactly likable. And for all they knew, I was still weak. A rat.

I pulled my blade from Ryder's chest, avoiding looking at his face. I tried to wipe the blood away, but it only smeared against more of the wet substance. I was covered in it from head to toe.

Fucking hells.

Thankfully, nobody else would be awake at this hour. I left Ryder where he lay, jogging back toward the castle. I snuck through the halls in the shadows, as silent as I had ever been. Walking felt like a dream. Moving felt like floating. I wasn't even confident that I had actually made it back to my room before I opened the door.

Wolf lay shirtless—again—in bed. I froze at the threshold, letting the door swing open.

He lazily glanced up at me before doing a double take. I wasn't sure if it was the blood covering my body or the panic on my face that set him off, but he jumped to his feet and closed the distance between us in a second.

Wolf. This felt familiar. Felt real. Felt safe.

"Huntyr," he said, pulling me by the arm and closing the door behind me. The sound of my name on his mouth was real. Intense. Intimate.

No, I was probably imagining it.

"He's dead," I breathed.

"Who's dead? What in all hells happened?"

"I had to kill him," I said, more to myself than to Wolf. "He was going to kill me if I didn't."

Wolf's hands grazed my body, running down my torso, examining every inch of me. "This blood..."

"It's Ryder's."

Wolf's hands found my face, cradling me. I didn't stop him. "Tell me what happened."

So I did. I told him every detail, though most of my words came out rushed and chaotic. I told him about Ryder sneaking up on me, attacking me, touching me. Fuck, even thinking about his grimy hands on my body made me shiver.

By the time I got to the end, Wolf had gone still. Scarily still. Inhumanely still.

"Say something," I begged, my voice broken and

167

distant. Normally, I would put more effort into appearing put together. To appearing whole.

Not tonight. Not with him.

"He deserved to fucking die," Wolf said finally. My eyes met his, a storm of unsaid words. "I should have ended him a long time ago for laying a hand on you."

I was so dangerously close to crumbling. To falling against him and letting him carry some of this damn weight. I was so fucking tired. The rush of adrenaline had left me a shell of a body, a fragment of a soul.

"Hey," Wolf said. "Tell me where his body is, and I'll take care of it. I want you to wash the blood off yourself and get in bed. You don't need to worry about this."

His words came out harsh yet quiet, his hands caressing me in a way that burned the back of my throat.

"He's in the woods," I explained. "To the right, just past the tree line."

Wolf's thumb brushed my cheekbone once. It was a promise.

He left without saying another word.

I didn't crumble on the floor like I thought I might. No, I found myself in the bathroom, filling the tub with hot water.

Stripping my bloody clothes off and throwing them into a pile.

Turning the hot water red with blood.

Draining it.

Filling it again.

I had gone through two tub-fulls of water before my

skin felt clean. I dipped my head under, letting the water flush over me.

It felt nice underwater. Quiet.

I would have stayed in there all night, actually, if it weren't for the fact that Wolf would be back soon. The last thing I wanted was for him to come back and find me naked in the bathtub, half-drowned in the dirty depths.

My body ached as I pulled myself from the tub, dressing in my clean clothes and crawling into bed.

I tried to wait up for Wolf but failed miserably, succumbing to the comforting darkness of the night.

I woke up in my bed, thirsty as all hells with a splitting headache. After managing to blink my eyes open, I glanced over to Wolf's bed, expecting it to be empty like it usually was.

Only to be met with beaming eyes.

"Good," he started. "You're awake."

I pushed myself up, my ribs screaming at me from the movement. "I'm awake," I repeated. "What time is it? Don't we have training today?"

"I figured you could use the extra sleep."

"And you?"

He shrugged. "I don't need the training."

Arrogant ass.

Memories of last night came rushing back to me. Ryder attacking me, Venom diving into his skin, all that blood...

"Fuck," I mumbled, rubbing my temples. "People are going to notice Ryder's gone. And if we're gone..."

"Don't worry about Ryder. Nobody will find him, and if they do, no one will care. He should have been expelled for what he did to Maekus. His punishment was fitting. I told your friends you weren't feeling well this morning. Nobody will suspect a thing. You have nothing to worry about."

His calmness sent a wave of unease through me. That, plus the way he looked at me...

"I should go," I said, slipping out of bed. Hells, I couldn't even remember getting dressed last night, but my boots were exactly where they usually were at the end of my bed. "They'll be worried about me."

Wolf's brows drew together as he watched me pull my boots on.

"You can take it easy, you know."

"Except that I can't," I retorted, my voice sharper than it needed to be. I finished with my boots and faced him. "You don't get it, Wolf. You're strong. You'll get into The Golden City without even trying. You're an angel, for fuck's sake. But me? I have work to do. I have people who are counting on me. I can't *take it easy* and expect to make it out of here alive."

I expected a rebuttal, some snarky remark, an insult. Anything. But Wolf only tightened his jaw and looked away.

"Right," I mumbled, heading for the door. "I'll talk to you later."

I fastened my hair into a bun behind my head on my way to the classroom. I didn't want to talk to anyone, especially not Wolf. Not now. I couldn't understand the way I was feeling. After last night, everything was blurred.

The line between hatred and need, the line between fae and monster.

Everything blurred.

I burst into the training room with my fists tightened.

Lanson, who was tied in conversation with Ashlani and Voiler, snapped his head in my direction. Everyone else continued sparring around the courtyard, unaware of my absence entirely. The sun rose above the walls of the castle, beating down on everyone, even in the chilled air.

I heard a satisfying thud of a fist hitting flesh, followed by a roar of victory from one of the males to my right, but I continued walking straight ahead.

"There you are!" Lanson called out, immediately jogging over to me. "I was worried about you. Feeling any better?"

"Yeah," I lied, lowering my head so he couldn't see my features. "Much better."

"Good, because there's something I wanted to ask you."

I shoved my hands in my pockets, waiting for him to continue.

"The apprentice ball is coming up. I'm wondering if you'd like to attend with me."

I stared at him in shock. Lanson was nice, sure, but to ask me to the ball? Attending those things was not a priority for me. Making friends was not a priority, either. And why would Lanson ask *me* of all people here?

"That's sweet, Lanson, but I—"

"Just think about it, okay?" His eyes were so large and innocent. I envied him, I really did. He didn't have the heaviness on his shoulders that I had grown so accustomed to. He wasn't from Midgrave. He didn't have to claw and beg just to make it through the day alive. Fae from the surrounding cities seemed... happy.

"Sure." I forced a smile on my face. "I'll think about it."

The morning went by as usual. Lanson took it easy on me while we trained, whether he knew I was sore as hell from last night's attack or not.

"Time for sparring," Commander Macanthos announced as he stormed into the courtyard. He wore the same training clothes he wore every day, but his long-sleeved top was replaced by one cut at the shoulders, exposing his sculpted and scarred arms.

I tilted my head toward the sky and silently thanked the goddess that he didn't notice my late arrival.

Commander Macanthos pushed past everyone until he reached the center of the courtyard. He held up a sheet of paper and read, "First up, I want to see Huntyr and Espek."

All hells.

Ryder's friend.

This could not possibly have come at a worse time. My body screamed at me to relax, to surrender. I'd fought in pain before, and I'd certainly suffered worse injuries than these. But the pure weight of exhaustion I felt now was lethally new.

I didn't want to take another beating.

But I had no choice.

"Fine," I said, stepping into the training circle. "Let's get this over with."

The fae before me looked angry. Angrier than Ryder.

Ryder hadn't looked angry with my dagger impaled in his body, though. He looked afraid.

I wasn't prepared when a fist came straight toward my ribs, making brutal contact with my already-bruised body. I doubled over, staggering to the side.

"What?" he hissed. "You can't handle a simple fight?" He laughed through gritted teeth. "Maybe Ryder was right about you."

I raised my fists.

He smirked.

"Go ahead," he taunted, waving me on. "Try me. Try to hit me, I bet you can't even land a punch with those—"

I jumped forward and aimed my fist toward his unprotected lower stomach. It landed, but my movements were slow and lazy. He grabbed my arm and twisted, forcing me to the ground with a grunt.

"Give up," he growled.

I sent my free elbow into his thigh as hard as I could, ignoring the pain that radiated through my arm. He wailed and stepped back, letting go of me.

I stood and instantly attacked, aiming low with a kick to his right leg.

But I wasn't as strong as I usually was. My kick was fucking pathetic. He caught it and threw me to the ground, landing on top of me mere seconds later.

"Give up," he said, jamming a fist into my stomach.

"No," I gasped.

He punched my jaw, split my lip.

Everything blurred.

"Fine. I guess I'll have to end this fight myself." He raised his fist again, and I closed my eyes, ready for the impact that would likely take my consciousness.

But it never came.

I opened my eyes again when a shadow covered us, blocking the sunlight that typically shined onto the courtyard.

Wolf stood above us. "I'm next," he snapped. "Get up."

I wasn't sure who he was talking to, but the fae climbed off me with a growl. "She's a waste of energy," he mumbled to Wolf, but Wolf didn't budge.

Didn't smirk.

"Get up," Wolf said again, this time directed at me.

I pushed myself to my feet, using all of my energy to remain upright. The world around me swayed, but after blinking a few times, everything seemed solid enough.

"She can't fight like this," Lanson argued, stepping into the circle. "She needs a break." He tried to grab my arm, but I shoved him away.

"No," I growled. "I'm fine. I can fight."

Wolf didn't bother looking at the commander. We both knew he wouldn't do a damn thing to stop this. This was what training was for: weeding out the weak so the strong prevailed.

Maybe I was much more fucking fragile than I thought. I certainly felt weak.

"What?" I demanded, holding my hands out on either side of my body. Blood filled my mouth, dribbling from my chin. "Afraid to hit a girl?"

Wolf's eyes moved across my face, no doubt scanning each injury. Each new weakness. His training uniform had barely been touched, and not a single bruise covered his dark, perfect skin.

He was an effortless predator. He won his fights with power and honor.

Me? I won mine with every last piece of fucking life I had left in me.

When he met my gaze again, though, something much colder lingered. "Not in the slightest, Huntress."

I had seen Wolf move, had watched him fight. But being the one on the other side of that undeniable strength was something else entirely. He moved with such precise speed, I barely had time to defend myself as he swung a fist toward my face, making contact with my jaw while he kicked my feet out from under me.

I landed on my back hard, the air rushing from my lungs. *Fuck. He really just punched me in the face. This was happening.* I scrambled back to my feet and re-adjusted my stance.

"If you want me on my back, you can just ask next time," I said. My words were barely audible as I fought to catch my breath, but a few fits of laughter confirmed that they were loud enough.

Wolf held my gaze; emotionless, ready. His eyes didn't leave mine, though, as I moved closer to him. They didn't wander to the knife in my hand, didn't observe my approaching feet.

What in the hells was he looking at?

"You don't know when to quit, Huntress, do you?"

"I know when to quit," I mumbled, swinging my blade to his side. He blocked it without so much as a grunt. "But I also know that when I quit, I die."

I could have sworn the corner of his mouth twisted upward, only for a fraction of a second, before he moved again.

This time, he did not hold back.

I attempted to jump over the leg he swung out again, but he was on me in an instant, grabbing me with an arm around the waist and tackling me to the grass. My body rolled over his once before he landed above me, bracing his body above mine while pinning me to the ground.

"Sometimes," he started, lowering his head until his face lingered just inches from mine, "we have to quit in order to survive."

Yeah fucking right.

Everyone was watching now, and I could hear even more laughter from the back of the courtyard.

I wasn't giving up without a damn fight.

I slid my knee up, trying as hard as I could to land a blow between Wolf's legs, but he realized what I was doing instantly, letting go and dropping the body weight he had been holding earlier. His entire body crashed against mine; he pinned me to the grass easily.

Every single inch of my body touched his. A dark storm

brewed behind his eyes, his breath mixed with mine in a rapid wave.

"Try that again, Huntress, and you won't like what I do next."

"Get off of me," I grunted.

"Tell me you're done with this fight."

"I'm not done."

I tried to fight against him, tried to lift my shoulders from under him, but he placed a harsh hand on my chest—right beneath my throat—and pinned me down. A snarl played on his lips, genuine anger this time.

Not playful. Not flirtatious.

"Tell me you're done."

No, I wanted to scream. I would never give up, would never surrender. Isn't that what Lord would have wanted?

Fucking angels. I swallowed a mouth full of bitter, vile blood and choked. I turned my head to the side and spit it out just in time.

"Fight's over," Wolf growled, pushing himself off me. I expected him to storm off, to forget I ever existed and go back to ignoring me.

But he grabbed my wrist and hoisted me to my feet. "You're coming with me," he insisted.

I tried and failed to yank myself from his grasp. "I'm not going anywhere with you," I argued.

There was nothing anybody could do as he threw me over his shoulder and marched out of the courtyard.

Even Lanson stood helpless, nobody willing to stand up against Wolf.

Cowards.

"Put me down!" I yelled.

He led us through the castle, through the stone hallways, away from the courtyard. I half-expected Lanson to storm out after me, but he didn't.

Nobody came. Nobody cared.

It was just Wolf and I, my face bleeding against the back of his shirt while he carried me.

"Hells!" I yelled as he finally set me on my feet. Though when I stood upright, I stumbled to the side, catching myself on the stone wall.

"You're a fucking mess, Huntyr."

I waited for the hallway to stop spinning before I answered. "There you go. Caring again."

"No," he said. "You're not turning this shit on me. You let people beat you up, you won't give up, you won't protect yourself. Why? This isn't helping anyone. You're slowly killing yourself."

A rough fit of laughter escaped me. "Isn't that what we're all doing?" I asked.

"No," he answered quickly. "It's not. I thought you wanted to survive this damn place."

"I do."

"Then start fucking acting like it. You want others to think you're weak? Done. Fair enough. But to let them beat you to a damn pulp? You're better than this. You're stronger than this."

"Am I?" I asked, my words coming out in a harsh breath.

"After what you did to that sorry bastard last night, yes. I believe so."

Silence lingered in the few feet between us. The truth of his words hit me harder than I would have liked. I didn't want to think about last night. Didn't want to think about Ryder's dead body, about what everyone else would think if they knew.

Wolf was right. I was a damn mess.

"Go to bed," he said. "And stop acting like you're nothing, Huntress. You're forgetting who you really are."

He turned and stormed down the hall, no doubt back to the courtyard, leaving me feeling more alone than ever.

CHAPTER

SIXTEEN

The courtyard looked different today. Instead of an open, grassy field for us to practice combat, targets with large red circles in the center lined the back wall.

"Today you will practice the art of throwing your daggers." Commander Macanthos spoke with a glint in his eye, one that both thrilled me and terrified me. "Physical combat is not enough to protect The Golden City from any outside threats. You must be able to hit a target from afar with pristine accuracy."

I bit my cheek to stop myself from smiling. Throwing daggers was a skill I had been forced to perfect in my years at Phantom. It was necessary for killing vampyres without getting your throat ripped out. It was also a skill I could practice here without having to take beatings to blend in. Marking the targets a few inches off center wouldn't be difficult.

"Once you've all learned to aim without killing one

another, we'll move onto wielding other weapons. Who here feels confident in their skills with a weapon?"

A few students to my right raised their hands, lifting their chins. I quickly glanced at Wolf, who stood next to the courtyard wall with his shoulder pressed against the stone. I didn't even have to wonder if he was ample with a weapon. Everything about him screamed that he was lethal with a dagger.

It was annoying as all hells.

I looked away before he noticed me glaring at him. My jaw was still sore from his punch, and no amount of scowling would make up for that.

Asshole.

"Good," Commander Macanthos continued, seemingly pleased with the confidence of the group. "Then it seems we'll have no problem with today's challenge."

My body stiffened. It wasn't any normal combat training day. *Today was a test.*

"Gather toward the targets." Commander Macanthos did not wait for us to follow before turning on his heel and marching toward the back of the courtyard to where the targets were waiting for us.

I never had much target practice in Midgrave. Aside from vampyres, that is. I learned quickly that missing my mark was not an option when it came to fighting those creatures.

This wouldn't be any different.

Commander Macanthos spun to face us when we were about ten paces away from the targets. "You," he pointed to Ashlani. "Stand in front of that target."

The air outside chilled.

Ashlani's eyes snapped open. She looked side to side before returning her gaze to the commander. "Wh–what?"

Commander Macanthos rolled his eyes as if this was just another day at training for him. "Don't make me repeat myself."

Even from here, I could see Ashlani's breath grow shallow as she hesitantly made her way to the target. She froze for a few seconds before turning to face us, her chin lifted with confidence even though her lip wobbled.

Fuck. I shouldn't have cared, but I did. Ashlani didn't deserve what was coming.

"Great." Commander Macanthos clapped his hands together. "The best way to practice throwing daggers is to up the stakes. Many of you are confident in your ability to throw, but some of you…" His eyes spanned the group of students before landing on me. "You."

My gaze did not budge from his. "Yes?"

"Let's see you hit the target."

A cry slipped from Ashlani's lips.

"With her standing there?" I asked.

Commander Macanthos did not answer. He crossed his arms over his chest and waited.

Great. Real fucking great.

I slid Venom from her sheath at my thigh slowly, feeling dozens of eyes watching my every move.

The students in front of me quickly slid out of my way as I stepped in front of the target.

In front of a squirming, petrified Ashlani.

I tried to comfort her by softening my gaze and looking

as confident as possible. I wasn't going to hit her. I knew that.

But she didn't. Neither did the other students, who practically radiated with fear. Lanson included.

"We don't have all day," Commander Macanthos pushed. "Throw it."

Anger laced my senses. Of all the students standing in this courtyard, why me? Why was he singling me out amongst everyone?

I channeled that anger into my senses. Ashlani stood as still as possible, which helped. I didn't raise my hand when Commander Macanthos asked who was skilled with throwing daggers, so I could get away with hitting the wall next to her.

I focused in, putting one foot in front of the other.

I raised my hand, pointed Venom toward Ashlani.

And I threw.

Ashlani flinched at first but sighed in relief when the dagger smacked against the wall just a few feet to her left.

I sighed too, releasing the growing tension from my shoulders.

"Again," Commander Macanthos ordered.

My eyes snapped to him. "What? Again?"

"You heard me. Until you can actually hit the target, you'll go again."

"And you really think it's necessary for Ashlani to stand there the entire time? There are other ways to practice!"

Hitting the target—what was left of it on the perimeter of Ashlani's head, anyway—would mean showing one of my greatest skills. Sure, I wasn't the only one here who could throw a dagger. But I wasn't entirely sure that the others could throw with as much accuracy as I could. Could Espek hit the target beside her head without nicking her? Could Lanson?

Somehow, I doubted it.

I marched over to the wall, avoiding Ashlani's chaotic and desperate gaze, and picked up Venom.

I wiped the sweat from my palm before tightening my grasp around the hilt.

One more throw. If I threw one more and made it close enough to the target, Commander Macanthos would relax.

That's what he wanted, right? To embarrass me? To show the whole class I couldn't hit the target with Ashlani standing there?

Commander Macanthos didn't know me. Nobody here did.

I made it back to my original throwing position, taking one breath before throwing Venom. It was quick—too quick to give me time for hesitation.

Ashlani screamed this time. Her legs shook beneath her as my blade barely grazed the edge of the target before falling to the grass beside her.

An audible sigh escaped Lanson behind me.

I looked to Commander Macanthos, who only stared back at me with determined eyes. "Again."

Ashlani cried out again. The sound of it rattled my bones, sunk my stomach.

"I can hit the target just fine without her standing there," I argued.

"What's the problem, then?" Commander Macanthos was testing me. Pushing me. Expecting me to quit.

Quit or kill Ashlani.

Sweat formed on the back of my neck. "This is fucking ridiculous," I mumbled.

"Is it?" Commander Macanthos uncrossed his arms and stepped toward me. Whatever personal vendetta he had today, I was sick of it.

"Throwing a dagger at Ashlani proves nothing. Anybody can hit a target if they try enough. Putting her life in danger is pointless."

He scoffed, not bothering to even glance at Ashlani before adding, "Ashlani, step away from the target. Huntyr here thinks she can disobey my orders."

Ashlani scrambled away from the target, making her way to Voiler before tears poured from her eyes.

I let out a breath.

"If you think it's so pointless," Commander Macanthos muttered, "then you'll have no problem standing there yourself."

This was it. This was the real fucking test. Did he think of me as a coward? Did he think I would be too afraid to stand in front of the target while one of my classmates threw the dagger?

Fuck. Him.

I bit my tongue to keep the stream of curses out of my mouth as I stomped over to the target. I picked up Venom and sheathed her at my thigh before I stood facing my classmates.

Most of them had trained for this. They could throw a simple dagger without gutting me.

I hoped.

I looked at Ashlani and gave her a small nod before scanning the other faces, waiting for Commander Macanthos.

"What about you?" the commander asked a student. It wasn't until I looked at him that I saw who he approached.

Wolf.

Wolf still stood uninterested at the edge of the courtyard. And his eyes were glued on *me*, even as the commander walked toward him.

"What about me?" Wolf responded.

"Care to show the class how to hit a target, angel?" Commander Macanthos was downright antagonizing.

But Wolf's jaw tightening was the only sign that he heard the commander at all. "I'd rather not."

Commander Macanthos halted a few feet away. "That wasn't a suggestion. Start throwing."

Espek choked on a laugh to the right.

I ignored him. I ignored crying Ashlani; I ignored Lanson who was now beginning to argue. I ignored everyone, actually.

I focused on Wolf.

He lazily sauntered over to the front of the crowd, standing about fifteen paces from me. He could have stepped closer, but he was making a point.

I glared at him from my place in front of the target. If he drew my blood while throwing the damn knife, it would be the last thing he ever did.

"Any day now," Commander Macanthos chirped.

Wolf's features flickered with distaste before he slid his own dagger from his waist. His eyes locked on mine. His black feathered angel wings glistened in the sunlight, making him look annoyingly gorgeous. His black training pants fit his long legs, matching the shirt that exposed the bulky muscles of his arms.

Throw the damn dagger, Wolf.

As if reading my mind, he smirked. And then—before I even realized what had happened—a dagger impaled the target just inches from my neck.

My eyes slammed shut. I blew out a shaky breath before opening them again, only to find Wolf's sharp eyes still piercing through mine.

"That is how you hit a target," Commander Macanthos praised. "Show them one more time."

Wolf rolled his eyes, finally looking away from me but still acting as if this was all a huge inconvenience to him. "Is that necessary?"

Commander Macanthos's eyes widened. "Yes," he spat. "Unless you'd rather have one of your other classmates take a—"

"No," Wolf interrupted. "I'll do it."

Fucking angels. Why did I feel *relieved* that Wolf wasn't letting anyone else throw?

When Wolf refocused on me, I could have sworn I saw light simmering beneath his eyes. I froze as Wolf stomped forward, his chin lifted and his fists clenched, to withdrawal his dagger from the target beside me.

He stepped close—closer than he needed to—as he yanked it free. His bare arm brushed against mine.

"Try not to kill me," I whispered, loud enough so only he could hear.

Wolf froze and looked away, shaking his head. "Careful, Huntress. There are many things I could do to you with this dagger, but making you bleed is not one of them."

He gave me a quick wink before walking away, leaving me frozen and irritated as all hells in front of the target.

One more throw.

That was it.

Lanson stepped up and whispered something to Wolf that I couldn't hear, but whatever it was, it made Wolf's features morph into something terrifying and amused.

It was a terrible combination.

I shifted on my feet, rubbing my hands together in front of me. When Wolf looked at me again, he smiled.

Then he sent the dagger flying. It landed so close, I felt the puff of air from the force. The dagger hit the target right beside my head, inches above my ear.

Too fucking close.

Everyone in the class froze, probably waiting to see if the dagger had hit me.

A loose piece of my black, curly hair fell like a feather, floating in the air until it landed by my feet.

Was he fucking kidding me?

I pulled away, yanking the dagger out of the target and marching over to Wolf.

"That's enough for now," the commander announced.

"Find a target and get to work. If you get stabbed, that's on you."

The students began silently dispersing as I stomped toward Wolf. "What the fuck was that?" I hissed, holding onto his dagger.

Wolf shrugged. "Your little boyfriend was worried that I would hurt a hair on your pretty little head." His eyes flickered to my curls. "I think you'll survive."

He leaned into my space and yanked his weapon from my grip. When he turned and walked out of the courtyard —leaving the entire class—I didn't stop him.

I turned to find Lanson watching my every move.

"Are you okay?" he asked carefully as I approached.

"I'm fine," I assured him, trying to act as if Wolf didn't have a way of pissing me off like nobody else. "He must have it out for me today."

Lanson mumbled some sort of agreement before we got to work, throwing our daggers at the target in front of us, thankfully with no lives actively at risk.

Wolf didn't come back for the rest of the day, and if the commander noticed, he said nothing.

And I wasn't sure if the pit in my stomach was relief, or something very, very dangerous.

CHAPTER

SEVENTEEN

M y interactions with Wolf grew cold before stopping altogether.

He didn't really care about me. I knew that. I wasn't sure what I was to him, what we were. He cared about me enough to protect me, to hide Ryder's body so I wouldn't be kicked out of Moira.

He cared enough about me to punch me in the fucking face during training, too.

But I put that behind me. I spent my days with Lanson, Voiler, and Ashlani, thankfully not fighting in front of the class anymore.

With each day that passed, I felt it more and more— the weight of our time here slowly dwindling away.

The sun set beyond the edge of the castle walls. Lanson and I sat in the grass, our feet stretched out before us, as the glowing orange sky took over my thoughts. Our fingers almost touched in the plush, cool grass below us.

"Do you think about it?" he asked quietly.

I snapped back to our conversation, not even realizing my mind had drifted. "Think about what?"

"What the final test will be? Why they can't tell us? Which of us will make it into The Golden City?"

I turned to look at him. Lanson was not the simple, clean male I thought him to be when I'd first met him. His mind spun in ways that made me want to ask him what dwelled inside.

He was fighting something in there, too. I just didn't know what it was.

"I've been trying to think about that all as little as possible, actually. Whatever's coming for us in that final test... I'm not sure I want to know," I admitted.

Lanson took a deep breath beside me, blowing it out loudly before looking back at me. "Bond with me," he said.

"What?" There was no way I'd heard him correctly.

"When the time comes, I want you to bond with me, Huntyr. We can get through the final test together. We'll make it to The Golden City together."

My pounding heart drowned my thoughts. "Why would you want to do that? With me, I mean?"

His eyes softened. "Isn't it obvious?"

Before I could respond, Lanson dipped his head and brushed his lips against mine.

The kiss was brief and light, and it all happened so fast. After two seconds, he pulled back and met my gaze. I was surprised at the tenderness there, the warmth.

"I like you. I've liked you since I first saw you. I know you've been getting stronger here, but if you bond with me, I'll make sure you survive, Huntyr. I'll take care of you."

I couldn't stop myself from laughing, shaking my head as I tore my gaze away.

"What?" Lanson asked, frowning. "I thought you would be relieved."

"No, it's not that," I stuttered. "It's just..." I took a long breath. All this hiding, all these secrets. Could I tell him? Could I tell him the truth?

"I'm here for you," Lanson whispered, brushing another soft kiss to my lips. I tried not to stiffen. "I'll always be here for you."

It would be so easy for me to give in to him. So easy for me to let him carry some of the damn weight, to let him see a small fraction of my dark, twisted soul. He had to know some of it, right? He had to suspect some of the secrets, some of the bruises that never healed, some of the shadows lurking in my eyes.

Could he see it? Could he sense how damaged I had become?

Maybe that was why he offered me his help. Maybe it wasn't because I consecutively lost every fight. Maybe it wasn't because I let people beat me up in training.

Maybe he saw the cracks of my soul, the broken pieces of my heart. Maybe he saw my tired eyes and pale skin, frail and dull.

Or maybe he was telling the truth. Maybe he saw it all and liked me, anyway.

He kissed me again—the third time—and moved his hand up to the base of my neck. He deepened the kiss, much different from the feathered questions that lingered between us before. This kiss was confident. Needy.

I kissed him back, only for a few seconds, before pulling away.

I hadn't thought of Lanson like that before, but now?

Maybe this was what I needed. Maybe I *could* finally trust someone. If we were going to bond, he would find out anyway. Now was just as good of a time as any to rip the truth out of the buried secrets.

"I have to tell you something, Lanson. I'm not as weak as you think I am," I whispered.

His eyes widened in shock. "I know that. I was just saying—"

"No, not like that. I haven't been entirely honest with you about who I am, about where I came from." He waited for me to continue. "I'm a fighter, Lanson. I've been trained to kill vampyres my entire life. I've been losing my sparring matches on purpose, appearing weak so people wouldn't look in my direction. I can fight, Lanson."

He stared at me for another moment before cracking a smile. "You're not serious."

I stared back with a straight face. "I've never been more serious."

The silence that lingered between us terrified me more than anything in the entire damn academy. Wolf also knew my secret, yes, but that wasn't by choice.

This? This was a risk. My heart pounded as if I had a blade pressed against the skin of my throat.

Lanson was the blade. Each second that passed without his answer pressed it deeper and deeper.

"Say something," I begged.

"Huntyr," he started. He turned and stared deep into

my eyes. "Hells, this is amazing! If you know how to fight, if you've been training, we could actually stand a chance out there when we bond." Excitement laced every word.

I sighed in relief. "You're not mad?"

"Mad?" he repeated. His hand came up to caress my cheek. "I knew you were different from the rest. I could feel it. And I understand why you lied about knowing how to fight. This isn't the safest place to show your true strengths."

I leaned into his touch, smiling against him. "If you really want to bond with me, you should know the truth."

He smiled. It was warm and genuine in a way that made my stomach flip. "You're secret is safe with me, Huntyr. Hells, I can't believe nobody else knows about this."

"Well, Wolf knows."

"Of course he does." Lanson sighed, pulling his hand away from my cheek. Lanson's sudden change in attitude forced me to lean after him.

"Not because I told him. He knew it before we arrived here."

"So you two knew each other? I mean, how close are you? What else aren't you telling me?"

My head spun, the anger in his voice sending me into a deep downward spiral I wasn't sure I could escape from.

"Lanson, stop. I promise I'm telling you the truth now! Wolf happened to see me in Midgrave the day before we came here, and I had no intention of ever seeing him again. Where is this coming from?"

He sighed. I fought the urge to reach out and turn his

chin to me. "The way he looks at you, the way he protects you, I just thought... I mean, damn, Huntyr. Everyone else in this place is terrified of him. Everyone but you."

His words grazed the edges of my heart.

Wolf scared me, though I would never admit it. He scared me to my core, scared me in ways I had never felt fear before.

But it wasn't because I thought he would hurt me. It wasn't because he was an angel, because he was stronger than anyone else here. It was what he made me feel for him that terrified me the most.

"I'm here with *you,* Lanson," I whispered to him. "And I'll get through this with you if you still want to bond with me."

I leaned into him and pressed a kiss to his shoulder.

Hells, I had no intentions of bonding with anyone. I figured I could get my ass kicked alone, and that would be just as painful as sharing the bond with someone else.

But Lanson? He was safe. He was solid. He was strong enough to win *most* of his fights during training, and he had done nothing but protect me and care for me the entire time I had been at this academy.

I could do this with him. Lord would never know; he never had to find out.

Lanson answered me with a kiss, gentle and safe.

I kissed him back until I couldn't feel the pain in my chest, the numbness in my soul, the knives at my fingertips.

CHAPTER

EIGHTEEN

An hour later, I returned to my bedroom.

"Where have you been?" Wolf asked before I had even shut the door behind me. It was the first thing he had said to me in days.

"Out," I answered. "Not like it's any of your business."

He leaned against his bed, still fully dressed as if he had just gotten back to the room. It had to be well past midnight.

"Hells, do you ever make anything easy?"

I paused and faced him. "Just stop," I said. "Stop pretending like you have to give a shit about me, Wolf. You go your way, I'll go mine. It's been working pretty damn well that way so far."

"Come with me," he said.

"What?"

"Come with me for the night. I have something I want you to see."

"I'm not going anywhere with you," I whispered, but I

knew he could hear it in my voice. The uncertainty. The doubt.

We both knew I wanted nothing more than to get as far away from this damn castle as soon as possible.

Wolf's jaw tightened as he looked at me. "Let's go." He walked out of the room and let the door close behind him, not waiting to see if I would actually follow him.

Probably because he knew I would.

I was darting out of the door and down the hallway before I could process my actions, before I could realize how pathetic and embarrassing it was for me to bend to him in this way, especially after I just agreed to bond with Lanson during the final test. At least he walked straight ahead of me, not antagonizing me for acting the way we both knew I would.

No, he walked with his shoulders back and his feet steady. Almost like he was... nervous.

"Where are we going?" I asked, catching up to him as he led us through the back doors of the castle and into the forest.

The same forest I had killed Ryder in not too long ago. I hadn't been back here since, and I didn't trust myself around the raw shadows of night.

"You haven't been yourself lately," he answered.

"What are you talking about? You don't know me well enough to make that observation."

I couldn't deny the hint of anger lacing his words. It tightened my chest, catapulted my heart.

"I'm talking about the fact that you're a killer,

Huntress. You're a predator. You carry sharp blades and even sharper teeth."

He kept marching forward, his thick black boots crushing the fallen leaves below. He didn't slow down for me. Didn't turn to see if I still followed.

I did.

"That was different," I replied. "What you saw me do in Midgrave, that was—"

"That was what? Somebody else?"

"No, it was—"

"What?" he asked again, his voice morphing into a growl that sent goosebumps down my arms. "What changed? Because I sure as all hells know you're not growing soft. Not here. Not now."

"I'm not growing soft."

"Really?" He spun to face me; I almost ran straight into his chest. "Because that lethal weapon I met in Midgrave sure as all hells wouldn't agree to bond with some random fucking fae."

My breath hitched. "You were spying on me?"

"Hardly. You two weren't exactly hiding."

Fuming hot embarrassment crept up my neck. "Bonding with Lanson will not make me weak," I explained. "It will make me stronger. He wields magic, he's strong."

"You're stronger."

"That's not the point—"

"That *is* the point, can't you see that? He's using you."

"He is not!"

Wolf's fists tightened and raised, and I fought the urge to flinch away from his sudden outburst of fury.

But just as quickly as that calm, collected mask fell, it rose again. He closed his eyes and took a long breath, his chest rising and falling as he dropped his hands down to his sides.

"All I'm saying is you're better off without him. He'll slow you down."

"Then what would you suggest?" I snapped. "Entering the final challenge alone? Not bonding with anyone? Because that's my only other option, Wolf. I don't exactly have fae lining up to share their magic with me. Unless you're offering, of course. But I already know you'd rather claw your own eyes out, so let's not go there."

His nostrils flared, his face morphing into a snarl. "Forget it," he muttered. "Let's just go."

He continued marching into the forest, leaving me breathless and distraught as I stormed after him. He didn't speak again until we approached the outer wall of the academy, hidden deep within the thick forest.

"Here," he said, holding his arms out to me. "I'll fly us both over."

I gaped at him. "Are you kidding? Are we even allowed to leave the academy grounds?"

"What's wrong?" he asked, smirking at me for the first time all night. Hells, I hated how much I missed that damn smirk. "Afraid?"

"Of getting kicked out of here? Yes, actually."

"Nobody kicked you out for killing Ryder, did they? You can trust me, Huntress. Let me carry you."

My body froze. I knew Wolf wouldn't hurt me. I knew he wouldn't jeopardize our time at this academy, either. He acted like he didn't care about a single thing in the entire world, but I could see through those walls. Hells, at times I caught myself *wanting* to see through them.

"Fine," I mumbled. I stepped forward and wrapped my arms around his neck, letting him hold me to his chest with an arm under my knees.

I waited for some sort of snide remark, but none came. Even as his massive angel wings lifted us from the ground and into the air, delicately dodging the surrounding trees as we ascended the wall.

"Where are we?" I asked.

Midgrave had been bad, with crumbling walls and homeless children living in the streets. But this? Not a single structure remained standing. The partially built walls harbored a few crouching individuals—fae, I assumed—but something eerie lingered in the darkness.

I immediately reached for Venom.

"The outskirts of Khaer."

"Khaer? I thought Khaer was one of the wealthiest cities in Vaehatis?"

"It was," Wolf answered, dropping his voice to a whisper as we crept in the darkness. He kept his body in front of mine, his eyes scanning the streets in front of us. "But nobody could survive them."

"Survive who?"

Instead of answering me, Wolf unsheathed the long sword from his hip. A gruntled, familiar groan came from my right.

I spun, gripping Venom. "Vampyres," I hissed. The creature hadn't spotted us yet, but it would soon. It crept and stumbled aimlessly, with decomposing skin and rotting leftover clothing now covered in grime and blood.

"They invaded a few years ago," Wolf explained, his breath tickling my shoulder. "They killed the thousands that used to live here. They tried to fight, but there were too many."

The vampyre turned in our direction, freezing when it sensed us. *Here we go.*

"Kill it," Wolf whispered. His hand slid onto my waist, lingering there for one electrifying second before sliding to my elbow, raising the arm that held Venom. "Unleash the beast, Huntress."

His lips brushing my ear, his hand hovering over my body, the creature approaching just a few feet away. It all made me feel something I hadn't felt in a very, very long time.

The vampyre let out a disgusting, wet roar of primal hunger before bolting in our direction. But I was ready. With Venom in my hand, I rushed toward it and slid the blade into the monster's chest before it even knew what had happened.

All too quickly, it was over. I pulled Venom from the mass of rotting flesh before the body crumbled to the ground.

"Good," Wolf praised. "Do that again."

Another vampyre stumbled into the street. Fresh blood dripped down the nasty thing's chin.

Fucking monsters.

I jumped over the body in front of me and leapt at the second beast, wrapping my legs around its waist and cutting both arms off in two swift motions.

Lord had taught me that move.

It wasn't enough to dismember them, though. I shoved him away and slid my knife into the second mass of rotting flesh for the night.

Again, it was over.

"Again," Wolf ordered.

I spun, finding him watching yet another vampyre that stumbled toward us.

"Are you not going to help me?" I demanded, though I could see it in his face. This wasn't for him.

It was for me.

"You don't need my help," he said simply. "You don't need anyone's help."

The way he looked at me sent my stomach dropping to my feet, but I quickly shoved those feelings aside, busying myself with the kill ahead.

And the next one.

And the one after that.

My body moved like it had at Phantom. I hit every mark with ease, feeling more powerful than I had in weeks.

By the time I pulled Venom from the eleventh body, my heart buzzed with life.

"Is this why you brought me out here?" I asked, wiping the grime of my blade on my pants before sliding her back into my thigh's sheath. "To do your dirty work for you?"

Wolf watched, his back pressed against a half-standing brick wall with his arms crossed over his chest.

But those eyes...

He stared at me with a heaviness in his gaze that made me want to drop to my knees. His mouth curved up on both sides, his teeth grazing his perfectly plump bottom lip. I stepped closer, trapped in his stare.

It wasn't until I stood a foot away from him that he uncrossed his arms, pushing himself from the wall.

He opened his mouth to say something, but not before both hands slid up to my neck, angling my chin up at his towering body. I froze in shock, let his hands move me, guide me, coax me.

"You're a fucking goddess." He dipped his head and brushed his lips over my jaw, my neck.

I tilted, giving him even more room as his hot breath erupted over my exposed body. Adrenaline pumped through my veins, heightening every single sensation. His hands on my body were making me think things I had never admitted, making me want things, want him—

"It's unfortunate that you'll be *nothing* after you bond with him." Wolf pulled away, walking down the street the way we came.

I stood there, panting, trying to piece together what the fuck just happened.

"Excuse me?" I called after him. "What did you just say to me?"

"Don't make me repeat it," he yelled over his shoulder. "It's embarrassing enough as is."

I pulled Venom from her sheath and lunged, a mess of anger and chaos and tragedy. The blade aimed directly at his back, and I wanted to dive it in—hells, I wanted to hurt him.

But he turned just in time, his wings blowing my hair across my face as he grabbed my wrist and twisted, pulling the blade from my hand.

"You're a coward. You're jealous that I may actually trust someone other than you."

He clenched his teeth. "You haven't seen me jealous yet, Huntress. If I were jealous, your little toy would be dead."

"Then what?" I cried. "What could I possibly have done to make you this angry?"

Darkness swarmed his eyes. "You feel loneliness and you lean on the first piece of shit who shows you any signs of affection."

I ripped my hand away and shoved his chest. "You don't get to say that to me. You don't get to have any opinion about who I do and do not lean on."

"He doesn't know you." Wolf's chest rose and fell with every breath. "He does not know how strong you are. Hells, he thinks you're a fragile doe, Huntress. What would he think if he saw you like this?" His eyes grazed my body. "Dripping in blood and fuming with hatred?"

He might as well have punched me in the gut. My mind spun for something to say, for an argument, for a truth. But I had nothing.

Wolf's words, as painful and horrid as they were, were true. And he knew I feared them, knew I hid that truth deep inside of me, buried underneath the façade of this weak, helpless female.

"Right," Wolf said without softening his sharp eyes. "That's what I thought."

I watched him walk away, leaving me in the street with my heart in pieces.

Until he stopped walking and turned around.

And all hells, I hated the way my stomach twisted.

"Are you coming? Because you can't fly back on your own."

I wasn't sure what changed. Wolf was sometimes flirty and arrogant and annoying, but he could also be cold and brutal and distant.

I walked toward him and let him pick me up, his warm skin electrifying my body as he held me. This beast, this wicked and forceful angel that had fallen from his place amongst the greats, had a dark side, too.

Only he was much, much better at hiding his.

CHAPTER

NINETEEN

"It's not working." I let my hands fall onto the table of the study. Hells, I had been in the study with Ashlani all day attempting to scrounge up the tiniest ounce of magic. Hours had passed, the sun had set, yet still... nothing.

"You're too hard on yourself." Ashlani placed both elbows on the long wooden table and leaned forward, her straight blonde hair falling over her shoulder as she looked deep into my eyes. "Relax a little. You'll get the hang of it soon."

I leaned back in my wooden chair. The room was filled with rows and rows of books, none of which seemed to help me conjure natural magic.

At least it offered us some privacy against all the eyes during the day.

"I have no idea how you're doing this so easily." I crossed my arms over my chest in defeat.

206

Ashlani smiled, holding her hand out and sending a tiny gust of wind into my face.

"Show off," I mumbled, unable to hide my smile.

She laughed too, and in the quiet study, the sound seemed to echo off the walls.

The wooden doors creaked open, and Voiler stepped inside. She made eye contact with us but immediately looked away.

"Hey," I whispered to Ashlani. "Should we ask her to come sit with us?"

Ashlani's mouth tightened. "Trust me," she started. "She doesn't talk much. We're better off on our own."

"I think you'd be surprised."

I waved my hand in Voiler's direction, grabbing her attention. "Hey, Voiler! We're practicing a bit of natural magic over here if you're interested in joining."

And I'm in desperate need of your help.

Ashlani groaned, and I shot her a warning glare as Voiler hesitantly made her way to our table.

"So," Ashlani started as Voiler sat down, hanging her bag over the chair behind her, "you and Lanson, huh? I can't say I'm surprised. He's had a thing for you since day one."

Voiler's eyes widened.

My mouth fell open. "Ashlani!"

"What? Everyone can see it! Right, Voiler?"

"Um." She glanced frantically between us. "He does smile at you quite often."

I rolled my eyes. "He does not."

"Not when the angel's around, anyway. He's jealous." Ashlani flipped her hair over her shoulder.

"Really? Did he tell you that?" I tried to seem uninterested, but she could see right through me.

"He didn't have to. He gets all tense and angry when Wolf's around. He's always asking about you when you're gone. Hells, I'm surprised he hasn't asked you to move into his own bedroom after Ryder killed his roommate."

My stomach dropped at the mention of Ryder's name, but I forced myself not to flinch.

"What's it like being roommates with a fallen angel?" Voiler interrupted. "I mean, you two must talk, right?"

I shrugged. "We don't say much. He keeps to himself."

"Oh, please." Ashlani leaned forward even more, dipping her chin. "He's gorgeous, and he follows you around like you're his. I can see why Lanson's so jealous."

A flush rose up my neck. "He's not—"

"What? Gorgeous?"

I leaned back in my seat, defeated. Ashlani and Voiler both smiled at me. "Enough about this, please! We have more important things to discuss here."

"Fine. Are you two going to the ball tonight?"

I groaned, tossing my head back. "I told Lanson I would go with him, though I'm not sure how drinking and dancing will help any of us pass the Transcendent. I need to focus on summoning magic, not socializing with the other students."

"What about you, Voiler? Are you going?"

She pursed her lips and shook her head, her jet-black hair falling in front of her face. "Dancing isn't my thing. I'll be catching up on sleep and trying to heal some of these bruises." She lifted her arm for emphasis, showing off the blue and purple.

"I'm jealous," I sighed. "Maybe I can hide, too, and nobody will notice."

"Oh, I'll notice," Ashlani added. "And Lanson will notice. You're going."

We spent the rest of the afternoon discussing the other fighters, magic, and the history of the vampyres. Voiler knew more than both of us about magic and where it came from, which didn't surprise me in the slightest.

She warmed up to us after a while, finally starting to lower that wall she kept so tightly around herself. I didn't blame her. We all had walls.

Even Ashlani, who I certainly didn't trust at first, was showing me the real female beneath.

I didn't want to see either of them die.

I prayed to the goddess that I never would.

The sun set as we made our way back to our rooms.

"Hey." Ashlani pulled us both close, lowering her voice to a whisper. "Have you heard about Ryder? I heard Headmistress talking yesterday about finding his body in the woods. I also heard her say they spotted vampyres nearby, much closer than they have ever seen them here. Maybe the vampyres were what killed him."

My stomach dropped. Wolf was supposed to hide the body. Until now, the rumors had been that Ryder couldn't handle the academy anymore, and he snuck out in the middle of the night. It was unbelievable, sure, but there wasn't a body.

Now, Headmistress could look for someone to blame. Ryder wasn't punished in the slightest for killing Maekus, but how many faults would Headmistress and the others ignore?

Voiler gasped. "What?"

Ashlani nodded. "Apparently, they found him half-buried and covered in blood."

I covered my mouth with my hand, trying to mimic Voiler's shock.

They wouldn't know. Nobody besides Wolf had any reason to think I killed him.

"Well, he deserved it," Ashlani added as we approached the bedrooms. "I'm surprised he lasted this long with that attitude of his. Males like him would never make it into The Golden City."

"Yeah," I added. "I'd hope not."

"Hurry and get ready for the ball." Ashlani paused at her door. "I'll see you later tonight."

I nodded, forcing a smile on my face before pushing my own door open. With Wolf gone, I let myself relax, collapsing onto my bed with a groan.

They're not going to find out it was me. If animals really got to him, his body would be in shreds. Nobody would even notice the stab wounds.

Hells. I looked at the clock on the wall. I had one hour to get ready for the ball tonight.

My nerves grew more and more palpable with every passing minute, even as I tried to brush them away.

Everything was fine. Everything would be fine.

CHAPTER
TWENTY

The dress I selected from the few options given by the academy fit my body perfectly, with long, tight sleeves that covered every inch of my skin from my wrist to my neck. The rest flowed to the floor with a layer of black fabric that melted against my body. It wasn't too tight that it constricted my movements, but it still hugged my curves comfortably.

I looked at myself in the mirror, sliding my hands down my waist.

I could count on one hand the number of times I had worn a dress.

I was never supposed to be pretty. Was never supposed to care about how my black hair curled around my face, almost always getting in my way. I was never supposed to wear nice things, to wear dresses, especially at formal balls.

But this was a new life. I had a new purpose, a new meaning.

211

Looking in the mirror, I didn't feel as out of place as I expected. I felt... a surprising wave of emotions.

This ball wasn't supposed to matter to me, either. If anything, it was another meaningless gathering of people I wasn't supposed to care about.

But deep down, I cared. I cared about the ball. I cared about this damn dress. I cared about the way my hair wasn't as shiny as it was before, about whether he would like the way the thin fabric of the long dress hugged my curves.

Lanson was kind and strong. I would bond with him, and he would help me get through the Transcendent.

Not Wolf.

I pictured how Wolf would react if he were here seeing me in this tight dress, a very different uniform than the casual training outfit I wore every day.

No, Huntyr, I thought. *You don't care what he thinks.* He wouldn't even bother attending an event like this one. He was too cool, too calculated.

The pit in my stomach grew. I wasn't supposed to be thinking about him. I was supposed to be thinking about my date, about Lanson.

I shook my head and turned away from the mirror.

Lanson was nice. He was considerate; he protected me, and damn, I was starting to believe that he actually liked me. Much more than Wolf liked me, anyway.

A rapid knock on my door stole my attention.

"Huntyr?" Lanson's voice rang out.

I scurried to the door, gripping the knob and opening it with a sigh of relief.

Lanson stood there with a bundle of white roses in his hand.

His eyes immediately landed on mine, only drifting after a second to take in the length of my dress. I couldn't stop the blood from rushing to my cheeks.

"Damn, Huntyr," he sighed. "You look... you look stunning."

"Yeah, well," I stammered, glancing down at my feet strapped into the slim heels, "the school provided the dress."

The shoes were awkward and unnatural. It would have been easy to kick them off, to walk barefoot through the castle, but I shoved my feet into the tiny prisons anyway.

"Still," he pushed. "Even in your training clothes, you'd be the best looking fae at the ball tonight."

His eyes flickered with an emotion that made my stomach flip.

"We better get going." I swallowed, turning to close the bedroom door behind me. I gave the space one last scan, taking in Wolf's perfectly made bed, before clicking it shut.

Lanson's hand immediately wrapped around my back. I reminded myself not to flinch away; he had no idea what lingered on the skin beneath.

Nobody did.

I'd made sure of that.

We walked in comfortable silence, eventually joining the lingering students waiting to be let into the ballroom on the base floor of the academy.

And I absolutely hated that I was nervous.

"Isn't it strange?" I asked Lanson. "We're supposed to

kill each other to get into The Golden City, and they want us to drink and dance and forget all our problems for the night."

Lanson laughed. "At least they're providing the drinks," he whispered, his breath brushing over the tip of my ear.

"It better be worth it," I murmured back, more to myself than to him.

And I meant it. The biggest social gathering I attended in Midgrave was drinking ale at the tavern with Rummy. This was out of my comfort zone. It was unlike everything I'd been trained to do.

I let Lanson lead me to the table of food and wine, not hesitating in the slightest when he handed me a glass of red liquid.

"Here," he said. "Relax a little, Huntyr. This is supposed to be a fun night."

I shot him a glare, rolling my eyes at the thought. "You really think anyone here is having fun when we're supposed to be training for survival? This is a show, a charade. They want to parade us around like puppets."

"You're cynical," he replied, leaning in so only I could hear him. "But I like that about you. Always on the lookout. Always with your guard up."

I ignored the way his words made my shoulders tense and turned to Ashlani, who skipped toward us with a white, glittering skirt flowing around her ankles. "There you two are!" she chimed, breaking any invisible tension that may have lingered between Lanson and me. "I was starting to think the two of you bailed!"

I took a long sip of my drink, letting it burn my stomach as I swallowed. "That's still looking like a pretty good option."

"This is a celebration, Huntyr!" she retorted. "Don't be such a grump."

As much as I hated it, she was right. I turned my attention to the room around me, filled with all sorts of luxuries and expensive foods I had never seen before. The boring, bare ballroom had transformed somehow, turning the dark walls of wood and stone into magical sheets of twinkling lights and white fabrics that would make you forget you were at this horrid place to begin with.

"See," Lanson said, watching me with a grin, "it's not so bad here."

"Fine," I admitted. "I'll try to have a good time, but I promise you I'm not dancing. And if any of those assholes try to beat me up again, I'm leaving."

"Deal!" Ashlani squealed, clapping her hands as she picked up another chalice of liquor.

Boy, was I wrong. It was the drinks. It absolutely, without a doubt, had to be the drinks. Because somewhere in the midst of Lanson whispering in my ear, of refilling my drink anytime it was nearly empty, and of the beautiful music growing louder and louder as the night went on, I ended up on the dance floor.

Dancing and twirling around like a damn idiot.

As if I actually belonged here. As if I actually stood a chance at having real fun.

I danced with Ashlani first, letting her bubbly laughter and annoyingly contagious smile drag me out there against my will. She clasped my hands, not letting go as she twirled me around, giggling and tossing her head back as we made our way to the center of dancing fae.

"You're smiling," Ashlani said. I was so dizzy, I thought I could collapse right there. "I've never seen you smile this much."

She was right. My cheeks started to hurt from it. "There isn't usually much to smile about, especially around here."

"There's always something," she replied, turning her attention to something behind me. "You just have to look for it."

I spun around, expecting Lanson to be standing right behind me.

And nearly froze when I saw Wolf, tall and annoyingly fucking handsome in a blacked-out suit that barely seemed to fit his long, sculpted limbs. I stopped dancing. Any smile lingering on my face disappeared, stripped entirely from my expression as I met Wolf's cold, empty gaze.

Only, it wasn't *entirely* empty.

I was taking the few steps toward him before I realized what I was doing, before I could talk myself out of it. I moved through the crowd, narrowly avoiding the other drunk, dancing fae as I kept my eyes locked on his.

"What are you doing here?" I asked. My voice didn't sound nearly as angry as I'd meant for it to.

Wolf's mouth twitched upward. "Celebrating. Enjoying myself. Same as you, it seems."

"You don't seem like the type that celebrates. Or like the type that enjoys yourself, for that matter."

He smiled fully, flashing his perfectly white and sharp teeth at me. "If you want me to show you a good time, Huntress, you only have to ask. With a *please*, of course,"

"Screw you," I said, turning on my heel to make my way back to Lanson.

A rough hand caught my upper arm, pulling me back to Wolf in one swift motion, as if it took little to no effort for him to move my entire body so easily.

"Careful," he growled.

His eyes locked on mine, holding my gaze for a few seconds before flickering down to my mouth.

I didn't move. I couldn't.

We were locked in time, stuck in space. Nothing else existed except him standing there, his grip tight on my arm, yet not painful.

For a second, I let my mind wander.

Maybe Wolf wasn't so terrible after all. Maybe he wasn't as big of an asshole as I had made him out to be.

And maybe, just maybe, he would let me find out what it would be like to kiss him.

"Huntyr." Lanson's voice from behind made me jump.

Wolf held onto me for a few seconds longer—much longer than he needed to—before releasing me. His jaw tightened as he shifted his gaze to Lanson, and I immediately felt the chill of where his arm had just been.

"Everything okay over here?" Lanson asked. His words were slow and calculated, though his eyes weren't on me. His mouth drew into a thin line as he stared up at Wolf.

Wolf's eyebrow raised, waiting for my response. I

glanced between the two of them, still lost in the slight haze of whatever we had been drinking for the last hour.

"Everything's fine," I replied, though my eyes were glued on Wolf.

Lanson laced his hand through mine. Wolf's electric eyes slid down my arm to our interlocked fingers, and his brows drew together.

"Come dance with me," Lanson murmured, though he said the words loud enough so Wolf could hear them, too.

I didn't have to answer. He was already pulling me, tearing me away from Wolf's intoxicating presence and into the crowd of ballgowns and half-drunk academy students, all trying to escape their twisted, imperfect reality for the night.

Stop caring, I reminded myself. *Stop worrying and definitely stop thinking about Wolf.*

When Lanson pulled my body flush against his in the center of the fae, I didn't object. Ashlani danced somewhere in the crowd next to us, her laughter filling the air and slicing through the steady flow of music.

"I hate him," Lanson said, any attempt to hide the distaste in his voice long gone. "I hate that he's here, and I hate that he's looking at you."

With my arms resting around Lanson's shoulders, I let him spin me, allowing me to get a glimpse of what he was talking about.

Sure enough, Wolf stood at the edge of the ballroom, his tall figure identifiable anywhere, with his arms crossed over his chest and his impossible, ice-filled eyes glued on us.

On me.

"Just ignore him," I said, pulling myself a little closer to Lanson.

I could have sworn I saw Wolf's jaw tighten at the movement.

Satisfaction rolled in the pit of my stomach. I knew Wolf didn't care for Lanson, but he didn't quite care for any of the students at this academy.

But why wasn't he watching the others? Why were his eyes glued on us?

Lanson's hands slid lower on the base of my back. He spun us around again, moving in tune to the music as it shifted from one song to another.

"I didn't take you for a dancer," he whispered in my ear, his lips brushing my skin in a way that sent chills down my spine.

I leaned into the sensation. "Tonight, I am," I said. I rested my head against his shoulder, letting him carry the weight of me. I had to admit, it felt nice, not having to carry it all.

Even if I was acutely aware of the eyes that lingered. One bright, sexy pair of eyes in particular.

"I like you like this," Lanson mumbled, his lips moving closer to my neck. "I rarely see you relaxed."

"I can't relax," I replied on instinct. "I can never relax in an environment like this. Not when so much is on the line."

His right hand moved lower, just above the base of my rear. "I'm here now. I'll protect you, Huntyr. You can trust me."

For a split second, I forgot about Wolf. I forgot about

my mission, about the damn tests. I forgot about everything except Lanson's hands on my body, about the music
moving through the air, controlling my movements.

Before I knew it, our bodies were right against one
another, not a single inch of space keeping us apart. "I'm
not supposed to trust anybody," I admitted. "I spent my
entire life reminding myself of that."

His breath, hot and constant, tickled my neck. He must
have sensed this reaction, must have felt how he practically carried my body through the crowd as his hands
roamed down my waist, gripping my ass in a way that I
never would have allowed if I were sober.

When he pulled away to stare at my lips, I let him.
Although his stare didn't send the same flare of heat
through my body as Wolf's.

I wasn't sure how much time passed. Wasn't sure how
many songs had come and gone as I lay enthralled in
Lanson's arms, wasn't sure how many times his hands had
wandered below my waist, wasn't sure how many times
his lips had brushed my neck.

Wolf's figure was no longer near the back wall of the
ballroom. I hated the way my stomach dropped when I
noticed it, but I didn't pull away from Lanson.

Lanson actually cared about me. Actually liked me,
even. He saw me as kind and special.

Unlike Wolf, who saw me as nothing more than a
fraud. One who needed protecting and coddling, one he
needed to swoop in and save.

I was beginning to relax at the idea of him leaving the
ballroom, storming off to whatever brooding he had left to

do this evening. Until he cleared his throat right next to us, causing both Lanson and I to stiffen.

"Excuse me," he said, his voice a sultry growl. "Do you mind if I have a dance?"

I froze.

"I do mind," Lanson said without taking his arm off my back.

Wolf's eyes had softened. They weren't as dark and distant. They were... warm. Pleading. "Huntress?"

"Just one," I said, answering for myself.

Lanson immediately stiffened, but I shot him another glare, and he eventually backed down. "I'll get us more drinks," he whispered.

And then he was gone, leaving Wolf and I alone on the dance floor.

"You don't strike me as someone who dances." I let him guide my arms to his shoulders.

"I don't." His wings created a barrier, keeping the other fae at least three feet away from us as he moved us around to the pull of the music.

"Yet you couldn't wait to get out here and interrupt me and my date?"

Wolf's jaw tightened. "I don't like him."

"That's fine. You don't have to dance with him, then."

His fingers tightened around my waist, pulling me an inch closer to him.

"You've been spending too much time with him."

My eyes snapped to his, a mere few inches lingering between his face and mine. "Excuse me?"

"You can't trust him. Something about him isn't right."

"And why is that?" I asked. "Does it have anything to do with the fact that he likes me and I like him?"

Wolf scoffed, averting his gaze to the ballroom behind me. "You don't like him."

"You know nothing about me, Wolf."

His eyes met mine once more. I caught myself staring at the white specks glittering in his blue irises, at the black hair that had grown longer since our time in Moira.

"I know more than him."

Wolf spun me around, forcing a gasp from my lips as he pressed my body to his. I suppressed the laughter that threatened to betray me at the sudden strength of his dancing.

He threw me around the ballroom like I was nothing.

"That's enough," Lanson said, interrupting us.

I shoved Wolf away from me, embarrassment flushing my cheeks. We hadn't even completed one dance, but it had been one dance too many.

"I'll take my date back now." Lanson stared at Wolf with his jaw set, his fists tightened.

"She's all yours." Wolf shot me a glare before leaving, his black angel wings following him out of the ballroom.

Hells.

"Come on. Let's get out of here." Lanson's words dripped in lingering lust and jealousy, a dangerous combination.

I felt lust, too, but not in the same way. Not all for Lanson, though I couldn't quite understand it, couldn't quite understand why I kept glancing over Lanson's shoulder, looking for someone else.

Looking for someone who didn't care.

I nodded, giving him the signal to pull me away.

And he did.

I didn't see Wolf again as Lanson guided me, half carrying me out of the ballroom and toward the outdoor gardens.

The cool night air immediately kissed my skin, waking me up.

We were the only ones in sight, the only ones away from the music and the dancing and the clouded judgements.

I finally stepped away from Lanson, who began murmuring about Wolf as he paced back and forth.

Males and their tempers.

"Why do you let him get to you?" I asked. "Hells, Lanson. I came here with you!"

"I don't like it," Lanson growled. His hands ran through his hair, messing up the slicked-back locks. "He behaves as if he owns you, Huntyr."

"Well, he doesn't."

"That's not what it felt like back there." Lanson shook his head with a scowl.

"What do you want me to say?" I asked. "I'm here with

you! I'm not with him!" I had never seen him this way; he dug his fingers into his scalp as if he could bury those thoughts, as if he could bury his anger.

But I could feel it from where I stood; heavy and hot and restless. "Look at me," I ordered.

Lanson shook his head without turning around, but eventually he pulled his hands away from his hair.

"Look at me," I repeated, more desperation seeping into the words.

He turned slowly, his eyes hesitating to meet mine.

I wasn't sure why I needed him to like me. Needed him to want me. Needed him to approve of me, to hate Wolf just as much as I did.

It was a familiar sensation—one I felt daily growing up with Lord. In a world where I didn't belong, in a world where my own parents were ripped away from me, I wanted *someone* to long for me. I wanted *someone* to accept me.

I wanted Lanson to *see* me.

Before I could stop myself, I stepped forward and slid my hands up his chest.

He stiffened at first but didn't back away beneath my touch.

I slipped my hands under his jacket, up to his shoulders, his neck, his chin.

I could see it in his eyes, the change. Lanson no longer looked at me like I was his entire world, like I was his to save. He looked at me as if he saw the truth in me; as if he noticed the darkness that always loomed over my head.

He looked at me like I was a broken, shattered mess.

Finally, he saw the *real* me.

We were too busy with ourselves to notice anybody else entering the courtyard, anybody approaching, anybody watching.

Until a slow clap from behind me made me jump.

I pulled away from Lanson and spun, finding Espek watching us in amusement.

"How cute," he hissed. "Though, I think you owe me something."

"Excuse me?" I hissed.

Espek stumbled forward, clearly drunk. Clearly angry.

"Get behind me," Lanson ordered.

I ignored him and hiked up my dress, pulling my blade from my thigh.

Espek looked at it before peering back at me. "So that's how you killed Ryder, then? Stabbed him to death with that toy right there? All but ripping him to shreds?"

"I don't know what you're talking about."

Lanson stiffened beside me.

"You know exactly what I'm talking about, rat. They found his body, and you're the only one stupid enough to kill him. You owe me a life."

My first instinct was to step in front of Lanson.

But Espek's eyes didn't move from me. Not for a second. He pulled his own blade from its sheath and took a bold step in my direction.

"Run, Huntyr," Lanson pleaded from behind me. "He's going to kill you!"

"I'm not going anywhere," I growled. I became vaguely aware of Lanson backing up behind me.

He wanted to run.

I wanted to fight.

"Stupid, stupid girl," Espek snarled. "You thought you could get away with it? You and your pet wolf?"

"Like I said, I don't know what you're talking about."

"She didn't kill anybody!" Lanson added from behind me. "Just leave her alone!"

Espek looked at him as if just realizing he was here. "You really believe that?" he asked Lanson with a scoff. "Maybe you should ask your little girlfriend about Ryder's body. He wasn't just ravaged by animals, you know. He was stabbed repeatedly before his body was left to rot."

My blood froze. I wanted to deny it. Hells, I wanted to. But something primal deep within me told me not to back down, not to let him win.

"Huntyr?" Lanson asked. "What is he talking about?"

Anticipation dripped in the air. I knew a fight was coming. I had killed Espek's friend, and he knew it from the start.

"It had to be done," I sneered, taking half a step closer to Espek. "He killed Maekus, and he was going to kill me."

Espek's eyes went wild. "Had to be done? Hells, I don't care what Headmistress says. He was stabbed over ten times! Those were not animal claws!"

I pictured Ryder's body, half-rotting in the dirt where Wolf left him. He deserved much, much worse.

"I did what I had to do!" Venom's weight in my palm reassured me.

"Liar."

I lunged first, throwing myself at Espek without caution. I didn't give a damn that he held a blade of his own, that he was a foot taller than me and twice my size.

I was getting sick and fucking tired of people underestimating me.

Espek met me halfway. I ducked at the last second to avoid the tip of his blade. He roared and spun around, throwing a fist into my ribs that never seemed to heal.

But this time, I barely felt the pain.

I sliced down across his arm, Venom skimming and slicing the sleeve of his formal top. He roared in anger and reached out, gripping my long hair and yanking my head backward.

My eyes burned with tears, but I was still satisfied from drawing the smallest amount of blood.

Lanson was yelling something in the background, but I was too focused on Espek to make out the words.

Was too focused on death.

"You think you're tough with this thing?" Espek yanked my head back further until my back nearly pressed against his chest.

Then he reached for my blade.

No.

I tried to yank my arm away from him, tried to claw at his face, kick his knees—anything.

But it was no use.

His hand found mine, holding tightly to Venom.

"Don't you fucking dare," I seethed with hatred.

He only laughed.

Where the *fuck* was Lanson?

Espek twisted my grip as hard as possible. I held on as long as I could; held on like Venom was all that mattered in the world. Because she was. Venom was my one reminder of home, of Lord, of my mission.

I needed her.

But she landed in the grass next to us, and I had never felt more fury in my entire life.

"What's wrong?" Espek seethed into my ear. I was sure he was pulling out hair, was sure I could feel my scalp bleed. "Not so strong without your weapon to protect you, are you?"

"Fuck you," I spat.

He laughed. "That's what I thought, little rat. Though, you're not the only one with a weapon."

I discovered the meaning of his words much, much too late. He maneuvered his free hand to grab his own blade, pulled my back against his chest, and dove the dagger into my torso.

Deep.

Adrenaline, shock, fury. Everything froze. I couldn't think. Couldn't breathe.

He pulled the bloody dagger out, finally letting go of my hair.

My hands instantly pressed against my stomach, against the piercing pain that hit me a few seconds later.

No.

I dropped to my knees.

Espek laughed again, and the sound of it was almost drowned out by the blood pumping through my ears.

And then I watched as Espek stepped toward Venom, picked her up, and summoned his magic.

A gust of wind rushed in his direction before I watched the sharp steel of the blade break.

He was using natural magic, manipulating the elements to shatter Venom.

The blade snapped with a gut-wrenching crack of metal.

If I hadn't already been bleeding, I was sure I would have fallen to pieces.

I didn't recognize the gruntled cry that escaped me, from somewhere deep in my body, clawing up and out of my throat.

"Enjoy fighting with this," he hissed.

My eyes landed on Lanson, who stood frozen in place a few feet away.

Shock pulsed through my body, warm blood poured from my hands.

"Huntyr." He held his hands out as if approaching a wild animal.

"Lanson, help me."

What was he doing? Why wasn't he helping me? I was vaguely aware of Espek kicking the handle of my broken blade and storming out of the courtyard.

Was vaguely aware of the horror dripping from Lanson's features.

"Lanson," I said again, barely a breath. *Hells, I was speaking aloud, wasn't I?*

"I can't do this," Lanson sighed, holding his hands at

his sides and backing up like I was a wild, rabid vampyre ready to pounce.

Not a bleeding girl who needed help.

Every movement hurt. I tried to stand, but the wound in my torso had sliced my muscles.

"Help me! I need to get to my room. I need to stop the bleeding!"

He shook his head. "You killed him, didn't you? You really are a killer, just like you said."

I laughed. Actually laughed.

"You're scaring me, Huntyr."

I quit laughing long enough to see the horror on his face. "Lanson," I breathed—begged. "I'm losing too much blood. I need you to help me."

I knew what panic looked like. I had seen it way too often when Lord would bring new trainees to Phantom.

The wide eyes, the open mouth.

I knew exactly what was going on in Lanson's mind.

My vision swirled. My body fell into the grass.

"I'm sorry," Lanson stuttered, backing away from me slowly. "I'm sorry, I'm sor—sorry. I have to get into The Golden City, Huntyr. If Headmistress finds out it was you... I can't... I can't do this."

"*Lanson!*"

"I'm sorry!"

What the fuck? Was this really happening? Lanson backed up even more, nearly tripping over his own feet, before giving me a look that felt somewhat like a mixture of both betrayal and disgust.

My vision spun again; dark tunnels threatened my eyesight.

I was losing too much blood. My limbs felt numb, my chest grew cold.

I was too lost to argue anymore as Lanson ran away, too afraid of the dark monster before him. Afraid of what he saw in me.

When my eyes fluttered closed, I didn't fight them.

CHAPTER
TWENTY-ONE

I tried—begged the goddess, even—to make it to that door.

I didn't know how much time passed, I only knew that everything in my body was telling me to keep going, to keep crawling.

I was so close, just a few feet away. But darkness swarmed my vision, welcoming and cool. I suddenly could not remember the last time I'd slept, the last time I'd relaxed, the last time I'd given in. How good would it feel to surrender to that darkness, to stop fighting, just for once.

Surrender. What a strange, foreign thought.

I quit crawling, limbs aching and blood dripping, and I gave in.

My hands shook, my legs wobbled. Lord stood behind me and watched, waiting for my next move.

It was my first kill.

Lord told me I was ready before he brought me out here. I never traveled this far outside of Midgrave. I didn't feel ready, but he knew more than I. If he thought I was strong enough to kill a vampyre, I could trust him.

Besides, I was thirteen years old. It was time I learned to protect Midgrave just like the other Phantoms. I wasn't just some kid who lurked in the shadows, following everyone's every move. I was a fighter.

A killer.

"You have to be fast," Lord whispered behind me. His words were sharp and fierce, his voice slicing through the freezing night air like a sword. "It will kill you if you hesitate for even a moment. I won't help you, Huntyr. You have to do this on your own."

I clenched my jaw and fought back the thoughts that came rushing to my mind—the thoughts that told me I wasn't good enough. Wasn't fast enough. Wasn't strong enough.

Those thoughts were useless. I was just as good a fighter as the rest of the Phantoms, and by the time I reached their age, I would be even better.

I would be the best.

I heard the vampyre before I saw it. I would have nightmares about the half-gurgling, foul sounds that came from the creature's mouth as it stumbled toward me.

My heart pounded so fast, I thought I was going to die any second.

My small knife felt too heavy in my now-sweaty hand.

"Focus," Lord hissed behind me. "Do not disappoint me, child."

I blinked as the vampyre stumbled forward again, moving faster than I expected. I had seen vampyres before, sure, but never so... close.

Never with nothing but my knife between us.

I raised the blade above my head, ready to pierce the creature's chest if it took one more step.

"Now!" Lord yelled behind me.

I didn't think. I didn't hesitate. I let out a scream as I jumped forward and impaled the hungry, disgusting vampyre in the chest, piercing its heart just as Lord taught me.

The blade sliced the decaying body with so much ease, I thought I missed the heart.

But the creature slumped to the ground a few moments later.

And I finally took a breath as I pulled my weapon from the dead body.

"Very good," Lord praised from behind me. Those two words were enough to set my entire world aflame. "Do that again."

CHAPTER
TWENTY-TWO

Someone lifted me from the ground.

Firm and strong, sculpted arms held my body close.

It was him. Wolf.

"Don't fucking die," he whispered. Not just once, I realized, but over and over again. As if the words would help me. As if the words would force the darkness out.

I closed my eyes again, resting my heavy head against his chest.

"Dammit, Huntyr," he muttered as he kicked the door open, carrying me into the bedroom.

I became vaguely aware of him setting me down on his bed. Became even more aware of him scavenging my body with his hands, searching for the source of the blood, no doubt.

He didn't hesitate, didn't even bother with the extra time it would take to lift my dress up and over my head. He ripped it off, leaving me in my chest wrap as he wiped at the blood, finally identifying the source with a stream of curse words beneath his breath.

"You're losing too much blood." He somehow sounded even angrier than usual.

His warm hands pressed on my torso, over the deep gash.

"What the fuck happened? Who did this to you?"

I tried to tell him, tried to remember. But my brain was so foggy, my mind felt so...

"No," he growled, moving to straddle me on the bed so he could keep pressure on my torso with one hand while leaning up to meet my eyes. "You do not get to die. You do not get to let them win. Do you understand me? If you close your eyes, I'll fucking kill you. Now focus, Huntyr. Tell me who touched you. Was it Lanson?"

Think, Huntyr, think.

I remembered the ball, the dancing, the fight.

Him.

Lanson had been so different, so... so cold.

And Espek did not even blink as he slid his blade into me, leaving me to die.

My chest ached, those stupid tears stinging my eyes. How could I have been so *naïve*?

Wolf was searching my face, waiting for me to say something. But I didn't have to. I was never very good at hiding my emotions.

Wolf's expression softened, then his eyes darkened with anger.

"He's going to die for this," Wolf said, turning his

attention back to my wound while he shook his head. "I should have killed that bastard a long time ago."

He moved, scrambling for something I couldn't see. He pulled his hands away from my torso, and I immediately missed the warmth.

"I should have known," I managed to choke out, my voice hoarse and scratchy. "I should have... I should have—"

"Stop," Wolf growled. I looked at him in time to see him slicing his own palm with a knife. Blood pooled, his blood this time, in his hand. "Hold still. I'm going to heal you."

I must have been delusional, because I thought he said he was going to heal me with blood magic.

But then he moved to prop my head up, holding his bloodied hand over my wound.

"Help her, goddess." He said the words so quietly, I almost thought I had imagined them.

Slowly, I felt it. Warmth radiated from his palm, more so than usual. It spread into my torso with a light that illuminated room.

"A little more," he mumbled.

I obeyed, holding still as Wolf worked. My vision blurred again, and my eyes grew heavy, but I fought to stay awake.

It must have been the angel properties making his blood magic so strong.

That, or the fact that I was on death's doorstep.

Wolf finally stepped away, gently lowering my head

onto the bed before rummaging through something on the other side of the room.

"Sleep," he said, returning with a towel that he used to wrap around my exposed, bloody stomach. "You'll feel better in the morning."

"Why are you helping me?" I asked, immediately hating the vulnerability in my voice.

Wolf paused long enough that I wasn't sure he would answer at all.

But then, in a softness I had never heard him speak in before, he said, "You are making me remember."

I woke up to the sound of Wolf growling. Literally growling, primal and dangerous and vibrating my bones. I stirred in bed, running a tired hand over my face.

"Get the fuck out of here," Wolf seethed.

I blinked my eyes open to find the door cracked, Wolf blocking my view with his outstretched hands. His bulky frame filled up the doorway.

"Please," Lanson's voice filled the room, pleading and painful. *Fuck.* "I need to talk to her."

"That's not going to happen," Wolf snapped. I had never heard his voice so lethal.

"I don't think you're the one who gets to decide that," Lanson responded.

A long silence filled the air. I envisioned the way Wolf was most likely glaring at Lanson, an entire foot shorter than him, and the way Lanson probably stared back, terrified and helpless.

I had to admit, the vision made me feel a little better, even if it was only in my head.

But the reality was that I had to face him eventually.

"Let him in," I whispered, pushing myself up to my elbows.

Wolf spun around, mouth agape as he looked at me. And then his brows tightened, eyes darkened. "Are you sure?"

"I'm sure."

I didn't have to be an expert in reading Wolf to know he didn't like it, but I reminded myself not to care.

This had nothing to do with him.

"Fine," Wolf said, stepping to the side and letting Lanson enter the room.

He looked disheveled as all hells, clearly hadn't slept at all. "Huntyr," he said, taking two steps to stand by my bed. His hands hovered for a second like he wanted to reach out, but he didn't. "I'm so sorry, Huntyr. I don't know what to say."

"You can start by explaining what the fuck is wrong with you," Wolf said from the doorway. His arms crossed over his chest, his legs spread.

He was a sight.

"Wolf," I warned, though he had a point.

"I don't know what happened," Lanson explained,

ignoring Wolf. "I panicked. I shouldn't have left your side, it all happened so fast."

"You left me there to bleed out," I stated.

"I know," he murmured. "I know, I know. I'm so sorry, Huntyr, you have to believe me."

"You told me I could trust you," I hissed. "Dammit, Lanson. I counted on you to have my back."

"I know!"

"What changed? You stood up for me before, so what happened? Was it Espek? Was it the way we fought?"

"I was just surprised, that's all," he whispered, stepping even closer. If I could flinch away, I would have.

"I opened up to you," I said, hating the way the back of my throat burned. "I told you my secret, Lanson, and now what? I'm supposed to think you'll fight for me? How can I ever trust you again?"

"Huntyr, please," he begged, closing his red-rimmed eyes. "Please, give me another chance."

"The only reason I'm alive right now is because of him." I nodded to Wolf.

Lanson's nostrils flared, a flash of anger betraying his features. "Don't say that. We can still get through this, Huntyr. We can still fight this together."

"How?" I spat. "How am I supposed to complete the bond with you when I see what you really are now, Lanson?" Tears threatened my eyes. "You're weak. You're a coward, and you run from the darkness."

He took a step back as if my words had physically hit him. "Me?" he questioned. "You think *I'm* the weak one?"

"Watch it," Wolf growled from the doorway.

"You've been lying to everyone this entire time, Huntyr," he hissed. "Me, included. You made me think you needed my help. You made me think you were..."

"What?" I pushed. "I made you think I was what, Lanson?"

"Soft," he said. "Kind. Like me."

I huffed. "I am nothing like you."

"I see that now. You're a killer, Huntyr. You're cruel and dark and violent. I may run from the darkness, but at least I do not wallow in it."

"Get out," I ordered.

His eyes widened. I knew he regretted his words the second they left his mouth.

But I didn't care.

"Get the fuck out," I said again.

He waited a second longer. Waiting for what? I wasn't sure. I sure as all hells would not change my mind.

"You heard her." Wolf opened the door as wide as possible. "Get the fuck out."

Lanson spun on his heel and marched out, but not before whispering, "You two deserve each other," with his fists clenched and teeth grinding.

Wolf closed the door behind him, nearly clipping the back of his heels.

"I've always hated him," he said matter-of-factly. "You're right. He's a coward."

I closed my eyes, feeling a sudden wave of nausea. "I'm an idiot," I mumbled.

"Don't you dare start with that, Huntress. Don't put this blame on yourself."

"Hells, I was bleeding out in the middle of the court-yard all alone, Wolf. He's afraid Headmistress will find out I killed Ryder. He ran away like a scared rabbit."

"Then let him," Wolf said, softening his tone. "He showed you what you needed to see. Be grateful it was now and not after you bonded."

I sat up and pulled my knees to my chest, resting my forehead against them as I groaned. "This is all such a shit storm."

"You should shower and get that blood off you. We have a lot of work to do today, only two weeks before the test begins."

My mind raced. "What?" I asked. "You mean, we? As in..."

"You lost your partner, and I'm available. As much as it pains me to carry you through the damn test myself, we've already established that I don't want you dying here. It's your only option."

I stared at him, unable to form words. He actually wanted to partner with me?

"You're willing to bond with me?" I asked. "I was under the impression you weren't interested in bonding."

"I didn't say I wanted to bond with you," he argued, moving to sit in the small chair at the edge of the room. "I said I would partner with you. Big difference."

"Why partner at all if you're not willing to bond?"

"I watch your back, you watch mine. Assuming our enemies will be running around everywhere during the final test, it wouldn't be the worst thing in the world to have someone watching my back. But bonding with you would mean sharing my emotions with you, and trust me, you do not want to feel what I feel." He shifted in the chair, leaning forward and bracing his elbows on his knees as he stared intently in a way that sent a chill through me. "Unless, of course, you'd prefer to die. Because your idiotic decisions are making me believe that."

"Of course not," I spat. "I'm just surprised. I thought you'd rather die than partner with anyone."

He shrugged. "You heard Headmistress. The odds of passing the Transcendent without a partner are low. It's you or nothing."

"You healed me last night."

He didn't blink. "Yes."

"Headmistress said that was rare. Close to impossible, even."

"Yeah, well. She doesn't know the power of angels as well as she thinks she does."

A small smile flickered on his lips, one that made my chest warm. "Thank you."

"It's our little secret, Huntress."

He stood and walked out of the room, giving me privacy to wash the blood from myself. It was incredible how much the wound had healed. I couldn't even walk last night, and now?

Wolf wanted to be my partner for the final test.

I actually had a chance to pass.

The pit in my stomach grew with every step I took toward the study chambers. After a day of hiding in my bedroom, Wolf all but forced me to get up. I couldn't let them think they had won.

Couldn't hide from the truth forever. Couldn't hide from *them*.

Ashlani and Voiler had snuck in yesterday after Wolf had left, and they insisted on finding out every single detail of what happened. Apparently, Lanson had barely spoken to anyone since the incident, and Espek didn't show up anywhere the next day.

My chest warmed when I thought about how much Ashlani and Voiler cared. I wasn't expecting to make friends here, but I was pleasantly surprised by them.

"Just remember," Wolf whispered, his hand falling to the small of my back as he leaned in, "you say the word and they're dead."

"I can fight my own battles, thank you," I hissed back with a scowl.

Wolf shrugged, his hand lingering on the door of the already-filled study chambers. "Doesn't mean I wouldn't be satisfied as all hells to cut a few hands off. Fingers, maybe. Toes."

I shook my head and pushed forward, interrupting the entire class with our entrance.

"Thank you for gracing us with your presence today, Huntyr. Wolf. Take a seat," Headmistress announced with maximum levels of annoyance before resuming her lecture.

Every single pair of eyes fell on me. The breath left my lungs, sucked out by the need to appear strong.

Emotionless.

Violent.

Wolf's hand on my shoulder, guiding me to the back of the classroom, was the only thing that caused me to move again. Arguably the only thing holding me up.

I dipped my head, avoiding everyone—especially Lanson—and let Wolf lead me to the open chairs in the back corner.

It wasn't until I was fully seated that I felt the eyes peel away from us.

Missing training yesterday was bad enough. But showing up with Wolf? If I didn't have a target on my back already, I surely did now.

My eyes scanned the front of the room, landing on Espek. From this angle, I could see the side of his face, bloodied and bruised to make him almost unrecognizable. He no longer held his head high with confidence. He stared at the ground, tense and nervous.

Wolf leaned in close. "I couldn't help myself."

Hells. I bit my cheek to stop from smiling.

"Like I was saying," Headmistress continued, "your magic outside of The Golden City is still weak. The bond will allow you to wield more power than you'll be able to on your own, especially when it comes to blood magic."

"Why would we need to wield more?" Ashlani asked. "What happens during the final test?"

"Nice try," Headmistress Katherine replied with a smirk. "You already know I cannot reveal any specifics regarding the final test. But this is what I can tell you: What you believe to be reality will change. What you imagine is and is not possible in the world will be altered. Magic will run wild all around you. Your best bet at survival, at standing a single chance against what you'll be fighting during the final test, is bonding."

I could have sworn I felt Wolf stiffen beside me.

"I suggest you begin practicing with your chosen partner. There are heavy risks involved in bonding with someone you are not compatible with. They could siphon all of your power and burn you out entirely. You both could lose control, consumed by the extra rush of magic available to you."

I felt Lanson glance at me from the row of seats ahead, but I kept my eyes glued on Headmistress as she explained the specifics of bonding, the magic words that a pair would repeat while sharing blood until their magic connected.

It didn't matter to me. Not anymore. I was a fucking fool to think I could actually bond with Lanson. Wolf was right the entire time; he was a coward.

A nobody.

He left me bleeding out, dying in the middle of the courtyard.

He saw the darkness in me and ran. Just like I always feared he would.

Heat crept up my chest, my neck, my face.

Lord would be so deeply disappointed with me.

Wolf's hand fell on my thigh and squeezed gently. I snapped my head in his direction, too surprised by the gentleness of the gesture to stop myself, and I raised my eyebrow in question.

He winked, which confused me even more.

But then my eyes landed on Lanson, who still stared at me, only now his eyes were looking at Wolf's hand on my thigh.

Now it was his turn to flush red.

Good. He's the one who should be angry. He's the one who should hate himself, who should be ashamed of his actions.

Fuck him.

As soon as Lanson looked away, Wolf removed his hand. My stomach dipped, causing me a rush of emotion I couldn't begin to decipher.

But in the midst of it all, I even thought I had heard Wolf muffle a laugh, too.

CHAPTER
TWENTY-THREE

By the time our magic lesson ended for lunch, I forgot all about Lanson and his betrayal.

It was time for me to refocus, to lock in on what was really important.

Lanson was nothing but a distraction. Without him, I had a chance of learning my magic. I had a chance of getting stronger, at preparing even more for the Transcendent.

It was time to make Lord proud.

I didn't realize Wolf had been walking behind me until his hand fell on my lower back. "This way," he whispered in my ear, close enough that his breath tickled the skin on my neck. "We have different lunch plans today, Huntress."

He sped up and turned down the next hallway, opposite the rest of the students. He led me away from Ashlani and Voiler, who would no doubt be waiting in the dining hall. But I didn't have much of a choice, and a few seconds later, I was following him down that same hallway.

We walked through a maze of different corridors, ones I was certain I had never been down before, until he pushed open a pair of old doors that led outside.

"Where are we going?" I asked.

Wolf turned and held his hands out, a smile flickering on his face. "This is your new classroom," he announced.

I took in the surroundings. Once I had fully pushed through the door, I realized we weren't out of the castle— not really.

Wolf managed to find another small courtyard, one that was still contained within the four stone walls but was much smaller than the courtyard we had been training in with the rest of the students.

This area was not pristine and perfectly groomed like the rest of the castle. An overgrown garden lingered in the far corner, and the grass in the back had grown taller. I could tell nobody had been in here for a while. The tall white walls were now coated in crawling vines and a thin layer of dirt.

I preferred it over the rest of the castle. It was natural and unkept, reminding me of Midgrave.

"My new classroom?" I repeated.

"This is where I'll be training you," he said. "Clearly, you aren't able to train like you would if you were alone. Too many prying apprentice eyes with your big secret."

I sighed and dropped my bag against the wall. "So, you're my teacher now? I mean this in the nicest way possible, but are you qualified for that? Maybe we should find a tutor who—"

"First, you didn't even try to be nice. Second, unless

you want even more people to know your little secret about being a trained vampyre assassin back in Midgrave, I'm all you have. And yes, I am qualified."

I put both hands on my hips, waiting for more.

Wolf stared back at me with those light eyes that I was finding less and less terrifying.

A certain beauty lingered in them.

"Fine," I sighed. "When do we start?"

His answer was immediate. "Now."

I barely had time to brace myself before Wolf catapulted himself toward me, tackling me at the waist and rolling me to the ground. His hand behind my head broke my fall, but he didn't even try to hold any of his weight back from crushing against me on the grassy ground.

"Seriously?" I barked.

"You have to be ready, Huntress. Always. Your enemies won't wait for you in the Transcendent, and neither will I."

He half-straddled me, bracing himself with an elbow. I tried not to think about how much of our bodies were touching, how much he could probably feel.

"Get off me," I hissed.

His expression softened for a second before that same annoying smile played on his lips. "Make me."

The constant weight of him pressed against my lungs, restricting their expansion. "Get off!" I said again, louder.

I tried to buck my hips, tried to rotate us to throw Wolf off his balance, but he slid his hands down my body and pinned my hips there, applying more than enough pressure to ensure I couldn't move.

"I said, make me."

This time, when I tried to wiggle beneath him, I didn't move at all. I only pressed my body further into his, which resulted in a unique type of smile from him.

"I'm stronger than you. I'm much larger than you. I know you can get out of this, Huntress. Think."

Fuck him. I could hardly think of anything that wasn't his body pressed against mine, his legs pressed against my outer thighs, the warmth of him spreading across my torso as his hands held my hips with an unbreakable force.

What would Lord do? What would I do at Phantom?

Wolf was right. I would never get him off me with sheer force. I needed something else, something unexpected, something...

With Wolf's hands on my hips, my own were free. I didn't stop to think whether my plan was a good one. I just acted.

I wiggled both of my arms free before gripping his hair and pulling as hard as possible. He grunted as his head followed my motion, yanking him to the side.

And throwing off his balance.

He quickly tried to recover, but I sent my knee between his legs, completely throwing his weight off me and onto the grass beside me. With my body free, I rolled in the opposite direction, recovering in a fraction of a second and pulling my body to a squat.

He was still recovering on the ground beside me, grunting and cursing things I couldn't make out, but I was sure I could guess.

"I thought you were going to train me," I breathed, still

fighting to catch my breath. "Not sit on top of me like some large brute."

He laughed humorlessly as he found his way to his feet. "You've still got some fight in you. That's good. I was worried you may have lost it all fighting with that soft fae of a boyfriend you had."

I didn't even wait for him to recover. I closed the distance between us and punched him in the stomach as hard as I could.

If he wanted me to fight, he would get a fight.

My fist connected with Wolf's gut, but he was prepared. He grabbed my shoulders and shoved me backward without a flinch of pain.

"Again," he said.

I came at him even faster, aiming a blow to the ribs.

He stopped me again, pushing me back even harder.

"Again."

An hour later, we were both dripping in sweat and fighting for breath. Wolf blocked nearly every single one of my advances, but the ones that I surprised him with left him wide-eyed and smiling at me like he was seeing me fight for the very first time.

My muscles burned. My lungs screamed.

"Come on," I said, hearing the chimes that our break was over. I jogged to my bag and picked it up, pulling out a small loaf of bread. I tore it in half, not even looking at Wolf as I held it out for him. We had been so busy training that neither of us thought to go grab any food from the dining hall. "Headmistress will kill us if we're late again."

Wolf didn't take my bread for the first few seconds. In

fact, I felt him approach me, but he stopped a foot away. I eventually turned to him, only to find him staring at the bread with his brows drawn together.

"What?" I breathed. "I didn't poison it, I promise you that."

"You should eat that," he replied without meeting my gaze. "You need to regain your strength."

"Don't be ridiculous." I pushed it in his direction. "You haven't eaten all day. Take it."

A few more seconds went by.

Did he really think I needed my strength? Or did he not want to share the bread with me for another reason?

Sweat dripped down his forehead, following the sharp lines of his cheekbones. His bright eyes glittered with a deep energy. I found myself wanting to know more about them, about the rare light that danced beneath them.

I threw the bread into the air. Wolf caught it against his chest with one hand.

"Come on," I said again. "It's time to get back to class."

His features softened, something nobody else would have noticed, before he finally bit into the loaf. Thank the goddess. I truly did not have the energy to decipher any more of Wolf's facial expressions today.

He followed me through the hallways back the way we came, not saying anything else as he ate the rest of his bread. It wasn't nearly enough to fill my growling stomach, nor would it be enough to fuel my body after the weeks of torture I had been enduring, but it was better than nothing.

By the time we made it back to the classroom, I had

mostly caught my breath. That didn't stop the fact that Wolf and I both were covered in dirt and sweat.

And that, once again, we were the last ones to enter the classroom.

And all eyes, once again, shifted to us.

I didn't think to wonder how the rest of the apprentices would take this, or how it looked that Wolf and I had shown up together—again—breathless and covered in sweat.

But the look of horror on Lanson's face put the idea in my mind.

Did they think we...?

A satisfied laugh from Wolf behind me only confirmed my suspicions. The fae in the front of the room began snickering as well.

Hells.

I stormed to the back of the study room, face burning red, and took my seat. Wolf slid into his seat casually beside me.

"This isn't funny," I hissed at him. "I told you I don't need to be drawing this type of attention to myself."

He didn't even try to hide his smile. It was a deep contrast to the worry that dripped on his face just a few minutes ago. "I believe it may be a bit late for that."

I rolled my eyes and sank into my seat, trying to disappear from the lingering eyes, trying to will the blood away from my cheeks.

Lanson was going to think Wolf and I were hooking up during the lunch break.

Half of me was mortified, angry that I would now be associated with Wolf even more than I already was.

But the other half of me saw that agony in Lanson's eyes and reveled in it, wanted to sink inside and take hold of that pain, wanted to shove within it and make it even worse so he could feel even a fraction of the pain that I felt when he betrayed me.

He could think whatever he wanted. As long as he knew I was no longer his friend.

The rest of the day went by as torturously slow as possible. My muscles ached as I sat in the cold, hard chair of the study room. I fidgeted and shifted, trying to get even a moment of relief from my burning body, but it was no use.

And of course, Wolf was steady as a rock beside me, as if he were perfectly comfortable and content to sit in the study room for the rest of his life.

I all but jumped from my seat the second the final clock chime rang, bolting through the halls and collapsing atop my bed before Wolf could even make it through the door.

"Can I ask you something?" He made his way to his own bed.

I grunted, barely finding the energy to speak.

"Who taught you how to fight?"

A dreadful silence filled the air. In all honesty, it was a surprise this question hadn't come up before. Wolf knew I was an assassin. He knew I was trained to kill, lethal to any vampyres who may have entered Midgrave.

But I didn't become an assassin on my own.

"Someone back home," I replied quietly.

"Your parents? A friend?" His voice sounded genuinely curious, but my heart had already sped up. I didn't like these questions. They felt too real, too close to the truth.

"My parents are dead."

Another silence.

"I'm sorry," Wolf replied. I heard him shifting, moving to sit on his mattress.

I turned to face him, finally opening my eyes against the lingering exhaustion threatening to take me under. "Someone found me as a baby and raised me as his own. He's the one who taught me to fight."

"To protect yourself from vampyres?"

"Mostly, yes."

"And you enjoyed it? Spending your life killing them?"

Enjoyed it? I hadn't enjoyed most things in my life. Aside from sitting on the rooftop with Rummy, everything else was borderline manageable.

I never thought about *enjoying* my training with Lord. I certainly didn't enjoy the punishments, the dozens and dozens of lashes on my back. I didn't enjoy the shame and guilt of losing any fights, either.

But those few seconds of pure bliss each time Lord smiled at me, each time he approved of my fights, each time he told me he was proud of me.

That made it all worth it.

"There wasn't much to enjoy in Midgrave," I answered. "We all struggled. I did what I had to do to stay alive."

Wolf nodded as if he somehow understood what I was trying to say. "And the one who saved you, is he an assassin as well? Is he the one I saw with you in Midgrave?"

For one split second, I debated telling the truth; telling Wolf about Phantom, about Lord. Maybe, just maybe, I could trust him, could confide in him with this big secret.

But then I remembered the look on Lord's face when he swore me to secrecy. He had worried me with his expressions many times in the past, but that one was different.

I couldn't tell Wolf. I couldn't tell any living soul about Phantom.

I already screwed up by trusting Lanson. That wouldn't happen again.

"Enough of the interrogation," I sighed. "I'm tired. I'll see you in the morning."

I closed my eyes and listened to the sound of Wolf's breathing. He eventually settled into bed, his breath slowing with each passing minute.

To my relief, he didn't ask any more questions about Midgrave or my fighting. I wasn't sure how many more questions I could dodge, especially under the growing weight of exhaustion.

Wolf already knew too much. He was on my side right now, sure. But so was Lanson at one point. Lord had always warned me against trusting outsiders, against letting anyone else in.

He was the only one I could trust. Lord was the one who saved me, the only one I could share this secret with.

It had to stay that way.

TWENTY-FOUR

"Don't even think about partnering with anyone else," Wolf growled in my ear.

I managed to sneak out of bed and to the courtyard for training before Wolf had even woken up, somehow thinking I could partner with someone else for sparring today.

Like the damn idiot I was.

Everyone else already had partners. Even Lanson had managed to find a new partner for sparring, a smaller male fae who kept to himself, leaving me utterly alone in the back of the courtyard.

Until Wolf arrived, anyway.

"Hells," I mumbled. "You're already drawing way too much attention."

"We've been over this, Huntress. Your plan to stay under the radar is toast. You're stuck with me, now."

I rolled my eyes and groaned. I guess it was better than

standing alone in the corner, waiting for the mentor to notice me.

And I had already trained with Wolf. I was learning the patterns of his movements, the flows of his punches.

"Fine," I admitted. "But if you make me bleed, I'll kill you."

I turned to face him, only to find him already smirking. "Careful, Huntress," he purred.

The surrounding groups had already begun warming up, throwing half-assed punches and running through basic combat movements.

My entire body still felt stiff from yesterday's training, but that would not stop me. With less than two weeks until the final test, I had no time to spare. I had to grow stronger. I had to step up.

I faced Wolf and held up my fists. He did the same, his signature smirk still lingering on his face. With the morning sun rising over the edge of the castle walls, I noticed the way his wings had a subtle tint of gray in the black feathers. His wings somehow managed to stay glistening, the feathers perfectly arranged in the confines of his muscular back.

Yet they never impeded his fighting, either. I caught myself staring, re-adjusting my gaze to his eyes.

He smirked. "You're staring."

He didn't wait for me to make the first move. In a flash, he stepped forward and kicked at my legs, trying to send me off balance.

It almost worked, but I had seen that move before. I jumped over his leg and sent a punch to his ribs.

My fist made contact, but Wolf gripped my arm and spun me to his chest before I could retreat. He pressed my back against his torso and slipped a hand to my throat, squeezing just enough to restrict my air supply.

"If I was a vampyre," he breathed, dipping his head to my neck, "you'd be mine."

The way his voice rasped sent goosebumps down my arms. His hand on my neck was hot and infuriating in a way that made me want to submit to him.

Fuck that, I thought to myself. *He's doing that on purpose.*

I leaned my head back onto his shoulder, giving him the impression that I wanted more of his breath on my neck, more of his hands on my exposed skin. I even pressed back against him harder, feeling the vibrations of his chest before I raised my elbow and sent it into his ribs.

Hard.

Wolf didn't have time to prepare for my hit. He grunted and doubled over, giving me the perfect opportunity to send another hit to his back, directly in between the base of his wings.

He dropped to his knees immediately with another growl of pain.

"Wow," I breathed. "If I knew the way to get you on your knees was by hitting you between your wings, I would have done that a long time ago." I chuckled and put both hands on my hips.

But Wolf wasn't done. He grabbed the backs of my calves and pulled my legs out from beneath me, sending me crashing onto my back in front of him.

He leaned forward and knelt over me, his black angel

wings on full display. "If you want me on my knees, Huntress, all you have to do is ask."

Deep down, I knew he was messing with me, trying to distract me.

Deep down, I knew he wasn't serious.

But the way his gaze flickered across my face, lingering on my mouth. The way his hand grazed the back of my leg, teasing beneath my knee.

If it was a distraction, it was a damn good one.

"Great," Lanson's voice interrupted us.

I scrambled away from Wolf and made it to my feet, brushing the dirt off my back as best I could.

"What do you want now?" Wolf asked with a bored sigh.

"You really can't keep this contained to your bedroom?" Lanson growled. His perfectly placed hair was now disheveled and messy. His clothes were clearly dirty, his eyes dark with exhaustion.

This wasn't the Lanson I knew. The Lanson I knew wasn't confrontational. He swallowed his grievances.

But he had always been jealous of Wolf.

"You don't know what you're talking about," I mumbled.

"Enough," he spat. Wolf rose to his feet beside me. "Stop lying to me, Huntyr. All you ever do is lie."

Ashlani was at his side, pulling onto his arm. "Stop this, Lanson," she whispered.

"I'm not lying," I said, louder this time. I wasn't sure why I felt such a strong need to defend myself, especially to Lanson. "There's nothing going on between us. I told you that before, and it's still true. Not like it's any of your concern."

He laughed, but it wasn't the same bubbly laugh I had heard before. This one was cracked and angry, filled with emotions that couldn't be contained. "None of my concern? Funny. That's not what it felt like when you were kissing me."

He was too loud, and the fighters around us started to look.

"Stop it, Lanson!" Ashlani hissed again.

"No," Wolf drawled, narrowing his eyes. "Please, continue."

Lanson's attention slid to him. His nostrils flared, his face turned red with anger. "Fuck you," he hissed.

Wolf didn't budge.

Lanson stepped forward toward Wolf. Too close. "You think you're so strong? You think you're better than everyone else here because you're an angel?"

Still, Wolf didn't budge.

"She's not who you think she is," Lanson hissed, pointing a finger in my direction.

I crossed my arms over my chest, feeling everyone's attention landing on me.

"You've said enough," Wolf said quietly. Lethally.

Lanson's eyes widened. "Have I? Because I know something about her that I think plenty of fighters here would love to know."

No. My heartrate sped up, my palms grew sweaty. *Don't you fucking dare.*

Lanson stepped toward me. "You trusted me to keep

your little secret, didn't you?" he hissed. "Well, I trusted you too, Huntyr. I guess we'll both be disappointed."

I didn't have time to react. With a flash of black feathers, Wolf attacked, flattening Lanson on his back and standing over his body with his fists clenched.

Lanson coughed on the ground.

"Don't say another fucking word," Wolf growled.

I staggered backward. Wolf was... he was defending me *and* my secret.

"Why?" Lanson coughed. "Why are you protecting her? She's a fucking serpent!"

Wolf kicked his ribs. We all heard them crack. He knelt next to Lanson's crumpled body and whispered something so quietly, I couldn't make it out.

But whatever it was, it seemed to scare the shit out of Lanson.

Wolf stood up and stalked away, brushing my shoulder as he whispered, "Let's go."

I hesitated for a moment, watching Lanson scramble onto his feet without meeting my gaze.

And then I turned and followed Wolf out of the courtyard.

I wasn't sure why I followed him. Maybe it was because we were a team now. Maybe it was because he was the only one in the entire damned academy that would protect me, or maybe it was the way I was beginning to actually feel safe with him.

But I followed him without thinking, without hesitating. My feet floated on the stone floor, as if Wolf led me instinctively.

"Will you slow down?" I asked, but my voice came out as a weak cry. "Wolf!"

He spun around too quickly, his jaw clenched and his fists tightened. He was angry, angrier than I had ever seen him.

"What's going on with you?" I asked. "Are you letting Lanson get in your head?"

"No," he barked. "That coward doesn't deserve to live. He shouldn't fucking talk to you like that."

I leaned my back against the stone wall and closed my eyes, running my hands through my messy hair. "I should never have trusted him," I admitted. "I'm a fucking idiot for thinking I could trust him. It was so obvious."

"Don't. Don't you dare put this on yourself."

I opened my eyes and stared at him. "This is on me," I admitted. My heart beat in my ears, my mind spun, spiraling into the dark place that felt like home. "This is all on me, Wolf. Lord told me not to trust a single fucking soul, and I didn't listen. He was right, he was fucking right, and he's going to kill me if the secret ever gets out—"

I froze. Wolf froze. *Lord.*

My eyes widened. Wolf saw it, too. Sensed how absolutely fucking screwed I was.

But he didn't ask any questions. He didn't question who Lord was. He didn't press on.

His heated gaze flickered to my lips.

I stopped breathing.

And then he was gone, storming back down the hallway, taking that small piece of my darkest, deepest secret with him.

CHAPTER
TWENTY-FIVE

"Voiler, you're sparring with Espek today." Commander Macanthos stepped back as the circle gathered around the training area.

Voiler had sparred a couple of times before. She won most, but Espek would not go down easily. He was cruel and untrustworthy. His size alone was enough to make anyone nervous in a sparring match, let alone Voiler, who stood at nearly half his height.

Fuck.

His face had barely healed, and satisfaction rolled through me as I surveyed him. He didn't appear nearly as strong as he used to, and without Ryder, Espek looked utterly alone.

Good. He was lucky he still lived.

I felt Wolf's body behind mine as I lingered near the back of the circle. I couldn't stop the uptick in my heart rate as Voiler stepped forward, assuming her fighting stance.

She had become my friend. I didn't want to see her hurt, even if it was just training.

I glanced at Ashlani, who was already looking at me with the same worried eyes.

You've got this, Voiler.

Espek threw the first punch.

No surprise there.

Voiler ducked effortlessly and rolled away, forcing them to switch sides.

Commander Macanthos stood watching with tight lips. He knew this was an uneven fight. He knew it, and he still chose her to fight against Espek.

I did not know what he was thinking, but you would have to be blind to see how unfair this was.

Voiler dodged the next few punches, which only infuriated Espek. His face flushed red, his breathing grew heavy as Voiler danced him around the sparring area.

When Voiler threw an elbow into Espek's ribs, he hissed in pain.

There we go, Voiler. More of that.

But Espek recovered quickly, grabbing her arm before she pulled away and throwing her to the ground like she was nothing.

He jumped on her in an instant, pinning her to the ground with a hand around her throat.

Come on, Voiler. She gasped for air; Espek's hand tightened.

I glanced at the commander. *End the fucking fight!*

Everyone froze. Not a single person dared to move, dared to breathe.

And then the impossible happened.

It all went down so fast, I barely noticed. Voiler reached toward Espek's thigh, where one of his own daggers was strapped, and sliced her own hand.

The blood hit the ground a fraction of a second later.

Espek didn't stand a chance as shards of ice formed in the air around them. They impaled themselves into Espek's back, piercing his heart, killing him.

The entire fight lasted a mere few seconds.

Voiler shoved Espek's lifeless body off her before crawling away, gasping for air. Ashlani knelt beside her, grabbing her shoulders and pulling her into a hug.

But my gaze moved to the commander.

"You have powerful blood magic," he said, nodding to Voiler. "It's rare for someone to wield so much control in a time of panic. Hells, most would have killed us all with those shards."

I held my breath. Voiler was the first one to kill another in sparring. And it was Espek.

"We'll resume sparring next session," Commander Macanthos announced. "And unless you have as much control over your blood magic as this one, I suggest you do not attempt what you have just witnessed."

And that was it.

Voiler had killed with blood magic, so effortlessly and precisely that we hadn't even had a chance to stop it.

Hells, maybe Commander was right before. Maybe I wasn't the only one wearing a mask in this academy.

The next day, Wolf and I trained alone in the secret courtyard. I liked it there. I could be myself, I could train without prying eyes, could actually grow stronger. Better.

It was what I needed considering the Transcendent was only a week away.

I sat in the grass, absolutely exhausted, and let my body relax. "You never told me why you fell," I started. "You're a fallen angel, I mean. What happened?"

He sighed but eventually made his way to sit beside me. He stretched his long legs out before him, leaning back onto his hands. His black wings grazed the tall grass beside me.

"There were many things," he explained. "But the ultimate reason had to do with my father."

"You didn't kill him, did you?" I was only partially joking.

Wolf laughed under his breath, moving to pick at the grass between us. I couldn't help but smile; he looked so young, so innocent. The corner of his mouth tilted in the smallest hint of a smile as he thought about what to say next.

"No," he replied. "But there have been many times when I wish I had."

Another silence lingered, the sound of snapping grass strands filling the air between us. This quiet grew heavy, though, as the weight of his words fell onto me, tightening my chest with an invisible fist.

"But he's an angel?" I pushed, ensuring my voice held a certain delicacy.

Wolf hesitated before answering, "Yes, my father is an angel."

"Is that why you're trying to make it into The Golden City?"

His chest rose and fell with a long breath. "I was born there, you know. I lived there for years. When I fell, I was exiled. I was told to never return. When I woke up the next morning, I was in the middle of Khaer, with no clue where I was. My white angel wings had turned black, and I had been stripped of all my possessions. That was a long time ago, but yes, I guess you could say that's why I'm trying to make it into The Golden City. This might be the only way back."

My chest tightened at his blatant honesty. He had been exiled from his own home? And he was forced outside to live with nothing and nobody? Hells, that couldn't have been easy.

"And you think they'll let you back in?"

He shrugged. "If I make it back fairly, yes. My father may not be thrilled, but The Golden City is big enough for us to live in peace. Besides, I have to try. It's... it's different there. I can't say my experience on the outside has been fortunate."

269

Another silence lingered. Wolf's eyebrows drew together, his bright eyes darkening in thought.

"What's The Golden City like? Is it as beautiful as they say?"

The corner of Wolf's mouth twitched, but his expression remained dark. "It's unexpected. It's constantly changing. There are always new threats, and the angels are very strict about keeping order."

"Is it true that there is no crime and no poverty?" Excitement leaked into my words. I couldn't help it. Imagining a place so unlike Midgrave made my stomach flip. If I were being honest, I struggled to imagine such a place. I grew up fighting to survive. The people of Midgrave were not inherently violent or aggravated, but hunger would make any sane fae do something they might regret.

People in Midgrave starved to death. In The Golden City, that would never happen.

"Trust me," Wolf said. His voice grew distant. "There is plenty that will surprise you about that place."

I closed my eyes and let my head fall back, breathing in the cool night air. It was nice to be here with Wolf, I had to admit that much. Even though every part of my body burned with exhaustion, even though my eyelids were heavier than they had ever been before, I didn't want to leave.

Not with him beside me.

We stayed that way for a while. The soft flow of air blew the tall grass, creating a soothing sound of comfort. Out here, we couldn't hear the constant voices that echoed through the massive walls of the castle. Hells, for once, I wasn't constantly listening to the sound of my heart.

It was nice.

"I have something for you," he said after a minute.

I opened my eyes and found him reaching for his bag.

"What?" I asked, my brows furrowing. "What are you talking about?"

But my mouth fell open as soon as I saw what he removed from that bag.

The familiar steel handle, the perfectly angled blade.

Venom.

"Hells," I breathed, taking the perfectly intact weapon from his hands. "But this was broken. I saw Espek break it himself!"

Wolf shrugged. "I know a fae not too far from here who specializes in wielding weapons."

I stared at him, my mouth hanging open. "Wolf... I don't know what to say." Tears threatened my eyes. I flipped Venom over, taking in the perfect emerald jewels and now-shining steel.

"It seemed important," he added.

"It—she was. This was the only gift he ever gave me."

"The male who raised you?"

My eyes hesitantly met his. "Yes."

His face hardened, but I smiled. Wolf didn't understand, but he didn't have to. This dagger was the only thing that reminded me of him, of home. Venom reminded me of my purpose here, reminded me of who I really was.

I was lost without her.

Before I knew what I was doing, I threw my arms around Wolf's shoulders and hugged him.

Wolf tensed at first but eventually wrapped his arms around my back.

We didn't have to be enemies anymore.

In fact, we weren't enemies at all.

Wolf and I ate our food in silence, with the entire dining hall to ourselves. All the other students were in bed by now, getting plenty of sleep before another grueling day at the academy tomorrow.

Everyone but us.

Wolf sat across from me at the end of the long wooden table, focusing on his meal and ripping a piece of meat apart with his white teeth.

I did the same, eating as much as my stomach could handle. With all the extra training from Wolf, I needed the fuel.

"Magic isn't as easy for me," I started in between bites. "It feels... it feels resistant."

Wolf ate the rest of his meal in two bites before he leaned back, eyes glued on me and brows drawn together. "You'll get there," he said. "You just need to focus enough."

Something glittered in his bright blue eyes.

"Your eyes," I said before I could stop myself, "is that because you're an angel? Do all angels have light in their eyes?"

He smiled, looking away and actually flushing for the first time since I'd known him. "No, not all angels. My eyes look this way because of the magic I possess."

"Lightning magic?"

As if on cue, light blared around his pupils again and flashed as he locked his gaze on me.

"Something like that."

I considered his words. "What type of magic do angels have access to, anyway? I never see you practicing natural magic or blood magic with the others. I know your magic can heal. What else?"

He shrugged with one shoulder. "I don't need to practice the way the rest of you do. I've been wielding magic for most of my life. Healing is one of the many gifts I have, but like anyone else here, there's a balance. I can't use it whenever I want, and it drains quickly when I use too much."

"Interesting."

"Every angel wields a slight variation. Some are seers, some are healers, some bend the earth. We all have different strengths, and I'm sure you'll find yours soon enough."

I sighed and continued picking at my food.

It wasn't just that I was afraid to show the other students my strengths. I couldn't do it. Aside from barely summoning some natural magic, I had nothing. The other students summoned fire and controlled wind.

But me? I controlled nothing. I *felt* nothing.

"Any more questions?" he pushed, leaning both elbows on the wooden table. "Or is it my turn to interrogate you?"

I also leaned forward, copying his posture. "I was not interrogating you. I was simply curious about the lightning that explodes in your eyes when you get angry or when you're entertained. That's a very valid curiosity."

Slowly, without looking away, the corners of his mouth slid up. His eyes scanned my face, raking over every feature.

"What?" I asked, suddenly feeling much too vulnerable.

A silent beat passed.

"You are a stunning creature, Huntress."

I sucked in a breath. It was so easy for him to say those words, so easy for him to stare at me with blatant amusement in his gaze.

I wanted to back up, to cover my face, to retreat. I felt too exposed when I was with Wolf, and after all the time we spent together lately, I was feeling things that made no sense at all.

Like the fluttering in my chest when he looked at me, the nerves when he entered a room.

"Dinner's over," I said, pushing my plate back and standing from the table. I cleared my throat and made my way to the door. "I'm going to sleep. Don't wake me when you come in."

And that was that.

I left Wolf and his torturously addicting eyes at the table gaping after me.

I only let myself smile when I was alone in the confines of my bedroom, where the darkness covered the blush on my face.

This feeling was more dangerous than any test, than any threat.

But this time, I didn't care.

CHAPTER
TWENTY-SIX

Two days later, I snuck away to practice the one thing Wolf couldn't help me with.

My magic.

I drew blood repeatedly, trying to give the offering that was required to summon blood magic. The angry, red skin on my palms wasn't healing fast enough for me to keep slicing. Blood smeared Venom's handle from my grip as I tried over and over and over.

Still, blood was required to summon the blood magic.

So blood would spill.

I rolled up the sleeve of my tight black training top and dove the tip of Venom into my skin.

Think, Huntyr. Focus. I thought back to what I had learned about blood magic.

Clear your head. Think of your intentions.

I pictured a small flame, one that could fit in the palm of my hand. I felt the heat of it, imagining the small orange

276

light flickering deeply enough to illuminate the dark courtyard.

Voiler had tried to help me again a few days ago, but it was no use.

This had to come from within. My blood had to call to the magic.

I closed my eyes. *Come on, blood magic. I know you're in there somewhere.*

Other students had succeeded overwhelmingly with summoning their blood magic. Even Wolf had managed to heal my wound with his blood magic, which was annoyingly gratuitous of him. Still, I remained shocked.

Focus on the flame, Huntyr. Focus on summoning the magic.

I thought about how the entire castle had been blessed by the archangels. I pictured them pouring their power into this place, into the stones of the walls, into the dirt beneath my feet.

Come on, Moira. I only need a small amount of your magic.

I let my blood drip and drip and drip. I took my knife and sliced even more of the skin on my forearm, offering more of my blood to the blessed lands of the academy.

Give me something.

Anything.

The silence became unbearable.

Still, I felt nothing.

"Hells," I mumbled to myself, aligning Venom's tip back onto my arm. Maybe more blood would do the trick.

If what was said about bloodlines being stronger with blood magic was true, perhaps the opposite was true as well. I was born from poverty. I was raised without even knowing who my actual parents were.

Lord surely did not have good things to say about them.

Perhaps they had been too far from the pure fae bloodlines that I had no magic left in my veins. Perhaps this entire seminary was a waste, and I could never wield blood magic like the others.

It had to be a possibility.

I pictured Lord's face, thinking about how angry he would be with me if I failed. The scars on my back were nothing compared to what he would do to me next.

Hells, if I couldn't summon this magic and get into The Golden City, I could never show my face around Lord again.

I was the one person he trusted with this assignment. I understood why, of course. In a world as cold and evil as this one, we all had to be careful about who we trusted.

Trusting people showed vulnerability.

Vulnerability would get you killed.

A wave of desperation fell over me. My entire body screamed with pain, whether it was from the dull ache of old bruises, or the new stings from the blood sacrifices, I didn't know.

Everything hurt.

Everything needed rest.

Rest was a luxury here, though. It was a luxury back in Midgrave, too. One I could not afford.

Every single day in Midgrave had comprised of fighting. If I wasn't slaughtering vampyres, I was training with the other Phantoms or being sent out on missions.

I still remember that first mission Lord sent me on.

He almost looked... nervous.

"You're ready for this," Lord had said. Of course, I believed him. I spent years fighting every single day.

And winning every single fight.

When I wasn't training with other Phantoms, I was training with Lord himself. He was the one who had taught me how to wield a blade correctly. He taught me how to hold a weapon in my hand—not too tight, not too loose. He showed me how to escape an opponent much larger than me, how to not panic in the throes of death.

Every single day, Lord had made sure I was ready.

And it all led to this.

If only he had been the one to teach me magic. I was certain Lord would have broken through to me.

He saw me like that. He understood even the deepest parts of me.

My chest ached. I had never been away from Lord for more than a few days, typically when I was sent out on missions.

I felt too far away from him. Too distant.

I closed my eyes and thought of his voice—commanding and violent—echoing off the stone walls of the castle.

I pictured him telling me exactly what those mentors had told me. I pictured him holding Venom, slicing my shirt, and cutting the skin above my elbow.

Letting me bleed.

And then I pictured the land below being infused with the blood, accepting the sacrifice to the archangels.

"Bleed," Lord would say. "Bleed and live."

I wasn't sure what changed, but suddenly, every ounce of my body was electrified with a new energy. It was unlike any rush of adrenaline I had felt before, unlike any thrill.

Static erupted from the tips of my toes to the ends of my fingertips, followed by a deep pull of dark, smokey magic that grew thicker and thicker, swirling and molding the surrounding air.

This was it. This was the energy Headmistress spoke of.

I was finally connected to the magic.

I pictured Lord giving up more and more of my blood for the offering. I slid the tip of Venom from my shoulder down my bicep, cutting more of my shirt, not even flinching as the contact stung.

Warm liquid poured from my arm.

I kept my eyes tightly shut.

Bleed and live.

The light buzzing in my body turned to a full-on roar, and any chill I had felt from the night breeze had morphed into a burning fire that overtook all of my senses.

Magic rushed through me.

I felt it as surely as I had felt anything else before.

Bleed and live.

Bleed and live.

When I ran out of fresh skin to slice on my left arm, I swapped hands, holding Venom in my other hand and slicing through the fresh, untouched sleeve of my right arm.

Bleed and live.

Lord would not be disappointed in me. I would give every single ounce of this blood to Moira if it meant returning home to him victorious.

Whatever Lord needed of me, I would fulfill.

I owed him at least that.

Fire.

Fire.

Fire.

I let the magic run through me, and with each drop of blood that fell to the ground, it grew stronger.

Fiercer.

Hotter.

My heart pounded, cutting out any other sounds that weren't the constant, rapid beating of blood in my ears.

I tossed my head back.

And I let go.

Fire erupted around me, so fierce and full of fury that I thought I was imagining it at first. My entire body relaxed as my magic—the blood magic—poured around me.

I no longer doubted the archangels; I no longer worried I wouldn't have enough blood to offer them.

This was it.

Fire roared in a circle around my feet, giving off waves of heat but never touching my skin. It spread outward, crawling over the dried grass, as if awaiting an order.

I waved my hand. Fire flew into the air.

Laughter bubbled my chest, mixing with the pure euphoria I felt from the release.

More. It needed more blood.

I cut my arm again.

More flames rose.

I moved to my torso, not bothering to lift my shirt as I cut a line across my stomach.

Another rush of adrenaline fueled me.

Laughter and the sputtering of flames and chaos filled that empty, hollow space in my soul until it all went black.

The rush of adrenaline stopped. The rush of magic ceased. As quickly as it began, it was over.

Voiler stood before me, nothing short of horror on her face. She must have put out the fire, must have stopped the magic that was only beginning to fuel my body.

I could feel how much power remained, how much my body liked the strength of it.

"What are you doing, Huntyr? You plan on burning this entire castle to the ground and taking everyone with you?" Her eyes were frantic as she looked at me, looked at Venom, who now dripped with my blood.

I looked down to see a pool of blood forming around my feet.

Hells.

I tried to take a step, but my legs surrendered beneath me.

Headmistress had said something about the boundaries of magic, especially blood magic.

Maybe this was what she meant.

I landed on the ground, in the small pool of my own blood. My arms were still bleeding, offering magic that the ground no longer accepted.

I was only slightly aware of Voiler trying to pull me to

my feet, was only slightly conscious as she left the court-yard, returning a few minutes later with Wolf.

"I'm sorry," Voiler whispered. "I didn't know what else to do."

"I'll take it from here, Voiler." Wolf's voice melted over me, like a warm breeze. "Don't tell anyone about this."

"Heal her," she whispered, more of a demand than a suggestion, and then she was gone.

"I don't need help," I insisted, trying to push myself up.

"You can't even stand." Wolf knelt in front of me, concern dripping from his features.

"I just need to make it to my bed." Exhaustion lapped at my body like waves at sea, ready to pull me under.

"Are you serious?" he demanded. "You're falling apart, Huntress. Here."

He threw my arm around his shoulder, even though we both knew he could pick me up without so much as blink-ing, and walked me silently out of the courtyard and down the hall to the bedroom.

"I don't know what happened." Each breath took more energy than I had to give. "I needed it to work, Wolf."

He removed my arm from around his shoulders. I thought he was going to drop me on my bed, but he led me into the bathroom. He gripped my waist and hoisted me onto the edge of the bathroom sink.

"What are you—"

He lifted my wrist and surveyed my arm, grimacing at every slice from the knife. "Are you trying to bleed yourself dry?"

My head grew too heavy to hold up. I didn't realize I

was falling into him until he caught me, sliding a hand around my neck and holding my face to his.

"I'm helping you. Lift your arms."

I objected, but he guided my hands above my head, moving both wrists together so he could use his free hand to peel my shirt up.

"No," I muttered, too numb to think, to feel.

Wolf still didn't know about the scars. If he saw them, he never asked questions about where they came from.

He stopped instantly, his eyes searching my face. He may have been harsh and rude and awful at times, but he would not undress me while I sat here objecting to it.

Unfortunately, the fight I had left in me slowly dwindled. And the way his fingers grazed my bare stomach made my chest do unnatural things.

"You need help, Huntress." His voice had softened, his breath now tickling my cheek. "I hate seeing you like this. Let me help you."

I clenched my jaw but nodded.

Carefully, tediously, Wolf lifted my sliced shirt. I hissed as the fabric passed the shallow gashes of my torso, the gashes on my shoulders. Wolf didn't seem to look anywhere but my shirt, though I could have sworn I noticed his breath hitch as the fabric slid the rest of the way off my arms before finally falling to the floor.

Leaving me in my chest wrap.

He froze, finally letting go of my wrists and letting my arms lower to my sides.

"Is it bad?" I whispered

Wolf reached for the towel and ran it under the water,

all without looking away. "You're lucky you didn't drain yourself completely."

I let my eyes flutter closed as Wolf began wiping the blood away from my arm, starting at my wrist and slowly working up to my shoulder.

"This isn't working," he mumbled. "There's too much blood. Here. I can only heal you partially, but I'll fill the bath with a healing tonic." He sliced his hand with his knife, bleeding once again, and placed his palms on my arms. That same healing warmth radiated from him.

"You shouldn't waste your energy on me. I'm fine." I knew how risky it was to use blood magic to heal, knew how much it could drain him if he wasn't careful.

Still, he kept his eyes on me as the deeper gashes in my body closed.

Hells.

"That will have to be enough," he muttered. "I can't use too much."

He moved away for a second, and a moment later, the bath began to fill.

Wolf returned with a gentle touch at my waist. "Stand."

He lifted me from the counter and set me on my feet before reaching for the waist of my pants.

"I can do it," I argued.

"No, Huntress." He ran his thumb up and down my hip bone in an oddly affectionate gesture. "You can't."

He knelt before me—for the second time in my life—and peeled away my boots.

One boot was off.

Two boots.

The water filling higher and higher in the bathtub became the only sound in the room, the only one I really registered, though I was sure Wolf could hear how fast my heart beat.

"Hold onto me," he whispered.

I did, gripping his shoulders while he carefully peeled my combat pants from my sweaty, bruised legs.

Soon enough, I stood in nothing but my chest wrap and my underwear. I should have cared. I should have felt embarrassed or ashamed or exposed.

But I felt nothing. Absolutely nothing, except the way his fingers carefully worked my body.

I didn't even realize my head had fallen onto his shoulder until his hand came to work his fingers through my messy, knotted hair.

"Come on," he started. "Let's get you in the bath. You need the healing salts."

Slowly, he lifted me in his arms.

Slowly, he let my body dip into the warm water.

A pathetic sound of relief sang from my lips as I let myself sink into the bath. Finally, I found a single ounce of relief from the numbness.

I pulled my knees to my chest and wrapped my bloodied arms around them.

I was too enthralled in the distraction of the warm, luxurious water to notice the way Wolf moved behind me, tracing the tip of my shoulder with his finger.

And then traced another scar.

And another.

I only noticed the intention of his actions when he dipped his hand into the water to trace my entire back.

"Huntress." His breath was a wisp of a shadow in my mind. "You do not know the violence that runs through my veins, begging me to obliterate anyone who lays a hand on you."

Goosebumps erupted down my arms.

I did not flinch.

I did not hide.

"It's complicated," I breathed.

And that was all I said.

Wolf's hands froze, and I knew he wanted to ask more. He wanted to know exactly who gave me every single one of those lashes. He wanted to avenge me, for whatever reason.

But tonight, I was far, far too exhausted to explain.

Wolf got to work scrubbing the blood off my arms, careful to avoid the larger gashes and taking his time cleaning the sensitive areas. He made no more remarks about my deformed back. He made no more comments about how dangerous blood magic could be.

He bathed me. Like a worried, attentive lover, he washed the blood from my tainted skin.

And for once in my life, I let him.

I t must have been at least an hour.

The water of the bath had turned cold by the time Wolf finished. He pulled me from the water and wrapped me in a towel, letting me dry off in private while he fetched me clothes.

His clothes.

Unfortunately for both of us, blood magic hadn't left me with many spare shirts. The one remaining outfit I had needed to be saved for training.

Either way, I didn't argue.

His clothes were much, much larger on me, which left my skin room to heal.

I even unwrapped my chest, not bothering to care how my breasts might look under Wolf's thin shirt.

I reached for the door of the washroom, but Wolf was there, pulling the door open and immediately meeting me at my side.

"Thank you," I breathed.

He guided me to my bed with ease.

"For helping me. For healing me. I know it's risky."

Wolf's features flickered in the dim light from the lantern. Everyone else in the castle had surely gone to sleep by now.

Somehow, it felt as if we were the only two people in Moira.

He helped me sit on my bed, letting his hands linger on my waist. "Anything for my deadly huntress."

It had to have been the overwhelming levels of exhaustion that made me reach out to his retracting hand, catching it before he could turn to his own bed. "Will you stay with me?"

He tensed.

My heart stopped.

"I'll always stay with you."

I moved over, giving him plenty of room to slide into bed beside me.

It felt so natural, it should have scared me. It should have forced me to think about all the times we surely had laid together, wrapped in each other's arms, because there was no way in all hells that it could have felt so natural.

But it did.

Even as I laid my head on his chest, wrapping my arm around his torso. Even as his hand fell on my back and then tensed.

I wasn't sure why I said the next words, but like everything else happening in this moment, they felt right.

"Not all of us wear our scars on our face for all to see, Wolf. Some of us like to hide, as if that will make the pain go away."

Wolf's hand teased under the bottom of my—his—shirt. The warmth of his palm flattening against my skin made me shiver.

"I see your scars in your eyes." The tips of his fingers circled. "I see them in your fight. I see them in your determination. I see them in your anger."

When tears burned my eyes, I let them fall.

"Just because your back may hold these physical scars doesn't mean you can't rewrite that story, Huntress. You're a fighter. These explain nothing if not that."

CHAPTER
TWENTY-SEVEN

I thought I was having an incredibly realistic, torturously sexy dream about Wolf. One that involved his warm, comforting body behind me, holding me in his arms, breathing onto my neck.

I thought it was all a dream until I remembered what happened last night.

My eyes shot open. Sometime in the night, we moved around in my bed. Wolf's arm rested firmly under my head, the other under my shirt and flattened against my bare stomach. His entire body pressed against mine, our legs intertwined together in our carnal, raw position.

Holy hells.

Class would start soon, and after last night, I was going to do everything in my power to avoid talking to Wolf this morning.

I tried to pull myself out of his grasp, but it only resulted in my body pressing deeper into his.

Wolf moaned lazily, tightening his hold on my body.

His thumb grazed the underside of my breast.

My breath hitched.

"One more minute," Wolf breathed, his voice dripping in morning grogginess.

I let my head fall back onto his arm. "You're going to make me late."

"Sleep." His fingers moved across my skin, and there was no way he didn't know *exactly* what he was doing.

I exhaled deeply, noticing every part of Wolf pressing against me.

And very aware of how hard he was.

Before I could stop myself, I rocked my hips backward into his.

He groaned, which only brought even more heat between my legs.

"Careful, Huntress."

This was bad. This was very bad.

His thumb grazed my breast again, and I all but arched into him.

"You're doing that on purpose." My hoarse morning voice cracked.

Wolf's satisfaction became clear when he pressed himself into me, not even attempting to hide his body's reaction.

Snap out of it, Huntyr.

"Okay," I sighed, interrupting whatever was happening between us and shoving myself away from him. "I need to get to the study. Voiler's probably worried about me after what happened last night."

He sat up, too, as I crawled over him and off the bed.

My body didn't feel nearly as sore as I thought it would, though after Wolf healed me, my wounds were hardly noticeable.

"We should talk about what happened." His voice was soft and tired.

"No, we shouldn't. I lost control, and it won't happen again."

I didn't give him any more time to argue. I finished getting dressed in the only clothes I had that were not ripped to shreds, slipped my boots on, and walked out the door.

Voiler and Ashlani were already seated at our table in the study before I arrived.

I half-expected Voiler to tell Ashlani what she saw in the courtyard yesterday, but nothing seemed out of the ordinary as I walked up to the table and settled in.

"Can you believe it?" Ashlani whispered to Voiler. "He's like an entirely different person now."

"Who?" I interrupted.

"Lanson. I've never seen him so angry. He can't even talk to me without biting my head off."

"Everyone wears a mask. His was just better at fooling us."

"Wow," Ashlani said, leaning in. "That was deep, Hunt."

Hunt. Rummy was the only one who'd ever called me that.

I missed her. My chest ached for home, for returning to the hell that was Midgrave. One day, I would return to her. One day, I would make it back. I would return to my life of protecting her and the people of that city with everything I had.

My eyes slid to Voiler, who already stared at me with soft eyes and an understanding smile.

"Come on," Ashlani said to her. "Let's go find some more books to stuff our faces into."

Ashlani and Voiler both stood from the chairs, but Voiler hung back while Ashlani disappeared into the rows and rows of books behind us.

"You okay?" she whispered, loud enough for only me to hear.

"Yeah," I replied with a soft nod. "I'm fine now."

And that was that. Voiler understood. I could see it in her eyes. She was like me, with secrets and darkness. But I knew she wouldn't tell anyone what she saw last night.

She disappeared behind Ashlani, leaving me alone at the table.

Though my solitude didn't last long.

A few seconds later, the door to the study swung open. Lanson sauntered through with his shoulders rolled back, his chin lifted.

I pushed myself from my chair and stood, either ready

to follow the others into the rows of books, or to fight Lanson if he dared approach me.

Either way, I was ready.

I stood tall as his eyes scanned the empty room before landing on me. Lanson looked at me with an expression I had never seen before, one of hatred and pride and cruelness. He was a stranger staring at me now from the other side of the study.

I fucking hated him. I hated him for tricking me into thinking he was good and kind. I hated myself even more for falling for it. I wasn't this person. Lord trained me to be better than that, to be smarter than that.

I was so distracted by Lanson's death glare that I didn't feel the body coming up behind me.

"Do you want to really piss him off?" Wolf's voice whispered so quietly in my ear, I almost didn't hear him.

And he was close, so close that if I turned to look at him, his lips would have brushed against me.

"What?" I whispered back.

Wolf's hands slid softly onto my hips from behind. He pulled me back an inch until I pressed against his chest. I almost pushed away, but the grip on my body held me still.

"Go with it," he said. "Weak, cowardly males like Lanson all want the same thing."

Wolf dipped his head from behind and skimmed the sensitive skin of my neck and shoulder with his mouth.

Hells.

"And what's that?" I asked. I fought to keep my voice steady with the sudden wave of heat pooling in my lower stomach.

One glance at Lanson told me he was watching every second.

"They want to feel like they're the only one who can give you what you want." His lustful voice vibrated against my neck as I tilted my head, giving him what *he* wanted.

His hands tightened against my hips, fingertips pressing into me with a possessive need before he slid a hand up my torso, pinning me to him from behind.

I exhaled and closed my eyes, buying into this show.

Wolf was right. Lanson had believed I hated Wolf, had believed I wanted nothing to do with him. That cowardly bastard might have hated me, but he hated Wolf even more.

I leaned against him completely as his hovering lips turned to fervent kisses against my exposed skin. It was nothing like the way Lanson touched me.

It wasn't hesitant or questioning or gentle. Wolf held me with a dominating need, one that weakened my knees and made me forget everything I was supposed to despise about him.

He kissed my neck and grazed my skin with his teeth, sending chills down my arms. He sucked the skin lightly in between kisses, and I rolled my head back against his chest. His mouth, so hot that I was sure my skin was burning, slid from my neck to my ear, where his breath sent chills down my spine.

"At least pretend to like the way I touch you," he whispered.

Yeah.

I was screwed.

295

I didn't even look to see if Lanson was still watching us before I spun in Wolf's arms, draping my hands over his shoulders and pressing my chest to his. His arms fell naturally across my back, holding me against him just as strongly as he had before.

Certain. Secure.

"What now?" I asked, my lips not even an inch from his.

Shadows swarmed his eyes. His chest rose and fell heavily against mine, the only sign that he was affected by our passionate touch.

"That depends," Wolf whispered back, eyes moving from mine down to my lips. "How mad at him are you?"

It was a deep question, one that went beyond the simple words that had left Wolf's mouth.

How mad was I?

Fuck, Wolf's hands on my body made me forget about Lanson altogether. I was suddenly reminded of the eyes that still lingered on us.

I swallowed before answering, "Very mad."

A fraction of a smile flashed across Wolf's wickedly handsome face before he dipped his head and kissed me.

No, a kiss was not a strong enough word to describe it.

It was a confession, a promise, a domination, an enchantment.

Wolf's mouth controlled me easily, slowly at first, as if he was giving me time to get used to it. After a few seconds, though, he seemed to quit holding back. His mouth moved against mine with a tantalizing heat, one that made me happy he was practically holding my body up against his.

I kissed him back, not worried if I was doing it right. Not concerned about whether he would like it or whether I was about to embarrass myself. Wolf guided me with the same conviction he carried all the time.

Only now, it was for me.

And I had to admit, it was damn sexy.

Our bodies fit together perfectly, as if my waist was made for his arms to hold. As if his shoulders were made to lift me, to support me.

We had touched many times before. I was no stranger to how a man's body felt against mine.

But this? This was devotional.

He moved to grip my ass, nearly lifting me off the ground with his strength. I moaned against him—not on purpose, which I was sure he'd give me shit for later—and slipped my hands into his hair, pulling.

The growl of pleasure that came from him made my legs even weaker. "Careful," he mumbled against my mouth, but he didn't stop.

No, he deepened the kiss further, if that was even possible. He devoured my lips until that wasn't enough, then he moved to devour my jaw, my neck, my collarbone.

I exhaled deeply when he gripped my ass again, this time wrapping my leg around his waist to hold me there. I tossed my head back as Wolf ran his tongue up the front of my neck, meeting my lips again with a light bite.

He kissed me, gentle and slow, before barely pulling away. "He's gone," Wolf breathed.

"Good," I whispered back, my voice hoarse.

We stood there longer than we needed to, wrapped in this intimate and vulnerable embrace in the middle of the study.

Too many unsaid words lingered between us, too many truths and secrets and lies.

Ashlani cleared her throat behind Wolf.

I shoved myself away, fumbling to straighten my top and my hair as Wolf just stood there, smirking at me.

"See you later, then," he said.

And then he, too, departed the study, leaving me breathless and on fire.

Ashlani and Voiler both stood, their arms filled with piles of books and their mouths hanging open.

"Shut up," I cut them off before they could even begin, but it was impossible to stop the smile from spreading on my face. "Do not say a word."

They returned to the table, the three of us pulling out our chairs and taking a seat as if I hadn't just been kissing the fallen angel. Neither of them asked questions, though I could tell Ashlani was ready to erupt with curiosity.

We dove into the books of history and vampyres and angels and war, but as we sat there studying, my entire body heated with every single memory of Wolf's hands on my skin.

I didn't see him for the rest of the day. Not in the dining hall, not in the courtyard. Not even in the bedroom, as I made it back later that night, lying in bed and perking up at every sound in the hallway.

No, Wolf was back to being his mysterious, disappearing self for the day, leaving me a pathetic pile of worry and curiosity.

Just as I drifted off to sleep, I let my fingers brush over my lips.

Hells. I was in trouble.

CHAPTER

TWENTY-EIGHT

Wolf's hands on my body taunted my mind. *And that damn kiss.*

It came out of nowhere. Wolf had been so hot and cold ever since I met him. He was either saving my life or ridiculing me, either pissing me off or healing me with blood magic.

But he was nothing like Lanson, that was for damn sure.

I didn't see Wolf again after that. I tried to control my thoughts, tried to rid them of his icy eyes and muscular hands, but it was near impossible.

I couldn't have been asleep for more than a few hours before a scream filled the hallway, echoing off the stone walls and closed doorways. My eyes shot open immediately as I reached for Venom, who was slipped perfectly beneath my pillow.

Another scream rang out, somewhere further into the castle.

I jumped out of bed and slid my boots on. Every beat of my heart pumped my body with fuel, with energy for a fight.

I crept toward the door and waited for a sound in the hallway, hearing nothing.

Only silence filled the air, along with the muffling of a few other students who were also awoken by the screams.

Where the fuck was Wolf?

A strange sense of worry filled my senses, mixing with the adrenaline and all but forcing me out of my room.

After a few silent steps forward, other students followed behind me as we all made our way down the corridors, trailing after the sound of the screams.

Just when I thought perhaps nothing was wrong, that maybe whatever happened had ended, I heard another scream.

I burst into an all-out run, Venom tight in my grip.

Suddenly, I was back in Midgrave, running through the streets and following any shout of terror I could hear.

Suddenly, I was back with Lord, with him yelling at me to move faster, quicker, stronger.

And it was damn good, because I turned one more corridor in that castle, and a vampyre jumped from the shadows.

"No," I hissed under my breath. "What in all hells?"

Someone behind me shrieked. I didn't.

I leapt forward, meeting the beast in the center of the hallway with Venom ready. This one was strong, still with most of its flesh intact. It must have turned rabid very recently.

I sliced it down, Venom finding its heart in one swift motion.

"Was that a vampyre?" Ashlani asked in the crowd behind me.

"Yes," I replied. "And there will be more. Get ready."

She whimpered in panic, but I didn't blame her. Those who hadn't fought these monsters up close wouldn't be prepared for the half-rotting flesh, for the rabid attacks and the smell of death.

Hells, that *smell*.

A grunt around the corner tipped me off to another creature lurking in the shadows. I ran, ready to fight, and found him sinking his teeth into someone's flesh.

Fuck. Fuck. *Fuck.*

I gripped the creature's head and sliced it off with one motion.

I stepped over both bodies and kept moving forward. If the vampyre had gotten that far, there was no use in trying to save the victim. Death had already taken hold.

I turned into the main hallway, where the front doors of the castle had been pushed open, only to find ten more creatures funneling indoors.

This wasn't happening. This *could not be* happening.

Vampyres had made their way into the castle.

CHAPTER
TWENTY-NINE

"Wake up!" I yelled, my voice echoing through the castle. "Grab your weapons! Vampyres are attacking!"

I didn't look to see if anyone else had jumped into action before catapulting myself forward to stab another vampyre in the chest.

What the fuck was going on? There weren't systems in place for this? Sirens? Warnings of any kind?

How could they possibly have gotten this far into Moira?

"Huntyr!" Voiler's voice rang through the castle. "On your right!"

I spun just in time to see another decaying corpse's jaws coming straight toward me.

I raised Venom, but Voiler was already there, leaping onto the creature's back and twisting its head from its body.

Hells.

"Thank you," I breathed.

She nodded. "You take the left side. I've got your back."

Ashlani cried out in horror and disgust behind us, clearly not used to seeing these morbid creatures.

"No," I argued. "I can fend them off. Go find the others. We need to secure the entire castle. There could be hundreds more waiting for us outside."

She hesitated at first; I could tell she wasn't comfortable leaving me alone.

"Go!" I urged.

But she clenched her jaw and ran back down the hallway leading to the bedrooms, where the others would get ready to fight.

I just had to hold the vampyres off long enough for the others to get here.

Wolf. Where was Wolf? Where was Headmistress? Where was *anyone?*

I crept forward until the hallway split in two. The right led to the courtyard, to the center of the castle. The left led toward the front gates.

I turned left.

Another scream rang out in the distance, one that made the hair on the back of my neck stand straight up.

Fighting these creatures in such a beautiful, protected castle sent an eerie wave of terror down my spine. This was much, much different from fighting these things in Midgrave, in the crumbling town of chaos and poverty.

These half-dead beasts had somehow managed to get into Moira Seminary, which was blessed by the archangels and protected by dozens of powerful, magic-wielding fae.

I shook my head. I couldn't think of that right now. The only thing I could afford to focus on was the next kill.

The next creature.

Soon enough, I was forced to focus on only the way my blade sliced into another demon's chest.

Cutting off another creature's head.

An arm.

Another chest.

I killed and killed, making my way down the hallway as I waited for Voiler to return with the other fighters.

Some goddess-damned help would be nice.

Two more vampyres approached. I turned, risking a glance over my shoulder to see if someone—anyone—was coming to help me fight them off, but found a hallway full of corpses.

No, it was just me.

Me and more bloodsuckers.

A roar of frustration escaped me. My shoulder burned as I lifted Venom again, diving the gore-covered blade into another vampyre's heart.

I moved to pull the blade out, but my hand slipped.

Fuck.

There was too much blood, making everything slippery.

The second vampyre sunk its teeth into my other shoulder.

I shoved it away, its predatory growl making me shiver as I scrambled to find Venom's handle.

The body around my blade crumbled. I pulled Venom

out just in time. But not before one of the boney, sharp claws sliced my thigh.

I stabbed the second in the chest before limping over both bodies.

Keep moving, Huntyr. That won't be the last.

Exhaustion tore away at my limbs, the gouge on my thigh burning. I was losing blood, way too much blood.

Where were the mentors? The protectors? The other fighters in this damn castle? Why was I the only one fending them off? The entire castle would be taken, I was sure of it.

I could fight a few vampyres, sure. But this?

There were too fucking many.

My movements grew sluggish, as did my senses. I was too distracted by the radiating pain in my thigh to notice the vampyre approaching behind me.

When its disgusting fingertips dug into my shoulders, I spun, but it was too late. The creature's weight had thrown me off balance, and we both fell to the ground with a thud, the decomposing body falling on top of me.

I cried out, immediately scrambling to get the creature off me, but not before its teeth dug into my bicep.

I tried to dig deep, tried to find some hidden source of strength deep inside of me to fight harder, to shove its crumbling body off mine, but I had already lost too much blood. My vision blurred, my limbs grew weaker with every agonizing draw of blood into the creature's mouth.

I hated it. I fucking hated this academy for allowing these vampyres to enter. I hated myself for allowing the damn thing to get this close.

"Huntyr!" Wolf's voice filled the hallway, a low boom that forced my eyes to shoot open.

Within two seconds, Wolf had found me. He ripped the creature's head from its body, throwing both to the floor beside me.

And then he was there, kneeling next to me, wiping the blood from my face, my shoulders.

"There were too many," I gasped.

"I know," Wolf said as he tore off a piece of his shirt, tying it around my thigh.

"I killed so many, but they kept coming."

"I know, Huntress." His eyes were dark, his brows drawn together in concern. "Stay awake for me. Don't close your eyes."

"I don't want to fight," I slurred. I couldn't tell if I had said the words out loud or in my delusional mind, but Wolf's eyes found mine, needy and desperate.

"Fuck," he cursed. "You're coming with me. We have to get out of this hallway."

I barely registered him lifting me, carrying me over the scattered bodies.

Wolf's heart beating against my ear became the one thing I held onto, the one thing that stopped me from slipping away into oblivion.

I fought. For him, I fought to stay awake. But somewhere in the castle, somewhere amidst shadows and death and fighting, my eyes fell closed.

And I was too far gone to open them again.

THIRTY

Wolf whispered in the distance, and I thought it might still be my dream, somewhere that wasn't reality.

Wasn't the castle.

Wasn't this horrid, vampyre-dwelling place.

I tried to blink my eyes open, but the light was far too bright. I shut them again and listened for Wolf's voice, focusing on him, on the one thing I knew was real.

"She wasn't supposed to get hurt," Wolf said.

"And it was your job to ensure she was out of the way, Wolf. You could have mentioned the fact that she would slaughter every fucking vampyre we sent in there."

"That wasn't the plan, and you know it." He sounded angry, confused.

What were they talking about?

"It all turned out as it should have. The girl is fine, and the job was complete. He only wanted to send a message."

Wolf growled. "She was seconds away from being devoured by one of your monsters!"

Whoever Wolf was talking to huffed. "Monsters? Really, Wolf? It had to be done."

"It didn't, and it won't happen again. You can get the fuck out of here and tell him that it's over. I'm doing everything I was told."

A pause filled the air.

"Fine," the male replied. "For what it's worth, I never intended for him to send that many vampyres. It was only supposed to be a couple."

"Just get out," Wolf sighed. "Before anyone finds you here."

What. The. Fuck.

Wolf knew about the attack? No, he partially *planned* the attack?

I heard a door shut before I forced my eyes open, squinting against the pain.

"Huntyr." Wolf stepped to the side of my bed. "You're awake."

"Get away from me," I said against my dry throat. "Get the fuck away."

He held his hands out in surrender. "It's not what you think."

"I said get back! Who the fuck are you, Wolf? You knew the vampyres were going to attack? No, you knew they were sent to attack?"

I sat up in bed and rubbed my fingers against my pounding temple. This was all too much, too much to process.

Too fucking painful.

Wolf was supposed to be on my side. He was the one that—despite every fucking thing in my life telling me not to—I actually trusted. I'd let him in. I let him see some of that darkness.

All for what? Another betrayal? Another stab in the fucking back?

"Let me explain," Wolf begged. I saw it there again: the desperation in his eyes. The same desperation I saw when he knelt over my body, right after saving my life.

Again.

I would be dead if it wasn't for him. Is that why this hurt so fucking much?

My vision blurred again, but not from physical pain. It was an ache deep in my soul, one that only resulted from me lowering those sharp, violent teeth and actually letting someone else in.

Pain exploded everywhere.

I stood from the bed, not bothering to put my shoes on, and stumbled out the door. Wolf yelled things after me, but I didn't stop. Tears burned my eyes. I didn't want him to see this side of me: weak. Broken.

Betrayed.

"Huntyr!" Ashlani's voice caught my attention. She stood down the hallway at her door, looking at me in horror. Wolf froze behind me.

I was seconds away from letting the tears fall. I didn't realize I had leaned toward Ashlani until her hands were on my shoulders, pulling me inside, holding me up. I vaguely heard her cursing something at Wolf, vaguely heard him cursing back.

And then the door shut behind me.

"What the fuck did he do to you?" Ashlani scanned my body with her eyes. Voiler immediately shot up in bed. "Did he touch you? Did he hurt you?"

"No," I sighed, but the tears fell down my face, anyway. Hells, it had been so long since I last cried. "He didn't touch me, I just... I needed to get out of there."

Ashlani guided me to sit on her bed. "It's okay," she sighed. "You're with us now. Take all the time you need."

I stayed in that room for the rest of the day until the sun went down through the small stone window. I drifted in and out of sleep, still healing from the attack.

Voiler explained that the Headmistress had been out of the castle at the same time the vampyres attacked. Wolf and Commander Macanthos killed most of them, while Voiler and the other students managed to kill the rest.

Hells.

The castle had felt eerie before, but now that we knew vampyres could attack at any moment?

Something wasn't right.

That, mixed with the pit in my stomach caused by Wolf's betrayal....

I felt sick. What in all hells was he doing? Why would he want vampyres to attack? Was it to weaken the other candidates? To show power?

And h*ow*?

Ashlani and Voiler both drifted to sleep on Voiler's bed. I waited until I knew they wouldn't wake before sneaking out of the room and creeping out of the castle. Blood still smeared the walls, the smell of death lingering as I walked further and further.

Air. I needed air.

It was too close to the Transcendent to let myself fall apart.

The moon shone down in full force from above. My feet moved automatically into the forest, and before I knew it, the trees above had swallowed me in darkness.

Right now, running into those woods and never returning sounded pretty damn appetizing. This had all gotten too messy, too complicated.

I should have listened to Lord. I should have shut out every single fucking person who tried to talk to me in Moira. I should have kept my head down like I was told, not partner with the fallen angel.

Shame, anger, betrayal. It all fueled my blood. I ripped through the thick forest, stomping forward as if every single step away from the academy would fix this mess.

I heard him behind me a few moments later.

It wasn't unexpected. To be honest, I was surprised he didn't bust down Ashlani's door to get to me.

I didn't turn around as Wolf approached, stopping just a few feet behind me. Every sense of mine became aware of him: of his breathing, of his scent, of the soft breeze from his wings as he tucked them behind his shoulders.

"I thought I told you to leave me alone," I breathed.

"You did."

"Then what didn't you understand, Wolf? Or are you here to torture me some more with your pretty fucking lies?"

He huffed. "You think my lies are pretty?"

I spun around, teeth clenched. That charm was useless now. The soft spot inside of me that used to light up at that smile was iced over, guarded with knives.

"What do you want from me?"

Wolf's smug smile slowly dissolved from his face. He looked so naked without it, so vulnerable. "You need to know the truth," he admitted.

"Stop." I held up my hands. "I honestly do not have the strength to hear any more bullshit from you, Wolf."

He shook his head. "It's not bullshit."

"And how am I supposed to believe that? How am I really supposed to believe that you're going to tell me the truth about everything? You knew about the vampyre attack! You—you helped them? I have no fucking clue why you would do something like that!"

"Because," he said, stepping forward and lowering his voice, "I've wanted to tell you for weeks now, Huntress. It's been fucking killing me that I wasn't honest with you, and I know it's too late. I know I fucked it all up. But if you're going to hate me anyway, I want you to hate me because of this."

I froze. "Because of what?"

"I only told you half of the truth before when I explained why I fell as an angel. It's because of my father, yes, but it's because of what he turned me into."

"What are you talking about?"

He closed his eyes, his entire body tense. I was about to curse at him, was about to brush past him and leave him here in the forest, but some invisible force made me freeze.

When he opened his mouth again, I saw them.

The razor-sharp vampyre fangs protruding from his teeth.

I gasped, stumbling backward.

"He forced me to turn. He used dark magic from the archangels and *forced* me to be his sacrifice. But angels are of a pure bloodline, and vampyres are not." Pain laced every word that tumbled from his lips, as if the words alone hurt him to speak. "I didn't think I would survive the transition, but I did. He forced me to turn into a vampyre, Huntyr. And when I woke, my wings were black. I was fallen. I could not be an angel and a vampyre. He turned me into an abomination."

Wolf could barely look at me.

"No," I mumbled, my body trembling. "It's not possible. Angels cannot be half-vampyre."

"It *is* possible," he pleaded, taking a hesitant step toward me. "Look at me, Huntyr. Look at what I am. I was not born this way, I was turned."

Fuck. Wolf stood before me, rigid and terrified and raw, with pleading eyes that made me want to retch.

"Why would your father do that to you? Why would he turn you into this?"

Wolf shook his head. "He wants power. He thought that by turning me into one of them, we could control them. Scarlata Empire fell, Huntyr, but it won't stay fallen forever."

My breath escaped me. "Your father wants you to control vampyres?" Pieces fell together in my mind. I knew what it was like to have a man controlling you. But this? This was evil. This was wrong.

He nodded.

"Was he the one who planned the attack?"

Wolf took half a step forward. "It wasn't supposed to happen that way, I swear to you."

"How can I believe you? How can I believe any of this? I don't trust you, Wolf," I whispered. "You lied to me about everything!"

His expression fell further. "I don't expect you to. I lost your trust. I accept that."

"Then why bother? Why show me this? Why follow me out here and tell me all this when you know I'll never trust you again?"

"I had to tell you the truth."

"But why?" My words cascaded from a whisper to a roar of unsaid words, of hidden emotions. "Why tell me you're a *vampyre* when you know what I am? You know what I do, Wolf! You know what I was trained for my entire life, what I was trained to kill!"

I unsheathed Venom from my thigh, turning her in my palm.

Wolf's eyes shifted to Venom, then back to me.

He fell to his knees.

"Wolf," I breathed.

He raised his chin, exposing his chest. "If you have to kill me, kill me. I deserve much worse than death at your hands, Huntress."

"Don't you dare," I whispered. "You're a fucking coward for this, Wolf."

"I'm a vampyre, you're a vampyre killer. I knew what the risk of telling you this truth was, and I'm willing to pay the price." His icy eyes glittered with intense lightning before he closed them. "Do it."

"But it's *you*!" My voice broke. I dropped to my knees in front of him, crumbling in surrender the same fragile way he did. "How am I supposed to look at you, beautiful and tragic, and shove this blade into your chest? How am I supposed to kill you when you're the only fucking person who's made me feel—" My words quivered, my hands rattled.

He blinked. "What? Who's made you feel what, Huntress?"

A sickening numbness spread through my chest, radiating down my stomach.

He knew exactly what he made me feel; he had seen it in my eyes, in the half-truths and passing touches.

Wolf's hands caressed my shoulders, his thumb moving to my chin, forcing me to look at him. With his other hand, he slid down my arm, shifting my dagger up to touch his chest.

All I had to do was apply the pressure. All I had to do was finish it, finish him.

I saw it in his eyes, too. He wanted me to do it. He had submitted to me fully, had given up on his side of the fight.

"A vampyre," I breathed. "How could you have kept this from me? You knew who I was, Wolf. You saw me in Midgrave." But my words weren't angry anymore, they were barely audible. No, I didn't have the energy to be angry.

Everything fucking hurt. My voice cracked again. The tears I had been holding back fell freely down my face.

Wolf's face softened too, as if that was even possible. He caressed my face, running his thumb over my wet cheeks. "I didn't plan this—fuck. I didn't plan to grow close to you. I swear to all goddesses, Huntyr, I never meant to lie to you. I would shove that dagger in my chest myself if I thought it would keep you from this."

A sob wracked my body. I couldn't do this. I couldn't kill him. I dropped the dagger to the ground beside us, and before I knew it, Wolf was holding me up, caressing me, pulling me to his lap.

He murmured against my ear, encapsulating me in his arms, spreading his angel wings around us. He held me tightly, as if holding onto me could take back the absolute chaos of pain and lies and betrayal.

I couldn't fucking take it anymore, couldn't take another betrayal.

"I-I need space." I mumbled through my tears and shoved myself away from him, horrified by the fact that a vampyre had been comforting me.

Wolf's eyes widened as he searched my face for answers.

I wiped my face with the back of my hand. "Just leave me alone, okay? I need to think. I can't handle this right now." When I rose to my feet and stumbled back toward the castle, Wolf did not follow me.

I hated him for lying. I hated him for taking care of me, for saving my life so many times. I hated him for standing up to Lanson and Espek and Ryder. I hated him for being here, for holding me while I cried.

And I hated him the most because I didn't hate him at all.

CHAPTER
THIRTY-ONE

Everything was falling apart.

I couldn't trust Wolf. Not only did he hide the truth from me, but he was a vampyre. He was an abomination. He was half a blood-sucking monster.

How was I supposed to put my life in his hands during the final test? How was I supposed to count on him to protect me?

Wolf didn't come back that night. I lay in bed above the covers, listening to the wind howl outside for hours on end. Each creak of stone in the hallway, each howl of wind outside the window, made my heart skip.

The Transcendent was starting today.

I couldn't help but wonder if Wolf was out there somewhere drinking someone's blood, or maybe he had run away for good, left me here to complete the final test alone.

Hells, maybe I would be safer alone.

By the time the sun crept through the tiny window in

our stone bedroom, I had convinced myself Wolf was gone. He was never coming back.

I would have to deal with it.

I sat up in bed, laced my boots on, and tied my black curly hair in a tight bun at the base of my neck.

My entire life, I counted on myself to survive. This was nothing different.

I took one large breath, swung my bedroom door open and—

"What in all hells?" I nearly tripped over the large body lying right in front of my door.

It was Wolf, his black angel wings tucked around him while he slept.

His eyes shot open when he heard me.

"What are you doing out here?" I asked, trying and failing to keep my voice at a whisper. "Have you been here all night?"

He pushed himself to his feet and cleared his throat. "I wanted to give you space."

I glanced down the hallway, ensuring everyone else's bedroom doors were closed before gripping his wrist and pulling him inside. "Are you serious right now?" I closed the door behind us and pressed my back against it.

He ran both hands through his messy, slept-on hair. "I couldn't leave you, Huntyr. You need someone to get through the Transcendent with, and I'm here. We've been practicing for this."

"That was before!"

"I still need to get into The Golden City. So do you. Nothing has changed—"

"*Everything* has changed! Goddess above, Wolf! Everything is different now!"

His shoulders slumped. "I don't expect you to forgive me, but let me do this. Let me help you through this test, and you'll never have to talk to me again once we get into The Golden City."

"How? How do I forget everything after last night and pretend like this is normal?"

Wolf took half a step forward. "You look into my eyes, and you feel your own heart when I tell you I will die before I let anything happen to you, Huntress. You're safe with me, and you might not want to believe it, but deep inside of you somewhere I know you can feel that truth."

There was no arrogant smirk, no teasing smile.

And damn it all, because he was right. He lied to me, but something inside of me urged me to trust what he was saying. He would keep me safe.

I didn't want to partner with Wolf for the Transcendent, but I also didn't want to die. Wolf kept secrets. He lied to me about who—*what*—he was. Even thinking about it now sent a vile taste to my mouth.

I could never fucking trust him again when it came to his intentions. But I knew one thing: Wolf would not let me die during this test. If I wanted to get into The Golden City, this was my best shot.

"Fine," I replied. "Get ready. We don't want to be late."

I spun around and slid out of the bedroom, leaving him there alone. I couldn't be around him any more than I absolutely needed to. Wolf had a way of infiltrating my every waking thought, of making me forget all the horrible things about him.

Fuck.

I hated that I still needed him, hated that I felt safe near him.

He was a vampyre, the one thing I had spent my entire life killing, training to kill.

Hating.

But Wolf was nothing like those vampyres I had slain so many times. He wasn't incoherent; he wasn't rabid. His body wasn't decomposing as he stopped at nothing to get my blood.

No, Wolf was more angel than vampyre, more god than demon.

He was a beautiful predator, hidden in plain sight.

Last night's revelation had shattered everything I knew to be true about the bloodsucking monsters. I had been with Wolf for weeks now, had been sleeping in this room beside him, and not once did he do anything but protect me.

Well, there was the time he punched me in the face during training to make a point, but that was different.

Even then, he was protecting me.

Wolf emerged from the bathroom wearing his training leathers. His muscles had leaned out in the weeks at the academy, and even the holsters on his thighs seemed to bulge against the sheer muscle of him.

"I know you don't trust me," Wolf said as he stepped toward me. "I don't blame you. But I will protect you,

Huntress. I spent every fucking day since I met you trying to keep you safe, and I won't stop. Not now."

I clenched my jaw, trying to swallow down the wave of emotion that followed. I didn't have the time or the energy for this, and I had cried way too much last night to let a single tear fall today.

"Let's just get this over with," I retorted. "We don't have to be friends, Wolf. We both do our parts to stay alive, and as soon as we're in The Golden City, we'll go our separate ways."

His nostrils flared, but he eventually nodded.

We both turned and funneled out the door, following the rest of the students silently into the study chamber.

Everyone dressed in their best leathers and tactical gear. Weapons strapped across chests, thighs, backs. The rest of the females had their hair tied back tightly, ready for combat.

It's ridiculous, I thought. We did not know what we were stepping into, only that it was dangerous. It was possible that no combat would be involved at all, but that's what was so terrifying: not knowing.

Nobody spoke as we all took our seats in the main study room, waiting for instructions from the three mentors that stood in the room's front.

Everyone looked grim. Hells, it was palpable.

Half of this room would likely be dead by the end of the week. Earlier in the academy, we would have bothered with snide comments or cruel insults, but not today. Today, we all looked straight ahead, chins up and fists tightened.

Nobody was getting through this unscathed. *Nobody.*

"You've made it this far," Headmistress Katherine announced, clasping her hands before her. "You've survived training that not everyone could survive. You've surpassed both physical and mental tests of combat and magic. Now it's time for your final test."

I fought the urge to slide my chair closer to Wolf's. I was a fucking coward for craving the enemy; I knew that. But I also knew that having him by my side during the Transcendent was my best shot at surviving. He had powerful magic, and I could barely summon my own. I needed him whether I wanted to admit it or not.

Commander Macanthos stepped forward. "Drink this and let the tests begin. Fail to drink, and you will surely die. When you wake, your life will not be the same."

What? The final test was to drink from this cauldron?

A few whispers filled the room, everyone just as confused as I was. I snuck a glance at Wolf. He swallowed, the only sign at all of his uncertainty.

"It's not poison, is it?" Ashlani asked.

"Drink," was all the commander said as he passed the cauldron to the first apprentice near the front of the room.

I didn't see a way out of this. Whatever would happen after we drank that liquid would be up to the goddess. Hells. If I went through this entire seminary only to be killed by some liquid, I would be better off dead. I could never face Lord that way.

"It'll be okay," Wolf whispered to me.

The first person drank from the cauldron, tensing, but

easily passed it to the second student. Then the third. The fourth.

Nothing seemed to happen.

"How do you know that?" I asked.

Wolf's hand fell onto my shoulder, his fingers splaying over the back of my neck. "I'll always come find you."

I turned to look at him, only to find a soft, broken smile on his face.

I couldn't stop myself. I smiled back.

Then I took the cauldron. My hands shook. Wolf was the only one close enough to notice.

Hells. There was no turning back now. All of this training, an entire life of killing and murder and fighting and bleeding. It all came down to *this*.

Fear threatened to paralyze me, but I focused on Wolf's hand on my shoulder. I focused on the adrenaline pounding in my veins, looking for a fight.

I put the cauldron to my lips.

I let the liquid pour into my mouth.

And I swallowed it.

I expected fire, death, pain. But none of that came. I passed the cauldron to Wolf, watching him do the same, before he, too, passed it on.

We all looked to the front of the classroom, where the first students took the drinks.

Only a few more seconds passed before bodies hit the floor one by one.

"Huntress," Wolf breathed next to me. Or maybe I imagined it? I tried to turn and look at him, but my vision blurred. The lights in the room grew much, much too bright, before everything faded to a deep, comforting black.

I let the darkness come.

I often felt strongest in its depths, anyway.

I reached for Wolf's hands before I fell, but he wasn't there. Nobody was. It was just me, just as it always was.

Just as it always would be.

"Huntyr, Huntyr! Wake up, Huntyr, we have to move. We have to go, now!" Wolf's voice echoed through the comforting, dark numbness. I didn't want to leave the soft caress of home, but something in his voice—something that hurt me to hear—forced my eyes open.

Fuck.

Fire erupted around us. We were no longer in the castle, no. We were now in a forest with thick, overgrown trees towering above.

Wolf was leaning over me, shaking my shoulders. He cursed as soon as he saw my eyes open, his pupils swarming with lightning.

"What—"

"Get up," he hissed.

I scrambled to my feet, hearing an anguished cry in the distance.

Someone stepped behind Wolf, weapon raised.

Wolf spun and swatted the weapon from their grip before snapping their neck.

Fuck.

I turned, looking for a path out of here, away from the chaos. Everyone fought. I glimpsed Lanson's figure in the distance, battling for power with another fae I didn't recognize.

Heat overtook each sense. Trees burned around us, limbs fell.

Wolf was right. We had to get out of here as fast as possible.

He grabbed my hand and pulled me, leading us through one of the few openings in the trees that weren't erupting in flames.

"Huntyr!" a female voice screamed out.

Ashlani's voice.

I spun, looking for her in the flames and chaos. "Ashlani? Where are you?"

Wolf tried to pull my arm, but I shook it free and continued back toward the fighting. If she needed help, I would help her. I would not have Ashlani's death on my shoulders, too.

A hand shot from the smoke and latched onto my forearm, fingernails digging into my skin.

I aimed Venom directly at their chest before recognizing the blonde, singed hair. "Hells," I gasped. Her face had been coated in blood, her eyes covered in smoke and her hair all but burnt off.

"You're hurt," I mumbled.

Wolf yelled something else behind me.

Ashlani's eyes widened; she must not have realized that she was injured.

She looked down at her torso. I followed her gaze.

"No," I breathed. Someone's dagger protruded from her stomach, so deep that only the handle was visible.

She looked back at me, a single tear slipping through the blood on her face. "It's okay, Huntyr," she cried.

Someone's war cry shook the surrounding air. Wolf's hands fell on my shoulders.

Another body fell behind Ashlani.

A vampyre.

We weren't the only ones fighting out here. We weren't the only danger to one another.

"Ashlani, we have to go," I urged, pulling her toward me. "We can patch your wound as soon as we get somewhere safe. Come with us!"

Ashlani's features cracked before her knees gave out. I tried to catch her as she fell against me, sinking to the ground.

More chaos, more screaming.

"We have to go," Wolf hissed behind me. "She's fatally injured. She won't make it!"

"I'm not leaving her!" I yelled. "Just help me carry her and we can help her when we get—"

"Huntyr," Ashlani interrupted me, her words slurring. "You have to go," she said. "You'll make it to The Golden

City, I know you will. You were born for this." The soft smile on her face was one that I had seen too many times.

Ashlani was too kind, too innocent. She didn't deserve any of this.

My stomach hurled. "I'm not leaving you!"

Her hands moved to grip the handle of the knife in her belly. Before I could object, she pulled out the blade.

Blood poured from the open wound.

"Go," she said, voice fainter now.

I shook my head. "I'm no—"

"Go!" she rasped.

Wolf was pulling me, holding me, carrying me through the scorching forest of death and teeth and evil.

But I couldn't take my eyes off Ashlani. She fell to her knees as Wolf dragged me further and further from the chaos. A few moments passed, and a scream split the air before I realized it was mine.

Ashlani fell to the ground motionless before her body was engulfed in flames.

No.

But Wolf kept moving, dragging me further and further away. When I stopped screaming, he set me down but gripped my wrist as we marched. When he stepped over a burning log, I followed, not even feeling the pain.

And then we were running.

He pulled me along, keeping me on my feet. I focused on my breath, matched my inhales with the pounding of my boots against the forest floor. The worst of the fire was behind us, giving us a clear view of the trees ahead.

It was infinitely dark. There was no moon, no stars

keeping the shadows at bay. Even my fae eyes struggled to see the next step.

But every time I fell in exhaustion, Wolf was there, pulling me up.

My lungs burned, and my muscles ached, but I welcomed the pain. It was the only thing I could hold onto that reminded me this was real. It wasn't a sick dream that I would wake up from tomorrow.

This was actually happening.

We had to have run multiple miles, covering ourselves in dirt and mud and scrapes from the thick forest, before Wolf finally slowed down.

"What is this?" I asked. "If this is the final test, what was that slaughter? Why did—why did—"

"It started with the vampyres back there," Wolf explained. He wasn't nearly as out of breath as I was. "They didn't know how to react. At first, it was us against them, but something changed. The first few fae went down, and everyone panicked. It's a survival instinct; you'll kill anyone who might possibly be your enemy if you don't think you can fight them."

I didn't think about Ashlani. Didn't think about Voiler. Didn't think about Lanson. Didn't think about the evil, catastrophic scene we had barely escaped from.

"Some of them are still asleep," I breathed.

"I know."

"They'll burn alive. That, or the vampyres will get to their bodies before they wake up."

Another breath. "I know."

Wolf kept walking, not missing a single step as we

maneuvered through the thickening trees and fallen logs. He didn't seem the least bit shaken from what we just witnessed.

"Where are you going?" I asked. "What's our plan?"

He stopped, hands dropping at his sides, and spun to face me. "My plan is to get as far away from whatever the fuck just happened, Huntress."

I flinched at the harshness of his words.

"Do you know what I thought when I found you unconscious? I had no fucking clue what was happening when I woke up. I thought... I thought..."

"Hey," I said, stepping closer. This was not the time to be pissed off at him for lying to me. This was life or death, and I needed him to survive. "I'm right here. We made it out of there, okay?"

He shook his head, refusing to look at me.

"Wolf," I repeated. I slid my shaking hands up his chest, feeling his rapid heartbeat beneath my palms. "Look at me."

He swallowed but obeyed, eyes meeting mine with a palpable heat. "I can't lose you. Not after all of this."

"You won't," I promised. "I'm alive, okay? I'm right here."

He shook his head again, as if refusing to see the truth. I reached out and grabbed his hand, placing it on my chest. Holding it there.

"I'm right here," I repeated. "I'm alive."

Wolf's eyes fell to his hand that now pressed against my chest, just over my beating heart. I needed him to be okay, needed him to believe this. Whatever happened back there was just one of many tests we were about to face.

I needed him to fight.

His brows drew together as he pulled his hand away. "We should find somewhere safe, somewhere with high ground."

"You could fly," I suggested, glancing up at the darkening sky.

Wolf shook his head. "Everyone will see me flying. We already know there are vampyres in these woods, and we don't need to draw any attention our way."

I bit my tongue. Wolf spoke about the vampyres as if he wasn't one himself.

He had been doing it the entire time we had been at this academy. Even before then, back when I ran into him in Midgrave. He acted like he was different from them, and maybe, in his eyes, he was.

But in mine?

I had no fucking clue what he was.

I turned away and focused on my surroundings, on the current problem. Wolf was right. As easy as it would be for him to fly above the forest, it was too dangerous. We couldn't trust the other students, and we sure as hell couldn't attract any vampyres.

The thick forest was damn near impossible to maneuver through. We couldn't take a single step without pushing through sharp foliage, but we had no other choice.

Until I heard the thin trickle of water running in the distance. It wasn't perfect, but it was a start. "Then we follow the sound of that stream, and we track it uphill."

Wolf nodded.

It was something to keep us moving forward, to keep us from becoming paralyzed in this massive fucking forest with no idea as to what was going on.

If we stopped, we would die. And we sure as all hells were not about to return to the chaos we just ran from. That much we knew.

I bent over, holding myself up with my hands on my knees while I took three large breaths. I tried not to picture Ashlani's burnt face as she called my name.

Fuck.

"Are you feeling okay?" Wolf asked.

Absolutely not. Not in the slightest.

"I'm fine," I replied, pushing myself back up. I didn't look at him. I couldn't. "Let's just keep moving."

And we did. For hours, we walked forward, following the sound of the stream uphill. We didn't know where we were, what would happen to us.

But we were together. That alone gave me a comfort that I was sure I would be paralyzed without. Ashlani was gone. Voiler was either alive or dead. Lanson had turned into a desperate killer.

I followed Wolf's heels through the darkness as we continued. He slowed his pace when he noticed me falling behind, but otherwise, we didn't speak.

Forward, forward, forward.

We would make it into that damn Golden City, or we would die trying to get there.

THIRTY-TWO

Without a fire, the frosty night grew unbearable. Wolf and I eventually found a small clearing beneath a large, thick tree, which offered us enough coverage from any fae who might summon their wings and fly above.

I was too exhausted to fight the need for sleep that approached with every passing minute, too tired to worry about vampyres or predators or anything else that might wait for us out here.

We needed sleep, even if it was a mere hour.

I sat on the cold ground with my back against the tree bark. My leathers did what they could to keep my body heat around me, but with the crash from the adrenaline earlier and the lack of substantial food, I grew weary with every second.

Wolf busied himself building a small trap so we could catch something while we slept.

I cleared my throat. "Can I ask you something?"

He paused and looked back at me, his wings swinging out of the way. "Anything."

"You're half vampyre, so does that mean you crave blood?"

He tensed. Even his wings seemed to tuck tighter behind his shoulders. He dropped the trap he was working on and faced me fully, giving me every ounce of his attention. "I crave blood, yes, but not the same way the monsters you kill crave it."

"But you drink it?"

Wolf rolled his head back, rubbing a hand at the back of his neck. He didn't want to answer. Of course he didn't. We both knew what the answer would be.

"Sometimes, yes."

"Can you live without it?"

He stilled. His dark eyes met mine. "No. I can't live without blood."

That was everything I needed to know. I tucked my legs up to my chest and breathed in the freezing night air. "I figured."

Wolf stood still for a second before approaching me. He took the few steps to my spot beneath the tree and knelt in front of me, inches from touching my knees. I would've flinched away if I had an ounce of extra energy to give.

"What are you doing?" I whispered.

He leaned forward, ensuring I had nowhere to look but him. "I would never feed from you, Huntyr. You have to believe that. There is no craving that would make me betray that. There is no amount of hunger that would force me to turn on you. I would die first, I swear by the goddess."

This was Wolf—the arrogant, prickly, dangerous, deadly angel that made everyone turn the other way. Wolf was dark and alluring and tempting, but this?

This was a plea. This was raw. Wolf begged me to believe him.

"Is it true what they taught us in Moira? You still have a soul?"

Wolf cracked the fraction of a smile. "What do you think?"

What *did* I think? "I thought I knew you," I whispered. "I thought you were a fallen angel. I thought you wanted to protect me."

He leaned closer. The heat of his breath had me leaning forward, too. "And now?"

I closed my eyes but didn't back away. "I think you hurt me. And I never thought you, of all people, would be capable of that."

When I finally opened my eyes, I saw Wolf staring at me, but it wasn't the same soft Wolf that had been there moments before. His walls had been rebuilt, the mask of arrogance and cold replacing whatever emotion had been there before.

My words hurt him. *Good. They should hurt him.* He hurt me ten fucking times over.

Wolf retreated, returning to finish the trap he had been working on setting. I didn't say another word. I didn't apologize, didn't backtrack.

It was the truth.

I leaned my head back on the tree bark and let my eyes flutter shut again. Everything hurt. The numbness in my body had morphed to a constant prickling from the freezing environment. Sleep wouldn't even be possible if it weren't for the sheer exhaustion washing over me.

I took a few long breaths and let the cold take over.

I wasn't cold when I woke up. Not in the slightest. I nuzzled deeper into the soft warmth beside me, not wanting to fully wake up.

Until I realized what—*who*—I nuzzled against.

I sat up with a gasp, pushing off Wolf's solid chest and sliding away from him.

He grunted and opened his eyes. "What is it?" he rasped with exhaustion.

"Nothing," I answered, running my hands through my hair. The sun had just risen; there was no way we had slept more than one hour. "I just—I didn't know—"

"Come back here," he demanded, re-closing his eyes and letting his head fall back on the forest ground.

I froze. "What?"

"It's freezing, and you're being stubborn. You need more sleep. Get back over here, Huntress."

Perhaps Wolf was far too delirious to realize just what he was asking.

"We've shared a bed before," he said, reading my thoughts.

"That was different," I replied. "I didn't know you were a bloodsucker then."

"I didn't sink my teeth into your veins then, and I certainly won't now. Come. Here."

Fuck. The utter demand in his words could not be denied, even by me. I was too tired to fight it, too cold now to make sense of how I felt.

So I moved closer to him and laid my head on his chest, wrapping my arms around his torso. He lifted the edge of his jacket and slipped my hand beneath, in between his shirt and the warmed leather from his body heat.

I couldn't stop the sigh of relief that escaped me.

Wolf said nothing, though. Didn't make any sexual jokes, didn't laugh at my obvious moment of weakness.

He just wrapped his arms around me, pressing my body to his, and fell back asleep.

With my ear pressed against his chest, I listened to the subtle drum of his heart. Listened to the constant pounding, the perfect rhythm.

"Huntyr," a familiar voice pulled me from my sleep. "Huntyr, wake up."

I blinked my eyes open, still wrapped in Wolf's arms.

But that voice sounded so familiar...

"Rummy?" I sat up, careful not to wake Wolf. "Is that you?"

Her familiar laugh, bubbly and warm, filled the space around me.

I stood up and walked toward the trees, finding her leaning across the bark in the same black leather jacket she always wore.

"Hells," I breathed. "It really is you. What are you doing here?"

She crossed her arms over her chest and smiled, as if she had meant to surprise me all along. "Happy to see me?"

"Happy?" I couldn't contain my excitement. I ran to her and pulled her to my chest, hugging her tighter than ever.

Rummy and I weren't much for physical affection, but I would make an exception this time. My chest swelled with happiness. She laughed and hugged me, too, wrapping her arms around my scarred back.

But when she pulled away, her smile had faded. "I came here to tell you something, Hunt."

My stomach dropped. "Tell me what? How did you even find me? We're in the middle of the Transcendent."

"I know. That's why I had to come find you myself. It's Lord."

I blinked. "What?"

"He's sick, he... he isn't in his right mind."

"What do you mean? What's wrong with him?"

"Maybe I should show you instead."

She turned and began walking deeper into the forest. I glanced over my shoulder, ensuring Wolf still slept soundly, and followed Rummy.

Lord needed me.

I couldn't wait.

"Wait up!" I called after Rummy. She maneuvered through the thick forest like she knew exactly where she was headed, like she had been through here dozens of times before.

Still, I ran after her.

In all the years I'd known Lord, I had never seen him sick. I had never seen him injured. Even when he fought off vampyres, he remained unscathed. The only blood that ever marked his skin was the blood of those killers.

If what Rummy said was true, things must have gotten very bad.

"This way!" she yelled.

"Are you sure you know where you're going?"

We wound through the thick trees. The bushes scratched my legs and tore at my skin, but I kept moving, kept following Rummy.

She slowed down ahead of me, giving me a chance to catch up.

And then I saw him.

Right in the middle of the clearing lay Lord.

"Hells." I rushed to his side, dropping to my knees. He was wearing the same black clothes he wore every day, but this time, they were ragged and torn. His dark skin had grown ashen, drained of the typical healthy blush.

I thought he would at least be happy to see me, but when he recognized who knelt before him, his face was stripped of all emotion. "Huntyr," he said.

"It's me, Lord."

"Huntyr!" He was yelling now, frantic and afraid. It wasn't like him.

"What happened to him, Rummy?"

I turned to look at Rummy, but she was gone. Nothing but dark forest remained where she stood moments ago.

"Huntyr!" Lord crawled to me, strong yet frail. His eyes were wide; I had never seen so much white in them. I caught his shoulders as he threw himself at me.

"Calm down, Lord! It's me!"

Lord continued to panic. "Huntyr! Huntyr! Help me!"

"I—"

Suddenly, it wasn't Lord at all falling toward me, gripping my shoulders.

It was Wolf.

His eyes searched mine with the same fearful expression I had just seen in Lord.

"Wolf?" I whispered.

"It's me, Huntress. It's not Lord, it's me. I'm here."

"I–I thought I saw..."

His piercing eyes scanned my face. "What? What were you seeing?"

"Rummy was here," I explained. "My best friend from home. She told me Lord needed me, that he was hurt. I didn't want to wake you. Lord looked so—"

Wolf's jaw tightened. "I've been with you this whole time, Huntress. Your friend wasn't here. Neither was Lord."

My heart stopped. "But I saw them."

I became acutely aware of Wolf's hands on my shoulders, of the way they stilled as the realization sank over both of us.

"This is part of the test," he whispered, glancing at the surrounding forest. "You were hallucinating, Huntyr."

I opened my mouth to argue what so clearly could not be the truth, but I stopped myself.

Rummy and Lord in the forest? It didn't make any sense. Why would I be tested this way?

Wolf's eyes widened as they settled on something behind me. I turned to look, but saw nothing.

No.

"Wolf, it's not real," I reminded him. "Whatever you're seeing isn't there. I'm here." I pressed my hands over his. "I'm real."

His eyes flickered between me and whatever he saw behind me. I saw the fight in his darkening eyes, saw him trying to decipher it for himself.

"Stay with me, Wolf. It's not real, remember that."

"Right." He looked at me and smiled, but it wasn't a genuine smile. I knew him enough to know that. "It's not real."

He flinched, pulling out of my grasp and jumping to his feet.

"I did everything you asked," he said to the invisible guest in the forest.

Wolf's hand fell to his sword.

"Wolf," I warned.

He rocked his head. "No, you can't do this to me!"

I screamed his name again, but he couldn't hear me. Not anymore.

His black wings spanned to their full length. "I knew it." His teeth clenched, his fist tightened. "I knew you would turn out to be a coward. I never should have trusted you."

He swung, his sword barely missing me. I crawled out of the way before jumping to my own feet and backing out of his reach.

He swung the sword a second time.

"It isn't real, Wolf!"

We were both screaming, both being way too loud in the forest's silence. Any creatures within miles would hear us.

Any *vampyres*.

"You can't take them!" He staggered backward now, fighting an invisible enemy. "The wings are mine!"

I couldn't just sit here and watch as Wolf swung his massive sword around, attracting all killer creatures to us with every shout.

I walked to the back of him slowly, trying not to draw any attention to myself, trying not to make a sound.

And then launched myself onto his back.

He stumbled even more with my added weight, but he did not fall. I wrapped my legs around his waist from behind and clung to his neck, even as his large black wings moved, trying to push me off.

"Relax!" I whispered directly into his ear, trying to calm

him. "It's me, Wolf! It's just me and you here! You have your wings! Nobody is taking them!"

A few seconds later, he stopped fighting.

"I'm going to climb off you now." I jumped to my feet.

Wolf turned slowly, eyes still wide when they met mine. "It's you," he whispered.

"It's me. But I have a feeling it won't be just us here soon."

A twig snapped.

"Hells," I breathed. "They heard us."

But it was not vampyres that catapulted out of the surrounding woods, teeth barring and claws gaping.

No, what we saw approaching was much, much more horrific.

"You're seeing this too, right?" I whispered, half-sure I was still hallucinating.

"Yes." Wolf's voice cracked. "I see them."

Two creatures, larger than any bear but with half-decaying bodies, sauntered forward. They sniffed the air as if they were looking for something.

Wolf and I stood in horror as their gazes locked on us.

CHAPTER

THIRTY-THREE

"Any chance this dagger takes them down?" I asked, my voice wavering. I gripped my weapon even tighter, trying to ignore the fear that seeped into my body, threatening to paralyze me.

"Sure." Wolf gripped the back of my shirt as we backed up slowly. "As long as it's a magic sword that will burst to flames inside of them."

Fucking hells. "Good, so we have a chance."

The beasts charged us in unison.

"RUN!"

Wolf and I burst into a sprint, maneuvering through the trees and tangled grass of the forest. The beasts behind us, however, didn't have to maneuver at all. Their pure strength burrowed through the trees, tearing through the shrubs.

This was it. We were going to die.

"You have to use your magic!" Wolf narrowly dodged a low tree branch. "It's the only way we'll kill them!"

"Are you kidding? We both know I can't use magic like you can!"

"I'll aim for the beast on the right, but you have to kill the one on the left." Wolf was already summoning his natural magic. I could tell by the wind that pushed at our backs, swirling around us with a mixture of dirt and leaves.

I stole a glance over my shoulder. "If I stop running, they'll kill me!"

"Not if we kill them first."

His words sounded incredibly confident, as if he had no doubt in the world that I could conjure magic and kill the beast.

But he had seen me try and fail with magic dozens of times. How would this time be any different?

Wolf stopped running, leaving me no choice but to stop with him. We spun to find the beasts barreling toward us, slobber dripping from their half-fur, half-bone faces.

"Now, Huntress!" he commanded.

Wolf held his hands out and roared, animalistic and bone-chilling, as the conjured wind blasted at the beasts.

He was buying me time.

Okay, Huntyr. Think. Become one with nature, become one with the elements. If I could conjure even the smallest bit of fire, I could blast them.

But I felt nothing.

Wolf held the wind, but it would not last. Even through his shirt, I could see his flexed muscles doing everything they could to maintain his power.

But with every passing second, that power slipped.

One beast roared, rearing on its hind legs.

"Huntyr!" Wolf yelled, half a plea and half a warning.

My mind drew a blank. I acted on instinct alone.

Bleed and live.

I gripped Venom and sliced my forearm—deep—as I waited for my blood to drip to the ground. I only had seconds before the beasts would break through Wolf's hold.

Bleed and live.

The wave of magic hit me with so much force, I was nearly knocked from my feet. Wolf lost his hold at that same moment, and the beasts came tumbling forward.

Wolf yelled something at me, but I couldn't hear him over the ringing in my ears.

It started in my feet first—the rampant ball of heat that searched for a release, like an animal of its own, seeking prey. By the time the wave of magic had reached my hands, I had one second to aim the power at the beast in front of me before it attacked.

Everything burst into flames, and I held the magic until I was certain that not one but both beasts had been eliminated.

When I finally relaxed, both creatures had turned to ash.

Wolf fell to his knees on my right, clutching his side.

No.

I could not even feel my body, but I ran to him, just in time to see him fall to his back, blood pouring from his abdomen.

I was too late. The beast had clawed him. Deep.

More rustling came from the trees. *That was not the end of this fight.*

Wolf grunted, pulling his hand away to survey the blood that came with it. Both of us heard the second roar of whatever creature lurked out there, no doubt also smelling this blood.

"Come here, Huntress. We have to bond. *Now.*"

THIRTY-FOUR

"What?" I panicked. "*Now* you decide you want to bond with me?" I screamed into the air, no longer caring who heard us. The damage was done. Wolf's blood poured from his abdomen.

Too much blood.

"Now, Huntyr, so I can use your magic to heal!" Wolf growled, baring his teeth. "Or you'll be left to finish this damn Transcendent without me!"

Fucking hells.

I knelt beside him, hands hovering his body. There was so much blood, I had no idea where to start. "Tell me what to do, Wolf."

He grunted in pain. "Combine our blood."

I frantically reached for Venom, not wasting a second before slicing my palm. With Wolf's entire shirt cut open, I had no problem finding an open wound and pressing my bloody palm over it.

"Now what?"

Wolf squeezed his eyes shut. I did the same.

Beasts grew closer with every second.

"Arte magica coniuncta, potentia nostra multiplicatur et floret."

He recited the words that would combine our magic, that would merge us together so he could pull from me. I didn't have time to think about whether it was a good idea, about whether he would drain me of my magic.

The words of the old language fell off his tongue as if he spoke the language himself.

I repeated the ancient words with him.

"Arte magica coniuncta, potentia nostra multiplicatur et floret. Arte magica coniuncta, potentia nostra multiplicatur et floret. Arte magica coniuncta, potentia nostra multiplicatur et floret."

Please, goddess, I begged. *Give to him what you have given to me. Heal him. Let him live.*

A rush of fire filled my veins, followed by a chilling, icy coolness.

It was working. My magic radiated from me, moving to him as if it belonged to him, as if it submitted to him.

As if he owned it.

"Wolf," I breathed. It wasn't painful, but my bones recognized this magic as leaving.

A bond worked both ways. If he took from me, I would have to take something from him.

Wolf grimaced, clutching his healing torso.

I felt the dam of magic raise, blocking anything else from pouring into him.

"You can't keep it all," I reminded him. "Stop fighting

it, Wolf. This is the only way!" I gripped onto his waist, just outside his own hands. "Stop holding back. I can handle it." My eyes pleaded with his.

I saw what he felt: the pain, the pure agony.

But it didn't matter. This was how the bond worked.

He tried to hold his emotions back from me, tried to spare me from whatever he felt. But we completed the bond. There was nothing he could do that would stop me from feeling it.

"You feel my strength," I reminded him. "You know I am not weak, Wolf. Pain is no stranger to me. You *know* I can handle it."

Something like pity fluttered across his pain-riddle features.

And then I felt it.

I barely made it to my feet before doubling over, wrapping both hands around my stomach.

Deeply rooted numbness hit me first, much deeper and much colder than I had ever felt it. My body recognized this as Wolf immediately, and I had no choice but to pull even more. A brief, agonizing pain in my stomach told me it was working; I was feeling what he felt.

The hunger came next.

It was demobilizing, all-consuming. I did not recognize it as hunger for a few seconds, only because it was so much stronger than any craving I'd ever felt.

And it wasn't for food.

Wolf stood up, finally stopping his stomach from bleeding with the help of my magic. He shared my strength now, my magic, my being.

351

"Huntyr," Wolf said softly, as if approaching a sleeping monster. "Are you alright?"

I swallowed and stood, trying to keep a straight face.

My stomach dropped. A storm of dread, hunger, and agony rushed in; emotions I had felt before, but never in so much force.

You don't want to feel what I feel.

I might have collapsed entirely under the weight of Wolf's bond if it weren't for the creatures in the forest moving closer.

We had to move. Fight or die.

Wolf sensed this, spinning around and drawing his sword.

He didn't have to tell me to take the left; I could feel his intentions without him opening his mouth. I pulled Venom out and crept forward, keeping my eyes fixated ahead.

"Come on," I said, forcing myself to stand up straight. "Let's kill these damn monsters and be done with this."

The next moments came in a blur of swords and daggers and bone and flesh. With the help of the bond, I was finally able to conjure natural magic.

And by the blessing of the goddess herself, it was not half-dead bears that cascaded toward us with their flesh-hungry jaws. It was merely more vampyres funneling toward us with the scent of fresh blood.

They were much easier to kill.

And kill.

And kill.

I killed until my entire body screamed in agony, until I

could no longer decipher my blood from the blood of my enemies.

Wolf fought at my side, not missing a single beat. His sword cut through the vampyres as if he were cutting air itself.

He, too, dripped in blood.

But we were alive, and I could feel his racing heart pulsing through my own veins with the power of the bond.

Bleed and live.

Another vampyre fell.

Bleed and live.

Wolf's sword sliced through three bodies at once.

Bleed and live.

We killed until only him and I stood in the forest, dripping in the blood of our enemies and staring at each other in equal amounts of horror, a horror we could share.

A horror that was ours.

CHAPTER
THIRTY-FIVE

"You're hungry," I said. It was not a question.

"I'm fine," Wolf replied. He didn't bother opening his eyes. Didn't bother lifting his head from the ground.

I sat beside the fire, my legs curled to my chest. At least I wouldn't have to huddle beside him for warmth this time. I was certain our bond would give away too many of my secrets if I got any closer.

After the adrenaline of the fight faded, after we found shelter to recover, after my heart settled, I was left to feel it all.

Wolf's emotions came and went like ocean waves, cascading against rock and sand and then retreating into the vast void of *him*.

Each time the wave came back, I fought to catch my breath. Sometimes it would be a crippling numbness that took over, starting in my chest and forcing the breath from my lungs. Sometimes, it came in waves of despair.

I wanted to ask him about this one, wanted to ask him why he felt so much heavy regret, but I kept my mouth shut.

I wouldn't want him asking me about my emotions, either.

This was simply the byproduct of the bond. We didn't have to make it anything more than that.

But the hunger... the hunger was the one thing I couldn't ignore, the one wave that never retreated.

It sat like a rock in the pit of my stomach, screaming at me to feed, clawing and begging for relief.

"Is this what it always feels like?" I asked.

He smiled, drunk with exhaustion. I became accustomed to seeing him this way. Blood smeared his face, and dried sweat clung to his messy hair.

"More or less," he replied. "But it's always worse after a fight or an injury. It's been a while since I've been restricted this way."

Don't ask. Don't ask. Don't ask.

I asked. "How do you usually do it? Feed, I mean."

Wolf pushed himself up, looking at me with the reflection of flames lighting his face. Another wave of despair hit me, forcing me to suck in a breath. "Before Moira, I would sneak into the streets and take the blood from fae men. I don't need a lot. It's often over before they realize what's happening."

"It doesn't kill them?"

Wolf's jaw tightened. "I've succumbed to the bloodlust once, a long time ago. But I've never crossed that line again. That's the difference between me and them,

Huntress. That's what makes me different from those monsters you've been raised to kill."

I found myself mesmerized by the way he spoke. Something dark, something hidden lingered in his gaze. His eyes focused on the fire, lost in some memory I would have killed to see.

"And in Moira?"

He huffed. "Plenty of sleepless nights sneaking off into town. I couldn't risk feeding from anyone and exposing my identity."

"But why?" I asked. "I mean, why hide any of it?"

He tore his eyes from the fire and looked at me, into my soul. My stomach dropped, and I could no longer decipher my own emotions from the ones flooding through our bond.

"I'm an angel with black wings," he said, a sad smile on his lips. "Have I not fallen far enough?"

I smiled back, hoping it would cover the crack that split through my chest. I was quickly distracted by the next wave of hunger crashing at my bones.

"Tell me something," Wolf said, tossing his own head back against the tree bark and shutting his eyes tightly. If I was feeling only a fraction of his hunger, I could only imagine what he felt. The constant agony had to be unbearable. "Distract me."

"I always liked you better than Lanson," I whispered. Fuck, I didn't mean for that truth to come out, but I didn't have time to think of a better one. Wolf's eyes shot open. "I mean, I always felt indifferent toward him. He was a pleasant distraction here, that's all."

Wolf's face softened. "Indifference," he repeated. "That's a safe way to feel about others. It protects you."

"So does anger. So does hate."

"No, anger means you care. Anger means there's a piece of you somewhere that's slipping. Anger happens when there is a battle still within yourself, when you're trying to cover up pain."

"Is that what you think of me? All those times we fought, did you think I was in pain?"

When he looked at me again, his light-filled eyes held hints of gold. "I see you, Huntress. I think you hold onto a lot of pain in your life, but I'm not sure why or from what. You are angry, yes, but you're protecting yourself. That's something I can relate to."

Hells, he had no idea.

Pain had made me who I was. Pain had turned me into something violent, something indestructible.

"You didn't want to bond with me," I started. "Is it because of your hunger? Is that what you didn't want me to feel?"

His head tilted to the side as he surveyed me. I felt too exposed, though I wasn't sure why. After everything we had been through, his eyes made me feel more naked than anything.

Maybe it was because I knew he was right. He saw me.

"That's some of it," he answered with a breath.

"And the rest?"

As if on cue, a wave of despair hit my gut, forcing me to grunt in pain. If he held that emotion inside without letting me feel it, he did an excellent job.

"You've been holding back," I breathed.

"Only a little," Wolf responded. His eyes had glossed over. "I can feel what you feel too, in case you forgot."

I stifled a laugh. "Really? And what is it I feel?"

A crack of thunder littered the sky.

"At first, I felt nothing. A numbness of sorts, I don't know. But under that, something lingered. Something... wicked."

I swallowed.

"I realized you're in just as much pain as I am, Huntress." He flashed his perfect teeth. "That's what makes us so similar."

I opened my mouth to object, to respond, to tell him he had lost his mind entirely. But when I tried to speak, nothing came out. I couldn't find the words.

A tickle of satisfaction lit up on my stomach—his emotions, not mine.

Rain fell.

Slowly at first, then more.

The raindrops hit the thick leaves above us before trickling down, scattering across the dirt around us and splattering on the shoulders of my jacket.

Wolf pushed himself up and crawled over to me, moving to rest against the tree right beside me. He put his arm around my shoulders and pulled me to him, spanning his wings around us to keep us dry.

"What are you doing?" I asked.

He stilled, as if he had been doing all of this without thought and just realized his own actions. "I'm keeping you dry. Now that we're bonded, I'm not risking you freezing your ass off. I'd like to be as comfortable as I can while we're stranded out here."

Hells. When he closed the remaining two inches between us, I didn't fight it.

Wolf rested against the base of the tree while I pressed up against his chest, my thigh flush against his as his hand tightened around my shoulder.

The comfort of his wings was warm and safe, I had to admit.

And the way his thigh radiated heat through my own training leathers...

"Stop that," Wolf growled.

"Stop what?"

"Thinking those things."

"You don't know what I'm thinking."

His fingertips lazily moved against my shoulder. I couldn't even begin to fight the chills that erupted down my spine; it was a physical reflex.

"Careful, Huntress."

My face heated. *Fuck that.* Wolf was toying with me now, testing how he could make me feel.

Two could play that fucking game.

I placed my hand on the top of his thigh and nuzzled closer against his chest. His thigh tightened immediately, but after a few seconds, he relaxed under my touch.

My entire stomach heated with a foreign fire.

I had to fight back a laugh. Feeling Wolf's... *desire*, it felt so vulnerable and wrong.

And I wanted to feel *more*.

I pushed away enough to twist around in the coverage

of his wings and slide my leg over his lap until I straddled him.

Another roll of fire lit up my body as I settled onto him.

"You're playing a very dangerous game," Wolf whispered.

I adjusted my hips on his. "Good," I murmured, lowering my forehead to his. "I've always liked danger."

Wolf's hands slid to the top of my thighs. He still hesitated, still held back.

I could feel how much he wanted more of this, could feel the raw desire burning in his bones.

"Stop holding back," I whispered, grinding my hips again.

Wolf's fingertips dug into my skin as he moaned. "I can't."

"Yes, you can. I can feel how much you want to." I slid a hand down his chest, feeling the trail of desire in my body as if we were one.

But with it came another insatiable craving. Mixed with the lust and the fire, it was hard to identify, but it was there.

The craving for blood.

Since we had been in this forest, we ate meat from a rabbit Wolf caught, but that didn't come close to subsiding *this* hunger.

I sat up but didn't leave his lap.

"Wolf," I said, looking into his eyes. "You need to feed."

His jaw tightened, and his teeth clenched. Desire crashed through my body.

"Stop reminding me."

I didn't know what the fuck I was thinking. I wasn't thinking straight, that much was certain. It was no longer Wolf and I as separate individuals fighting for the same outcome. Lines were blurred somewhere, boundaries were crossed.

Wolf's hunger became my hunger.

Logically, I *knew* I hated vampyres. I *knew* I should hate Wolf.

But physically, I craved for him to feed just as badly as he craved it himself.

I gripped his chin and forced his eyes to mine. "Feed, Wolf." He tried to look away, but I gripped his face tighter.

"No, I'm not leaving you here in hopes of finding a fae before something—"

My blood froze. Time stopped. Everything disappeared except Wolf and I together in this forest.

"Feed from me."

THIRTY-SIX

Wolf shoved me from his lap and crawled out of reach, pausing with his back to me a few feet away, but I could feel the way his body reacted to my words. He craved me like a starving animal, finally on the verge of relief.

"You said you could control it," I added. "You're injured, and you need to heal. You can't finish the Transcendent like this, Wolf. You look like shit."

"Thank you for that detailed description of my appearance, Huntress." The familiar flirt in his voice was gone, replaced by a wall of painful restraint.

I crawled over to him, touching his shoulder from behind. "You need this," I whispered. "You want this."

He glanced at me over his shoulder. "This isn't about what I want."

"Look at me."

Wolf didn't move.

"I said look."

A few torturous seconds went by, and I thought he was going to ignore me entirely. Wolf was rigid and restrained, very different from the casual confidence he usually held himself with. Eventually, though, he turned around, sitting on the wet forest ground in front of me.

"I don't like vampyres," I explained. Wolf snorted, and I found great relief in knowing his personality wasn't entirely gone. "So I need you to know I'm not taking this decision lightly."

"I can't do that to you, Huntyr. I won't."

I smiled at him gently. "I don't think you have much of a choice. You're not leaving me here alone to hope you'll find someone else to drink from. You'll take what you need, and it'll be over. I'm not sure how much more of your hunger I can feel."

A wave of shame interrupted the hunger funneling through our bond.

"Stop that." I held out my wrist. "Just get it over with, okay? Drink it."

Wolf tried to turn his face away, but I sat up on my knees and placed a hand on his face.

"Feel what I feel," I whispered. "Feel how much I want this, too."

"You only want this because you can feel my hunger."

I picked up his own hand and put it on my chest, just over my heart. I searched his blue eyes and the light that simmered within; I begged for him to see the meaning behind the words as I said them. "*Feel* how much I want this."

I lifted the dam that held the ocean of emotions I held

back. I thought of the way Wolf kissed me in the study, the way my entire body surrendered to his touch when his lips landed on my neck. I thought of the way he fought with me like I was strong, not some fragile girl who needed protecting. I pictured his finger scattering across my cheek as he tucked away loose strands of my hair. His powerful arms as he carried my bleeding body through the hallway.

Wolf filled an ache in my chest that I never thought would leave.

I didn't feel indifferent to him. I fucking *hated* how much he made me feel.

Wolf sucked in a breath, eyes fluttering. "Huntress," he muttered. Just when I thought I had shared too much, had sent too many truths through our bond, Wolf's free hand wrapped around my waist, pulling me flush against him on our knees.

I wrapped my arms around his neck. His lips came close to mine. They nearly touched as we froze between breaths.

I didn't just feel his body against me. I felt the heat and desire and longing that he felt.

"You're a vampyre," I breathed.

He nodded. "Yes."

"I don't trust you."

The lightning in his pupils simmered once more. "And I'll spend the rest of my days trying to change that, Huntress."

Hells, it was impossible to hold back any longer.

"Are you going to kiss me?" I whispered. "Or are we

going to keep torturing each other for the sake of our pride?"

Wolf smiled. "Careful." And then his lips were on mine.

It was not a kiss disguised as a delicacy or a kindness. This was a kiss of survival, one of pure starvation. Wolf's hands moved to my neck as he held me still, devouring me with his mouth.

And I wanted him just as badly. I clawed at his jacket, pulling him closer as if our entire bodies touching was not enough. I wanted more of him, wanted to satisfy the heat and desire that erupted like a volcano.

Wolf moved against me with powerful force, not bothering to be gentle. Why would he? He could feel how badly I wanted him.

I bit his lower lip, pulling it into my mouth. Wolf let out an animalistic growl and pushed me onto my back, immediately covering me with his body.

He slid between my legs, his hips settling just below mine as he let his weight press into me. I wrapped my legs around him, clutching him closer.

He kissed me again, his mouth finding my jawline and his teeth grazing my earlobe.

I wanted more. Hells, I wanted so much more.

"Wolf," I grunted, trying to grab his attention.

He didn't stop.

"Wolf!"

He moaned a response, his kisses finding my chest, my collarbone.

"Feed," I whispered, pulling his face up to meet me.

His body stilled against me.

"Huntress." It was a groan of complete and utter surrender, one that melted my stomach and heated my core.

"Don't make me tell you again."

I wasn't sure why I thought I could have the power in this situation with my back on the wet forest ground and Wolf's entire body pinning me there, but I needed him to understand.

This wasn't a mistake. It wasn't a half-drunken idea in the heat of sex.

It was *my* decision.

He pulled back so I could see his face. "I'll only take enough to satisfy the hunger."

I nodded.

"And if you want me to stop, you say the word, okay?"

I nodded again.

"I need to hear you say it." His voice cracked.

"Yes, I'll tell you if I want you to stop."

And then he was kissing me again, devouring me like he had never kissed anyone before in his entire life.

When his teeth grazed the sensitive skin of my neck, I shivered.

Wolf's hand found my chest, just above my breast, and held me there, as if he were holding himself back.

I only felt the heat from his touch, let him feel my own desire as it flowed through our bond.

He moaned, hardening above me as he kissed my neck.

And then his teeth sank into me.

I jumped at first, surprised by the feeling of teeth sinking into my flesh, but Wolf opened the floodgates of his bond once more, throwing all the desire and lust and longing through me.

I could feel how turned on he was. Could feel the core of heat in his own body, growing and growing with the taste of blood.

Of *my* blood.

Somewhere in the mix of Wolf's hardness grinding against me and the pull of his mouth against my throat, I moaned.

Wolf moved against me again.

My hands slid under his shirt, grazing up his bare back on either side of his wings.

He took another drink. Another.

It was a dangerous wave of submission, of heat and truth and wanting.

And it all ended too soon. Wolf's fangs retreated from my neck.

I tightened my legs around him, arching my back to get closer to him.

He kissed the bite of my neck until I couldn't feel the pinch of his teeth lingering.

Still, I wanted more.

"Huntress," he said, pulling away and pushing himself up with his arms. I instantly missed the weight of him. "I–" He stopped himself, but I could feel the emotions before he had a chance to hide them from that thread between us.

It was different than lust. It was sweeter than desire.

"Thank you," he said. He leaned down and placed a soft kiss on my forehead.

"Wait," I said, trying to pull him back to me as soon as he moved away. "You don't have to—"

"Yes, I do." His words were harsh enough for me to freeze. "It's not that I don't want to take this further, because trust me, Huntress, I do."

"Then what's the problem?" I breathed.

The darkness crept through the bond. "I can't. Not here. Not like this."

I wanted to ask more questions, but brutal embarrassment stopped me. Hells, could I not scrape up even one last ounce of dignity?

I let Wolf retreat, let him sit with his back to me, grateful that the rain had now slowed so I didn't need the shelter of his wings.

I had let a vampyre *feed* from me.

And I actually fucking enjoyed it.

THIRTY-SEVEN

"It's not worth it," I argued. "We can find The Golden City without giving away our location to everyone else in this damn forest. You said it yourself. It's too dangerous."

"We've been out here for days," Wolf responded, expanding his black wings. "I'm running out of patience. We don't even know if we're heading in the right direction."

He had a point. If Wolf could get a vantage point of vision from the sky, we could shave days off our journey.

Weeks of endless wandering could be saved.

"Fine," I breathed. "But don't stay up there long."

"Careful," Wolf teased. "It's starting to sound like you're worried."

I rolled my eyes. After last night, we were well past the point of subtle flirting. I pleaded to the goddess that the added strength from a long night of rest would help me hold back some of my emotion so he couldn't feel how much those words still affected me.

"Hurry up," I snapped. "I'll be waiting with Venom."

He winked and launched into the air, his wings blowing my hair into my face as he disappeared above the tree line.

I wiped at my neck, where the skin began to bruise from Wolf's teeth last night. *Hells.* I woke up sweating, wondering how much of that was a sick, twisted dream.

But it wasn't a dream. It was very, very real. My stomach dropped at the memory.

Part of me wanted to curse myself for being so vulnerable, especially with one of *them.* Wolf was the enemy, was everything I grew up hating. But the other part of me burned with a fresh wave of desire each time I thought about what had transpired between us.

Nobody ever wanted me the way Wolf did. It differed from anything I had ever known, and I could *feel* how real it was.

Wolf couldn't fool me like Lanson. Not with the bond. I could feel his emotions, his thoughts.

But then morning came, and we were back to being Wolf and Huntyr. Sassy. Arrogant. Bickering.

It's better this way, I reminded myself. Anything else would be messy and unreliable and risky. I had a mission to complete, one that didn't involve falling for a rare, wicked creature.

A few moments later, Wolf landed on the ground with a thud, a smile illuminating his features.

"What?" I asked.

"We're close. We're closer than close, Huntress. We're getting into the damn Golden City today."

We moved like we had all the energy in the world, bustling through the woods without a single care as to what could lurk around us. This was it. We'd made it this far, survived the horrid nature of the damn magical forest.

We were so fucking close.

Wolf led the way, cutting down any branches that separated us from approaching our prize. Whatever he saw in that sky must have been marvelous. I hadn't seen him light up this way the entire time we were in Moira.

His excitement spread to me, too. Courtesy of the damn bond.

We laughed and panted as we got closer, closer, closer.

Two hours later, we stood at the tree line. Wolf bent beside me, lowering his eyesight to match mine as we peered through the branches.

Towering white walls sat at the top of a hill, no more than one hundred paces away. White brick on top of white brick created an impenetrable fortress, one that we could not even begin to see beyond.

Not unless Wolf wanted to fly above, which was out of

the question. We were desperate, yes, but we had *some* sense left.

We did not know what waited for us. An eerie silence lurked. No birds chirped. No leaves wavered.

Only our beating hearts and panting breaths filled the air.

I knew he could feel it: the anticipation of a fight.

Something was coming.

"It has to be a trap, right?" I whispered. "There's no way we will waltz in there without a fight."

Wolf's jaw tightened. "I don't know what to believe out here, but I certainly don't trust it."

The walls were too clean. Too white. Not a single speck of dirt, not a single misplaced stone or faded brick.

It was too perfect.

"I'll go out there first," I started. "And if you see any arrows or blood-sucking demons coming my direction, yell."

"Absolutely not," Wolf scoffed. "You're not going out there alone."

"If we both go, we could walk into a death trap. One of us will mitigate risk."

"It isn't *worth* the risk."

I spun and faced him, scanning his face. "This is the whole reason we're here, Wolf."

His eyes glared into mine, intense and filled with a fierceness that made me shiver. "I don't care. You stay here. I'll go."

"Seriously? How is that any different from me going?"

"I won't have to sit here and imagine all the ways you could get hurt. Please, Huntress."

I took a long breath. I didn't want to see him get hurt either, but I had to keep my mind on the end goal.

We were too close for distractions. "Fine," I answered. "But if you see or hear anything, you get back here immediately. Okay?"

Wolf gripped my face with both hands and placed a harsh kiss on my mouth. It wasn't romantic or filled with desire like the kisses last night. This one was a promise. A lifeline.

He pulled away and marched out into the opening.

I watched every step with my hand on Venom, ready to pull it. Ready to kill anything or anyone who came after him.

My fae ears twitched toward a breaking stick to my right. I glanced and saw nothing, immediately returning my eyes to Wolf. My heart had never beat so quickly in my life.

Lord had trained me to be calm, collected.

But it was always *my* life at risk. I hadn't been trained for this. Hadn't prepared to watch someone else step into danger.

Wolf kept moving. He was halfway to the wall. A little further. Anticipation spilled from my veins.

We were so fucking close.

And then all hells erupted.

THIRTY-EIGHT

Fire split through the grassy land that separated the thick, magic forest from the walls of The Golden City.

At first, it came in a small trickle, feeding through the gap like a stream of water. But as soon as the wave of heat reached my feet, it burst into the sky, creating a wall of flames.

I screamed and leapt away from the source.

Someone controlled this fire, aimed it at us. This was no mere coincidence. I opened the bond, searching for Wolf.

Beyond the flames, he roared in pain, only for a second, before a massive gust of wind sliced through the valley, blowing fiery flames and fuel in a chaotic cyclone.

Natural magic.

Hells.

"Wolf!" I screamed. "Someone's doing this to us!"

Another gust of wind put out the flames for a few seconds before they came back.

Stronger this time. Bigger.

Wolf burst through the hot wall of fire and met me at my side, sword still in hand. The tips of his wings had been singed in the flames, some of the angel feathers still burning. I felt a flare of pain through our bond, but quickly blocked it out.

We didn't have time for pain.

"We have to get out of here!" he shouted. "We have no protection out in the open."

"No! We did not travel this far just to turn back now!"

He felt it, too. I know he did. We were so damn close to ending this entire fucking disaster.

A wall of fire could not keep us from The Golden City.

Nothing could.

That's when we heard the laughter.

Lanson staggered forward from the thick cover of the forest, though I could hardly recognize him through the bloody pulp that used to be his face. His hair was dark and matted with dried blood, and his clothes had nearly been scorched entirely from his body.

"Lanson?"

The fire cooled as he stumbled toward us. "This is it, isn't it? The ultimate battle to see who is strong enough to penetrate these damn walls?"

"I've been waiting a long time to kill this bastard," Wolf whispered in my ear. "Please, goddess, let it be now."

I held my hand out to stop him.

"Why are you trying to kill us?" I asked. "We all want the same thing!"

"We're all dead," he muttered. "Can't you understand that, Huntyr? None of us will make it out of here alive. There's no way over that damn wall."

"You don't know that," Wolf hissed. "Did you even try? You can barely stand."

"You two just arrived. I've been here for days, watching everyone else attempt to cross. Vampyres take some. The brutal fall takes the others."

I stilled. "That can't be true."

"No?" I had never seen Lanson so unhinged before, so violent. "See for yourself, then."

"How are you still alive?" Wolf asked.

Lanson shrugged. "I realized something."

When he stumbled forward, I raised Venom. Lanson didn't seem to care.

"Everyone is dying because they want to get into The Golden City. They can't stand the thought of not making it, of being stranded in this cursed forest to die. But not me."

"You don't want to get into The Golden City?"

Lanson laughed again, though it ended in a coughing fit with blood running down his chin. "You." He stepped toward me.

Wolf growled, raising his sword.

"You think you're so much better than the rest of us? You'll end up on the ground just like them. You're a weak coward, just like the vampyres."

A few muffled groans rang through the forest behind him.

The forest spurred into flames again.

When a vampyre darted—faster than I had ever seen any vampyre—from the trees and tackled Lanson, the flames ceased completely.

"Huntress." Wolf's voice dropped dangerously low. "On your left."

I glanced to find the entire forest bustling with movement.

Vampyre movement.

I immediately backed into him. We could fight a few vampyres, sure, but this?

I bumped into his chest and turned, only to find an equal amount of the bloodsucking creatures to our right.

We were trapped.

"You have to fly us over," I thought aloud. "It's the only way we leave this fight alive!"

When he didn't respond, I turned to look at him. His right wing expanded fully, the burnt feathers falling to the ground, but the left wing...

The back of it had burned completely. He couldn't even expand it from the tight position behind his shoulder blade.

Goddess above. Wolf was burned so badly by Lanson's fire, he couldn't fly.

"What do we do?" I asked. He could heal himself, but the vampyres were only feet away. He wouldn't have the time, and I wasn't entirely sure either of us had enough magic left.

Wolf squeezed his eyes shut. When he opened them again, he wasn't really there. He had gone somewhere else in his mind, somewhere I could not fully follow him in the darkness.

"I'm going to stay back and fight as long as I can, Huntress. You're going to get into The Golden City, regardless of whether I'm alive to see it."

CHAPTER
THIRTY-NINE

I t took me two full seconds to understand what Wolf meant, two more seconds to curse at him with the harshest words in our language, and one second to slap him as hard as I could in the chest.

"Have you lost your mind? That's not even a question, Wolf. Do you really think that lowly of me?"

"No," he answered. "I don't think lowly of you at all, Huntress. Can't you see why I'm doing this?"

I shook my head. We didn't have much time.

"I don't care why you think you're doing it!" I screamed. "I'm not leaving you, Wolf!"

"You have to!"

"No!"

We stood there, chests rising and falling and eyes wild, in the chaos of death and claws and decay.

"I'm not going anywhere without you," I added. "Not after everything."

He hesitated, and I thought for a second he would try to argue with me again.

But then he smiled; the sad version of his smile, not the epic one. "Okay," he said. "Then we better fight like all hells, because I'm going to be pissed if I saved your life all those times for nothing. I kept count, remember?"

I half-laughed, half-sobbed as I rotated Venom in my grip.

And then I turned.

And I fought like all hells.

CHAPTER

FORTY

With Wolf at my back, I slaughtered every vampyre who ran at me. Blood dripped from my face, running into my mouth, but I didn't care. A vampyre bit my arm, but it didn't slow me down.

I stabbed and pulled Venom from corpse after corpse after corpse.

And we weren't making it any closer to the damn wall.

"We need a new plan!" I yelled. "They're coming out of nowhere!"

Wolf grunted in pain. "I'm open to ideas!"

"Stay behind me." I stabbed another vampyre. Then another. "I think I can use my blood magic one more time."

"No!" Wolf argued. "You'll be drained. It's too risky!"

"I don't have much of a choice, Wolf!"

For the first time during the Transcendent, terror shook my voice.

We were running out of options, and we both knew it.

The sound of Wolf's sword slicing through flesh rang true behind me. It was the constant sound of victory, and as long as I heard that damn sword killing the beasts, I would keep fighting.

As long as he was here, I would fight.

"I have to try it, Wolf!"

"Fine, then I'm trying with you."

His burnt, feathered wings brushed my back as he moved closer to me.

"On three!"

Wolf's sword rang again, buzzing in the air, mixing with my dwindling adrenaline.

"One!" Teeth grazed my shoulder, too close to my throat.

"Two!" Wolf's back now fully pressed against mine, his remaining wings being ripped by the claws that closed in around us.

"My heart bows to you and you only, Huntress."

A tear fell down my face. "Three!"

Everything I knew went black.

CHAPTER

FORTY-ONE

I knew something was wrong the second I opened my eyes. I could feel the emptiness in my soul.

For one, it was too quiet. Not a single leaf rustled in the wind.

I pushed myself up from the ground and immediately found Wolf lying a few feet away on his back. His wings were completely shredded and burnt. His eyes were closed.

And he wasn't fucking moving.

He lay in a pile of ash, and as I crawled to him, I realized everything around us burned. The vampyres were gone, scorched along with everything else.

We fucking did it.

"Wolf." My throat burned, my breath hitched.

But he still did not move.

No, there was no way he'd drained himself. There was no way he had used all of his blood magic on *this.*

"Wolf!" I screamed, shaking his shoulders, pounding his chest. "Wake up, Wolf! You don't get to leave me here!"

I shook him again.

Again.

Something inside of me broke, a tether had snapped.

"No!" I yelled. "I'm not doing this alone! I'm not doing this without you!" I didn't care who heard. I didn't care how pathetic and broken I sounded.

Wolf and I were supposed to do this together. I fought for him. I pressed forward for *him*.

Without him, I was a fraction of a fae. I had no chance of making it into The Golden City.

And I didn't fucking want to.

I lowered my head to his chest and wept. "I will never fucking forgive you for this, Wolf Jasper. *Never*."

His chest did not beat. It did not rise and fall with his breath. He did not laugh or give me a snide comment in return.

Wolf was gone.

"My heart is yours, you bastard! You can't leave me!"

My breathing stopped. I didn't care how many of those monsters crept closer to us, didn't care how little time I had left.

I told Wolf I wasn't leaving him.

That wasn't changing. Not now.

I didn't leave his side as I turned and raised Venom. My hand shook. My fingers bled.

"Come on!" I screamed, more to the goddess than to the vampyres. "Come on and end this, you fucking cowards!"

The vampyres came first. Ten of them, maybe more, I wasn't sure. I stabbed as many as I could, trying not to falter away from Wolf's body when the others bit into my shoulder, my ribs, my thigh.

I screamed in pain but did not fall.

Thunder cracked the sky, rain pouring down in heavy droplets, one after another.

I couldn't even breathe without inhaling the crying sky.

I fought and I fought and I fought.

The agony of teeth and claws and slashes in my body fizzled away. That comforting numbness took over. Took over everything, actually. I didn't have to think about moving, about which monster to kill.

My vision blurred.

Something rammed into my side. More claws, more blood.

I fell beside Wolf, losing Venom in the chaos of decay.

I didn't cry anymore. I didn't care.

More thunder filled the sky.

I turned to Wolf, laid my head on his chest.

More teeth, more claws, more killing.

The very last thing I thought about before my eyes closed for good was not Lord. It was not the drive to kill one last vampyre. It was not anger or resentment or grief.

I thought wholly of *him*.

CHAPTER
FORTY-TWO

D arkness caressed every inch of my body. All the pain I felt moments ago disappeared. In fact, I couldn't feel my body at all.

I tried to blink, but that helped nothing. The darkness around me looked the same whether my eyes were open or closed.

The next thing I felt was an all-consuming wave of... of comfort. Of peace.

"Death awaits you," a female voice grazed over my skin.

I snapped my attention around, trying to find the source of the voice, but it was no use in the void of nothingness.

"Who's there?" I asked. "Am I dead?"

The female voice hummed, and my skin warmed at the sound. "That is up to me to decide."

I waited for more of an explanation, but none came. "Who are you? What's happening?"

"I am Era, Goddess of Vaehatis. You've died outside the

walls of The Golden City, and it is up to me to decide if you shall continue living."

Wha—

"You died protecting the half angel. Why risk your life for him?"

It took me a few seconds to answer. This was... this was the goddess? I was speaking to Era herself? And I was dead?

"I had no choice," I replied. "I couldn't leave him, and I wasn't going to make it in without him."

A gust of wind blew my hair across my face in the black void, followed by a flash of blue light.

Then I could see. The wind blew and blew and blew, not letting up as the light swarmed in a funnel, spinning and spinning before halting entirely.

Revealing Era, Goddess of Vaehatis, standing before me.

No, not standing. Floating in the shadows. Her skin was dark and velvet, her hair waist-length and flowing around her in a blanket of glimmering blue light. She radiated in power. I fought the urge to bow, to look away in the presence of her beauty.

She looked straight at me with nearly iridescent eyes. "You did have a choice," she pushed. "He offered his life for yours, and you turned it down."

Fuck. Was Wolf dead, too? Did he manage to survive the chaos of the vampyres?

"No," Era answered, reading my thoughts. "He did not survive. He is in this void, same as you, awaiting his fate. I am the one who decides who is worthy of The Golden City. I am the one who controls the souls who continue living."

EMILY BLACKWOOD

If I could feel my body, I was sure it would have electrified. "He deserves to get in," I explained. "Wolf is the one that should make it, not me. I cannot enter The Golden City without him."

She floated closer to me, her midnight power illuminating the darkness. "He is half a vampyre."

"Yes, he is."

"Yet you love him."

A sob filled the air around us, and it took me a moment to realize it was mine. Love.

Was that what the flip of my stomach was every time he entered a room? Was that the warmth I felt when he unlaced my boots for me, the pull in my heart when he tended to my wounds?

How quickly he could piss me off, how rapidly I forgave him, even though I pretended to stay angry?

Was that love?

"Yes," I admitted, breathless. "I do love him."

Era eyed me, and I could feel her gaze piercing the space in the void as sharply as a dagger would. This was it. This was the moment I died, or I continued living.

But my words were true. I did not want to make it into that place without him.

"Your heart is pure," she breathed. "His heart is dark, but you have shown him the light. There is something I need from you."

"Of course," I stuttered. "Anything."

"You will not understand what you see when you wake up, but you must trust yourself. Yourself, and the boy. Your heart tells the truth, and you must not abandon it. I will see you again, child. Very, very soon."

"What does that—"

"Hang in there," she interrupted. *"You will understand in time."*

Her blue light faded before I could ask any more questions, before I could make sense of the encounter.

Era, Goddess of Vaehatis, let me live.

Hands held my face as I opened my eyes.

Familiar hands.

Strong hands.

"Wake up, Huntress."

Wolf.

My eyes shot open, finding him leaning over me with his blood-stained face. His wings were no longer burnt and bent. His black feathers had regrown, fully healed.

Alive.

Breathing.

"Is this... Are we...?"

"Dead? No, not as far as I can tell, though I'm not sure we should be relieved. I saw—"

"The goddess," I finished for him. "I know, I saw her too."

I sat up and looked around. We were now on the other

side of the massive white wall, but it was no longer clean, no longer perfect.

It was as if the sun did not even shine on this side of the wall.

"What is this?" I asked, my brows pushing together.

"This is The Golden City."

FORTY-THREE

I never thought I would go back to Midgrave, but this place reminded me of it. The familiar crumbling stone structures, the fallen buildings, the rats scurrying in the streets.

Wolf and I walked silently around the perimeter of the wall, looking for any signs of life, of angels, of anything.

Death. That had been the ticket into The Golden City. That had been the one thing we needed to get beyond that impenetrable wall.

This whole time, the goddess herself was the final test.

Our wounds had been healed, though my bones still ached from the trauma. We tried not to think about who else might lurk in The Golden City, who might wait for us.

Everything was wrong.

There were no glamorous lights waiting to greet us, no comforts or luxuries. This place was filthy. It reeked of death and decay.

And vampyres.

I followed Wolf as he turned down one street, pushing through a door and entering an abandoned dwelling.

He shut the door behind us, barricading it with an armchair.

Then he turned around and ran his hands through his hair, cursing under his breath.

"What are we supposed to do now?" I asked, trying not to panic. "This can't be it, right? There has to be some mistake; there's no way this is The Golden City."

He closed the distance and placed two hands on my shoulders. "We're going to figure this out, Huntress. You're right, there's no way this is where we end things."

"We should see the archangels, at least. They must be here somewhere!"

Wolf nodded, something dark flashing beneath his eyes. "Yes, you're right."

I exhaled, allowing myself to relax for the first time since before that battle.

And then I stepped forward, wrapping my arms around Wolf. He tensed at first but quickly moved to hug me back.

"Does this mean you forgive me?" he whispered against the top of my head.

I gasped, stepping away. "You heard that?"

He shrugged, sliding his hands to my face and bringing his lips close to mine. "And my heart belongs to you, too, Huntyr Gwenevive."

A sob of relief wrecked my body. Not just at his words, but at him.

He was here, warm and solid against me, holding me, talking to me.

"I thought you left me," I whispered to him. His forehead pressed against mine, his hot breath on my lips.

"Careful," he teased, that playful flirt back in his voice. "It's starting to sound like you care, Huntress."

I laughed, tears streaming down my face, and kissed him.

My hands shook as I placed them on his chest. He covered them with his own, holding them to his bloodied, torn shirt. This kiss was gentle and soft. It was vulnerable. Easy.

I pulled away, my lip quivering. "I should clean this blood off of me."

I saw the restraint on Wolf's face, but he didn't fight me as I pulled away and surveyed the room, looking for anything to cleanse my bloodied, battered skin.

Whoever used to live here must have been wealthy. A large bed sat with massive wooden posts in the middle of the room. The bed was still made, covered in a thin layer of dust.

A perfectly placed desk sat on the far wall, with a broken mirror placed above it.

I moved past it, inching toward a doorway in the back of the room. The door had broken from the hinges, but I cried in relief when I saw a full washroom inside. At least this place wasn't a total loss.

I quickly found a small cloth and began wiping my hands, doing what I could to scratch the dried blood and caked dirt from my skin.

And then I saw a drip from the piping in the shower.

If there was still running water here, it may restore all lost faith I had in the luxuries of The Golden City.

I turned the handle.

And all hells, water poured from the ceiling. I nearly cried in relief.

Steam radiated a few moments later, and my knees shook.

Running water.

Wolf appeared in the doorway. "Is that—"

"A hot shower? Yes." A laugh shook my body. "Yes, it is."

He smiled too, and for a brief moment, there was a crack in the wall of grief that had been cascading around my heart.

"I'll give you your privacy," he said after a moment. "Take all the time you need."

I didn't bother asking him to try to re-assemble the broken door. He would respect my boundaries. What little was left of them, anyway.

After a few calming breaths, I stripped off my blood-soaked clothes. My boots were practically molded to my feet, but I eventually got them off too, sighing in relief at the sudden freedom.

Steam filled the small room, calling me forward. I stripped off the rest of my clothes, leaving the brutal pile on the ground, and stepped into the shower.

"Hells," I mumbled as the water cascaded around me. The heat enveloped my torso, my shoulders, the back of my neck. I took a long breath and finally put my face beneath the water.

I didn't have to look down to know that the water around my feet would be red and black, a reminder of the last week. More blood I tried to rub away only revealed a new healing scrape or scar. My arms were covered in claw marks, bite marks, and gashes.

This was supposed to be the end. It was supposed to get better now; it was supposed to be easy.

I had a mission to finish for Lord.

Emotion hit me like a punch to the chest. That was the whole reason I was here, wasn't it? I was supposed to finish this for him.

He needed me.

How ashamed would he be if he knew I had surrendered to Wolf? Had let him feed from me? Had died for him?

I wasn't sure when I started crying, but before I knew it, hot tears melted with the steam from the shower. I tried to let the heat relax my muscles, but more pain followed.

Always more pain.

Always more suffering.

I hated this. I hated that I never caught a break, and when I did, it wasn't going to last.

I mean, Wolf wasn't going to last, right?

I sensed him behind me without having to turn. Before Moira, I would have cared. I would have fought to cover myself up, to stop him from seeing my mangled body, the scars on my back.

But I was too tired to keep those walls around my heart from crumbling.

"Huntress," he whispered, barely loud enough for me to hear. "You're crying."

I didn't bother fighting it. "It's not the first time you've seen a woman cry."

"No," he said, closer this time, "but that doesn't mean I like it."

I tilted my head toward the water and let it fill my mouth.

"You don't have to worry about me," I answered after a few moments. "I can take care of myself."

"I know you can," he said.

I vaguely heard him stripping his own clothes off, vaguely sensed him entering the shower.

But when his soft hand fell onto my bare shoulder, I crumbled.

"Huntress," he murmured, wrapping his hands around me from behind. "It's okay."

"No, it's not okay. It's the furthest damned thing from okay."

One of his fingers began tracing the lines of my back, the many scars that all remained in different stages of healing.

And then his lips were on me, hot and healing, bringing me back to life. Pulling me away from the darkness I was mere seconds from slipping into. Wolf's hands glided from my shoulders to my wrists, brushing the rest of the dried blood away with the water.

Then he moved to my back, doing the same.

He slowly spun me around, guiding me with the softest touch I had ever felt from him. He did not mention my red-rimmed eyes. He did not mention the light sobs.

He merely got to work wiping the blood from my chest, my stomach.

Wolf knelt to his knees before me, his black wings spanning across the wet ground as he ran his hands over my thighs, my knees, my calves. Normally, I would have loved to make a comment about how good he looked on his knees, but I could not bring a smile to my face. I could not force my body to laugh, not now.

But he knew that.

Nothing was more intimate than this: two war-riddled, broken creatures naked and exhausted, cleaning the blood from their ripped and bruised skin.

Still on his knees, Wolf looked up at me. Water pebbled on his thick eyelashes. "I meant what I said, Huntress. My heart bows to you and you alone."

I sank to my knees with him, only for the first time realizing how completely naked I was. My entire body flushed against him and his hardness pressing into my thigh.

Tears still slid down my face, but hells. Wolf's hands were there, wiping the tears away, kissing the fiery trails of them.

Making me forget. Making me *feel.*

"Wolf," I breathed, letting him tip my head back to kiss my jaw, my neck.

"Hmm?" he hummed.

"I don't want to go back to how life was," I admitted. "I want to feel again."

He pulled back and looked at me with dark, intense eyes. "Then let me help you," he said.

Whatever restraint he had while kissing me before dissipated, leaving two injured, hungry predators naked in the shower.

But I didn't feel like a predator. Not here. Not with him holding me, caressing me, looking at me like that.

He kissed me like his life depended on it. I kissed him back, my hands winding in his hair as I slid onto his lap, straddling him and pressing my body into his. My nipples skimmed along his warm chest, creating delicious friction, while the hot water falling on my back accentuated the heat between us—melting and blending our wet bodies.

I moaned as his hand lowered to my ass, gripping tightly as he nibbled the bruised skin from his bite only one day before.

My stomach tightened at the memory, the water suddenly feeling much too hot with the fire inside me.

"Bed," I breathed, wrapping my arms around his neck and sliding my fingers into his hair.

I didn't need to say anything else. Wolf lifted us both effortlessly. I wrapped my legs around him as he walked us out of the shower, out of the washroom, and over to the bed.

He lowered us with an absurd amount of grace for someone who had just fought in battle, and he braced himself above me with an arm next to my head.

But then he paused.

"I need you to know that I wanted this from the first time I saw you kill a vampyre." He lowered his lips to mine, kissing me softly. "You are strong." He kissed me again. "You are brave and incredibly difficult at times, but you are worthy of so, so much more, Huntress. You always have been."

I sucked in a breath when his free hand slid up my bare torso, cupping the underside of my breast.

"What happened to us hating each other?" I gasped. "What happened to the mean, terrifying Wolf who wanted nothing to do with me?"

He murmured against my skin as he lowered his lips to my collarbone. "He met a very violent huntress who swallowed him whole. The terrifying part is that he wouldn't want it any other way."

I pulled his face back up to mine and crashed my mouth to his, clashing teeth and tongues and claws as I surrendered to him.

Wolf's wings splayed around us as he devoured my naked body, first with his hands, then with his mouth. He moved down the bed, trailing hot kisses down my chest, before pulling one of my hardened nipples into his mouth and teasing me with his tongue.

I arched my back against him and moaned, wanting more.

Wanting *him*.

With a growl of satisfaction, he moved down my body. His hands grazed my thighs with an impossible delicacy while his mouth slid down the middle of my abdomen, leaving kisses in his wake. He kissed me lower, lower, lower, worshiping every inch of me until he knelt on the ground beside the bed.

He hooked both hands under my knees and pulled. I gasped but didn't object as he spread my legs with his hands, running his tongue on the inside of my thigh.

Goddess, save me. I had never been with a male like this. I had never been so unguarded.

Wolf trailed his mouth all the way to my core, leaving me writhing for the release only he could provide me with that perfect, torturous mouth. Just before he gave me what my body begged for, however, he pulled back.

"Perfect," he breathed. He stared at my body, not like I was broken. Not like I was scarred and damaged and hurt. Not like I was weak, but like I was the most magnificent creature he had ever laid eyes upon.

His expression tightened my chest, bringing a fresh wave of tears to my eyes.

But then he brought his mouth back to my body, and all thoughts vanished from my mind. Wolf's tongue moved against me, swirling across my sensitive peak and ravishing my core, consuming every ounce of restraint I had left.

He picked up one of my legs and tossed it over his shoulder, digging his fingertips into my skin and deepening his feast.

I moaned again, letting my eyes shut.

"Look at me while I devour you," he muttered as he pulled back. "I want you to remember who gives you this pleasure, Huntress. Me." He licked me again, slowly and torturously. "Only me."

A whimper of submission escaped me. A warrior on his knees before me, devoting himself to me, adoring me.

Only him. It was *always* only him.

And then he picked up where he'd left off, drinking in every ounce of me, teasing my clit with his tongue in ways that made me dizzy.

But I didn't look away, not once. Not as my toes curled, my hands tightened in Wolf's hair, my entire body shook, my release overtook every part of me, giving me a relief I had needed for far, far too long.

And then Wolf stood, his cock thick and needy with anticipation. I could do nothing but stare at him in awe.

I licked my lips. There was nothing I wanted more in that moment than to feel him inside me.

He easily adjusted me on the bed, lining up with my entrance. "Tell me you're mine, Huntress. Tell me you belong to me, and nobody can change that."

"Fuck, Wolf," I begged. "I'm yours, so painfully yours."

He slid into me, and I gasped at the feel of him, at the way he filled an empty, missing part of my soul. His sculpted chest flexed as he moved deeper, deeper, deeper until he had filled me entirely. I gripped his neck as he held my thighs around his waist.

His eyes darkened as he watched himself pull out ever so slowly, smirking at the glistening wetness, and lifted his eyes to me before thrusting back in. Hard.

I moaned, arching against the bed, but never broke eye contact—couldn't if I wanted to.

His gaze held me in a vise.

"You're mine," he repeated as he picked up the pace, pumping in and out with a torturous rhythm.

"Yours," I breathed. "I'm yours." It was all I could say.

Wolf consumed every other possible thought in my mind, leaving me breathless.

He pushed forward, slipping an arm around my waist and shifting me backwards on the bed. His body covered my own, and I realized just how much I needed the feel of his skin against mine, his strong arms bracing over me, his wings covering us both, keeping us in this warm, needy cave of lust and desire.

But it wasn't just lust. It wasn't simply desire. Not anymore.

I needed him like I needed air. I would crawl for him if he asked. I would beg for him; he only needed to say the words.

"Careful, Huntress," he mumbled against my mouth as he kissed me. "I can feel those pesky emotions of yours, and you're seconds away from stripping me of all my restraint."

"Who said I wanted you restrained?"

Wolf paused, and then—as if he had been holding back his emotions this entire time—he sent a flood of them through our bond.

And then I saw *images*. Pictures of me sleeping in bed at Moira, pictures of me with my back turned to Wolf, pictures of me laughing with Ashlani, dancing with Lanson, all came crashing through our bond, followed by images of me injured and bleeding, me crawling into his lap in the forest, his teeth sinking into my skin.

Everything came crashing into my mind with such a warmth, such a deeply rooted adoration, I gasped at the physical feeling.

Wolf showed me his emotions—how he really felt about me this whole damn time.

I blinked away my tears and pulled his face back down to mine, not wanting him to see just how much his emotions affected me.

Another kiss, hungrier.

Needier.

And then he resumed the rhythm, pushing himself inside me while I arched against him, grinding my hips against his.

"Huntress," he moaned, his entire chest vibrating. He pounded against me again. "Huntress." Again.

He did not speak my name ordinarily; he worshipped it.

"Huntress."

The headboard knocked against the wall.

"Huntress."

His voice cracked.

"Huntress."

Suddenly, I did not know my name at all, only the words from his lips. The way he spoke it was the only way I wanted to hear it for the rest of eternity.

Pressure built inside me all over again, and I knew then that he would send me over the edge.

So I let him guide me there, his perfect, divine body giving me everything I didn't know I needed.

My soul kneels to yours.

But in that moment—as Wolf roared in release along with me—my soul did not just kneel.

It bowed.

CHAPTER

FORTY-FOUR

When morning came, I wanted nothing more than to wrap myself in Wolf's scent and drown in it.

"You never talk about him," Wolf stated, his finger trailing the side of my face as I blinked my eyes open.

"Who?"

He swallowed. "Lord."

I sat up in bed, pulling the sheets with me. I had slept better than I had all week, nuzzled in Wolf's arms until the sun rose. Even then, I didn't want to leave. There was a certain safety in Wolf's arms that I couldn't find anywhere else.

But this conversation quickly pulled me back to reality. I had mentioned his name to Wolf once, weeks ago.

And he remembered.

"There's not much to talk about," I replied. "I've probably already said too much, actually."

"Come on," Wolf said, tucking a stray curl behind my ear. "You don't have to be like that with me. Not anymore."

I tried to look away, but Wolf stopped me.

"It's complicated," I breathed.

His thumb brushed over my cheek. "I can tell. He's the one who gave you those scars, is he not?" Dark shadows flashed across his eyes, but he quickly recovered.

"It's not what you think."

"Isn't it, though? He hurts you, Huntress."

"He saved me."

Wolf stilled, waiting for an explanation.

I knew I could tell him the truth, but this? This was something I had never told anyone, not even Rummy. She had pieced it together herself, sure, but I didn't tell her the intimate details of each lashing.

Each punishment.

Each praise.

I was pathetic. I knew I was. I wanted nothing more than Lord's approval, and I would do anything to please him.

Everything in my life, I owed to Lord.

Until now, anyway. How many times had Wolf saved my life? He had literally died for me, though neither of us knew then that dying was the ticket into The Golden City.

"I don't remember my parents," I started, "but Lord tells me the story often. He found me in the forest. Our camp had been ravaged by them. Vampyres. I was the only one alive. For whatever reason, they left me. I was only a baby."

Wolf didn't blink. Didn't move.

"Lord took me in. He trained me as his own. He already had a small group of assassins that worked beneath him, and together they would take out pretty much anyone for the right price. But soon after he found me, he started Phantom. He recruited the deadliest fae and taught them to be weapons."

"He raised you in Phantom?"

"He raised me to survive." There I was again, defending him.

"He forced you to kill, Huntress, and don't try to tell me they were just vampyres. We both know that is not the truth."

I gave Wolf a soft smile. "I did this all for him," I said, though the words were quiet and weak. Maybe it was because I realized how pathetic it sounded now. "If I turn my back on him, Wolf, I have nothing. Nothing."

"That's not true," he argued. "You have everything without him. He hurts you, Huntress. This?" He reached around my shoulder and let his fingers trace one of the many, many scars. "This is not love."

My throat burned. I fought tears. "You don't know what you're talking about."

Wolf leaned forward and kissed my bare shoulder. "I know you, Huntress. He raised you to be a killer, and you've succeeded beyond anyone's expectations. I mean, hells. Look at what you've accomplished these last few weeks. It's no wonder why he chose you to get into The Golden City." He kissed me again, higher. "But you deserve to be around people who really love you. Who will protect you against anything, against anyone."

"Like you?" I asked, half-joking.

He met my stare. "Yes." His voice did not quiver. "Like me."

He kissed me deeply, intertwining his fingers in my hair, before pulling away. "We should get dressed. As much as I'd love to stay hidden away in this room with you, we need to find out what's happened to The Golden City."

I groaned, knowing he was right. The night had been a nice break from reality, but that's all it was. A break. We were supposed to be living in luxury with the elite fae and angels. This? This was the furthest thing from luxury.

My clothes were still on the washroom floor, dirty and covered in filth. So when Wolf tossed me a pair of clean trousers and a tunic from the dresser, I squealed in relief.

I had just finished putting them on when voices rang out from the hallway.

I froze, glancing at Wolf. He stared directly at the door, unmoving.

We were not the only ones here.

"Wolf?" I whispered.

He looked at me then, reluctantly. Heart-breakingly.

"Wolf," I said again.

He didn't answer. Didn't move. Didn't seem the least bit concerned as the voices grew closer and closer to our room.

"I'm so sorry, Huntress," he said.

"Wha—"

The door burst open, flying with so much force it *shattered* against the wall behind it.

Three men walked in.

407

Men.

No, they were not creatures of this realm. They were creatures of light, omitting energy as if they were the sun and the moon all in one. The male in the front of the group had long, white hair that fell to his waist.

White angel wings blended with the light, creating an iridescent rainbow of pure magic.

Angels.

"Wolf," the one in front, the one emitting light from his very being, announced. "I see you've completed your mission. I must say, he expected you two much sooner, but we'll take what we can get."

I recognized his voice. He was the one speaking to Wolf in our room after the vampyre attack in Moira.

Wolf said nothing, but his growl filled the room in deep vibrations of predatory instinct. Everything in me told me to run, yet I couldn't look away from this creature's beauty.

His golden eyes slid over to me. "So, this is her?"

Wolf stiffened. "This is her."

"Who are these people, Wolf?" Desperation leaked through my words, the type that made me look weak. "Why are they here?"

And why wasn't he fighting them? Why did he know them?

Wolf's nostrils flared. He still couldn't look at me.

The angel approaching me laughed. "Oh, sweetheart. Did you think Wolf here was your friend?"

My stomach dropped. I remained silent.

Venom was in the bathroom with the rest of my clothes, far out of reach.

Not like it would matter, anyway. These were angels. They were not fallen like Wolf, but rather standing here in their true, ethereal forms.

I lifted my chin. "What's going on here? What do you want?"

The angel glanced at Wolf. "You didn't tell her?"

I could hardly contain my rage, my confusion, my heartbreak. "Tell me what?"

The angel laughed. The walls of the room shook with the vibrations of it.

"Tell. Me. What?"

More laughter. Wolf avoided my gaze like he would drop dead just from looking at me. I hated that I felt it— the snap in my chest that felt much worse than dying, felt much worse than any blade slicing through flesh.

This pain was one that could not be seen by the eye, but would scar, nonetheless.

And now, it bled.

"Get the princess," the angel ordered. "It seems we have a lot to catch up on."

FORTY-FIVE

The men who flanked me were stronger than anyone I had ever gone up against, Wolf included. They gripped me so tightly that I was sure they could snap my bones, yet they did it so effortlessly.

"No!" I yelled, thrashing against them.

They did not bother grabbing Wolf. No, he went with them willingly in a way that made my chest tighten.

Whatever trust I had in Wolf vanished with every step we took. They dragged me from the room and down the hallway, outside of the house.

In the daylight, I saw so much more detail as they walked through the chaos of crumbling walls and falling buildings. We walked over garbage and bones, some of which I was sure belonged to fae at some point.

"Is this The Golden City?" I asked. "This was where we were supposed to end up after Moira?"

"Yes," one of the men in my ear hissed. "This is exactly where you were supposed to be, Princess."

I flinched from his breath, trying my best to get as far away as possible.

I thought angels were supposed to be kind. I thought they were supposed to be good and powerful and righteous.

But every inch of my body that touched them repulsed in a way that was worse than even the rabid vampyres. At least those beasts looked like my enemies.

An enemy who looked like a friend was much, much more dangerous.

"Why are you calling me that?" I seethed.

More laughter came from them. More rough dragging through the streets until we appeared at an archway in the cobblestone, one of the few structures that remained standing. Through the arch, a series of steps led underground.

I prayed that the real Golden City lay hidden through this archway, but the knot in my stomach warned me against it.

Nothing good ever came from deep, dirty, underground hideouts.

"After you." The guard to my right gripped my arm even tighter.

I hesitated for a mere second, but it was enough for one of them to shove me forward, sending me tumbling down the stairs and busting my knees open on the stone ground at the bottom.

I wasn't sure why I still expected Wolf to be at my side

in an instant. I was very certain, though, that the crack in my chest from his indifference hurt much worse than the blood that now dripped from my knees.

In fact, I liked the pain that now radiated down my legs. It was a pleasant distraction from the absolute betrayal that was seconds away from immobilizing me.

The worst part was that he could *feel* it. I didn't have the energy to try and hide my emotions of betrayal from our bond. He felt all of this, and yet he did not even flinch.

"Up," one of the males ordered. I got to my feet, not bothering to look for Wolf. Not daring a glance at his eyes; I knew I wasn't strong enough to see what would be there. "Walk."

I walked forward, into the underground tunnel that felt more like death than death itself.

And I had never felt more alone.

My heart raced. Perhaps death would have been better.

What would Lord think? Surely, he had no clue what would come of this. Hells, maybe he sent me here because he knew I would be strong enough to survive it.

If that was the case, I questioned his decision-making. I was not strong. Not strong enough for this, anyway.

"This way!" the angel ordered, leading us through a path of dark underground tunnels that eventually opened to a dimly lit, circular room with a throne in the center.

A fucking *throne*.

Iron and blades melded together, creating the massive structure in the center of the room that screamed power.

That wasn't nearly as terrifying as the male seated upon it.

Massive white wings, larger than even Wolf's, lazily fell over each side of the iron-wielded throne. The male seated upon it nearly made me squint by the power pouring from him. Similar to the angel who had taken us, his magic radiated around him in a way that made me think I could touch it if I just reached out and—

No. These were enemies. Every single ounce of this was wrong.

"Well." The male on the throne lifted his chin, greeting us in response. I did not look to see how Wolf reacted as we were ushered forward, only feet away from the center of the room. "You've finally made it, son. I expected you to be dead by now."

Wolf stepped forward. *Son?*

He had told me that his father waited for him inside the Golden City, that he was the one behind the vampyre attack, but this?

The angel on the throne shifted, noticing my confusion. Wolf stepped to the side of the throne, his black wings now resembling the angel's in every way except color.

And the other resemblances were...

"My name is Asmodeus," the male began. "I am the archangel of the goddess, and my son here has taken his sweet time in delivering you to us."

Wolf's arms crossed behind his back as he turned to face me.

Still, he did not meet my eyes.

Wolf was the son of an archangel.

"It's been twenty-four years. I can say I've been waiting for this moment for a very long time."

He stood, and I immediately straightened as he took a step in my direction.

"Waiting for me?" I tried to keep my voice from shaking, but it was no use.

He smiled. It was perfect and evil and rancid all at once. "Yes. Do you know why I've been waiting for you?"

I clenched my jaw.

"No? Well, it's quite a story, really. You see, your mother was a powerful woman. She owed me something, and she has yet to fill her debt. I'm hoping you can help me with that."

"How could I possibly help you fill a debt?"

He stood a foot away from me now, scanning my features like he had never seen a creature like me.

"You are the heir to the vampyre throne, the new Queen of Scarlata Empire."

I wasn't sure why such a powerful creature would need to lock me up, and I certainly wasn't sure what I did to deserve a stone cell in the underground dungeon.

This was not at all what I had imagined of The Golden City.

But that had turned out to be the least of my damn problems.

An heir?

No, they had it all wrong. In order to be an heir to the vampyre throne, I would have to be a vampyre. My parents would have been vampyres.

Neither of those things were true.

I sat on the stone ground for hours, contemplating everything that had just happened.

The archangel didn't explain much, and I quickly learned that he had no intentions of making my stay here comfortable. He hated me.

The archangel hated me.

Yet he believed I needed to fill a debt for him, one my mother owed him.

No, this was all wrong.

Had Lord known about this? Was that the whole reason he sent me here?

I shook my head, rubbing my now-filthy hands across my temples. Lord would have never sent me here if he thought these people would capture me.

If he thought Wolf would betray me.

Fuck. I had been trying to think of anything but Wolf for the past few hours, but I failed miserably. I couldn't keep his touch from my memory. Hells, it had only been last night that we were laying in each other's arms, confessing our love and surrendering to each other in ways I never would have imagined.

And each time that perfect, torturous face appeared in my mind, I wanted to retch.

I ran through every single interaction I'd ever had with him, trying to decipher the lies. There were so many damn signs, I should have guessed that he would lie to me again.

He was a vampyre, and he was working for the damn archangels.

Before yesterday, I wouldn't have imagined that archangels would be capable of something like this; something so brutal and wrong. Hells, the entire Golden City had crumpled.

How was this possible? How did the Headmistress at Moira Seminary not know that she was sending everyone to their death, whether they made it into The Golden City or died in the Transcendent?

We died.

We were *dead.*

And now we were in a very different version of this hell.

It only got worse when the sound of his now-familiar footsteps approached in the stone corridor. I had grown accustomed to the way his boots sounded on stone. How many times had I gotten excited when he entered a room? How many times had I instinctually looked for him at the sound of those footsteps?

"I don't want to talk to you." I curled my arms tighter around my knees, burying my face in them.

His footsteps stopped outside my cell. I didn't bother looking. He did not deserve to see my face; he did not deserve to have my understanding.

I never wanted to see him again.

My chest tightened at the thought. I was a coward. A

coward and a damn fool for thinking I could trust anyone, especially after what happened with Lanson.

Had I not learned my lesson?

"Fine," he said. His voice sounded tired and hushed, as if he were still hiding. Hells, that was probably all a lie, too. I wouldn't be surprised if he were the one running this entire operation with the archangels themselves. "I'll talk, then. You'll listen."

I squeezed my eyes shut, trying to blink away tears. My chest only tightened even more at the sound of his wings fluttering. This wasn't fucking happening.

"I never meant to hurt you, Huntress."

"Bullshit!" My words echoed from the stones. "And you don't get to fucking call me that, not anymore. You don't get to call me anything, actually."

How many hours ago had he been worshiping that name with his cock buried inside me? How many times had I let him trick me with his flirtatious grin and his arrogant teasing?

How stupid was I to let that happen? To trust him? To believe that someone might actually care about me?

"Just listen!" he hissed. "I had a job to do in Moira, much like Lord gave you a job. You wanted to get into The Golden City, anyway. I only ensured you would make it there." My head spun. My stomach rolled. "He forced me to do it, Huntyr, but you likely would be in this situation without me, too."

"No," I said, pulling myself to my feet and walking to the entrance where Wolf stood. His hair was a wreck, his eyes accompanied by dark rims. "I certainly would *not* be in this situation, Wolf. Maybe you did have orders. But tell me, were your orders to take me to bed, too? To make me trust you? Or was that just part of your own personal game?"

I blinked away the remaining tears. No, he didn't get to see me cry anymore. He didn't deserve to see me with my walls down, with my heart open. Only hot, electric rage pulsed through me. I let it spread, covering any soft feelings of adoration that may have remained, and I pushed that through our bond.

My anger would burn away the loving touches, the subtle gestures. My anger would repair the damage, would make me whole again.

Not him. Not apologies or amends. Not friendship, not love.

Only anger.

Wolf's bloodied forehead fell against the bars of the cell. "Everything between us was real."

"Do not insult me further with your lies." I shook my head.

A silence lingered between us, heavier than anything he could have said. Even if his words were true, they held no merit.

Wolf said he would protect me. He said he would have my back.

Yet he *willingly* led me into a trap.

Foreign emotion welled in my chest. I snapped my attention to him. "Stop that," I hissed. "You don't get to show me what you're feeling anymore. You lost that right."

"We are still bonded, Huntyr. Let me show you how sorry I am," he pleaded, gripping the bars of my cell.

I shook my head and built invisible walls around my heart, shutting him out. "I don't care how sorry you are," I whispered. "It fixes nothing."

"Maybe not," he replied. "But I can help you out of this. I can fix this."

"What do they want with me?" I pushed myself up and stepped into the small amount of light filtering into the cell so Wolf could see my face, so he could look at the person he had betrayed.

His brows drew together. "He wants to control the vampyre kingdom."

"But there is no vampyre kingdom. Not since the king and queen died."

"That's what you've been made to believe. The truth is that the kingdom has risen from the ashes. What he said is true. We have known this for years; it only took us some time to find you. You are half-fae, half-vampyre, and your mother was the vampyre queen. Your real name is not Huntyr Gwenevive, it is Huntyraina Fullmall Gawerula, daughter of Claudia Fullmall Gawerula."

I scoffed, shaking my head. Huntyraina Fullmall Gawerula. It didn't make any fucking sense. The vampire queen had no heirs. It was part of the reason the kingdom fell. Lord saved me from dying, he didn't take me from the vampyre kingdom. "That's not possible."

"You are twenty-four years of age, Huntress. Your vampyre cravings for blood won't kick in for another year.

You're stronger than any mere fae. You don't remember who your parents really were—"

"It isn't possible!" Panic clawed at my chest, digging a hole and tunneling deep inside of me.

"It is." His words held a certain tenderness that made me hate him even more. "I can even taste it in your blood. Your blood magic is more powerful than anything I have ever seen. You are the heir to the vampyre kingdom, Huntress. You *must* help him take control, or he will kill you for standing in his way."

FORTY-SIX

WOLF

Cherries.

That smell of her sweet, alluring blood ripped through me with every goddess-damned breath, igniting my senses and squeezing my heart until I was sure it would cease to beat. Her specific scent wafted through the air, even from corridors away.

My father didn't seem to notice it the same way I did. He wouldn't. He didn't crave her blood. He wasn't utterly obsessed with her.

Well, he was, but for different reasons. He talked and talked and talked, droning on about his plans for us over the next few days.

I paid no attention to that. Huntyr's agony, hatred, and betrayal ripped through the funnel of our bond. *Good.* I focused on that instead of the cherries, trying to remind myself of those sad, blue eyes when she found out who I really was, what I had done to her.

She fucking hated me. I could live with that for now. At least she was still alive.

Above the ground, vampyres crawled throughout the city. It was the reason I agreed to keep her locked in that cell. If any other vampyre even dared to come close to her, even smelled her for a second, I would eradicate them.

Her blood belonged to me.

My father stopped talking. "Are you listening to me, Wolf?"

Fuck. I slid my gaze to his. "I'm sorry, what were you saying?"

His face contorted in disapproval, but he continued anyway. "Did she show any signs of her power while training in Moira Seminary? Have you seen anything?"

Goddess, yes, I saw something. I saw her ripping herself to shreds, bleeding herself dry in an uncontrollable draw of power that nearly burned the castle down. I tasted it, too. Drinking her blood was like drinking life itself. She did not know how rare her abilities were. We were damn lucky that nobody else in that academy saw what she could really do.

Another wave of Huntyr's emotions infiltrated my gut.

I never planned on falling for her. I never planned on everything getting so fucked up.

My father wanted to control her, wanted to wield her special power for his own good. I already dragged her through this nightmare, delivered her to these monsters. I would not give them that, too.

"No," I answered. "No, I saw nothing. She's only

twenty-four years old. It could be months before her full powers manifest, along with her vampyre cravings."

My father's eyes became narrow slits of untrusting light. "It appears you two have gotten close. Closer than merely allies to gain entry to The Golden City."

"I'm just doing my job." I kept my voice even, bored. I flipped my hand over on the armrest of my chair and surveyed the skin around my nails. "She trusted me to get her here, did she not?"

A long silence rang through the throne room. I forced myself to sit still, to not squirm beneath the angelic power.

Most others feared my father. As one of three archangels serving under the goddess, he possessed more power than any angel or fae could fathom. He could do whatever he wanted, could control anyone or anything.

And he loved control.

Me? I feared him too, but not as much as I despised him. Ever since he turned me into this—this fallen angel, this vampyre—I saw him for what he really was.

Evil.

"She cares for you," he continued.

Still, I remained silent.

"But your mission is not over. Your orders were to deliver her and convince her to help us rebuild Scarlata Empire. That cannot happen if she is not willing."

"She needs time," I argued. "You're keeping her locked away like a prisoner after she found out she was betrayed by the one person she—" I stopped myself before I could say more. *The one person she loved.*

My father huffed and nodded. "Feelings like that don't

just disappear, son. If she cared for you before, there's a chance she still does."

I raised an eyebrow, feeling a fresh wave of her emotions. "I seriously doubt that."

He waited a few moments, tapping his finger against the armrest of his velvet throne before pushing himself to his feet. "A simple test won't hurt."

He smiled and my stomach sank.

"What test?"

He was already heading toward the long corridor that led to her cell. "Follow me. Luseyar, you too."

Luseyar, my father's errand man, immediately stepped in line. I pushed myself up as well, following closely behind both of them as the smell of cherries grew thicker and thicker.

When we turned the final corner to her cell, I balled my fists, piercing my skin with my nails to keep my face straight.

Don't react. Show no signs of attachment.

"What the fuck do you want?" Huntyr asked. Her words were powerful, but her voice was tired and dry.

My father tsked. "This will be simple. I'm going to ask you a few questions, and if you refuse to answer, your friend will be punished."

What the—

Luseyar gripped me by the arm and shoved the handle of his sword into my back until I was forced to my knees just before Huntyr's cell.

Then I felt the cool blade at the back of my neck.

Any other sword would not scare me, but Luseyar's

weapon was not one forged by fae or men. This light-omitting weapon was forged by the goddess herself and could end my life in a fraction of a second.

I froze but kept my gaze down. Huntyr moved in front of me, scrambling to her feet.

"You think I care what happens to your son?" She spit the words out like poison. "He betrayed me. Hurt him all you want. I'm not telling you anything."

A ripple of pain fluttered through our bond. Her pain. It would be nearly impossible to keep her walls up while she was this weak, while I was this close.

My father sighed behind me. "I've waited a very long time for you," he said. "I am a patient man, you see, but I grow bored with these games. As you know by now, I'm planning to rebuild Scarlata Empire. But I need you and your magic in order to do that."

She laughed in his face. "I'll never help you." *That's my Huntress.*

"Show me the magic you wield," my father barked. It was an order from an archangel—one that vibrated the steel of the cage in front of my face.

She raised her chin in defiance. "No."

Luseyar applied pressure to his angelic sword and slid it down my back, just between my wings. Burning hot agony ripped through my skin that was sliced open with barely any effort. My shirt fell from my body like it was never there at all. I grimaced and growled against the pain, but I did not move.

Don't fall for this, Huntress. Keep hating me. Keep wishing I were dead.

"Care to change your mind?" My father stepped forward until I could see him from the corner of my eye. I dared a glance at Huntyr, who stood tall on the other side of the bars.

Her beautiful black curls fell awry across her face, and her eyes looked red from crying. *Fucking hells.*

Still, she looked into the face of the archangel before her and shrugged. "Keep hurting him. This is getting fun for me."

Luseyar's blade sliced me again, this time just touching the base of my wing and slicing a few of the feathers there. The pain rattled my entire body, worse than any pain that could ever be inflicted on my body alone.

I cried out in pain and dropped my head, gnawing on the inside of my cheek. I would not ask them to stop. I would not ask Huntyr to give them answers.

I would rather take a lifetime of this pain than betray her further.

"What makes you think I have magic at all?" she challenged.

"My son here tells me you have none, but consider this a hunch."

I felt a wave of fear and helplessness through the bond —empty and shattering. When I lifted my head, Huntyr met my gaze, and her eyes widened with something that was not hatred.

"I'll ask you one more time before Luseyar here removes Wolf's wings from his body. Quite agonizing, I've heard."

"What?" I snapped, turning to my father. He would torture me to get information, yes, but take my wings?

He wouldn't.

Huntyr remained silent, and I felt even more of that fear flood from her.

"Show. Me. Your. Magic."

Huntyr's eyes now glistened in panic. Her gaze slid from my father to me, to the blade that now flirted with the flesh just above my left shoulder blade.

Don't break, Huntress. Not now. They're bluffing.

She shifted on her feet. Her breath hitched.

My father's dark, chaotic laughter gutted me. "Who knew the new Queen of Scarlata Empire was so cold-hearted, she would let an angel's most prized possession be sliced away from their body? Perhaps I was wrong about you."

I held my breath, but I felt Huntyr's relief flutter through me.

"Though if you truly never cared about my son, you won't mind him without his wings, anyway."

No.

Luseyar raised the sword.

I looked at Huntyr and sent her one last wave of all the adoration consuming me, sent her every good thought and loving emotion I had left so she wouldn't feel as much of the pain that was about to rip me to shreds.

Huntyr screamed.

The sword sliced through the air.

Made in the USA
Middletown, DE
26 August 2024

59733771R00257